Murder in the Diocese

The Maggie Monroe Series: Book Four

Helene Mitchell

GREEN SWEATER GIRL
COLUMBUS, MONTANA

Praise for the *Maggie Monroe* series

"Forty years of working in prison systems left me curious to read Helene Mitchell's Maggie Monroe books. I found them to be intriguing and captivating. From the first page I was enthralled with the eccentric, mysterious, and engaging characters. The books kept me guessing on 'who did it' while the small details brought me into the storyline. Highly recommend!"

— **Pam Sonnen,**
Idaho Department of Corrections Deputy Director (Retired)
Prison Consultant

Ms. Mitchell takes one on a wild ride of sex, orphaned babies, murder, church politics, infidelity and more. Her depiction of small town police forces, local politics and the interaction with corrupted church officials is really interesting and thought provoking. Join Detective Maggie Monroe and the rest of her crew as she takes on a case with all sorts of twists and turns! It's a good read.

— **D.D., Eagle, ID**

"Helene Mitchell brings the 'extra panache' with her *Maggie Monroe* books. She weaves a PERFECT tapestry of unpredictable mystery plots with colorful, imperfect, and unconventional characters. After working four decades in law enforcement, I thought I had seen it all. Then along came Helene Mitchell...you will absolutely love these books!"

— **Mike Moser**
Ada County Sheriff's Office (Retired)

"Thirty years in law enforcement, I have seen all kinds of criminal behavior. Helene Mitchell's *Maggie Monroe* books spin those behaviors into quirky mysteries. Fun reads!"

— **Shaun Gough**
Gooding County Sheriff

"Instantly draws you into the story! Unable to quit reading until you get to the end! Full of surprises and can't wait to read the next book in this series!"

—**Sharon**
Amazon Customer

Murder In the Diocese. Wow, what a story! Helene Mitchell writes another Maggie Monroe mystery. Part of the suspense—the real mystery—is the tie-in to the Church's clandestine cover-up of its clergy. Her telling invites the reader to come along as one door after another is opened—or closed—to reveal what you could not see coming. Finish the book. Put it down. Set it aside. You, too, will say, "Wow! What a story!"

— **Tom Decker, Chaplain US Army Retired**

This is a work of fiction. Names, characters, businesses, places, events, locales, and incidents are either the products of the author's imagination or used in a fictitious manner. Any resemblance to actual persons, living or dead, or actual events is purely coincidental.

Copyright © 2024 Green Sweater Girl Publishing, LLC

All rights reserved. No part of this book may be reproduced or used in any manner without written permission of the copyright owner except for the use of quotations in a book review.

Edited by AnnaMarie McHargue and Anita Stephens
Designed by Leslie Hertling and Eric Hendrickson

Library of Congress Control Number: 2024921943

ISBN (paperback): 979-8-9895968-5-0
ISBN (ebook): 979-8-9895968-6-7

www.gailcushman.com

Green Sweater Girl, Columbus, Montana

Dedication

To the thousands of victims of abuse, shame, and lies, by people in authority, and the cover-ups that follow.

They have become fat and sleek.
They have also excelled in evil matters.
They have not taken up cases,
Such as the case of the fatherless, so they might prosper,
And they have not defended the rights of the needy.

–Jeremiah 5:28

Author's Notes

Murder in the Diocese is a work of fiction, about serious crimes and cover-ups, and when exposed, leads to truth and eventually justice. In my novel, a Catholic local diocese covers up a crime and tries to protect the Church's interests at all costs. In this case a local church hierarchy looks out for themselves, regardless of who else it may damage. Recent press releases by the Holy See indicate that the Vatican is taking these abuses very seriously, and I pray that this culture of deception will cease to exist.

Although *Murder in the Diocese* relates a fictional tale of cover-ups within the Catholic Church, by substituting the names of other institutions and their hierarchies for the words "Catholic Church" and "diocese," the similarities in cover-ups become obvious. The Boy Scouts of America, Enron, and Watergate are all contemporary examples of hiding the truth from the population at large for no other reason than protecting high-ranking persons and the organization from ridicule and possibly prison.

By way of background, the Catholic Church has a history of well-documented scandals that expose a loosely connected assortment of support groups for clergy including treatment centers, hospitals, and retreat centers. If an investigation discloses his whereabouts or law enforcement tries to draw up charges against him, the church relocates him, and he starts anew. Bishops have moved priests easily from place and place, no questions asked. Email and cell phone numbers are changed accordingly. No one knows where these priests go or why, and the diocese doesn't address the rumors, rather insisting that the clergy has a right to be protected, and it is their duty to protect them.

Beyond the issue of transferring errant priests, they are given absolution. They confess their sins to a priest who absolves them of the transgressions. It doesn't matter if it is lying, a sexual indiscretion, pedophilia, womanizing, or thievery, these sins are absolved. The priest promises to make a thorough and complete recovery and all is forgiven. If he breaks his promise, he will receive more treatment, followed by chastisement, and another absolution.

With these moves, the priests save face and protect their retirements, meager as they might be, and may spend their final days of the priesthood in prayer and attending 12-step meetings. If rehab is successful, they may be reassigned somewhere else like a Catholic school or other non-parish position. If not, they are sent to treatment centers, which, while expensive, are a better option than ousting a priest from the brotherhood and having him, as well as the bishop, ridiculed by his parishioners.

The issues of abuse of power with the rite of absolution have been with us in many forms for thousands of years. While I doubt that *Murder in the Diocese* will correct any of this, it is on my mind. I hope you enjoy my book.

Helene Mitchell, 2024

Cast of Characters

Basin Police Team, subdivision of Reno Police Department
Maggie Monroe: *detective, recent staff addition*
Jack Shetland: *officer*
Johnny Tucker: *chief of police, Basin*

Diocesan Personnel
Bishop Connor Llewellyn: *bishop of the diocese*
Father Ralph Loren, Vicar General: *building his ticket to be a bishop*
Glenna, Administrative Assistant: *shelters the bishop through a sense of humor*

St. Gertrude's Parish
Father Rene Leclerq, Pastor: *workaholic, controls many facets of the diocese*
Father Patrick O'Grady, Associate Pastor: *plagued with ulcers*
Father Matthew Hope, Associate Pastor/Principal of High School: *athletic priest who loves his job*

Holy Father's Parish
Father Paul McGraeth, Pastor: *will do anything to become a bishop*

St. Anthony's Parish
Father George Murphy, Pastor: *senior priest in the diocese: understands that finances rule parish success*
Father Javier Pablo (JP) Shannon, Associate Pastor: *nearing retirement, doing his parish work between the 1st and 18th holes*

Our Lady of Perpetual Tears
Father Joseph (Josey) Zabalapeda, Pastor: *junior priest in the diocese and a day trader*

Others:

Angel: *dedicated to God, but God continues to test her*

Gwendolyn Harte: *wife, mother, and teacher, anticipating having a peaceful summer when she makes a discovery at Mass*

Clancy Harte: *husband, father, and attorney, wanting to protect his family*

April Harte: *Gwen and Clancy's daughter, a wrongly accused student*

Andy and Michael Harte: *Gwen and Clancy's sons, ages eight and nine, who work to solve the mystery*

Junie May Layne: *A former graduate of St. Thomas More High School*

Chapter 1

Angel
Saturday

Praising God and cursing Him at the same time, Angel fell to her knees. Wasn't she one of the faithful, one who prayed without ceasing? Hadn't she always attended Mass? Hadn't she always thought of Him first? Hadn't she sacrificed enough? Thank God, the babies looked healthy. Thank God, the pain was over. But why two? And one darker than the other. A black baby and a white baby? Wasn't one baby punishment enough? Why had they picked today to be born? Couldn't they have waited until next week?

Angel, as her stepfather called her, knew little of childbirth, babies, or caring for them. She did not believe in abortion. Babies were God's creation. She would not, could not destroy them. As a youth, she aspired to greatness and disciplined herself to achieve her goals, but these past years had worn her down. Now in her late 30s, she struggled with saying *no* to people, and her obsessive work habits had begun to exhaust her. She compensated for her passivity with gruffness, which others considered aggressive behavior. And these babies, they were unwelcome. She would never say unwanted, but they were unwelcome.

Hail Mary. She looked at the babies. Two. She didn't know there would be two. And the race thing. How could that be? Shouldn't twins look alike? According to her calculations they were due in four weeks, but they chose today to be born. Wearily, she recalled that violent night. At first, he had been gentle, teasing and smiling, then suddenly he changed and had become angry, brutal, even vicious. With his anger she became more passive, hoping he would leave. But her docility only made him more violent. He forced himself on her, then threatened her. She knew that revealing the secret would destroy all that she had worked for.

She had not seen a doctor during her pregnancy and relied on WebMD to learn about prenatal care. Later, she went back to the Internet to see how to deliver a baby, and had even purchased new, sterile scissors to cut the cord. No one had to know. She could ignore seeing a doctor; what did they know anyway? Tell you to push the baby out, pat you on the back, and send you home. This way, it was between her and God. Throughout her pregnancy, she had not drunk alcohol. Of course, wine didn't count. Nor did the daily Blood of Christ. And she didn't smoke. When the babies finally made their appearance, she severed the cords with her new scissors and tied them tightly. She then wiped the babies' mouths and noses free of mucus. From what she could tell, they appeared healthy. So, at least there was that. Praise God.

But the two babies. One white, one black. Had God played a joke on her? An unfunny, thoughtless joke? God was kind. This wasn't in His nature. *I am white*, she thought to herself. How could I have a black baby? Was he African American? *No, that's impossible*, she thought. He had dark hair, but his skin was so light. Could he have been black? She didn't know anything about him. *God had played jokes on her before, but why now?* All the fingers and toes were intact. She counted them twice. It made no sense. She would look in the Scriptures and perhaps she would discover the answer. Judas was black. At least she thought he was black. She was confused on so many levels. People said that God only gives you what you can handle. Had God forgotten that rule this time around? She thought so.

Chapter 2

Angel
Saturday

Mass would begin in a little over an hour. If she left now, she could deposit them under a pew. Some kind soul would take them to the hospital, and she would be free of them. "No one has to know whose they are," she repeated to herself. "No one has to know." She was exhausted and needed to rest, but she forced herself to get dressed. She wanted to get to Mass on time.

Angel started to clean herself and the babies. She ran water until it was hot, then cooled it. It needed to be warm, not hot, she remembered as she carefully washed them, and gently patted them dry. They finally were free of the mucous that surrounded them for eight long months. The towel she used was rust stained but clean. *I should have bought a new towel, too*, she thought. Her mind was in overdrive. The only thing she knew how to do was to make them look better, more appealing. *Please let someone want them. I want them to be wanted.* She thought of Mary. Jesus had been born of a virgin. True, she wasn't a virgin, but maybe she was a chosen one, like Mary? A holy one. She frowned.

She rambled to herself in her mind. *Shit, I only have one blanket. I didn't know that I would need two. What am I supposed to do now?* She saw her new scissors and decided to cut the blanket in two, clipping the dangling threads.

3

After, she had two jagged halves. The blanket had been too large for a single baby anyway. *I should have bought a new blanket as this one will scratch them. I should have thought of diapers, too. I was not prepared. Praises that I have an extra rosary.* She knew nothing about babies, bottles, or diapers, but she did know about rosaries. She knew the rosaries would protect the twins and bring them luck.

She kissed the two rosaries and placed one with each baby as she bundled them up and placed them in a cardboard box. They whimpered a bit. "Shut up," she snapped. "Shut up. Please don't cry." She shuffled out the door to her pickup and placed the box on the floor of the front seat. "No one can know. No one can ever know."

Angel somehow bolstered the strength to attend Mass that day but was too weak to do her normal routine. She entered the sanctuary and placed the babies in the rear of the church, knowing that someone would sit near the door, anxious for an early exit. Someone always sat there. She positioned them under the kneeling rails sure that eventually they would make a fuss. She thought this was a good plan as the babies needed to be found, and soon. She had two chances: one at the 5 p.m. mass and another at the 7 p.m. service. They were silent now and breathing easily, but as soon as someone discovered them, the questions would come. People would wonder who they belonged to and worse, they would ask why one baby was black and one white. They would wonder who could have left them there. They would feel sorry for the babies and take them to the hospital. No one would know they were hers, and she couldn't let them find out.

St. Gertrude's was one of the super-churches, semi-circular interior with room for over 400 parishioners who flooded each of the five weekend Masses. The stained-glass windows and muted bulbs darkened the room, but the candles illuminated it enough to allow people to read. Angel loved candles and the aura that they created at St. Gert's. Burning candles symbolized prayers ascending to heaven and lots of candles meant lots of prayers. She looked around. No one was there yet. She dropped two quarters into the prayer box and lit two candles, one for each baby.

As planned, once she placed the babies beneath the kneelers, she made her way to another section of the sanctuary. She thought over the events of the past few hours. Away from the babies, she knelt on a kneeler and prayed that they would be found by somebody young, someone with other children, someone who would love them. Of course, with her luck, some ancient, do-gooder would find them and kick up a fuss during Mass.

Before she left the sanctuary, she remembered that she failed to leave their names in the blankets. *I should have remembered, but now it's too late. Marie and Louis would be good names. Marie and Louis, her mother and her father. I'll get the names to them somehow.*

Maybe my luck will change. Angel prayed, "Glory be to God. Glory be to God."

Chapter 3

Gwen

Saturday

Hail Mary, full of grace, the Lord is with thee. The few parishioners who gathered recited the age-old phrase. Rosary beads jangled against the backs of the wooden benches and prayers ascended. Some would be answered. Some wouldn't.

Gwendolyn Harte settled into the pew waiting for Mass to begin. A born Lutheran who had converted to Catholicism as an adult, she struggled with the concept of Mary and how Mary could be without sin. She had read and reread the literature that the priests offered her but couldn't manage to pray the Hail Mary. She sat quietly and listened to the drone of other parishioners who semi-articulated the prayers as they thumbed the beads of the age-old Catholic prayer. Her mind drifted as she sat waiting for the priest to enter. Who would recite Mass today? Would it be the French priest who avoided looking at the parishioners as he talked? Would it be the professional Irishman who feasted on Rolaids? Or would it be her boss, the Iron Man, who doubled as principal of St. Thomas More, the local Catholic high school? They were all different, and each had his own agenda and responded to the Holy Gospel in dissimilar ways. One could argue that the word of the priest was the Word of God, but if that were true, why were they constantly contradicting each other? She fought these thoughts as she readied herself for whomever might show up.

Gwen and her husband, Clancy, and their three children had relocated to Basin two years before. Basin was a small city of about 250,000, a suburb of Reno, Nevada, and it was a far cry from the 700 people in Hawley, their previous home. It seemed colossal with its paved streets, sidewalks, mall, and traffic lights. Hawley had no stoplights, but in Basin, one flashed on nearly every corner, tempting motorists to run red lights in order to get where they were going faster. The ever-present inversion contrasted to the clear, starry nights of the mountains. Their lives in the city varied from their existence in Hawley, but Gwen's jobs were the same: wife, mother, and teacher. She enjoyed going to work, teaching school, returning home, playing games with her kids, and holding hands with her husband. Simple things made her happy.

She attended Mass alone today. Clancy had traveled toward Lake Tahoe to fly fish in one of the state's many fast-running streams. Their children were spending the night with Granny, and she was looking forward to a little R&R that Mass afforded before the gang returned home. She sat near the back of the church so she could make a quick getaway. She was already thinking about her comfy spot at home where she would stretch out in quiet to eat popcorn and watch a new Netflix movie. Attending Saturday night Mass would allow her to sleep in on Sunday, one of the benefits of the Catholic Church. She rose as the fat French priest entered. The gossip mill rumored that he was 37 years old, but he looked ready for AARP. He was stooped, wizened, and shaped like an hourglass with large hips and paunchy chest. He wore his tightly cinched belt high on his waist, which drew attention to his bulging stomach that sagged beneath. His body looked distorted, even comical. Eczema patched his red-faced nose and cheeks. His complexion was spotty, making Gwen wonder if he had been tested for skin cancer. His pale, shiny hair was streaked with gray and covered his shoulders. It might have been clean, or it might have been greasy. One couldn't tell. A good haircut would do wonders for his appearance. She thought he looked especially off today. Perhaps he was a little under the weather. His robe masked his physical being. He looked clerical, except for the Birkenstocks that peeked out of his robe. He wore no socks.

As Father Rene Leclerq strode in, he stared straight ahead, as if in a fog. Gwen automatically reached for the kneeler and started to pull it down. It snagged on something and wouldn't budge. She tugged again and looked down but didn't see anything. She ducked her head down to look closer and noticed a navy-blue piece of cloth that blended in with the carpet. And it moved. Oh. My. God. Oh, my God. She leaned down for a closer look and picked it up. It was a baby. A dark-skinned baby who couldn't have been more than a few hours old. She glanced behind her and to the sides. No one was within five rows of her. She had arrived 20 minutes earlier and had seen nobody except the few early bird parishioners who were reciting their Hail Mary's. She leaned down to check for a bag or note—anything that might explain the presence of a newborn under her kneeler. She laid the baby on the pew and scrunched under the kneeler. She didn't see a note or bag, but she spied another blanket. And another baby. This baby was fair skinned with blue eyes staring up at her. It was also but a few hours old. Twins? One black and one white? That can't be. Oh, my God. She gazed around again in all directions but saw nothing that would explain the presence of two babies. In fact, the whole rear section of the church was empty, and she sat alone in the pew. "This is impossible," she thought to herself. She touched their faces and thankfully they were warm, and alive, both shifting slightly at her touch.

After she had placed both babies on the pew, she tiptoed to the rear of the church to see if there was anyone who might explain the presence of two babies. She checked the women's bathroom, the entryway, and the cry room. She looked outside the doors of the church. No one. Confused, she returned to her seat. The babies were not moving, eyes shut, rasping restlessly. To whom did they belong?

The priest was mid-way through the Mass and about to begin serving the Eucharist. His squeaky voice grated on her ears, but she was not listening anyway. Before Gwen proceeded to the altar to receive the Holy Communion, she placed them back on the floor. Perhaps her proximity frightened their mother away and she would reappear while she was at the altar. She glanced around as she walked down the aisle, searching for someone who might have recently given birth. This was the 5 p.m. Mass, known for its elderly patrons. Two wheelchairs, a half a dozen walkers and canes in every pew. No mother was to be seen. Perhaps the mother was ill or in her car. When she returned, the babies hadn't gone anywhere. Their sticky eyes tried to open, but they made no noise.

Nothing in Gwen's historical toolbox told her how to manage what was mysteriously set before her. What do you do when you find two babies? Did anyone know? One thing was sure. Hail Mary, full of grace, was not going to solve this problem. Gwen placed them carefully back on the pew, one on each side and bided her time until Mass ended. Hopefully, someone devout would come over and claim them. Her eyes moved from side to side, from baby to baby, from black baby to white baby and back again. Could it have been a coincidence that two mothers left two babies? Her eyes alit on the statue of the Virgin Mary toward the front of the church. A miracle birth, two? God help her. Gwen was a convert. Miracle births? Two miracle births? These babies should have been in the incubator at the hospital.

When Mass finally ended, the priest and his entourage departed. No one looked her way. No one stopped.

Gwen sat still, remaining in the pew, uncertain of what to do. Nearly everyone had vanished, even those with walkers and canes. The usher was gathering the wayward bulletins and tidying up before the next Mass, which would begin in less than one hour. Gwen beckoned to him as he approached, "Excuse me." No answer. She cleared her throat and repeated a little more loudly, "Sir, excuse me."

"Did you need something?" he asked. That was an understatement. Of course, she needed something. A mother would be good.

"Uh, I have a little problem here. I sat here in this pew, but when I went to put the kneeler down, I found, uh, I found two babies. Both are only a few hours old," Gwen noted. "They might be twins. I don't know." His nametag read, "Frank Bilbaostrigo, Senior Usher."

"Babies? Whose babies?" Frank Bilbaostrigo exclaimed as he sidled between the pews to have a look. "Well, I'll be. They are babies, all right. And one is black, and one is white. I'll be," he exclaimed again. "Who do they belong to? They're not yours, Mrs. Harte, are they?" Gwen was surprised that he knew her name. He grinned, as though he had caught her in a secret. Gwen didn't know many people at St. Gertrude's, but Frank apparently knew everybody.

"Of course, they're not mine, and I don't have any notion who their mother is. I don't know how they got here or to whom they belong. Could you find Father Leclerq and ask him to come here, please?" Gwen was becoming concerned that she was going to be responsible for these babies. She continued, "I peeked into the blankets and didn't find any identification. No note or anything. This one is a girl, pointing to the darker of the two, and that one is a boy. The only thing in the blankets is a rosary. One with each baby. But I want to get them out of these blankets. Not only are they filthy and damp, but I am guessing they are scratchy wool, the kind you get in the military or when you are going camping. They're not the kind you should wrap newborn babies in. Plus, they aren't wearing diapers or anything else. Could you help me carry them into the cry room? It is brighter in there, and maybe if we unwrap them, we can find identification inside the blankets."

They each picked up a baby and headed toward the cry room and placed both in the crib. Gwen stripped off the wrappings while Frank set out to retrieve Father Leclerq. The well-formed twins might not have been full term but were well developed and had all their fingers and toes, but no identification. Some toddler-sized paper diapers and a couple of scruffy, but sort-of-clean blankets lay on a folding chair. She folded the babies into the too-big diapers and wrapped them up in the softer, cleaner blankets. They had been silent during Mass, but now were becoming a little fidgety. They gurgled rasping noises that babies make and stretched their arms and legs to work out the kinks of their nearly nine-month cramped fetal positions. She guessed they were about three or four pounds each but maybe born a few weeks early. They did not wear hospital bracelets and did not appear to be medicated. Their cords were cut and tied off with string.

Frank returned sans Father Leclerq. "He's disappeared," Frank stated. "In fact, everyone has disappeared. It's you, me, these little bambinos, and a few people moseying in for the next Mass. Did you find any identification?"

"No, only these dirty blue blankets and the rosaries. I guess they were not born in a hospital. They were born somewhere else, and the mother abandoned them here. Isn't the church one of the Safe Havens under the law that allows mothers to abandon their babies if they don't want them? The law was designed to keep babies out of trash bins. I remember reading about it some years ago. Are you aware of any pregnant girls in the parish who were about to give birth?"

Frank looked around and shook his head. "I don't know who the mother might be, but what I do know is that the 7 o'clock Mass will begin in about 20 minutes. The 5 o'clock Mass mainly has older folks, but families attend the 7 o'clock Mass. This room will fill up with a whole bunch of kids, and there will be a lot of questions and a lot of germs. Why don't we put them in your car? Can you transport them to the hospital? We could call 911 and get an ambulance, but that would cause a lot of questions. I know I shouldn't speak for Father Leclerq, but I don't think he'd want this type of publicity. It is also a health issue. The hospital will know what to do. Perhaps they can locate the mother. I'd go with you, but I need to get home to my wife. She's got the flu. I'll call you later to find out what the hospital suggested." She reluctantly agreed and gave Frank her cell phone number.

Frank and Gwen bundled the two up and carried them out to Gwen's car. Gwen squinted in the sunlight and held the blanket over the eyes of the girl baby. Frank instinctively did the same with the boy baby. The sun shined brightly. It was a typical evening in June, about 75 degrees with a hint of a breeze. The lack of clouds made it perfect. They placed the children on the floor of the back seat of her SUV. As an afterthought, Frank ran back into the church and picked up the two blue blankets and took them out to Gwen's car. They used them to wedge the babies in place.

The parking lot was filling again, but Frank didn't see anyone who looked like a new mother minus her new children. Gwen's children were older, and she had no infant-safety system. She knew it was against the law not to strap children in their seats. She thought to herself, *Drive slowly. The last thing I need is to get pulled over by the police. Of course, now that I think of it, maybe that would be good luck.*

Chapter 4

Gwen
Saturday

Gwen Harte maneuvered her SUV up to the emergency room entrance and honked the horn. No one came. The semi-circle in front of the automatic doors was vacant with a couple of signs that read, "No parking." A valet-less valet stand held a sign reading: "Closed Saturday and Sunday nights." *I'll risk it*, she thought. *What's the worst that can happen?* She set the brake and exited her car. She somehow picked up the two babies and toted them inside. They were asleep, but their eyelids jumped as she moved them. She stepped up to the admissions window while balancing the babies on her waist and opened her mouth to tell her story. The clerk replied, "Take a number." She did not look up.

"But...," Gwen stammered.

"Are you bleeding? If not, take a number. Triage will see you when your number comes up." She sounded as if she had been there all week. Her ashen hair stuck out from her attempted ponytail, and her hands were stained from a leaky pen.

"But..."

"Look, Ma'am, we'll see them as soon as we can. Take a number and get out your insurance cards." More loudly she said, "Number 422, please."

Gwen took number 428 from the number dispenser and obediently carried the babies to the waiting area and manipulated them into a chair. The hospital was a paradox. The chrome arms on the black vinyl chairs gleamed in the bright sun-lit room, but the tattered magazines were askew on the floor, table, and chairs. An overflowing toy box contained a variety of toys reminiscent of a second-hand store's toy department. The security guard absentmindedly fiddled with a hand-held computer game and critically eyed the visitors on the lookout for anyone scheming to hijack the emergency room. A sign on the wall boasted, "Your Emergency Is Our Emergency." *Definitely not feeling that now*, Gwen thought.

The babies had been cleaned some, but sallow, splotchy mucous and afterbirth stuck to their bodies. They looked the same, yet different. One woman, waiting to be seen, vacillated her gaze from Gwen to the babies and back to Gwen who returned the stare. Having one black baby and one white baby was sure to raise some eyebrows in or out of the emergency room.

In about 15 minutes, the clerk called number 428. Gwen carried the little bundles up to the counter to hand them over dutifully. The triage nurse asked her a couple of questions and eventually figured out that they weren't hers as Gwen had answered every question with "I don't know; I found them." The triage nurse's nametag identified her as "Luella."

"May I see your identification, please? Who is the mother?" Luella demanded curtly.

Gwen handed over her driver's license. "I don't know who the mother is. I found them at St. Gertrude's Catholic Church at Mass." Luella glared at Gwen.

"I see," Luella responded. "And who is the father?"

"I don't know. I found them at St. Gertrude's Catholic Church at Mass." Gwen answered while Luella tapped her pen and raised her eyebrows.

Luella needed more information for her forms and continued her quest. "I see. When were they born? Where are their mothers? Why are they different races? What's that about?"

"I already told you. I don't know. I found them at St. Gertrude's Catholic Church at Mass," Gwen could feel her rage building.

Luella was not happy with Gwen's answers and continued. "You realize that we can't help you, don't you? Newborn babies who are not born in the hospital are not allowed to be admitted as newborns. You are aware of that, aren't you?" Luella added more eye moves and mouth twists.

Gwen's patience was wearing thin. "No, I am not aware of that. I found these babies. I cannot care for them and can't leave them on the street."

Luella sighed and said, "I'll check with the charge nurse. Do you have insurance? Could I see your cards, please?"

It was Gwen's turn to sigh. "I have insurance, but these babies are not on my insurance plan, because I found them. They are not mine. How many times do I have to tell you?"

Luella persisted, "You must be a guardian. Are you the legal guardian?"

"I am not. I found these babies at Mass 45 minutes ago," Gwen reminded her again. "Look, Luella, I don't mean to be rude, but I found these babies. They are not mine. I don't know what to do with them. I need some help here. I don't blame you for not believing me. I'm not sure that I would believe me, but I need some assistance."

Luella smiled and wrote something on the form. "This is very rare. The Safe Haven law says we must take abandoned babies, but as far as I know, we have never had any abandoned children and haven't established a protocol." She told Gwen to move her car before heading back into the emergency waiting room. "The staff will look them over and decide how to deal with them. We will consider you as their next-of-kin until someone tells us differently." She finished filling in the form noting Gwen as next of kin.

How could Gwen be next of kin? She was merely a Good Samaritan doing a Christian deed. Luella wrote out the triage report and noted in large red letters that there was no insurance. She called for an ER nurse.

Gwen continued to balance the two babies on the counter as Luella pushed the door-opening button. Within minutes of returning from moving her car, another nurse appeared and helped her carry them behind the stainless-steel doors of the emergency room. Her name was Linda. She repeated the same questions as Luella, and they discussed whether the babies were twins since they appeared to be of different races. Linda was certain they could not be twins. Gwen didn't know if twins could be of different races or not. Other nursing staff threw in bits of experience and knowledge. The consensus was that no one knew whether twins could be of two races or not. Linda took their vitals and began to clean the babies. Their healthy color and their persistent whimpers conned Linda into some formula. Someone gave Gwen the emergency number for Health and Welfare. She called it and got a recording. *I am glad that I wasn't being beaten*, she thought as she pushed buttons through the menu to emergency children's services. She left a message with her cell phone number requesting Health and Welfare to call her back. She provided Linda's name and the emergency room number.

The emergency room was sterile with shining stainless steel at every turn. The nurses smiled, but they too reflected steel sterility. Every medical gizmo lay at their disposal, but would any of their fancy machines produce a mother for these babies?

Gwen pondered their introduction to life. Tiny, innocent, and unwanted. How could someone discard them? How could someone not want these babies? Babies were a gift from God, magic in most people's books. One minute you have a fetus, and the next minute you have a baby. Joyful. Truly a miracle.

She remained with the babies for an hour and watched the nursing staff come and go. They used thermometers, took blood, gave sponge baths, put on diapers that fit, and attached wires that extended from the babies to monitors. They were efficient and polite, and Gwen knew they were in good hands. The preemie bottles were measured in CCs, and the babies struggled to get a few drops of the formula down. The nurses finally wrapped them in blankets: one pink and one blue with matching caps. Gwen decided to go home to change her clothes. She would return tomorrow to see how they were doing. She gave Linda her phone number on the way out.

Chapter 5

Gwen

Saturday Evening

When she arrived home, she couldn't think of anything except those two babies. Her mind wandered all over the place: from Mass to Father Leclerq to Hawley to her own children. The phone rang, and her first thought was, *Thank heaven*! Health and Welfare. The Caller ID read, "Restricted."

"Hello. Thank you for calling me back," Gwen started, not waiting for the caller to identify herself.

"Are they okay?" the hoarse voice rasped. "I want them to be okay. Take good care of them, please. When you get them back from the hospital, safeguard them as your own children. Tell them that I love them. I named them Marie and Louis. Raise them with God, Mrs. Harte." Click. The caller hung up. Gwen checked the caller ID again. Restricted.

Stunned, Gwen sat down. *Who was this person? Why is she giving her children to me? I have a life. I have a husband, three children, a job, and enough to do without twin babies.* Her head spun as she thought about what had transpired.

The phone rang again. She checked the caller ID. Restricted, again. "Who are you? Why are you giving me your children?" she almost shouted into the phone.

"This is Violet at Health and Welfare responding to your call."

Gwen's conversation with Violet was as calamitous as the one with Luella. Violet asked questions for which Gwen had no answers. Violet couldn't answer the questions that Gwen had. Gwen described the phone call that she had received. It was disturbing that the caller knew that Gwen had found the babies and had turned the babies over to the hospital. She indicated that she wanted Gwen to keep the babies. How did she know who had taken them?

"The babies are safe for the time being, however, I have no available foster homes in Basin right now. It is Saturday night, and the hospital will take care of the babies until Monday. In addition, it will be difficult to secure a foster home for two newborns. We don't know about their family. For the moment, Mrs. Harte, you are their next of kin. Did you call the police?"

"No, I did not call the police, and I am not the next of kin. I drove them to the hospital and called you." Gwen was becoming irritated.

Clancy and Gwen had undertaken the responsibility of being foster parents once before. A 14-year-old boy tried to commit suicide with a pistol but missed his brain and severed the optic nerve blinding himself instead. They cared for him while the child welfare workers investigated the family and the child. The department needed to learn the whys and wherefores of the attempted suicide before returning him to his home. Clancy and Gwen dealt with the delays, broken promises, and tangled red tape. They knew the system. The department had rules, but there were many ways to circumvent them. A resourceful social worker could accelerate the process. A genuine, dyed-in-the-wool bureaucrat could cause a foster family to jump through hoops forever. Social workers could make the foster family's life as easy or difficult as they desired.

Violet persisted, "The mother evidently knows you. She might have chosen you on purpose or was glad you found them. She called you, didn't she? They'll stay in the hospital for the weekend. Monday, I'll expedite your case to certify you as foster parents, if you will assume that responsibility."

Gwen stammered a bit, "Well, uh, I don't know. I must talk to Clancy. We served as foster parents once before, but that was a few years ago. That boy was a teenager, and it was for only a few days. When do you need to know? What will happen to them if we don't take them?"

"You've already been foster parents? Oh, good. That makes it easier. The mother contacted you once and may call again. If she does, please assure her that the babies are safe. You should call the police and request that they keep an eye on your house in case she comes by. You could request a tap on your phone to allow them to trace the call should she call again. I'll have the department designate you as a foster home first thing Monday."

Gwen thought it was inconceivable that Health and Welfare and Violet would assume that the Harte family would just take these babies in. Her thoughts were running rampant, *Health and Welfare has decided that we're going to be responsible for these babies. First, the hospital decided I was next-of-kin. Now Health and Welfare announces that we're playing finders-keepers. What will be next, the hokey pokey?*

Gwen didn't express those thoughts, but suggested to Violet, "Don't you want to see them, and wouldn't you want to meet us before you just sign them over to us?"

"Patience, Mrs. Harte. I'll see them on Monday. They're in good hands now, and I can't do anything more this weekend. The system works slowly. You must be a fine woman, because you found them at church, didn't you? If you were a bad person, you wouldn't go to church," Violet responded brightly.

Gwen's head was churning. She could not believe what was happening. It wasn't that she didn't want to help. It was just that this wasn't what she had in mind for the week. But these newly born children, Marie and Louis, had never been held in the arms of someone who loved them. She wondered what Clancy and their three children would say. And what about them being of a different race? *How could I explain that when I didn't even know it was possible?*

"Okay, Violet, call me Monday. I don't know about being a foster home, but if we get certified as a foster home, we'll keep them for a few days starting then. Meanwhile, I'll call the police and file a report, but what do I file? A missing person's report. A found person's report. I have never done this before. And, before I forget, may I have your cell number please? Your number did not come up on my caller I.D."

"Just call the police and tell them you found the babies. You wouldn't want to be charged with kidnapping," she chortled at her private joke. "I'll talk to you Monday." Click. Violet hung up without leaving her phone number.

Chapter 6

Detective Maggie Monroe
Saturday Night

Sheriff Maggie Monroe was exhausted. She had been looking for a job in law enforcement for two weeks with no success. It was a Saturday night and she had exhausted her pool of law enforcement agencies. She and her husband Brick were enjoying a glass of wine, both frustrated with the whole hiring process, wondering what would come next. She had recently retired from her position in Barrier, a one-horse town that no longer had any horses. It had a good hotel, a casino, and of course a brothel. It backed up to the Sierra Nevada Mountains with plenty of both character and characters. Brick, prior to their marriage, had moved to Barrier as an escape from Los Angeles and the big city ways in order to teach school but ended up as the high school principal. They were the community's "power couple" with a lot of influence.

While Maggie served as the elected sheriff, Brick had been readily available to assist and advise her on "catching crooks," as she liked to say. The County Commissioners had allowed her one paid deputy, KG Garrison, nicknamed Cagey. She had called in Brick three times for assistance, first during her first week of being a sheriff, when the beloved priest had been killed. Second when an ex-convict was seeking revenge, and third when a brothel worker was killed, amid other complications. His expertise and her badge had allowed them to solve all three cases.

A Marine, Brick had always been a picture of health, but suddenly he wasn't. The VA's thorough evaluation had diagnosed a brain tumor, which had destroyed glandular function in his pituitary from exposure to burn pits during his first tour in the Middle East. They said his multiple injuries were inoperable, yet they had hope that he could continue his normal life, but he needed to be closer to a VA facility. The five-hour, twice weekly drive to Reno had exhausted them both. Reno's VA was excellent, and it specialized in burn pit syndrome. It was a perfect move, except Maggie had been unable to find an acceptable position in law enforcement.

After Brick's diagnosis, with his apparently failing health, they pulled up stakes and moved to Reno, finding the small town of Basin, a small suburb close to the VA for his weekly visits. Maggie had no prospects for work when they arrived but applied for positions with the Washoe County Sheriff's Office, the Nevada Highway Patrol, Reno Police, and finally with the much smaller Basin Police Department. She was told "No," repeatedly. As a former sheriff, she was overqualified for most open positions, which were at officer-level, and she wondered if the upper management unit considered her experience and qualifications a threat to their male-dominated hierarchy. None of the law enforcement agencies were hiring, they said, and disinterested because they were looking for someone younger, who was trainable in their methods of law enforcement, which she saw as a way of keeping the "good ol' boy" network alive and well. As sheriff, she answered only to voters, and she was the boss, albeit for a tiny department in a tiny county. Brick teased her by calling her the "High, by God, Sheriff," and he meant it.

Maggie wanted to stay with law enforcement and in the state retirement system for health and retirement benefits, especially with Brick's illness. But things didn't seem to be going her way. As a last resort she and Brick talked about private detective work, which didn't appeal to her. They were about to go to bed when Johnny Tucker, the Basin chief of police called her. "You still interested?" he started, sounding tired and frustrated. She hesitated. Yesterday he had not been interested, but tonight he was. It was nearly eleven o'clock. What was going on?

"Well, yes, I am. What's the position?" she asked.

"It's a detective position. Not high paying and I'll assign a patrolman to you, you know, so you won't be in any danger," the chief said. "It'll mostly be minor cases, misdemeanors, or family issues. No murders or anything complicated, those go to our experienced officers."

"You do know that I'm experienced, don't you? I was a sheriff for twenty years, and we handled everything. We didn't have a big office and staff like here, so my deputy and a half and I handled everything, even murder."

"Yeah, yeah," the chief said, brushing her off. "We'll give you a shot and see how it goes. You'll be the only woman on our staff and don't have any uniforms, so you can wear civies. Just make it professional, Detective Monroe. Can you start tomorrow?"

The truth was that Chief Tucker had been served with a discrimination citation for not having females on the staff, except for clerical help, and he hoped that hiring Maggie would get the county attorney off his back. "Tomorrow," he repeated. "Can you make it tomorrow, even though it's a Sunday?"

Maggie didn't like the sound of this job, but knew she had to get her foot in the door somehow, so agreed. "Does that mean I can't wear my bikini?" she answered, flippantly.

Chief Tucker smiled at her quick response, but answered shortly, "Bikini, no, but something that makes you look like you know something about kids. Be here first thing so we can get all the paperwork done; I've got something right up your alley."

"Maggie didn't know what he meant, 'to wear something that made her look like she knew something about kids', but she would figure it out. Sounds good, I'll be there. Is 6:00 too early for you?"

Chapter 7

Brick and Maggie

"Who was that?" Brick asked. "It sounded like one of your feelers worked." Brick was lying on the couch; he had grown weaker lately and prone on the couch seemed to be his most comfortable position these days.

"I guess I could say 'hallelujah,'" Maggie answered. "It's something. That was Chief Tucker who called, the Basin Chief of Police. He wants me to start tomorrow in a detective position. He said he had something 'right up my alley,' and I'm not sure what that is, but I'll show up tomorrow and 'wow' him with my ability and experience."

When Brick was first diagnosed with illness related to his tour of duty in the Middle East as a Marine Corps officer affected by the burn pits, she had read everything she could find about the diagnosis and it all sounded gloomy. His health was up and down, but this week, he had been a little better, almost back to his usual self. She was ready for him to be well. The VA had given them some hope, but he continued to have difficulty. But this week had been a good one.

Brick laughed. "He wants you on Sunday? Well, you 'wow' everyone you meet, so I'm sure it will be fine. I have another appointment at the VA on Monday, PT, I think, but I can get there on my own. I'll call the VA today to arrange transportation. They keep offering me a ride, but we've never needed it, but now I'll take them up on it. You do your 'wow' thing and catch all the crooks in Basin so that we can soon live in a crime-free city." Brick had often teased Maggie that her job as sheriff was 'catching crooks.' And she was pretty good at it.

Chapter 8

Gwen
Sunday

Gwen's plan to sleep-in evaporated when she awoke that morning. She attacked her Sunday tasks with fury, consumed a pot of coffee, scrutinized the paper, washed four loads of clothes, then took in the morning news shows. She couldn't help but think of the mother and wondered how she could have missed seeing her at church. She called the police after she arrived home last night, but they delayed their visit until Sunday morning. They hadn't shown up yet.

The phone rang. "Hello?" she responded somewhat hesitantly, not knowing who would be calling. The caller I.D. again read "Restricted." What good does it do to have caller I.D. if everyone is unknown? She whispered a prayer that it would be the mystery caller again announcing her name and that she would be right over to pick up the babies. "Hello?" No one answered. "Hello?" Silence. She shouted into the phone, "Hello?"

"Mrs. Harte?" A bristly voice scratched her ears. It sounded familiar, but she couldn't quite place it. She was silent for a second, debating whether it was a repeat visit from the mystery caller. "Mrs. Harte? This is Father Leclerq. Are you there?"

"Oh, Father Leclerq. Am I ever glad to hear from you? Yes, this is Gwen Harte. Wait, don't you have Mass today?" she stammered. She had called the church earlier and left a message but didn't expect an answer so soon. She thought he would be at Mass all day. She continued anyway, "Thanks for calling. I went to Mass last night and left with two babies." That didn't quite come out right. "I mean, I found two babies under the kneelers during Mass. No one was with them. They are newborns, just hours old. One is African American, and one is Anglo, but nobody was with them. Frank Bilstrigo, the usher, suggested that I should take them to the hospital. We looked for you, but you apparently left in a hurry."

"You mean, Frank Bilbaostrigo?" he corrected her. "I recited the Masses yesterday. Father O'Grady takes the Sunday Masses."

"Yes, that's right, Frank Bilbaostrigo. I took the twins to the hospital, and now they have them. I called Health and Welfare, and they think the babies should stay with me and my family. Some mystery caller called and told me to take care of them. I don't know who it was. I thought maybe you were she when you called, but it wasn't. It was you." She was babbling.

"Frank told me a little, but not much. Do you have any idea who they belong to?" Father Leclerq probed. "I mean, they aren't yours, right? Did you see anyone? Do they have any identification?" He was asking the same questions that the hospital and Health and Welfare had.

Gwen wanted more answers. "No, I didn't see anyone. I guess I am more interested in knowing if you saw anyone. I mean, did you see anyone before the 5 o'clock Mass who looked as if they had recently given birth?" That was a stupid question. Mothers who had given birth looked like anyone else except exhausted. Besides, how would a priest know what a new mother looked like? Father Leclerq seldom looked anyone in the eye. She doubted he would notice anyway.

His answer was predictable. "No, I didn't see anyone who might have given birth. Most of the parishioners at the Saturday Mass are older, so a pregnant, younger woman would have stuck out." He paused and snickered at his pun. "You keeping the babies is a good idea. I'll check around with the staff to find out if they know of anyone who might have abandoned them.

Abandoned babies are not good for public relations. I would like to see them though. If St. Gertrude's is the mother, does that make me a father?" He chuckled again. They talked a bit more and hung up. Gwen told him that she would call him to let him know when she had them.

Gwen had had no contact with the police since they moved to Basin, a Reno suburb, and even though they had lived there for two years, she still expected the western types she had known in Hawley. She was thankful when two officers finally appeared at her door. Detective Maggie Monroe and Officer Jack Shetland introduced themselves. They were a far cry from what she imagined.

"I'm Detective Monroe, and this is Officer Shetland. We're responding to your call about finding a set of twin babies. Are you Mrs. Harte?"

Gwen shook the detective's hand and introduced herself, "I'm Gwen Harte, and I'm happy you're here. Please call me Gwen."

The detective responded, "And call me, Maggie." Officer Shetland just placed his hand on his overladen belt and said, "I'm Jack."

Maggie Monroe was tall, taller than Gwen, about fifty years old, and obviously athletic. She was fit and looked like she could handle herself, yet had a gentle nature about her. She wore black slacks with a gray sweater, and a single chain with no pendant hung around her neck. She had pulled her long hair tightly into a bun at the nape of her neck. Her hair was brown with streaks of gray that could have been either natural or placed there by a hairdresser. She had a pretty face that didn't require make-up, and her complexion was clear with laugh marks at the corners of her eyes. She held a pair of glasses in her hand and switched them to shake hands with Gwen. She spoke slowly and seemed to consider her words before she spoke. She did most of the talking and took notes in her small notebook. She didn't have a badge or name tag.

Officer Jack Shetland looked like Mr. Clean gone bad. He had shaved his head bald, even though there wasn't much to shave. He had one of those faces that did not reveal his age. He could have been 25 or 55. He would probably look the same at 80, with a rounded face, darkened bags under his eyes, some skin lumps and a few creases. At six-foot-three and weighing close to 250 pounds, he was formidable in his police-issued blue cotton shirt and serge pants. Around his middle he wore a wide leather and metal belt that held two cell phones, a pistol, an official police radio, walkie-talkie, digital recorder, and pager. A large Leatherman knife housed in a leather case, a night stick, a circular ring of 50 or more keys with an expandable wire, and a set of handcuffs also dangled from the belt. *No wonder the police supposedly eat donuts*, Gwen thought flippantly. *They need the girth for all the equipment.* His radio cord extended from his belt to his neck and was clipped to his shirt collar. The earpiece in his right ear enabled him to monitor the police radio traffic. As Gwen spoke with them, he occasionally paused and cocked his eyes as if he were listening to the traffic instead of her. He wore three identifications on his shirt: a police badge, the required plastic ID badge, and a silver metal nameplate reading Jack Shetland. Characteristically polite, he ended every sentence of their conversation with the word, "ma'am." He stood at parade rest throughout their conversation with his hands behind his back, head alert, eyes front.

Gwen invited the two officers in and related her story about how she had discovered the babies and the rosaries. She disclosed the phone call and her conversations with Luella and Violet. The officers listened, asking a few questions.

Maggie started, "We stopped at the hospital to see the babies just before we came here and talked to the nurses. I have never seen or heard of twins of different races and thought we should introduce ourselves to them before we came here."

"They are cuties, aren't they," Gwen said.

"Yes, they are. I have a set of twins myself, now at UNLV, so I have a special place in my heart for twins and was a little curious about this pair. You say that you don't know anything about them?" Maggie had dealt with cases of all kinds, but she had never dealt with abandoned babies.

Gwen shook her head, "Not really, like I said, I found them. They were naked, but each had a rosary, so we wrapped them in blankets that were lying in the church nursery. I can't imagine anyone leaving these special babies alone. No identification, no message, nothing that might help to find their mother or father."

"If you think of anything else, give us a call. We don't have much to go on, only that the mother is Catholic and perhaps she gave birth to babies of different races. She's out there somewhere, and we need to find her," Maggie said, rising and nodding to Jack indicating it was time to go. "I'm new to the department and I don't have business cards yet, but you can reach me through the police station." Maggie stood up and reached for Gwen's hand, "Just to reiterate, my name is Detective Maggie Monroe, and we'll be in touch."

***

Gwen wanted to peak in at the babies and drove to the hospital and found her way to the nursery. The staff had positioned the twins beneath heat lamps to reduce jaundicing and had connected them to miscellaneous monitors. Gwen noticed that their heartbeats fluctuated greatly and wondered about that. "How are they?" Gwen mouthed through the glass to the nurse. She motioned to the nurse, whose nametag read, "Shelley," to come out.

Shelley was willing to talk and passed into the waiting area. "They are comfortable but are little jaundiced, so we decided to heat them up a bit. Are you the lady who found them?" Gwen was uncertain if it was a guess or a rumor. Rumors spread fast in hospitals.

"Yes, I am." She looked at the monitors they were connected to and asked, "Why are their heartbeats fluctuating so much? Is that okay?"

"It's pretty normal. They will settle down soon. You shouldn't worry. We are keeping a close eye on them. So, you are the lady who found them?" Shelley asked again.

Gwen acknowledged, "Yes, I found them, and now I feel responsible for them even though I don't have any connection to them. Has anyone else come by?" She hoped that the mother would make an appearance.

"A few people dropped by this morning, but only one young girl. I was busy and didn't pay too much attention. I guess she might be the mother. She was black though, and since one of these is white, I didn't think there would be a connection. And the police, a woman detective and another officer. They asked a few questions and left."

The signs on the incubators read, "Baby Boy X" and "Baby Girl X." Gwen told Shelley the names of the babies were Marie and Louis, and she penciled them in. Even though they had been abandoned, they deserved more than an "X."

Chapter 9

Gwen
Sunday Evening

The Harte Family moved from Hawley to Reno two years ago and embraced an entirely new lifestyle that they hadn't known so far. Gwen hailed from a middle-class family in Oregon but headed south in search of the "right job" after graduating from college. None of the jobs that crossed her path seemed right for her, that is, until she found the Marine Corps. Around the same time, she also found her soulmate Clancy. He had been raised in Connecticut and enrolled in college after a rather imperfect high school career, when he discovered alcohol, automobiles, and women, "all in the first week," he joked. His grades were abysmal, but the Marine Corps saw potential. Although he decided he had made a mistake on day one of boot camp, he somehow flourished under the weight of expectation in the Corps and quickly became a sergeant. When he and Gwen met, he had been a sergeant, she a second lieutenant. Corps rules being what they were, they were not allowed to fraternize. They both worked in supply, where he worked for her. She had been in the Marine Corps for five months, and he had been in the Corps for five years, but that was how the Corps operated. In his wisdom, Clancy applied for Officer Basic School with flight school. He was accepted, and their paths crossed again. This time they "fraternized" and, after a brief courtship, married.

The Marine Corps had been good to them. Once Clancy finished his education, their options opened wide. They transferred to base after base during their early years but learned quickly that they were spending too much time apart. They both decided to leave the Marine Corps to take advantage of the GI bill that offered to pay for graduate school. While he went to law school, she earned her master's, both studying in the light of their kitchen night after night. They were closer than they'd ever been in the Corps and decided to try somewhere new together now that their graduate degrees had been earned. They explored multiple available opportunities, and Hawley made the short list. They lived there for 11 years before making a move.

Clancy and Gwen had three children: two boys and a girl. Andy and Michael were eight and nine, and April was 15 going on 35, preferring to be an adult without the experience of growing up. Her grandmother nicknamed her AWA, April-with-an-Attitude. Michael and Andy were stereotypical all-American boys, riding their bikes, shooting baskets, playing football, and knew everything about everybody in the neighborhood. Andy was the joker, always ready with a pun or riddle, while Michael was the more serious kid, always considering more than what he was shown.

Hawley was a small mining town of about 700, positioned south of Las Vegas. It was a beautiful place to live, but it had been time to move forward, or as they quickly learned, fast forward, as life in a big city tends to demand.

Gwen taught English and drama at the local school, and Clancy opened a law practice but supplemented their income working part-time in the public defender's office. He attracted his share of junk law, which included whatever walked in the door: divorces, real estate, domestic cases, and estate planning. He didn't turn much of a profit, but the cost of living was low, and there was no place to spend money even if he'd had more. They were almost three hours from a McDonald's, a dry cleaner, or a movie theater. The general store limited their purchases to long underwear and Levi's, or an occasional colored bandana as a fashion accessory. Pendleton wool shirts in all shades of blue filled the shelves in the winter with tank tops reigning in the summer. In the same store, they could purchase groceries, alcohol, plumbing supplies, bird cages, blankets, school mandatories, and almost any other "necessity."

Before making their big move, they lived a quarter mile from the National Forest, enjoyed deer and elk outside their front door, and clear, smog-free skies every morning. They all came to cherish the hummingbirds that ate from the nectar feeders constantly. Of course, no place is perfect, and they had to learn to deal with winters that were no better than brutal. The year before they moved, 62 days had passed without seeing the sun. This was the final blow. Since April was entering high school, the time to try something new was perfect. Hard times for the miners and the loggers had diminished the size of the town. The law practice and the school also shrank. A move seemed to be not only appealing but eventually necessary. The move was a culture shock for all five, but they were rewarded with winters that were lovely.

Clancy researched the various law firms and finally decided to hang out his shingle as a sole practitioner. He would pick up a little of this and a little of that. He was a good lawyer, and people always needed a good lawyer. Teaching jobs were thin, but Gwen finally got a job teaching English at St. Thomas More High School. The pay was rotten, but the kids and teachers were nice with few, if any, discipline problems. As a bonus, their children could attend Catholic schools without tuition. Gwen's students accepted her and voted her as "St. Thomas More Teacher of the Year," which they announced at the end of the school year Mass. April experienced more difficulty especially since the freshmen cliques had been formed in the 8th grade at the junior high school. While in Hawley, April complained that there was nothing to do, and now in Basin, she grumbled the same thing: nothing to do.

The Harte's had not yet developed a solid friendship circle because of their preoccupation with school and trying to find work, but also were busy squishing 11 years' worth of past lives into a new house that didn't have any storage. Gwen's mother lived nearby, and they all enjoyed visiting her regularly. The children had never lived near a grandmother, making time with her something new to look forward to. She indulged them with shopping trips, homemade cookies, and treats, and gave Gwen some free time to pamper herself with some of those things that she hadn't previously been able to do.

Clancy and the kids were home when Gwen returned. The noise in the house announced that everyone had a wonderful time. Granny had made snickerdoodles, and the remnants of cinnamon wafted through the entry. Clancy was fishless, as usual, but he had stories to tell. One thing she had learned in Hawley: fishing and hunting trips were not about the animals, rather about the stories that go with the outings. Clancy's stories were predictable, about the ones that got away or the ones that didn't. While they fixed a dinner of hamburgers, baked beans, and carrot sticks, they discussed steelhead and the river, and April reported who did what to whom while at Granny's.

Gwen waited until the conversation slowed down and quietly announced, "My turn. I had a visit with the police last night, and I have some news," she paused and frowned, waiting for a response.

"What? What did they want?" Michael said. "What did you do wrong, Mom, rob a bank?"

"Nothing wrong. I went to Mass Saturday night, and you won't believe what I found." They all looked at her with surprise. "Make a guess." April guessed she had found money. Andy guessed she had found a dog and got up from the table to look outside. And Michael guessed a turtle, which he had been lobbying for recently. Clancy eyed her suspiciously but didn't offer a guess.

"Then, what?" they cried in a sort of unison when no answer seemed forthcoming.

She relayed her finding the babies, her trips to the hospital, the anonymous phone calls, the phone calls from Violet and Father Leclerq, and her visit with the police. The concept of babies was foreign to Michael and Andy, but they were fascinated by the tale. April viewed the concept of babies as babysitting money, but worse, infringement on her free time. Her thoughts were nearly clear to everyone: money would be good, but loss of free time would be bad.

They discussed the babies and their fates. "Can we keep them?" Michael and Andy wanted to know. April didn't say anything but still was thinking "babysitter." Gwen proffered the request from Violet that they become foster parents.

Clancy looked at Gwen as if she had lost her mind. "You must be kidding. Foster children? Now? For how long? Been there, done that, remember? Shouldn't we talk about this?" Sometimes his sense of reason was completely too unreasonable. "You don't know anything about these babies. They could be drug babies or black-market babies. You must be nuts." She had not considered those possibilities, but she already knew he wasn't going to win this one. "In addition, what about the mother? And the father? Where do they fit in? They might come calling."

"Clancy, Darlin', they are babies," she cooed, "just babies. And we're not talking about forever. A few days or maybe a couple weeks." He loved being called "Clancy, Darlin'." His real name was Thomas, but his older sister had called him Clancy after he learned the song, "Clancy Lowered the Boom" as a young child. His version was "Clancy Lowered the Broom." The nickname Clancy stuck, and he barely answered to anything else.

She knew time was calling for a more rational approach. "Clancy, my love, it isn't for a lifetime, it is until either A) they find the mother, or B) they are adopted by someone else. Remember that the mother gave them to us. We don't know who the mother is, but whoever she is, she chose us. I don't think I can wash my hands of them. April recently earned her driver's license and will be a big help." She tried to appeal to his sense of reason, and she knew she could appeal to April by mentioning that she could help by driving the boys to swimming lessons and baseball practices. "That'd be great, Mom,

I'd love to help out." She smiled her quick up-down teenage smile, which meant she was placating her mother. It was the same smile that earned her the AWA nickname. April was less enthusiastic about helping with babies than driving the car, but Gwen was looking for support, however it came.

Clancy returned, "I think you are forgetting option C. Health and Welfare might not find anyone, and we will have them forever." Gwen knew she was going to have to work harder, but Clancy continued, "And D, we already have three children, and if my math serves me correctly, three plus two equals five. Five children."

"It is summer vacation, and we're all out of school. It would be a good experience for all of us to be involved in foster care and to take care of these babies. Louis and Marie are off to a rough start. How can we turn our backs? Do unto others and all that jazz. What is the right thing to do here? What is the message that we want to give our own children? One, two weeks, tops. You'll see." Gwen was now appealing to his conscience. "Let's drive over to the hospital, and we all can take a look."

He finally agreed, "We might as well have a look. It won't hurt to look," Gwen smiled at him and grasped his hand.

All five jumped in the SUV to go to the hospital to peek at Marie and Louis. The blue blankets were still on the backseat floor and the kids tossed them on the driveway. "Yuck. What are these?" April asked.

"Those are what Marie and Louis were wrapped in, I'll take care of them later," Gwen answered.

Gwen had taken to using their names instead of the more impersonal "the babies." When they all arrived at the hospital, they found Shelley and another nurse feeding them. They did look cute, tightly wrapped in pink and blue blankets with little caps to keep their tiny heads warm. Michael and Andy made faces at them through the glass and were ready to take them home right then. April merely stared at them with no comment. She already had plans for the summer, and she wasn't sure how much time she'd be willing to give up and pitch in with Marie and Louis. Clancy and Gwen asked the nurses if they could hold them. Shelley agreed but made them scrub thoroughly before touching them. It was lucky she had not seen them wrapped in the dirty, wool blankets. Gwen could tell that Clancy was slowly giving in. He grinned when he held them. "You forget how little and helpless they are, don't you? They grow up too quickly." He looked out the nursery window at Michael, Andy, and April. Gwen thought she could see a tear in his eye, but he wasn't about to let it fall. "I'm not sure about having them permanently, but let's talk to the social worker about keeping them as foster babies for one or two weeks, tops. Agreed?"

Chapter 10

The Catholic Diocese
Monday

Bishop Llewellyn convened the Monday morning meeting: "Hail Mary, full of grace, the Lord is with thee. Blessed art thou among women, and blessed is the Fruit of thy womb, Jesus. Holy Mary, Mother of God, pray for us sinners, now and at the hour of our death." The bishop didn't always start with the Hail Mary, but he was in a hurry today. He had a 12:15 tee time in a foursome that included the mayor.

Four Catholic churches made up the Reno Catholic Diocese. St. Gertrude's parish, the largest, known as a super parish, lay in the center of the city, drawing members from throughout the entire city. Three priests served this congregation, Fathers Rene Leclerq, Patrick O'Grady, and Matthew Hope, who doubled as principal of the Catholic high school. The vast building, designed in a circular shape, allowed over 1,500 people to be seated at once. Thomas More High School was positioned near the church.

Holy Father's parish sat in the heart of the older, historic section of town. Father Paul McGraeth served as the lone priest of this parish, but several deacons and nuns rounded out his staff. It had a small, but loyal, congregation.

The third parish, St. Anthony's, lay near the city limits of Reno, and called itself a traditional Catholic community. Ready for retirement, Pastor

George Murphy, who was the moneyman of the diocese, steered the helm. Javier Pablo (JP) Shannon, who was feisty and nearly retired himself, assisted Murphy.

The final in the quartet of churches was Our Lady of Perpetual Tears where the bishop placed a neophyte priest, Father Joseph (Josey) Zabalapeda, in charge. This parish lay in a more rural area with many young families attending Mass.

All seven priests met, or were supposed to meet, with the bishop of the diocese twice a month, on Monday. Also attending these meetings was the vicar general, the executive officer, in military terms. He was the one who determined what happened in the diocese. If you wanted something, mention it to the VG, who would talk to the bishop. "They" would decide. It didn't matter if the bishop approved of the idea or not, if the VG wanted it, it happened. The two women in charge of parish education and the Catholic Schools set aside this time on their calendar, but of course they were not usually invited to participate in the discussion. No minutes were kept.

The VG created the June agenda with expected topics: 1. Budgets. 2. A new round of background testing for those who dealt with children. 3. The final selection of the editor of the diocesan newspaper, and 4. The assignment of committees for the various projects for the forthcoming year. The parish priests sometimes mentioned one or two other issues, but would be finished by 11:15, plenty of time for the bishop to dump his cassock for more comfortable wear suitable for 18 holes of golf.

Bishop Connor Llewellyn arrived three years ago, making him a newcomer by community standards. Anyone who hadn't taken his first breath in Basin was considered a newcomer, regardless of how long he had lived there. Bishop Con, as he liked to be called, was about 65, round of body, and happy. His balding head was fringed with white hair, and he wore frameless glasses. He sometimes jiggled when he walked and always jiggled when he laughed, which was often. His training was in education, and he had been selected as a bishop after having built a school in a poverty-stricken area of Southern California. The school became a symbol of the strength of the Southern California Catholic Church, and the media spotlighted him for his fundraising methods and innovative thinking. He was a jolly soul and was on several community committees as the Catholic representative. He liked to fish, ski, and golf, and when this diocese needed a new bishop, he announced that he was interested, and the committee selected him on the first ballot. Bishop Con earned his Ph.D. before entering the priesthood. He had been an excellent social studies teacher and a good football coach, but management was not his forte.

The meeting started with four priests present: Fathers O'Grady, Leclerq, Shannon, and Murphy. Absent were the Vicar General Ralph Loren, Fathers Hope, Zabalapeda, and McGraeth. It was not unusual for any of the pastors to be late, if they showed up at all. They controlled their own schedules and interruptions were a way of life. Who knew where McGraeth and Zabalapeda were, but you could be sure that Father Matthew Hope was pumping iron at the local gym. He spent at least two hours a day working out. His primary assignment as principal of St. Thomas More High School allowed him extra slack to manage his own schedule in the diocese, and that included as much gym time as he could manage.

Bishop Con stuck to his agenda with Father George Murphy taking the lead in the conversation. They spent 30 minutes discussing finances. Were the collections up? Did they have any deep-pocket donors? Were the priests on top of the day-to-day operations of the parish? Did they need help from the diocese? The annual diocesan fundraising had fallen short as the multiple cases about pedophilia had risen, so there would be no extra money for conferences or trainings. The priests tended to be tight mouthed about their parish finances and rolled their eyes as they listened to the drone of Father George Murphy and the bishop. They had no intention of letting the diocese know if they were flush or in arrears, and they kept the names of their big donors close to their chest. In a sense, they competed for the same purse and restrained from saying anything about their own situations.

Father Murphy, the senior priest, was an accountant at heart, and prided himself in accuracy with his funds. He was a virtuous man, and his parishioners doted on him. His somber persona did not lend itself to great fundraising abilities, but the money he guarded was accurate to the penny. Father Murphy had been around the diocese "since Christ was a Detective" as he liked to say, long enough to know that the main issue of any parish's survival, and thus his survival, was finances. He meticulously scrutinized his books, kept his finances solid, and freely gave advice about bookkeeping. He understood investments and interest rates, although he didn't dabble much. It was okay to let some areas in a parish slide, but finance was not one. He protracted his words, and the priests joked that he could turn the word "God" into three syllables.

Father Ralph Loren strutted in before Father Murphy ended his financial soliloquy. He was diminutive, but his demeanor portrayed him as larger. At first glance he could have doubled for Tom Cruise. Some female parishioners expressed that he was drop-dead gorgeous; too bad he was a priest. His blue eyes were his most remarkable feature and with his jet-black hair, he was striking. People teased him about his name, reinforced by his fashion consciousness.

"Good morning, gang. I'm sorry I'm late," he announced as he seated himself beside the bishop. He leaned over and murmured something privately to Bishop Con. Bishop Con smiled and nodded, and Ralph picked up the agenda and asked, "Did I miss anything? I'll take it from here."

"Only George with his usual diatribe about money," Father Rene Leclerq bleated. "The rise and fall of the Catholic Church according to George." Father Rene stammered the last two or three words. He was junior to Father Murphy and feared that he might have stuck his foot in his mouth. He retracted his words quickly, "Sorry, George, no harm meant."

Father Loren picked up the agenda and took over the meeting. "Okay, gentlemen, where are we on the agenda? Is there anything more on Item 1, the Budget?" Hearing nothing, he continued, "Item 2 is background checks.

They are due. Last year, the legislature took a stand on background checks for anyone who works with kids. The bishop requested that you go one step farther, especially when considering the pedophilia cases. He wants DNA checks for teachers, principals, counselors, aides, teachers, and, you got it, priests. We know that you have already had them, but here we go again. The diocese will not fuck around on this issue." Father Loren paused and smiled at his pun. He looked around to see if anyone else smiled. No one did. He continued, "The works. This is not a choice; get it done, gentlemen. I talked to the Gov, and he cut us a deal. It will cost about $35 a head rather than the usual $48. Thank God. Figure out how you will pay for it."

The bishop interjected, "Thanks be to God that we haven't had any pedophilia issues here. We don't want any surprises. The press would love to attack us, but we don't want to be caught with our pants down." Everyone chuckled at the bishop's pun.

Father Loren twisted his mouth, looked around, and continued with the agenda. "Next, let's talk about committees. We have four committees, four parishes, and four pastors. The committees are Finance, Spiritual Growth, St. Thomas More High School, and Social Justice. The bishop and I will assign you to the committees and take care of all publicity that comes out of the committees. Any volunteers, before I, I mean we, assign you?"

Father Javier Pablo Shannon spoke first with a smirk on his face. "McGraeth, Zabalapeda, and Hope aren't here. Let's assign them first. The most demanding committees are Social Justice and the high school. Give McGraeth the high school and Zabalapeda Social Justice. The Iron Man gets body building, that's all he does anyway." Father Shannon delighted in assigning work to others that he did not want to do.

Father Shannon, too, was a golfer, and spent many afternoons on the course. He avoided as many duties as he could at St. Anthony's. He considered the hours on the course his work, good for parish relations. He had served as pastor in several parishes through the years, but the parishes always shrank in size and monetary health. The diocese relocated him from parish to parish regularly, and now the diocesan leadership was anxiously awaiting his retirement. He also was more than ready to spend his mornings and evenings on the golf course. He was amusing and a decent golfer but paid little attention to social services and parish health. He could always sweet-talk a wealthy parishioner into paying his golf fees in return for special favors, like private Masses or cutting through red tape for annulments. Father Shannon charmed all he met with a warm smile and a hearty handshake. He had a quick wit, and a somewhat dirty mind. The combination of his cleverness and droll humor sometimes made people uncomfortable, but he was so likeable that they were quick to forgive him. Despite his 75-plus years, rumors flew about him and his womanizing. No one ever seemed to know for sure, but there were always stories of this or that lady friend who accompanied him on his weekend golf trips or joined him for a late dinner and the buzz was often hot and heavy. He hailed from Dublin, Ireland. His mother was a headstrong, working-class Mexican who had immigrated to Ireland from Mexico when she was 18. His father was a strong Irish Catholic. They married, had 12 children, and were each given Latin first names to go with the Irish "Shannon." Father Shannon, at age 17, left Ireland to attend seminary in the U.S. and never returned.

The vicar general agreed with him. "That sounds good. Now, who wants spiritual growth and finances?"

Father Leclerq interrupted. "No, I want to volunteer for the high school. I think I could make a big difference leading that committee. I've met several kids from there over the years so think it would be a good match. All the kids in my parish really like me."

"That's charitable of you, Rene," the vicar general answered.

"Okay. Does anybody else want to chair the board of the high school? It is an easy gig, and you get to have tickets to all the games and events. I'll even throw in a new TMHS t-shirt. If not, it belongs to Rene. You will need to attend all the school board meetings and keep on top of any controversies that arise. So, should we give Social Justice to McGraeth or Zabalapeda?" Ralph voiced.

The group looked at each other, and no one said anything. "Zabalapeda had Social Justice this year, so let's give it to McGraeth," Father Shannon volunteered. He, too, wanted to move this meeting forward so he could get out on the course.

"That leaves the Spiritual Awareness and Finance Committees. Which do you want, George?" Father Loren asked.

"I'll take the Finance Committee," Father Murphy answered, grimly. "I have had it for years, and I think I do a good job."

Father Loren said, "George, the bishop and I want to shake things up a bit. We are going to give you the Spiritual Growth Committee. It fits right in with your efforts to grow your parish. I checked your membership role, and you are down about forty people in the last few years, which translates to a few thousand dollars. You and JP will be great." The bishop nodded in consent.

Father Loren continued, "That leaves young Josey Z with finances. That's a good committee for a young priest. Our finances are in decent shape, thanks to George. He can't screw anything up." The bishop smiled and nodded. He loved it when the vicar general ran the meeting. He would get out to the golf course early.

The third item on the agenda was the selection of a new editor for *The Crusader*, the diocesan newspaper. Ralph reminded the other priests of the process, "The former editor moved, leaving a void in the diocesan staff. We interviewed four candidates, and today's the day. We've got to make the final selection of the editor. The next edition is due out in two weeks, and it's ready to fly, but the following edition has not been started. Who do you like?"

Father Javier again led the discussion, "One applicant is Hispanic, one a woman, and one of the other men has no recommendations. So, I nominate the blond guy, Cor-butt, I think was his name." He looked around to see their reaction.

"Corbin," the bishop corrected him.

"Yeah, whatever. Cor-bin." Father JP slumped down in his chair and decided to cover his tracks, "I am pretty sure the Hispanic is gay." Father Javier Pablo Shannon denigrated his Mexican roots as often as possible. He dubbed himself JP. Anyone wanting to taunt him called him Javier. People often wondered about his name and heritage, and he enlightened them by saying, "If they call me Father Shannon, they know me from church. If they call me JP, they're long-time friends. And, if they call me Javier, I know they're assholes. Make your own decision as to what to call me."

The bishop glared at him and responded, "Now, now, Javier, don't let your prejudices show here. We are looking for quality writing and someone who will get the job done. Who's the best candidate, sex and race aside?"

Father O'Grady countered, "I think we need to choose that woman. Look around, this room is filled with men. On top of that, she's a lot more qualified than Corbin, more experience, and more education. A woman's touch would bring a new flavor to this group." He had finished one pack of antacids and opened his second. "Anybody want one?" Father O'Grady had developed ulcers in the past year and now included antacids in his diet.

Father JP grinned. "A new flavor. Do you want to suck on her instead of those antacids? You'd like a woman's touch, wouldn't you, O'Grady? Why don't you go out and find a good piece of ass?"

O'Grady turned red and quickly retorted, "At least I could find one who was worth looking at. You'd be screwing the hole on the golf course." The other priests sniggered at this verbal bantering.

The vicar general resumed with the agenda. "Okay, we have a nomination, and Corbin looks good to me. Any objections?" Obviously, Steven Corbin was the VG's first choice, too. "He's the one. I'll call him. Second choice will be Jose LaFecha, he might be Hispanic, but he can write. The female has great ass-tits, I mean assets, but I agree with JP, a woman might spin a different web."

The vicar general adjourned them, "Boys, I guess that's it for today. Is there anything else that is 'good for the order?'"

"Yes, as a matter of fact, I have something else," Father O'Grady began. "It's small, but I need a favor. I got a speeding ticket the other day. I need it to go away. Anybody here know somebody at City Hall?"

"How about the mayor, will he do?" The bishop thought this would be a good excuse for another round of golf.

"I would guess so. Do you think you can get it fixed for me? I've maxed out the points for my insurance, and if this goes through, either somebody will have to drive me everywhere, or I'll have to get a bike. Can you imagine me, peddling my ass to Mass each morning? How about that for a homily topic: Pedal your ass to Mass." Father O'Grady laughed at his little joke.

"I'm golfing with him today. Don't worry. I'll get it fixed." The bishop looked at his watch again and smiled. *11:05. Thank God for Ralph Loren*, he thought.

Father Rene Leclerq lifted his hand in the air. He intended to tell the bishop in private, but he could see that the opportunity would not present itself, as the bishop kept looking at his watch. "It hasn't hit the papers yet, but somebody dumped some babies in church during the five p.m. Mass on Saturday. We don't know who their parents are. One is black, one is white, and they were abandoned under a pew in the back of St. Gertrude's. No note, no box of diapers, no nothin'. A rosary and a blanket for each. Do any of you know who might have left them?" He looked around, and hearing nothing, he continued, "My best guess is that it was an unwed mother, black, probably an RF." He used the denigrating term that the priests used among themselves for those who attend daily Mass meaning "Religious Fanatics."

"Does this mean, 'Congratulations, you're a father. Have a cigar?'" Ralph wisecracked. "That's really interesting though. You have no idea who they belong to? Where are they now? What's with black and white, I thought twins looked alike."

Rene laughed his uncomfortable nasal laugh and responded, "One of the parishioners discovered them under the kneelers and deposited them at the hospital. The hospital should take it from here. I don't think there is any problem, but I wanted to let you know that they were found."

"Thanks for the heads up, Rene. Try to keep it out of the papers, will you? They could do a number on this issue with their current media mood. I can see a headline now: 'Catholic Church Fathers Twins.' God, how I hate the media. Who is going to pray before we adjourn?" George volunteered and began a prayer that was sure to last much too long.

Chapter 11

Father Josey Zabalapeda
Monday

Joseph Zabalapeda had missed the bishop's meeting. He had stuff to do. He set out the "Office Closed" sign and plopped down at his desk. He knew he would be missed but justified his absence and thought to himself. *The bishop and his lackey, the VG, look down their noses at the priests who do the real work of the parishes. They hound us constantly about finances and social justice. They don't have a clue. Marcy's gone this week, and I need to catch up on my email.*

Father Zabalapeda was born and raised in the Northwest, the son of a Basque sheepherder and his wife, who was second-generation Basque. They became acquainted at church functions and married when she was 15 and he was 18. The local priest refused to perform the ceremony because she was pregnant with their first child, so they married in a civil ceremony.

A large group of Basques emigrated from northern Spain and worked as sheepherders in the western part of the U.S. throughout the early part of the 20th century. Small communities grew into larger ones, and they fostered the Basque heritage and language. They discerned that education provided upward mobility, especially when combined with a strong work ethic. This was the path to economic and social success. Many Basques began their lives in America as sheepherders and ended up owning the ranches and other businesses as the area grew. They ran for public office and began to gain importance in the larger communities. They retained their heritage by cultivating interest in their language and customs. Largely Catholic, they used the church as a basis of cultural unanimity: language, dress, and especially marriage. Through the years, they prospered financially and culturally, and continued to preserve the uniqueness of their civilization.

The strength of the Basque community is that they never saw themselves as second-class citizens. They educated their children and took pride in their communities. They saw the American dream as attainable and took aim.

Joseph Zabalapeda was the youngest of ten children, with the other nine being girls. He spent his summers helping his father tend sheep, but those years growing up had been rough. Too many kids, not enough money. Lamb stew six days a week. His Basque upbringing taught him to dream of something better, something that would bring him wealth and security. His Catholic roots encouraged him to consider the priesthood. These two concepts were incongruent; nevertheless, he aspired to have both.

As a child, he distributed communion to his older sisters using Necco candy wafers after they knelt before him in confession. He learned a lot about women during those confessions and employed this knowledge to terrorize his sisters. And when his abysmal grades in high school guaranteed that he would receive no scholarships, he blackmailed his older sisters to pay for his tuition in exchange for keeping secret their childhood indiscretions. He worked at a variety of jobs, waiting tables, selling used cars, running mall security, and staffing Direct TV phone lines, to make ends meet during the lean years. He even sold sperm and plasma and prayed to the Virgin Mary that the sperm sale would never come back to haunt him as a priest. He wasn't sure if it was a sin or not, but he went to confession anyway. So far, so good.

Josey was the youngest of the priests attached to the diocese, and they teased him about being the new kid on the block. The priests could not pronounce his Basque surname, and they dubbed him Father Joe Z, which they quickly abbreviated to Josey. He relished his new moniker, and soon everyone called him Josey.

Josey inherited the best of his family features. He was about six-foot-two and held his weight at 180 pounds, running three miles daily upon rising. His olive complexion and thick, black, wavy hair and black eyes made him look older than he was. One night while drinking with his college roommate, he gained a tattoo on his left shoulder that read *PERFECT* interwoven into an infinity sign. He wasn't sure what he had been thinking when the needle hit his skin. He thought it likely that he hadn't been thinking at all and kept it covered. He didn't want his parishioners to think that he was perfect. He never considered himself perfect, although in some areas, maybe. It was a close call. "Lord, it's hard to be humble when you're perfect in every way," Mac Davis warbled. It was Josey's song.

The parishioners accepted him. His fluency in Basque, Spanish, and English meshed with the parish diversity. And while his Portuguese was on the iffy side, he certainly could bluff in a pinch. His parishioners invited him to dinners and quinceañeras for the celebration of the 15th birthdays of Latin girls, and he partook in the Basque and Portuguese festivals that occurred throughout the year.

In college he majored in finance but performed poorly in anything finance related, so decided to become a priest. "At least I will always have enough to eat," he reasoned. Living with 10 women, he developed a cynical view of women with no intentions of marrying. Being a priest seemed the ideal job.

Josey took Mondays off. This morning he surfed the Internet, checking his stocks. A college friend had introduced him to day trading when the tech stocks were booming. It quickly became a passion. Young priests, he learned quickly, don't have much social life, so he needed a hobby. He took pleasure in his avocation, especially when he reaped rich rewards. With a handsome stock portfolio, he wouldn't have to worry about the pitiful diocesan retirement plan. Two years ago, he earned some big bucks doing his day-trading. He had turned a $5,000 inheritance from his father into $87,000 in a matter of days. His philosophy was uncomplicated: Pay attention to world events and don't be afraid of success. A little luck also didn't hurt. The $87,000 had eroded down to $24,000 through some recent stock market fluctuations, but Lady Luck would kick it over the $100,000 mark. He was sure of it. That was his goal. Turn a $5,000 investment into $100,000. Hard cash. Then he could turn that into $500,000. Easy-peasy-lemon-squeezy.

Josey delved into stock sheets like good juicy novels and kept up on Internet reports. He had his eye on several tech stocks, but GrayBonePhone7 Technology had piqued his interest. The company yielded a good profit last quarter and was about to split. He had already bought and sold them a few times. The research lauded them, and he knew they had been on the upward spiral. He keyed in his password to the chat room and tapped in a couple questions about GrayBonePhone7. The responses zipped back: *Hit it hot, earn a pot*, *You can't lose*, and *GrayBonePhone7 is phantom-tastic*. All positive responses. "When they split, I can double my money in a few days," he mused. "I could use a good break like this one." With a few clicks of his mouse, he moved half of his Digitoma stock to GrayBonePhone7 and bought 340 shares, which were under $35.00 each. He poured himself a cup of coffee and opened the mail. The usual: a couple bills, credit card offers, and a Catholic news magazine. He read another report about GrayBonePhone7. He glanced at his computer. It had bounced up to over $36 in a mere 15 minutes. "That's $300 smackeroos in 15 minutes. I'm a genius. A flippin' genius. Lord, it's hard to be humble," the golden oldie reverberated in his brain. The reports indicated it was a great company with an aggressive CEO who had worked for one of the main technology companies in Silicon Valley for several years and knew the players personally. His team had developed an innovative technology that would make the current phone system obsolete. Easier, faster, no more dialing or remembering numbers, all that jazz. Phone technology was booming. Every major tech company had zeroed in on advancing phone technology. Maybe he should invest a little more, the rest of his $24,000? He also retained about $3,000 in his checking account. He could invest that, too. That might raise his personal coffer up to $30,000 or even $40,000 by the end of next week. Click, click. He owned an additional 400-plus shares.

Chapter 12

Detective Maggie Monroe
Monday

Detective Maggie Monroe was happy. Mostly. Finally, she had a real job and a real case, something that she hadn't a week before. Brick seemed a little better, and her life seemed to be looking up. The doctors had discontinued two of his drugs and said he would consider removing the other three if his health continued to move in the right direction. They redid his schedule of appointments, from every four days to once a week, still intrusive, but Brick and Maggie thought that life was improving. She called her kids and told them the good news. Sean and Jimmy had just graduated from college and Sammy would be a sophomore. Life was good, or at least better.

Her Sunday had been busy, transferring her credentials from Barrier, and getting sworn in by the police chief, who seemed to think she had never responded to a crime before. She was about ten years older than he and had at least ten years more experience, but he treated her as if she were a rookie. There was no need to make his attitude an issue because she knew he would figure it out.

She liked her partner, Jack. He was "by the book" and he looked the part of a serious police officer, although he carried too much hardware on his belt, she thought. She had never had trouble handling her "clients" if they became unruly, but she appreciated his size and professional demeanor. He seemed to have a good attitude and a good sense of humor, and she looked forward to working with him.

The police station office didn't have a desk for her, but Chief Tucker set up an area with a folding chair and a rickety card table, saying he had ordered a new desk and chair which would arrive in a few weeks. He didn't offer her a police pistol, so she asked for one, but they were "fresh out," he said, "besides her cases wouldn't require any show of force, and Jack would assist her if she needed a weapon." She disagreed with him, but she was beginning to understand that this was an all-male office, one where women, no matter how competent and experienced, weren't exactly welcomed.

Things were different here, that was for sure. She had been raised in Barrier and knew the politics and the people in that community. As a sheriff there for nearly twenty years, she had faced a variety of cases, including those related to a local brothel that always brought interesting work to her office. Her first week, after having been sworn in as the Barrier sheriff, a murder landed on her desk. Certainly, a couple of abandoned babies didn't compare with the murder of a beloved priest, yet maybe they were more important, and she could prove herself to the chief.

Monday morning, she gained access to a computer, and dove into it. The computer was much newer than the one she had used in Barrier, and she made good use of it, logging into the Nevada law enforcement network, checking the laws for abandoned babies. She didn't have any other clues and needed to think through what to do next. She frowned thinking this might be a nothing case, but perhaps something else, more interesting, would be thrown her way later in the day. She drove to St. Gertrude's hoping to catch the priest and look at the "crime scene," the pews where the babies had been found, but the church was locked, and no one seemed to be around. She drove back to see Gwen.

Chapter 13

Angel
Monday

Angel didn't know much about her mother. She was raised by her stepfather, and except for the few times when he drank too much beer, he refused to talk about her. From what she was able to piece together after these drunken rants, her mother had worked as a server in a small waterfront diner on the southern California coast. She was pretty with long black hair and black eyes and had fallen in love with Angel's father, Lou, but he had moved on before she could tell him she was pregnant. Charlie, her stepfather, who worked as a civilian cook at the local Navy Base, took pity on her, and together the three became what seemed like a little family. But Angel's mother had bigger things in mind, and only two short years later, struck out on her own leaving Angel and Charlie behind.

Angel was all things average, with the exception of her tiny, squared off, sized four feet. Charlie nicknamed her Angel, teasing her that "all the angels have small feet." Soon everyone called her Angel, which was a name she liked. Buying shoes was a nightmare, and even in the winter she wore sandals. She didn't mind the teasing but always hoped that her feet would grow. They didn't.

The name, though, brought with it more than images of round, pink-cheeked cherubs. It brought a standard that Angel worked tirelessly to live up to: Angels were faultless, they never sinned, and they always dwelled with God.

As the years passed, Charlie continued to care for Angel. He taught her to cook and helped her with her schoolwork. He paid attention to her. He wanted her to help him stop missing her mother and persuaded her to take her mother's place in some areas of his life. He told her that they were a necessary part of being in a family, of loving each other. He wanted her to sleep in his bed. To keep him warm. To make him feel better. He divulged that her mother liked intimate things, like kissing and touching and she should, too, and he showed her how to do them. It was a family ritual, that's all, he explained. She had no one to ask, and Charlie thought it was all right; therefore, it must be.

Afterwards she felt guilty for her uncertainty. She went to confession where the priest gave her absolution. She should say a few *Hail Mary's* and *Our Fathers* to atone for her feelings of guilt. When she confessed to the priest about what Charlie wanted her to do, he demanded that she demonstrate. She should touch and kiss him like she had Charlie. He smiled and nodded and told her that it was good and showed her other ways that might please Charlie. He advised her to stay intimate with Charlie and report back to him. He reminded her that refusing to obey a priest was a grave sin and could result in eternal damnation. The priest counseled her to return to confession regularly.

The priest told Angel that she should not tell anyone else of her sins, her confessions, and the absolution. They were secrets. Charlie warned her not to tell anyone else either. So, she didn't. "If you are obedient, God will love you more," they counseled. For good measure, they added, "God sends disobedient angels to hell." She obeyed like a good Catholic and the angel she was.

Angel grew to accept and enjoy Charlie's advances. He worked hard and took care of her after her mother had left. He deserved to be treated kindly. Angel, in turn, devoted herself to keeping her stepfather happy. She had her

Charlie all to herself until he died when she was 17. It was then that she dedicated herself to God.

***

Angel abhorred controversy. Her life had been complicated enough, and she resented entanglements. Babies would have complicated her life, and she spent the morning meditating on life's many twists and turns. Her conflicted memories of her mother abandoning her, her father's leaving, her stepfather's desire, and her sins haunted her.

She was still recovering from the babies. Her milk was starting to come in, and she ached all over. Angel sat down, poured herself a large glass of Chablis, and since she had no one to talk to about the babies, she prayed. She prayed for mothers, for fathers, for her babies, and for the woman who found them. These babies needed a good mother, one who would not desert them like her own parents had deserted her. She rationalized that she had not abandoned them. She had merely given them to someone who could care for them. She didn't know the woman who found the babies, but someone told her that she was a teacher at St. Thomas More High School. A teacher. That was good. She had seen her at Mass and other church functions. Angel approved. This Harte woman would be just what her babies needed—a good mother.

Angel finished her wine and lit two candles, one for each baby. She knelt below the crucifix on her living room wall and again began reciting her prayers. She left the candles burning, as perpetual prayers for the babies. No one knows, and no one will ever have to know.

Someone had given Angel two Persian cats for company, silver tabbies named Shah and Pshaw. They had the run of the house and required extra work that Angel had neglected to do over the past several months. She had litter boxes in the bathroom and kitchen, but they were difficult to change. She couldn't bend over when she was swollen with babies inside her, and they had been filled with cat excrement for several weeks. The cats resorted to leaving their waste wherever they wanted. There were piles of newspapers, magazines, dirty clothes, and trash covering every surface; the scented candles she placed in every room did little to erase it. She needed more candles. She had pondered hiring a cleaning person, but she was too embarrassed about the current state of her house. Her life was her own, and she wanted no one to know about her business, and besides, it was nobody's business how dirty her house was. She wanted people to recognize her for doing God's work, not for her housecleaning. She would get around to cleaning the house and emptying the litter boxes sometime soon.

Once she felt a little stronger, she'd also need to handle the mess the babies made in the bathroom the day before. But that, too, would have to wait. Her stepfather never taught her how to clean, and she saw no reason to learn now. Enough scented candles and air-fresheners could work miracles.

Angel deliberated over calling the father of the babies to reveal that they had been born. He hadn't shown any interest in her or her pregnancy. She saw him regularly, but he never mentioned it. Did he know about the babies or want to know? She added some prayers for fathers in her prayers, refilled her wine glass, and dialed the phone.

Chapter 14

Gwen,
Monday Afternoon

Violet met Gwen and Clancy at the hospital with a fistful of papers to sign before they drove Louis and Marie to their home on Monday morning. The hospital confirmed that the babies were healthy and out of any danger of infection. Violet and her office had been easy to work with and expedited the foster parent application and provided one crib, some baby clothes, a case of diapers, infant car seats, a case of formula, and a debit card for other things the babies might need. They were loading the car when Detective Maggie and Officer Jack showed up with a few questions, but Clancy suggested they postpone the questions until the babies were settled in their new home. The two police officers agreed and agreed to come by later.

The Harte house was not set up for babies. The 2,000 square foot house consisted of three bedrooms, a den, a living room, kitchen, two baths, and a laundry room, plus the three-car garage. The realtor called it a split-bedroom house. Clancy and Gwen's room lay on the south side of the house. The other two bedrooms were situated on the north side. Michael and Andy shared a bedroom, and the three of them, much to April's annoyance, shared a bath. The split level proved a smart choice as it limited the amount of bickering that Gwen and Clancy had to endure. Of course, it also meant that they had no idea what was going on just a level away. Maybe the kids were trying to kill each other. Who knew?

The home was not enormous, but Gwen and the family maneuvered the large sectional to just fit in the smallish living room. It almost worked, but that was before the addition of a crib. Where could that go without displacing one or two of the other kids? For now, the crib would sit in the middle of it all until Gwen could rethink the furniture. That would not be today. Today she needed to focus on the babies.

As soon as everyone arrived home, the boys leaned into their new responsibility of watching Louis and Marie. They wanted to hold them, and pet them, and treat them like their treasured stuffed animals. Eventually, April came out of her room to have a look, so there were plenty of hands for holding and feeding them. April volunteered to do any shopping they might need, which, of course, necessitated her driving to the mall.

Gwen and Clancy had forgotten how much work tending babies was, especially two at once. Double duty on diaper changes, picking them up, putting them down, and feeding. As if conniving, the babies alternated their demands, sleeping and crying, crying and sleeping. The two four-pound packages demanded and received the attention of five full-sized, full-time servants. It was a good thing that school was out for the summer, as multiple hands were available to take turns managing every whimper or wail. Gwen also couldn't help but notice that the constant ringing of the family phones was adding to the confusion. The family was inundated with a constant stream of inquisitive minds calling to seek information or offer advice.

Frank Bilbaostrigo called. Edna was feeling better. Could they see the babies? Sure, later in the afternoon.

And if that weren't enough, people randomly started showing up at the front door. First came Father Leclerq. Gwen had never had a face-to-face conversation with him except for the compulsory "good morning" handshake after Mass, so his unannounced appearance felt like an intrusion. He wasn't anybody's favorite priest, at least not anybody she knew. On the dislike-to-like ten-point scale, he fell on the lower side. He was a priest and perhaps a recluse. Gwen didn't think that he was unfriendly but wondered how he became a priest with such paltering people skills.

Father Leclerq was clearly an introvert and seemed discontent and always wore an agonized look, which made Gwen and probably others uncomfortable. His contradictory homilies pronounced hell, fire, and damnation vacillating with altruism. As he rambled, he wavered from the Gospel, sometimes both sides in the same sermon. Nonconformity vacillating with compliance. Optimism vacillating with negativism. Confidence vacillating with insecurity. Gwen's instincts told her that he entered the priesthood because he was fleeing something. A lost love? An unhappy childhood? A demanding parent? Psychology 101. She wondered what it was.

Gwen answered the door saying, "Father Leclerq. Wow, this is a surprise. Please, come in. Would you like something to drink? Do you know my children: Andy, April, and Michael? Andy and Michael attend school at St. Gert's, and April attends St. Thomas More." She did a double take when she realized that he was a good three inches shorter than she was.

He followed her into the den without comment. Her children dutifully smiled and nodded, not knowing if they should fall to their knees or remain seated. They remained seated. At least they didn't say anything stupid.

"I don't think I've met your children and, thank you, nothing to drink," he answered without emotion, pushing back his unkempt and slightly greasy hair from his eyes. Gwen couldn't help but notice that he had dribbled coffee or water or some other unknown liquid on his black shirt. He glanced at the children and nodded in their direction. His voice was a little raspy, which grated on Gwen in the close quarters of their home. "I came to see the twins that you found. I like children, but I don't know many. I often don't see them except when they are baptized or making their First Communion. Sometimes they are completely grown up before I see them again. They come around when they get married or have their own kids to baptize. I wanted to see these new children of God." Typically, he stared off into space, not looking at anyone as he talked.

"Here they are. This is Marie," Gwen stated, gesturing toward the tiny brown baby. "And this is Louis. I wish I had more to tell you. They arrived with a scratchy blue wool blanket and a rosary for each baby, but other than that, we know nothing about them. One person called and told me to take good care of them and raise them with God. I assume she was the mother, but she didn't identify herself. Do you have any ideas?"

"Did she give her name?" he queried, not answering her question. "Or any other identifying information?"

"No name, no anything. She appeared to be giving these babies to us. I hope she calls back."

"May I hold one?" he asked. He reached out, took Louis in his arms, and held him next to his black shirt. Louis nearly disappeared in the arms of this large-chested man. He held him for several minutes in silence.

Gwen didn't know what to say, so she said nothing. Andy filled in the gaps with his question, "Hey, Father, did you ever wish you were a father?" Andy and Michael looked at each other and started giggling. April poked Andy, and both boys clammed up. Father Leclerq raised his eyes to the question but didn't answer. He passed Louis to April and picked up Marie. "They are tiny, aren't they?" he muttered after a few minutes, as he returned Marie to Gwen. "Thank you for letting me hold them. I hope that you get to keep them."

Gwen opened her eyes wide, "Oh, Clancy would love that," she retorted sarcastically. "He isn't all that crazy about having new babies in the house and certainly isn't up for a permanent arrangement. It's a lot of work. We had forgotten how challenging they are, but we're having fun. Are you sure you wouldn't like something to drink or perhaps even stay for dinner? I am about to put chicken on the grill. Potato salad and chocolate cake. It doesn't get better than that, and there is plenty."

Father Leclerq answered flatly, "No, I must be going. Let me know how they're doing and if you make any progress finding their mother. Thank you, again." With that he was out the door.

April summed it up. "I think Father Lacking-in-Charisma is a better name. Mom, he has zero personality, I swear. Do you remember the day he did Mass at TM? We thought we were all going to evaporate into our own boredom. No emotion, no energy. Dreary, sad, lonely, pathetic, what other words can I use?" She threw her hands melodramatically into the air.

"Don't be critical, April. He is responsible for a lot of people and all that goes on at St. Gert's. He's a busy man." Gwen silently agreed that he didn't have much charm today. Or ever. She expected a blessing for the babies, but he didn't offer one.

About 15 minutes later, Frank Bilbaostrigo and his wife, Edna, knocked on the door with their adult daughter, Junie May Layne. Frank hesitated at the door and was the first to speak. He carried the two blue blankets in his hand, "These two blankets were lying on the driveway. Are they the ones that the babies were wrapped in when you found them? They look the same. Did the police want them to help them identify the mother or who the babies belong to?"

"I didn't think of that," Gwen said. "Let me put them in the laundry room. Please come in."

"I hope you don't mind that I came, too," Junie May commented. "I heard about these dahl-ing babies and couldn't wait to see them. It's not every day that sweet twin babies are left in church. Thank heaven."

Gwen and her family had heard of Junie May but had never encountered her. Gwen knew that she served on every committee and attended every meeting at St. Gertrude's, but somehow had missed meeting her. "Glad to meet you, Mrs. Layne," Gwen replied. "I have heard lots about you."

Junie May was built like an upside-down pear, busty with spindly legs. Her olive skin displayed a few middle-aged wrinkles, which she tried to minimize with heavy make-up and bright red lipstick. Her jet-black hair revealed her Basque heritage with wisps of gray at the hairline making her suspect of hair color enhancement. She wore a red satin shirt and mid-thigh black shorts with black patent leather high-heeled sandals that accented her pigeon-toed feet. Hooped earrings dangled below her chin line and matched her silver necklace and the several bracelets that clanked on her arms.

"It's Junie May. Everybody calls me Junie May," she began as she extended three fingers for a handshake. She raised her wrist as her hand glided toward Gwen's. She drawled her words but never took a breath. "I'm glad to finally meet you. You're a teacher, aren't you? And your children are gor-geous. What is it that you teach? I attended TM. What a great school it is. You are in the best school in the state. I was senior class treasurer and runner-up for homecoming queen. Your house is gor-geous. It isn't very big though, is it? I don't think I have ever been on this street before. I live on the Southside area of town and have lived there for most of my life. What does your husband do? Isn't he a lawyer? Is he with one of the big firms? There are lots of TM grads who are lawyers. I am sure someone would take him. Don't you love it here? I would never live anywhere else. I don't know how people can exist in those small towns. They just don't seem to measure up."

Gwen didn't know how to respond. Clancy didn't need help getting a job. They had never lived in the city and knew many people who had never lived in the city and those folks got along fine. The three kids stared at Junie May in awe.

"Thanks," Gwen answered. That seemed to satisfy her.

The trio sat down on the couch, and Gwen handed them the babies. Junie May continued to ramble on about TM, answering and asking questions in her one–person conversation. The three of them oohed and aahed over the twins, holding first one and then the other. Andy and Michael kept them entertained with their impressions of babies. April rolled her eyes at her brothers' antics and retired to her room.

Junie May retrieved an armload of baby necessities from the car. The boys opened them item by item, rolling their eyes and making faces the whole time: receiving blankets, layettes, toys, and a bathtub. They would all be put to beneficial use. Junie May continued to carry on her monologue, ignoring the fact that no one else spoke. "What did you think when you found these babies? I'll bet you were shocked. I was shocked to learn they were of two different races. How does that work? They must have different fathers. Or different mothers? What did the hospital say? Do they have any birthmarks? They are very well developed for newborn twins. I have seen twins that are much older that don't have fingernails and not nearly this much hair. Did Health and Welfare give you a crib? I suppose they will give you everything you need. That's the government for you. Did you sell your house in Hawley, or are you moving back?" No one paid much attention to her ramblings after a few minutes.

Edna interrupted her as she picked up the rosaries on the table. "Are these the rosaries that were left with the babies? They are quite extraordinary and expensive. Rosaries like these can cost up to $500 each."

Junie May interrupted her mother. "I saw a rosary once that cost over $1,000. It was made with real pearls and was quite old. I don't remember where I saw it. Don't you love St. Gert's? Everybody there is kind and generous. It is such a loving community." She continued her gibberish.

Gwen didn't know much about rosaries and quipped, "I expect that would make for heavy praying." Her protestant background did not lend itself to knowledge of rosaries. Gwen owned one, but it was not in danger of being worn out. "That's a lot of money. If you can't buy it here, where would you get one like that?"

Edna, on the other hand, had a vast knowledge of rosaries. "You might find one in a specialty shop, a large Catholic gift shop, or the Vatican. I don't know, but these rosaries are distinctive. They are rarer than the usual, run-of-the-mill rosary. They are probably significant to the person who put them in the blanket." Edna was a go-to-daily-Mass, cradle-Catholic type person. She probably actually used her rosary.

Junie May continued, "I saw this type when I went to the Vatican for the first time. Have you ever been to the Vatican? I've visited twice. The next time I go I'm going to try for an audience with the pope. He is South American, you know, but, nevertheless, he's a good man. They'll select a Basque pope sometime. I'd love that. I'll bring you a large crucifix next time I go. It would look grand hanging right over that chair. You could move that awful picture and put up a crucifix. Do you have any crucifixes in this house? Father Rene would be glad to bless them. I could help you can find them on the Internet, eBay, probably."

Gwen's good humor was dwindling. Didn't Junie May ever stop talking? And thank you very much for the comment on the picture. It had been her grandmother's. The Internet was a good idea. Gwen had never been rosary shopping and decided to search the web for hints about these rosaries.

After what felt like a decade, Frank, Edna, and Junie May finally departed, so the family was able to dig into Gwen's promised dinner of chicken and potato salad. Clancy had warmed a little to having the twins there and took his turn holding and feeding them after everyone ate. They didn't cry much and opened and closed their eyes with sleepy blinks.

Chapter 15

Detective Maggie Monroe
Monday

Detective Maggie Monroe and Officer Jack Shetland had not previously worked together and wanted to get acquainted before they made their first visit as a team. They sat in the car talking for nearly an hour, sharing their experiences and philosophies, hoping not to be at odds with each other if something unexpected arose. They mulled over the babies, wondering together about the babies and where they might belong, and agreeing the three main issues didn't seem to be related. Abandoned. Two races. Catholic Church. Maggie had never worked a case regarding abandoned babies before, nor had Jack. They both knew that lots of babies were abandoned for myriad reasons. And the babies appeared to be twins, but at the same time, they were of different races, which didn't make sense and was a puzzle for both of them. But the third issue, the babies being abandoned in a Catholic Church could have a lot of ramifications and narrow possibilities down to a few.

Jack was Catholic, a cradle Catholic, born and raised in the Church by a devout mother who attended daily Mass. "I don't know who would leave babies in the church at Mass. I mean, it's a given that babies are important to us Catholics, and abandoning them is akin to leaving them in the desert to survive alone. You never know who might take them. A child molester or rapist or murderer. Who knows? We should talk to the priest and maybe even the bishop to gather whatever ideas they might have. They are good people and will do whatever they can to help."

Maggie agreed with part of his statement, but remained silent. Her experience with the Catholic Church priests and bishops was different. Should she tell what she knew to be true? The last priest she had dealt with had been into child pornography. She had been repulsed by it then, and the repulsion had continued, even these twenty odd years later. "Yes, you are right. Who knows who will turn up? Let's go see what the Harte family is like. I see some movement in there, so maybe they are done with dinner."

They knocked on the door and Clancy answered. She heard April and the boys arguing over who did what, reminding her of her own kids, Sean, Jimmy, and Sammy. Kids were kids, she thought.

"Good evening, officers. Any progress?" Clancy asked. Gwen was right behind him.

Maggie introduced herself and Jack to Clancy and he shuffled the baby in his arms to shake hands with each of them. "Don't get me wrong. We are enjoying the change in routine, but wondering if there will be an end anytime soon. I don't mean to sound unkind, but I don't think we can make this permanent. This would be five children. Five." He clicked off on his fingers: One. Two. Three. Four. Five. And I don't think we have room for more than the three we have."

Maggie looked at the babies lying on the couch and frowned, "I understand, but we don't have much to go on, more accurately, we don't have anything to go on. We talked to the hospital nurses, and they didn't have any ideas either. We called all the obstetric doctors in the area, but we got nothing from them either. HIPAA restricts them from helping us much, but at least they know we are looking for something or someone, and maybe someone will come forward. We went to St. Gert's to check the pews where you found them, but we couldn't rally anyone. No cars in the parking lot, and we don't know where the priest lives. Are you sure you didn't see anyone?"

"No, nobody. I sat in the back to make an early escape and was the only person back there. I don't know where Father Leclerq lives either, but he dropped by this afternoon," Gwen said. "The head usher Frank Bilbaostrigo and his wife came by, too. You might check with Frank because he seems to know everything."

Officer Jack looked surprised, "The priest came by? Father Leclerq? Really? He's not a very congenial priest. O'Grady wouldn't surprise me, but Leclerq?"

Gwen answered, "Yes, Leclerq. He called earlier, then dropped by. He seldom speaks to me at church, so it surprised me, too. Maybe he has a heart after all. He didn't say much, but he came. I haven't heard from O'Grady. He's not well, from what I understand. Stomach issues."

Jack said, "That sounds like Leclerq, not speaking, but I'm still surprised he showed up. I know Frank, and I'll call him. I go to St. Gertrude's, too, when I go to church, that is."

Chapter 16

Gwen
Monday Evening

After the police left, Michael, Andy, and Clancy dedicated themselves to assembling the crib. The wooden white, full-sized pen dwarfed the tiny babies even with both in it. Junie May had included a pale green crib sheet. Gwen and April dressed the twins in stereotypical pink and blue nightgowns as they settled into the evening. The den was adjacent to their bedroom where they would be able to hear them when they awoke. Clancy and Gwen prepared themselves for a sleepless night. Gwen set the alarm to ring every two hours hoping the babies would awaken and sleep at the same time. Maybe a Hail Mary would be in order for this trick.

Gwen intended to search the web for information about rosaries but decided to put it off until morning and maybe even have April do it. She and the Internet seemed to be inseparable friends.

Together, they fed the babies at 11 p.m. and hoped they would make it until 1 a.m. Clancy fell dead asleep, but Gwen merely dozed. She groggily fed them at 1 a.m. and returned to bed, hoping for a couple extra hours of shuteye before she had to get up again. The house was quiet, but suddenly it didn't feel quiet. Her eyes burst open. She looked at the clock. It was 1:54. She listened. Did she hear something or not? She reached over for Clancy who groaned, but his eyes also flashed open. It was a scraping noise, slow and muffled. Clancy sprang to his feet, hitting the floor with a thud. He turned on the bathroom lamp and grabbed the Derringer from the nightstand. "Be quiet," he warned Gwen.

Gwen wasn't about to argue. The scraping noise became a thwack followed by the sound of bushes being broken. Someone was clambering through them. Someone had broken into their house. Gwen rushed to the crib. It was empty. No babies. She screamed, "Clancy, they're gone!" She dialed 911 while Clancy surveyed the exterior.

But they weren't gone. Both babies lay in a chair by the window. They were crying the newborn whimper and trying to open or shut their eyes. "Oh, Clancy, they aren't gone. They are here, and I think they're okay."

April joined them in the living room, sleepily demanding, "What's going on?" Gwen was holding Louis, and April picked up Marie and gently rocked her.

"Someone broke in through the window and tried to take the twins. The kidnappers or burglars or whoever they were jimmied the window and got into the house. He moved the babies from the crib to the chair and was trying to get the window to stay up when your dad turned on the lights. He jumped out the window and left. I called 911, and the police should be here soon. I think the babies are okay."

The police arrived within five minutes. Gwen hoped Detective Maggie or Officer Jack would come, but then realized it was unlikely since it was the middle of the night. The night shift officers searched the exterior of the house before entering to ask some questions.

The houses in Harte's subdivision lay close together. But one of the main buying points of the house had been the wide array of shrubbery that acted as a barrier between homes. Every week a new flower or bush bloomed. The previous owners planted hedges near the house that were large and bushy and normally served as a deterrent for people jumping in or out of windows at 2 a.m. Now, broken branches on the manicured shrubs looked like they had been hit with baseball bats.

The two police officers entered the house and introduced themselves to Gwen and Clancy. Their badges announced Officer Ben Smith and Officer Ben Weston. *Hmm,* Gwen thought, *interesting name combination.* She also noticed the arm muscles that bulged beneath the sleeves of their police uniforms and was grateful to be on the right side of the law with these two. Before she could even offer them a seat, the duo began peppering them with questions: "Do you have any enemies or people who don't like you? Do you have any idea who would break into your house? Do you know why anyone would want to take the babies?"

Gwen summarized the babies' story. "I found them."

"You found them?" Ben Smith asked. "Oh, yeah, we heard something about that. Twins? Different races, right? Weird."

"Yes, you heard right. I found them at St. Gert's Catholic Church. At Mass. But now Health and Welfare has left them with us. The Safe Haven Act allows people to abandon their children legally if they leave them in a designated place or with a health care worker. The church is one of those designated areas. I guess that makes us the designated receivers. I don't know. The hospital named us 'next of kin,' and Health and Welfare told me 'Finders-keepers.' So, here they are." Louis was asleep again, and she tucked him back in bed. "They are about two days old and apparently have been abandoned." She went to the kitchen to warm some formula for Marie and bring back some coffee for all.

Marie began to whimper, and Clancy took her from April. Although they knew the babies were of different races, the officers seemed surprised.

"These two are brother and sister?" Ben Smith inquired. He was the taller of the two. "They sure don't look alike." An understatement at best. "I've heard of that before. Brother and sister of two different races, but I always thought they were adopted. I thought that happened with dogs not people. I don't think I've ever heard of human twins of different races. How could it be?"

April came to the rescue, "I checked it out on the Internet earlier and got a little information. I don't know how accurate it is. If the parents are of a different race, the children could also be of different races. They could be multi-racial. Or, if a woman ovulates and releases two eggs in the same month, and she receives sperm from two men, there could be two fathers. Sexual intercourse can be a couple days apart. The concept of two different fathers is called super-something. Superfecundation, I think. Or it could be superfetation, which is when a woman who is already pregnant, becomes pregnant again. DNA testing has improved greatly in the past few years. Scientists can prove if there are multiple parents. It's rare, and the circumstances must be right, but it can happen. Until DNA testing was available, people denied that it happened or blamed it on lots of other things, like witchery or even the devil."

Gwen was stunned at April's explanation. Where and when had she learned all that? She guessed that this proved there was something good about the Internet. Gwen had studied English, not science, and was never a whiz at understanding Mendel, his peas, or his dominant-recessive gene laws. She knew it would take some extra effort to understand superfetation and superfecundation, but she would work at it. Other people were sure to ask the same questions.

The two police officers listened to April's explanation with wrinkled brows and wide-open eyes, apparently confused by both the explanation and a young woman giving it.

Officer Smith said, "Well, you can tell that to Detective Monroe, she's all over this case, I understand. She's new on the force and seems to know what she's doing. I'm sure she'll call tomorrow. In the meantime, we'll check outside again."

The pair bid farewell, and went outside, researching the exterior of their home. Finding nothing of consequence, they returned to ask April more about superfetation and superfecundation, taking notes as she talked. "Thank you, April. We'll give this info to the detective."

Chapter 17

The Catholic Diocese
Tuesday

On Tuesday mornings after the Monday priests' meeting, Bishop Con and the vicar general met to resolve any problems that had come to light and to line out the schedule for the week. The bishop scheduled two rounds of golf, but his schedule for today and Thursday remained clear.

The bishop was old school. He left the parishes alone. If he didn't get wind of complaints and they made their tithes to the diocese, they were free to run the parishes without interference. He was outgoing and enjoyed a good laugh and tried never to get too serious with the pastors. "Buy 'em lunch and a coke, tell 'em a joke," was his management style. Let the VG handle the complaints. His life was good.

The bishop started, "What do we have on the docket this week, Ralph? I'm golfing on Wednesday and Friday afternoons. This morning I have a golf lesson, but I'll be back before lunch. Do you want me to handle any of the business left over from yesterday?" Before allowing a response, he continued, "Next week I travel north. And in two weeks, I'll tour the eastern part of the state. I hope I can find someone who wants to play golf with me. Last time I visited, I had to golf alone."

Ralph Loren, as usual, was organized and mapped out the bishop's schedule. He sat erectly in his chair with his legs tightly crossed. "We don't have much left over from yesterday, but you need to call Zabalapeda and McGraeth to inform them of their new assignments. I think you should call the Iron Man, too. We both know he was pumping iron, but someone needs to remind him that he is a priest. He'll tell you he was tying up loose ends after graduation, but we know better. I'll call the new editor of the newspaper and let him know he has a job. I'll have my administrative assistant call the others to inform them that they didn't get the job. They'll take rejection better from a woman."

Bishop Con griped, "I didn't like JP's comments about the Hispanics. He sometimes gets out of control. You should talk to him and remind him to be kind. Also, did you notice I called him Javier? He always says, if you call him Javier, he'll know you're an asshole. I think I'll call him Javier from now on." He relished the thought and chuckled aloud at rankling Father JP Shannon. "The majority of new Catholics in our state are Hispanic. He needs to put a clamp on his mouth even if he doesn't like them. For the record, I agree that a woman should not be the editor. An editor learns a lot of inside information that we might not want revealed. Plus, women are known for their loose lips." The bishop smacked his lips together as in kissing. "Loose lips sink bishops." He and Ralph chuckled at his little joke.

Ralph interjected, "JP's mother is Hispanic. He must have some deep-rooted anger to put them down as he always does. I don't think it would do any good to reprimand him. Instead, maybe we just point out his biases to him, or try to ignore them altogether. He'll retire soon, and the problem will disappear."

The bishop nodded and continued, "I got that speeding ticket fixed for O'Grady. The mayor doesn't mind making them go away but doesn't want it to get out. Would you call O'Grady and tell him to keep it quiet and slow down? He'll listen to you better than me."

"Absolutely," Ralph replied, making a note to himself. "Now, what about those babies? We don't want them causing us problems."

Bishop Con also visualized the potential headlines and reminded Ralph, "We need to keep eyes and ears open about these babies. A headline like that could explode in our faces. We haven't had any negative publicity for a while, and I don't want to start now. The papers would blow this out of proportion. I don't know why any bird-brained woman would leave her babies in a church. If Rene's right, she's probably an RF and thinks Mother Church means 'Mother Church.' Why didn't she just take them to the police station?"

"If I know Rene, he will have it under control. He'll deal with it. We won't hear anything else about it, in or out of the press," Ralph said.

The bishop responded, "That's good. I think I will give him a call to remind him to get it crammed under the carpet." He looked at the to-do list that Ralph had given him. Four phone calls and golf would be calling.

Chapter 18

Father Josey
Tuesday Morning

Father Josey Zabalapeda's administrative assistant, Marcy, called. "Father Josey," she declared, "I forgot to have someone deposit the collection. It is probably in my bottom drawer. That's where they usually put it. The deposit slips are in the checkbook. It should be about $1,500. Could you take it to the bank or ask someone else to do it?"

Marcy was a good administrative assistant, always thinking ahead. He responded, "Of course, I'll take it. Don't worry. I can take it right now."

He considered Marcy and hoped she was okay. She had been ill several mornings for the past few months and said she needed a week off for her mental health. At age 30, Marcy turned the heads of many men but remained unmarried. She wore her curly, black hair cropped short and her deep-set, black eyes smiled at everyone she met. Everyone liked her. Josey noted that she had gained a little weight recently and prayed nothing was wrong. Perhaps she was not paying attention to her health. She had dropped out of college after two years intending to become a nun but decided that the final vows were too restrictive, and she wanted a husband and children. Josey felt fortunate to have her as his girl Friday and would be glad to have her back when she returned.

He signed off from the Internet, picked up the collection, and counted it out. It totaled $1,843.62. Higher than Marcy thought. He opened the door to his pickup before it hit him. *Why don't I invest this week's collection in GrayBonePhone7? By the time Marcy gets back, it will have doubled. This will be a great pick-me-up for her. I'll deposit the collection in person and transfer it online to my own account. Then I'll swap it back to the church when it doubles. I can make a little scratch for myself and add in a few extra bucks for the parish.* The week's collection was larger than most weeks, but not large by the super-parish standards. "If I double it, we will have $3,600. I could probably keep $600 of it for my bother," he thought aloud. He drove his pickup to the bank to deposit the cash. *No one will be the wiser,* he thought. He checked his wallet to make sure that he had debit cards for himself and the parish.

He paused as he fingered the debit card. His bad angel loomed over his tattoo. *It isn't stealing,* he thought to himself. *I'm in charge of the parish and therefore in charge of the finances. If the finances go south, I obviously will pick up the pieces. It's perfect!* He laid his hand on his shoulder where his tattoo was and flipped the bad angel away.

He passed through the drive-in window to deposit the money. One of his parishioners staffed the window. He handed her the debit card and the bag filled with the parish offering. "Good morning, Father Josey. It looks like a good collection this week. I always worry that someone will steal this money before you or Marcy deposit it. I'd hate to see that happen to the parish collection. You work too hard for that."

Josey smiled at the teller, but his conscience took over. Taking this money was stealing. It was taking hard-earned money and using it differently than its intended use. Maybe this wasn't what he should be doing. He was unsure. It was a tough decision. He saw a sign behind the cashier that read, *Money Used Wisely Isn't Spent Foolishly.* It sounded like a Yogi Berra-ism, he thought to himself. *This is a wise use of the money. Everybody knows that it takes money to make money. To make my parish thrive, I need more than $1,800 a week. I'll do it. I know I'm not perfect, but this plan is pretty close.*

His cell phone jangled as Josey returned from the bank, "Josey, it's Bishop Con. We missed you at the meeting Monday."

Josey's color rose as his Catholic guilt set in. "Uh, I had some work to do and thought it needed to get done. Marcy's gone this week, and I've got extra things to do." He didn't enjoy lying to the bishop, but a few Hail Mary's after confession would take care of this little peccadillo. Our Lady of Perpetual Tears was Josey's first church as pastor, and he didn't want to rock the boat. He could be sent off to one of the remote parishes where it snowed day in, day out, or where the Internet was limited and unreliable. How would he ever be able to day trade? "I was headed over to your office to find out what committee you decided to put me on."

"That's why I called," the bishop answered. "I wanted to tell you in person. Congratulations! You're the new finance guy. This is a great assignment."

"Finance? That's great. I thought you would put me back on Social Justice. I figured George would stay on finance because he's been doing it a long time. I never dreamed of finance. What do I do?" Josey's conversation was rambling, and his mind turned flip-flops as he talked with the bishop. Talk about an honor! A full committee while in his first parish. Everybody knew the finance committee ran the operations. This was too good to be true.

Bishop Con continued explaining, "This is an easy one. You don't have much to do. You will attend the diocesan finance meetings and represent the pastors regarding finances. You studied finance in college, didn't you?"

"Yes, sure, I studied finance before I decided to enter the priesthood. It is my first love." He immediately corrected himself. "That is, after God and doing God's work, of course." His finance courses had been difficult, and he never comprehended many of the concepts. Claiming that he majored in finance played better with the girls. Accounting didn't quite have the same effect on women. Accounting majors were mostly nerds and, besides, it wasn't his cup of tea anyway; you had to be precise, or the problems were wrong. There was no room for creativity. On the other hand, with finance, you could be creative. He retook a few classes and graduated with a 1.8 grade point average. Although 4.0 GPAs were nice, you didn't need a 4.0 to be successful. He had rationalized his grade point with the law school adage "A-students make good judges, B-students make good lawyers, C-students make good money." With D's, he must be a genius, he convinced himself. When he applied to the seminary, they frowned on his grades, but the dean voided a couple unimportant classes and turned his 1.8 GPA into a 2.8 GPA, which permitted him to matriculate without restrictions. The diocese needed priests badly, and the seminary didn't care what your major was. They were seeking warm, male bodies.

"Of course, doing God's work," the bishop rolled his eyes to himself. "As usual, the diocesan budget is tight. No extra money for anything. The pastors need to have a strong voice on this committee to affirm that the money is used for the pastors and not eaten up with trivial things. A couple of charities out there are chasing the diocesan dollars, and we don't want the charities to steal our money. They can raise their own. CCP, Catholic Charity Plus, is the worst. It is aggressive and wants our money. They claim their mission is to take care of one-parent families, especially racially mixed children, but it wants us to give it money. To put it bluntly, it is a royal pain in the ass. I am sure you can get some advice from George on how to say 'no.' Ralph is always willing to help, too. You will be doing what you like to do. We are doing each other favors. You'll do a good job, Father Josey."

Chapter 19

Angel
Tuesday Morning

Angel had prayed all night. Her breasts hurt. She searched WebMD but didn't find anything that would help, other than sage tea and cabbage compresses, but even those seemed unlikely. They sounded too much like an old-wives tale. She used cold packs alternating with hot packs. Both helped initially, but then neither did. She wanted to get on with her life. She hoped that she would be able to go to confession soon. She lit more candles, praying to reduce the pain.

Angel roused early on Tuesday morning uncertain of her decision to abandon the babies. She couldn't control her thoughts. Were they okay? Were they in the same home? Did they sleep well? Had they grown any? Her breasts continued to ache and burn, and she was miserable. She cried out, "I've got to have something to help with the pain and pressure. I can't go to the doctor. God help me. The voice of one crying in the wilderness." She would have to bear it. God's punishment never ended.

Angel skipped her shower and dressed quickly while gulping down her usual breakfast of a peanut butter-banana sandwich, orange juice, and coffee on her way to work. Her office contained a single filing cabinet, a bookshelf, a cluttered oak desk, and a too-big swivel oak chair with a leather seat and a smaller second chair, which was loaded with more papers. The office furniture showed signs of age with scratched and marred surfaces after many years of service. She tried to keep it tidy because of the constant parade of visitors, but it didn't work out, and the disarray grew. Every now and then, she dumped a pile of miscellany into a box and stowed it in the closet to keep the gossip down.

She thought a little about the father of the babies. That long-ago day had been terrible. A nightmare. They served on a committee together. It was something about the Catholic moral code, and they had worked late. Just the two of them.

She had seen him around but had nothing in common with him. No reason in her mind to get to know him better, especially since she knew she was smarter than he, although that's not something he would ever admit. Neither of them enjoyed people very much nor had many friends. He was athletic, charming, and handsome, while she was less than pretty, chunky, and somewhat dowdy. Their childhoods were startlingly different; his had come from what sounded like a loving, wholesome family, while she had endured Charlie and his advances. She was fair with blue eyes and, although his complexion was darker than hers, she would not consider him as having dark skin. He had black hair, and his deep-set black eyes seemed to pierce through her. They had both seen the world and were committed to their faiths and careers. God above all. No matter what.

They had been thrown together to work on a committee that neither of them had any interest in. Other members of the committee had gone home, and they were left with cleaning up. He started prying into her personal life, asking some personal questions, questions that he had no right to ask. She thought he was nosy, but at the same time, she thought he could be trusted. No one knew her history.

One thing led to another. It was as if he somehow knew her innermost thoughts. But how could he know? He prodded her to tell her secrets—the secrets of her childhood. She did and immediately regretted it. When she began to leave, he grabbed her arm and crushed her breasts with his hands, forcing her in pain to the floor. He sneered, "Your father called you 'Angel?' You're no angel. You're a violation of God's commandments."

He slapped her across the face, keeping her down. Before she knew it, he was on her, inside her, raping her. She had never known such pain or such humiliation. It hadn't been that way with Charlie. Charlie was always gentle. But this one wounded her. Unremitting, stabbing pain, and shame. When he was done, he threatened her. If she told anyone, anyone at all, he would expose her secret to everyone, and she would be ruined. She should not go to a priest to receive absolution. No absolution for her. She was the devil. He left her splayed on the floor and disappeared out the door. He never spoke to her again. About anything. They had worked together on projects since, but he never acknowledged her in any way. To him, she was invisible.

The following evening, she pleaded with God for absolution. God, of course, forgave her. He always did, which is why she preferred to talk to God directly. She could tell Him everything. God gave her a throbbing headache as punishment. And now, as another punishment, God had given her twins, and of different races. These babies were her penance.

More important things demanded her attention today. She couldn't allow herself to think of the babies, plus she knew Mrs. Harte would take good care of them. God would forgive her for giving the babies away. He forgave the thief on the cross. Why wouldn't He forgive her? She forced herself to think about other things.

Hail Mary, full of grace...

She lit two extra candles, one for each baby and ceremoniously positioned them on her desk. She would let them burn all day as prayers for the health of the babies. She then poured some sacramental wine into her coffee mug and sipped a little. It was tasteless, but it was part of her prayer ritual.

At early morning Mass, she spent more time on her knees. She once traveled to the Basilica in Mexico and observed people crawling for miles to atone for their sins. Their bleeding hands and knees left a trail of blood in the streets. Perhaps if she increased the pain in her knees, the pain in her breasts would go away.

After her prayers, she meditated about her predicament. She needed advice. She needed to go to a real confession. She needed to confess to giving away the babies and all the lying. Any priest who heard her confession wasn't supposed to tell anyone, but she knew that wasn't always true. Anything heard in confession was open for discussion when shared. She would have to wait it out. The pain would go away soon. Surely, it would.

Chapter 20

Father Paul McGraeth
Tuesday Morning

Paul McGraeth came through the door like a storm. The bishop had recently reassigned his associate pastor to another diocese due to his heavy drinking. This left Paul the sole priest in the 500-family parish. No nuns, two incompetent deacons, who worked when they couldn't find a good game of gin rummy, and a staff of ancient crones, the Religious Fanatics crowd. The RFs. Holy Fathers, the matriarchal church of the diocese, deserved better. He deserved better.

At age 55 with 30 years as a priest, Paul McGraeth had taken only one sabbatical. When he entered the priesthood, the church promised him a sabbatical every five years, but the promises of the church didn't always become reality. He suspected he had prostate cancer because he was spending more time in the bathroom but didn't want to mention it because cancer was not on his personal agenda. He needed a sabbatical, that was all. He would talk to the VG this week.

He and Ralph Loren had always been friends, but since Ralph's promotion to vicar general, he had become increasingly pompous. He used to arrive on time for every meeting and event, but now he came late, which allowed him to make an entrance. He used to go out for a beer with the boys on Sunday nights; now he dined with the bishop. He used to wear blue jeans and a t-shirt; now it was all slacks and Ralph Lauren.

Paul had passed through a variety of stages during his years as a priest. His womanizing stage allowed him to peck at all the pretty girls who came to pre-marriage counseling. It was rather a joke with him. He held a private female-only session for some of his pre-marriage "counseling" when he and the bride-to-be would have a bedroom tumble. He told them that having a fling with the priest would keep God in their marriage and strengthen it. Sleeping with the priest who performed the marriage was merely another part of the ritual of marriage. It was one of those unspoken Catholic mysteries. Cradle-Catholics would do anything for a priest. He would give them a song and dance about going to hell if they tattled to their husbands and mostly, they bought it, hook, line, and sinker. The ones who didn't, he warned them that he would put a crown of thorns on their marriage. That usually shut them up.

Only once had a bride alleged fraud on his part. Her name was Francie, and she wanted an annulment shortly after her wedding. She came to him in confession and begged him to "counsel" her again. She was a beauty with long black hair and long, long shapely legs. Oh, those legs. Her body screamed "seduce me," and he had. Nine months later she gave birth and claimed him as the father. He conferred with the chairperson of the church council, who had called a friend of a friend, and a few days later DNA proved otherwise. It had cost him a chunk of change, but it was better than having a kid with his last name.

He had passed through the financial planning stage, which focused on money and investment schemes that would net a large return. He used a broker and did okay for himself. He would have plenty of money when he retired.

During his traveling stage, he hooked up with a cruise line and became the cruise pastor. The cruise lines paid nothing, but he traveled the world and visited every continent. Traveling was wonderful. He took a friend with him from time to time as he found it much more pleasurable traveling with a companion.

But now it was the age of electronics and at first, he had resisted. It seemed like such a waste of time, but the parish council had given him a computer and insisted that he learn to use it. He hadn't realized how much he could learn and after a few months he admitted that he loved the Internet. It was a way to relax, enjoy a few sites during the evening and found he spent more and more time on it. Through various social media outlets, he had met a few "friends" who seemed to have the same interests as he did and every night at 7:00 p.m., he spent time with his friends. It became an addiction.

But the stage that wasn't really a stage dealt with his sexuality. He was gay, or perhaps bisexual. He couldn't be sure. He enjoyed sex with both men and women, but preferred men. At least until a gorgeous woman danced into the picture. He started out in high school, screwing the naïve, love-starved cheerleaders, using his good looks and glib manner to seduce them. He quoted authors such as Emerson, "Give all to love, obey thy heart… nothing refuse." He led them to believe that this was a Bible passage, proving that they should have sex with him. None of them bothered to look it up.

During college, he enjoyed sex with a few women, but if his fraternity brothers seduced him, it gave him immense pleasure. Seminary classes were all male, which limited his options: erudite Catholic men. It was with those men that he learned that he truly preferred males, especially athletic ones. When his parents found out about his sexual orientation and promiscuity, they disowned him. He wasn't proud of his lustful thinking and thought that his vow of abstinence would cure it. It hadn't.

Paul struggled to be an abstinent heterosexual like most of the other priests he knew. He "counseled" a few women now and then, and when women flirted with him, he gave them a wink. Sometimes more. He had an affair with the wife of one of his deacons but broke it off after a few months. She announced to the bishop that she was pregnant, and he immediately shifted Paul to another parish. Moving was a pain, but it had saved his ass.

Father McGraeth's longest partner was Father Mark Simon, an Episcopal priest whom he met at an ecumenical service in a small town. Their six-year long relationship continued until they were both transferred to new parishes and distance prohibited their seeing each other regularly. Father Mark had left the priesthood, and now he and his current partner owned a wedding chapel in Las Vegas.

Father Paul McGraeth was popular with his parishioners. He was smart, good-looking, funny, meticulous, and organized. He remained fit with a daily workout and watched his diet. *No paunch for Paul,* he reminded himself, as he admired his slim physique in the mirror. He wore his salt and peppered black hair short with longer sideburns. He fancied himself as a dark-haired George Clooney and considered himself a Renaissance man, knowledgeable in a myriad of areas. He wore a goatee in the winter and shaved it off in the summer saying, "I need to breathe." He enjoyed gourmet cooking and bragged about his soups. He converted his extra bedroom into a bachelor pad complete with a jetted tub, a refrigerated wine cabinet, high-end computer station, internet, and large screen TV. It wasn't the ideal arrangement, but it would do until he was selected for bishop, which was sure to happen soon.

The bishop in Minnesota astutely placed young Paul on the bishop track. He fulfilled a tour in Rome to familiarize himself with the culture of the church and became fluent in Latin and Italian. He served a tour in South America, where he became fluent in Spanish and Portuguese and where he also completed his doctorate. He had pastored both large and small parishes and filled every assignment that came his way. He was a top contender in the running for vicar general last year, but Ralph Loren pulled some strings and beat him out. Luckily, he still had an ace in the hole: his brother in Anchorage.

The phone rang as Paul walked into his office. "We missed you on Monday, Paul," the bishop began. "We took care of business quickly, and we even finished early. I wanted to tell you that you have been assigned the Social Justice Committee."

Oh, shit, McGraeth thought to himself. "Can't do it, Con," he announced to the bishop. He didn't want any committee and this one met at night, and it would interrupt his time on the internet with his friends. "I don't have time. I'm the only one here. You gave me two incompetents for deacons and took the nuns away. They weren't any good anyway. They were screwing either the choir leader or each other. I don't know which. Maybe both." He continued his rant, "The RFs who work here are always smiling and filled with the 'Joy of the Lord,' but the quality of work is horrible. They sing hymns non-stop when they are working, and, in all honesty, they make me sick. Besides having to cover for all their shortcomings, Social Justice is due for an overhaul, and I have no time and definitely no interest. Get yourself another boy to help with the sick, lame, and lazy."

The bishop paused for a second, stunned. He didn't know what to say. Few priests talked to him this way, and it caused him heartburn. The bishop was a few years older than Paul, but Paul knew how to push his buttons. He knew that the priests swore among themselves, occasionally in his presence, but usually they didn't swear with such vehemence. "You mean the infirm, the hungry, and the homeless, not sick, lame, and lazy, Paul. Show some compassion. I don't have anyone else. You'll have to do it. Why don't you plead your case to Ralph? Maybe he can find someone else." They finished their conversation and hung up.

Paul shook his head thinking of the conversation. The bishop avoided disharmony whenever he could. It was typical: Give it to Ralph Loren. Let him get ulcers over these obnoxious priests. He can borrow some antacids from O'Grady. *Ralph Loren can go to hell, as can the bishop*, Paul thought as he hung up the phone.

Chapter 21

Gwen
Tuesday

Morning arrived early at the Harte household. The babies awoke starving, of course, and Andy and Michael clamored out of bed to see if they had grown. Monday had been a long day and a longer night. Clancy and Gwen had barely closed their eyes after the police departed, and while the babies had not reawakened during the night, Clancy and Gwen were groggy.

"That was fun. Your promise of two-or three-weeks tops happened all in 24 hours. What a long night!" Clancy grumbled reminding her of their contract. "I don't know who these babies belong to, but if this is a hint of what lies ahead, they're going to have a rough life."

Gwen agreed. "I never dreamed that anyone would try to snatch them. We must find the mother. If she doesn't want them, okay, but she has an obligation as a mother and to us. We deserve to know what lies ahead for these little guys."

As the sun came up, they filed outside to assess the damage. The screen was ripped off, and its frame was twisted. The window latch was smashed, but somehow the glass had not broken. Some bush limbs had snapped off during the intruder's hasty retreat, but the shrubbery would recover. Paint would conceal the scratches on the wall, and they could fix the window frame and replace the lock. The bushes would heal.

The Harte family devoured a noisy breakfast of scrambled eggs and bacon while speculating who, what, how, and why. They knew when. They discussed leaving the doors locked or unlocked and watching for strangers in the neighborhood. In Hawley, they never locked the doors, because no strangers came around. Everybody knew everybody and watched out for each other. Andy and Michael volunteered to patrol the perimeter on their bikes after breakfast.

The phone rang. It was Violet from Health and Welfare, "How is everything?" she chirped. "How did you manage through the night?"

Gwen related the story of the break-in and attempted kidnapping, and Violet shrieked. "Oh, my heavens. I'll be right over." Oh, happy day. Time to get dressed.

Violet swept in within the hour. She was laden with baby clothes and formula for Louis and Marie. A tall, portly woman, Violet wore her thick, grayish hair in a bun, piled high on her head. Her clothes could have been called frumpy, but she looked comfortable. Today she wore a lavender skirt with a matching blouse and a too-long lavender jacket. Her shoes qualified as good sensible shoes but would never make the designer window displays in Paris. She poked and prodded the babies and made a few queries about the break-in. Gwen wondered how old she was and settled on 50.

"Did you lock your doors last night? Did you see anyone? Did you call the police? Do you have an alarm system?" Gwen wondered if Violet thought they had broken into their own house and assured her that they didn't know who the intruder was. They visited for a while switching babies back and forth. Violet promised to draft a report about the incident and mail them a copy.

Andy and Michael began perimeter duty watching for unknown, shady characters who might be lurking around. Their imaginations brought about images of unsavory villains with long black coats, stovepipe hats, and handlebar moustaches, right out of some teenaged mystery novel. Andy wrapped himself in a blanket and announced that he was an undercover agent, reminding them that it was a pun.

April logged onto the Internet, seeking additional information on superfetation, super-fecundation, and rosaries. She volunteered to drive to the library for research, if necessary. Gwen smiled to herself, *I never thought I would see her researching rosaries.*

Soon everyone was busy with their assigned tasks. The boys guarded the perimeter while Clancy left for work. Gwen assigned herself to the babies and called the window repair person. April offered to drive to the gas station to fill the gas tank in case they needed a full tank today.

Gwen was starting to bathe the twins when the phone rang. It was Junie May Layne. "Any luck yet in finding out who the mother is?" she inquired. "I have my suspicions, but I am reticent to say who. You know, Gwen, evil people live in this world. Evil. How has your husband adjusted? I can't imagine my dear husband being such a good sport, although he usually is. He is a banker and extremely high up in his position. He loves babies as much as I do, but he is reticent. I can't believe anyone would abandon such adorable babies." She had the oddest way of drawing out her words yet spewing them out rapidly. You had to listen closely to understand her.

Gwen cringed at the word "reticent." It was included in every sophomore class vocabulary list, yet it wasn't a commonly used word. She guessed it was the one word that Junie May learned in her TM English class. Was she one of those people who never moved beyond high school?

"No, we are searching for some ideas," Gwen reported, not mentioning the break-in. Junie May would find out soon enough. "Health and Welfare, law enforcement, and the church are all investigating. I am sure someone will identify herself. You and your parents are active in the parish. Do you know any pregnant girls or rather girls who may have given birth?"

Gwen was immediately sorry that she had raised the question. "No one that I know of," Junie May answered, "but these young girls are sneaky. There was the Baldwin girl, who had a premature baby as they say. I don't think it was a preemie as it weighed almost 6 pounds. But the Baldwin family didn't reveal who the father was. She matriculated at TM but didn't make the cut. She's back in public school and will probably end up being a store clerk or something. Thomas More takes only the top students, as I'm sure you are aware. But that was last year. And there was the Clayton family. Their daughter was Christina. She also went to TM. The Clayton's adopted a little brown baby. But I know better. That baby wasn't adopted. It was theirs. They tried to keep it a secret. Christina is back in public school, too. We don't put up with that type of thing at TM."

Gwen tried to cut her off. "Thanks anyway, Junie...."

Junie May didn't miss a beat, "And there is the Farina girl. She was a, you know, the 's' word. She did what she wanted. I don't know who she gave her baby to. Evil, I tell you. I will call a few people and see what I can find out. I know everybody. The teachers at TM love you. Did I ever tell you that I went to TM and was the treasurer of the senior class and runner-up for homecoming queen? That was a long time ago though, but I still know everybody who has gone to TM. I'll call you back or maybe drop by. I would love to see those babies again. Don't worry. I won't say a thing about these babies. I'll keep it zipped, zipped, zipped." She made the zipped lip motion across her lips and locked it with a key although Gwen couldn't see her. She hung up before Gwen could say goodbye and good riddance.

The window repair person arrived and began fixing the window frame. Although the glass was not broken, he recommended a new window, which she rejected.

The next phone call was from Father Leclerq. "Gwen, Father Rene here," he drew out each word as if it were a chore. Nobody that she knew called him Father Rene, always Father Leclerq. "How are your babies? I was praying for them and decided to call. Do you need anything? I mean, can the church help you in any way? I sort of feel responsible since you found them at St. Gert's. Let me know." Click. Short and sweet. He hung up on her before she could respond to his questions or tell him that Detective Maggie and Officer Jack wanted to see the church. April's moniker for him, Father Lacking-in-Charisma, gained merit. "Well, Father Lacking-in-Charisma," she said to herself, "at least I know you are alive."

Clancy called a couple times during the morning, but Gwen didn't know if he was checking on her or the babies or trying to stay awake. He called again at lunch, volunteering to bring something home to cook on the grill, along with a little baby formula for an appetizer. Yum.

The next phone call was a little disconcerting. Gwen had developed the habit of checking the caller ID, and this one read, "Blocked." Gwen thought it was probably a telemarketer, but she answered as a question, "Hello?"

A deep voice articulated, "They are the devil's own. Give them back to God."

"Holy shit," Gwen cried aloud. She didn't recognize the voice and wondered if it was a computer, that AI business she had read about, or a real person. Gwen slammed down the phone and called Clancy, followed quickly by a call to the police station where she was immediately connected with Detective Monroe.

"We'll be right there," Maggie reassured Gwen. In the past three days, Gwen had spent time with mystery callers, a priest, Health and Welfare, the hospital, and two different versions of her friendly police department. Plus, Junie May. In addition, a variety of well-wishers and curiosity seekers sought them out. The media had not called, but they were sure to get wind of this soon.

Detective Maggie Monroe and Officer Jack Shetland arrived within the hour. Gwen was glad to see them. Maggie's mere presence calmed Gwen, while Officer Shetland's overbearing physique seemed frightening, yet reassuring. His mere appearance would frighten most intruders away.

Maggie asked Gwen about the caller. "It was such a weird message," Gwen said, as she handed them the scrap of paper where she had penciled the message word by word: *They are the devil's own. Give them back to God.*

"It's spooky, as if he or she wanted me to get rid of them, almost like he hated them. I think the first caller was a woman, and this one was a man, but it could be the other way around. Both voices were disguised somehow, maybe Artificial Intelligence, I don't know, but it's spooky and I don't like it. The first caller sounded like she knew them, was connected to them in some manner. This one sounded like he hated them. I wonder if the first caller was the mother, and this caller was the father. Or vice versa. It makes no sense to me. It isn't much to go on. I can't identify the voice."

"Try, Mrs. Harte," Maggie implored. "We have no clues right now, so anything you can tell us will be a help. Was the voice raspy, deep, squeaky, smooth? Higher or low pitched? Did you hear any noise in the background? You must remember something. What do the words mean?"

"I think the voice was deep, but it might have been altered or deepened. It didn't sound natural, possibly a computerized voice, like he was talking into a glass. The message was brief, 'They are the devil's own. Give them back to God,' which doesn't mean anything to me. I didn't hear anything in the background, but I hung up quickly, so I might have missed anything that was there. I'm sorry I am not more help."

"Are you sure he didn't say anything else?" Maggie queried.

"I'm sorry, Maggie. It was merely a voice, a weird, threatening voice. I am quite sure it was a man, but it could be a deep-voiced female. He blurted out the words and was gone before I had time to remember that I would need to identify the voice. I wish I could tell you that he had green or purple hair, but I can't." Gwen could have kicked herself that she hadn't listened better.

Maggie turned toward Jack and suggested, "Maybe we should tap their phone. With two phone calls and a break-in, it sounds like someone is trying to get their attention. How do you feel about a tap, Mrs. Harte?"

Before Gwen could answer, Andy and Michael crashed through the back door. "Mom, we saw him. He was in a car. He drove by, and then drove by again. He had a black hat on and looked mean and evil. I am sure it was him."

"Slow down, fellows, what are you talking about? Him who? Did he do something to you?" Officer Shetland stooped down and placed his hands on his knees as he looked them in the eyes.

They looked at him and backed up a little in awe of his size. They stammered as they answered his questions. "The guy who broke in. It was a b-b-bl-black car with writing on the door like a taxicab. It didn't have the thing on top though," Andy motioned like a taxi dome. "It might have been a delivery car."

"Show me," the Officer Shetland said, and the three of them headed toward the front door with Maggie close behind. "Yeah, nothing on top," Michael agreed. "The guy had a baseball cap on. He looked mean."

"Why do you think it was him?" Maggie asked, following them to the door. "I mean, did you talk to him, or did he stop in front of the house or anything?"

"No, he didn't stop. We just know." Both boys nodded adamantly.

The officers looked at each other. It didn't sound like probable cause for an arrest warrant. Maggie made a note in her notebook and sighed, "Thanks, guys, excellent work. We'll take it from here. Keep up the good work, but if you see him again, don't try to talk to him. Tell your mom and she'll call us." They didn't want another problem added to the one they already had.

Chapter 22

Father Josey
Early Tuesday Morning

Just after the opening bell rang on Wall Street on Tuesday morning, Father Josey Zabalapeda added another 700 shares of GrayBonePhone7, a few cents under $37.00 per share, using his entire $26,000. He looked at the parish account. The parish checking account balance was up, over $6,000. After he added the $1,800 from this week's offering, it would total over $7,800, and the building fund contained another $15,000. *All the bills are paid. Why not add to the parish coffers with a little GrayBone magic?* he thought to himself. Two hundred and ten shares. Click. Done.

He keyed in his password to enter the day traders' chat room and read an extensive list of subjects searching for people chatting about the curious upward-bound stock GrayBonePhone7. He lurked around the online chat room, clicking here and there, looking for his chat room buddy, DBLUP, to see what he knew. He and DBLUP had chatted before. DBLUP disclosed that he was a stock market analyst with facts and figures that were unavailable to many. He mentioned that he had earned fortunes three separate times by day trading and knew what he was talking about. He confided to Josey that he once rolled a $50,000 investment into over a half a million and repeated it again the next year. Between the periods of prosperity, DBLUP revealed he had lost a few dollars, but that was insignificant compared to his gains. DBLUP divulged that although he wasn't currently employed, his resumé included several different large investment firms. He had garnered knowledge from the best. Most investment firms were too conservative for his tastes so, he left them and worked his own portfolio. DBLUP liked GrayBonePhone7; no, rather he loved GrayBonePhone7. He predicted that it was the most promising stock out there. Other day traders were chattering about GrayBonePhone7 and some other stocks, but Josey and DBLUP coded their conversations. We don't want too many people in on this sweet deal. DBLUP confided, "We want the price of GrayBonePhone7 to remain low and stabilize to cash in on this bonanza." They both clicked off the chat room.

After lunch, Josey checked his stocks again. "Glory be. God is good." GrayBonePhone7 was up to $42.00. The church now had $8,800. His $26,000 was now worth over $30,000. Not a bad day's work. He reread the reports. They predicted a split on Thursday that would double the number of shares. If the trend continued, they would be back up to $42.00, maybe $45.00 in no time at all. "DBLUP is right. Won't Marcy be proud? No pissant raffles or bingo games for Our Lady. Our Lady of Perpetual Tears will soon be the Lady of Perpetual Joy. Maybe I can give Marcy a raise or buy her a new computer. I might even take her out to dinner, she'd like that. We can paint classrooms or buy the latest videos for the kids. Maybe add a room. Ride high, my GrayBone, ride high."

Josey plunked his baseball cap on his head and stepped out the door for his morning run. The mail carrier was coming up the walk, and the two collided.

"Hey, Padre, where you are going in such a hurry?" the mail carrier greeted. "You got to officiate at a funeral?" It was a poor joke, but the priest laughed.

"No, no funeral. I'm going for a run to start my day off right. This is one of God's great days. Yes, indeed. Seventy-five degrees, no wind, a beautiful sky. Did we get anything important?"

"Just the usual. I thank God every day for credit card offers. I would be out of a job if it weren't for these *$50,000 cash, zero percent interest, no transfer fees* letters that I put in nearly every mailbox on my route. It looks like you got a couple, and the church got a couple. Someday I might fill out some of those interest-free checks and take off for the Caribbean with no forwarding address. Free money. God bless credit card companies." He kissed the mail that he held in his hand before handing it to the priest and retracing his steps down the sidewalk.

"And God bless you," Josey automatically responded. Josey turned and went back inside to put the mail on his desk. The mail carrier was correct. There were four credit card offers mixed in with the usual ads, a couple bills, and a newsletter from the diocese. Nothing important. Josey tossed them all on Marcy's desk.

Josey's head cleared during his run. He sat down at his computer and entered the chat room again. The GrayBonePhone7 secret was out, and it was the "stock of the day." He and DBLUP chatted again for an hour, "I wish I had a little more money," Josey typed to DBLUP. "I could make a bundle on this. The opportunities are massive, and most people don't take advantage of them. If I had a windfall, I could clean up." The chat room continued its rumbling that GrayBonePhone7 would split on Thursday afternoon. DBLUP said he had observed it all morning and was confident in his prediction.

Josey returned to the rectory to shower and change his clothes. As he was getting a diet soda out of the refrigerator, the mailman's "free money" comment struck him like a lightning bolt. His mind was racing. *Why didn't I see this before? I must be going crazy. I can write a check on the credit card account, deposit it in my checking account, do an online transfer to my day trade account and purchase extra shares of GrayBonePhone7. As soon as it splits and regains the price, I will repay it without anyone knowing. DBLUP thinks it will happen within the week. I will have enough money that I won't have to worry ever again. But just this once. Now is the time.*

He went over to Marcy's desk and picked up the advertisements. They were identical: two from a credit card company and two from a national bank. One each in his name and in the church's name. Not that it mattered. He was the church as far as they would know. He took the advertisements from Marcy's pile of mail, opened them, and read them thoroughly. Each offer was for $50,000, zero percent interest for 90 days, with no upfront fees. Register on the Internet, and you were good to go. Instant money.

He turned his computer back on and checked again. GrayBonePhone7 was on the rise. It started the day at a little over $42 and was now at $52.50. It was going places. Definitely. He would do it. He would open those credit cards accounts today and transfer money into GrayBonePhone7 first thing tomorrow. God is good. Thank you, Jesus. He dialed his cell phone.

Chapter 23

Gwen
Tuesday Morning

Gwen finished feeding Louis and Marie as April ran into the den. She threw herself down on the couch. "Mom," she sobbed, tears streaming down her cheeks, "I talked to Audrey. She wanted to know why I hadn't told her that I was pregnant. She said someone called her and told her that I had babies. Oh, Mom, who would have said such a thing?"

April had not adjusted to the move from Hawley as well as Gwen and Clancy had hoped. She knew she was pretty but making new friends for a teenager was tough. Her confidence translated to arrogance, at times, which is why the moniker AWA, April-with-an-Attitude, stuck. She came from a long line of Irish peasants whose genes guaranteed that she could survive any famine. Unfortunately, those same genes also meant that she struggled with her weight. She wasn't fat, but the doctors predicted that she would always have to count calories. Gwen had counted them since she was 14, as had her mother before her. April was probably no different. She got good grades, did her homework, and played on the JV soccer team. Most of the other players had been in club soccer since elementary school and were better than she was. She mostly warmed the bench. Teenage cliques were difficult in most high schools, but at TM they were lethal. Most of the students came from moneyed families and looked down on the scholarship students. Her only friends were Audrey and Jenny who were also new to TM and helped April hold the bench down. Their bench-sitting cultivated a triangular friendship, but they were excluded from the pre-existing cliques.

"Audrey said what? Your babies? Who told her that these were your babies? You set her straight, didn't you?" Gwen was furious. She sat down next to April and hugged her. "Who would want to say such things? Was she saying these things to be mean?"

April sobbed the answers, "She wouldn't tell me who. She heard the rumor this morning, but she said that everybody knows it. I told her the babies weren't mine, but she doesn't believe me. She said that I was included in the school prayer chain. People are praying for me and my sins. Everybody thinks that I gained weight last year, and when I was absent from school during finals, I was having babies. She said Father Hope knows and is shocked. She told me that he was going to call me. What am I going to do? What will I say to him?"

"That's easy. You'll tell him the truth," Gwen answered, "and I'll talk to him. He is sure to believe me. He knows I found the babies. And Father Leclerq knows I found them. Why would I lie about finding Louis and Marie?"

April wasn't listening. "She wanted to know if I was going to keep them or give them up for adoption. Father Hope told her that it was against the rules to have a pregnant girl at St. Thomas More and I'd be kicked out of school." Father Hope was not only the principal but also Gwen's boss.

Gwen asked, "Did she talk to Father Hope? Who else did she talk to? I'll call him."

"I don't know. I don't know. All I know is my life is ruined." April's face was streaked with tears as she sobbed.

St. Thomas More had existed for about 35 years. The long-standing supporters were the insiders. Those whose parents had not attended St. Thomas More or who had not sat through eight years of Catholic School were considered outsiders. The school motto was "Faith, Hope, and Charity," but the "charity" aspect was void when it came to friends. The rumor mill functioned as the modus operandi. Reprimanding a student for gossiping created animosity, because gossip ran rampant with faculty, students, and parents because it was "the way we do things at TM." While the students at TM were smart, urbane, and matriculated into good colleges, the gossip mill created a school as uncharitable as any Gwen had seen. The teachers were personable enough, but she, too, was an "outsider." Of the 25 teachers, only about 10 were insiders, making the majority of teachers outsiders, an interesting dynamic within the faculty.

Gwen's seniors read *A Man for All Seasons* shortly before school let out. The school's namesake, Sir Thomas More, challenged the authority of King Henry VIII. Sir Thomas More was ultimately beheaded, but the standards that he defined in the early 1500s were certainly to be applauded in American society today: doing the right thing in the face of controversy, standing up to authority when it was wrong, elevating principles above personal ambition. A person of action, not words. Gwen thought of Sir Tom as she pondered the issues surrounding the TM gossip mill.

Gwen returned to tending the babies while April continued to weep. "April, don't worry, I'll call Father Hope. I'm sure that he can stop this rumor. Don't worry, you haven't done anything wrong. Our taking care of these babies is the right thing to do. The other girls are probably jealous that the babies aren't at their houses."

The phone rang, and Junie May began, "Hi, Gwennie. Junie May here. I wanted to check in." Gwen was uncertain why she was checking in. She bristled at being called Gwennie, and she had not indicated that Junie May should call her.

"Okay. Hi, thanks for calling." She didn't mean it. Her mind was on April, and she didn't want to be bothered with Junie May. "This is not a good t...," but Junie May cut her off.

Without taking a breath, Junie May reported, "I have been inquiring about pregnant girls at TM, and no one knows of anyone. Does April know if any of the girls at TM were pregnant this year? I don't think any of *our* girls would get pregnant while still in high school. Some people thought that a couple of the girls at school gained weight this school year. Do you know who they are? It could be one of them, but I don't think any long-established TM girls would get pregnant, as they have been taught better. Did you have high school girls get pregnant back in Hawley? I would guess you did. Our girls know better and are from such good families. Certainly, none of them are African American."

She was right about that. TM was a very homogenous school. The staff, administration, and student body were white except for a few exchange students who were accepted to make TM appear more ethnic-friendly than it was.

Junie May continued, "When I was in school at TM, there was one girl who got pregnant. She was a, I won't say it, the 's' word, not a good girl. We didn't want girls of her ilk at our school. I was one of the school leaders, because I was the homecoming queen runner-up and senior class treasurer. Not sure you knew that. I knew what was going on behind the scenes. The priest, who was principal, got rid of her in a flash. He never revealed why, but we all knew. How are the babies? They are dahl-ing, and I am sure your family would enjoy having them permanently, wouldn't you? Do you plan to keep them? How does April like them?" She stressed April.

Gwen interrupted Junie May. She didn't like the tone of the conversation. The easiest way to get a word in edgewise with Junie May was to interrupt her. "The babies are fine. We have no idea who they belong to. The church and the police are looking for the mother." Gwen also wanted to remind her that she had found the babies.

"Junie May, I hate to break this off, but this is not a good time to talk. I am feeding the babies, and it takes two hands. We can talk later." How much more abrupt could Gwen get? "Thanks again for the call." She hung up without waiting for a response.

"Who was that? Father Hope? What did he say? Did he expel me?" April sounded a little frightened. She was sitting up on the couch clutching a pillow against her body.

Gwen took a seat beside April, "No, it wasn't Father Hope. It was Junie May Layne. She called me twice today and came over yesterday. She's not exactly the silent type she claims to be. She's right in the middle of all this. I don't know her, but she is a very meddlesome woman. She's very involved with TM and told me yet again that she was senior class treasurer and runner-up for the homecoming queen. Like 30 years ago. Give me strength."

Chapter 24

Angel

Tuesday, Early Morning

He slipped on a no-logo black athletic sweatshirt and sweatpants and pulled a gray baseball cap low over his eyes. He quickly jogged four blocks out of his way and hailed a taxi, which he instructed to take him across town. He released the taxi and backtracked three blocks to a white depression-era house. He moved around to the back and let himself in.

The house was a mess. Dishes filled the sink, and newspapers covered the table. Two empty wine boxes topped a pile of trash that nearly blocked the door on the stained indoor-outdoor carpet, and a partially empty gallon of Chianti sat on the counter. "Tasteless shit," he said aloud. The blinds were drawn shut causing the house to seem dingier than it already was. Cat urine reached his nostrils, and he first coughed then gagged. The antique oak furniture, which could barely be seen under the piles of junk, looked old and shabby. "What a pig sty. God, how could I have touched her?" he chastised himself. Fat scented candles flickered on the counters and table, but they did not come close to masking the stench.

Angel was reading the paper when he entered. She was clad in a robe and slippers with her feet propped up on a kitchen chair. A half-full wine bottle and a coffee cup rested on the filthy oak table in front of her. She hadn't heard the door. She jumped to her feet as he came in, astonished at his intrusion. Feeling shaky and weak, she sat down again. She had dreaded seeing him but simultaneously wanted to see him. She didn't know what to say and mumbled, "What?"

"Why didn't you tell me?" he demanded, grabbing her shoulder, and threatening her. She shrank at his gesture. "I had a right to know. And one is black, and one is white? What's that about? I'm white. It isn't earthly possible for me to father a black baby. The black gene must have come from you. How do you know these are mine, you lying whore? Why didn't you get rid of them? Those babies are from the devil. You must get rid of them. You should have done it already. Your pregnancy was not God's will. It was your will. You seduced me and should have done something about it." His face bulged red with rage, and a vein in his forehead popped out as he spoke. "Does anybody know? This cannot get out. If it gets out, I swear to God, I will kill you. We both will be ruined."

Angel was appalled at his tone, and she cringed at his gesture. Too exhausted to fight back, but too exhausted not to, she shouted, "I didn't seduce you. You raped me, remember? I am not black, and I don't have a clue. God made them. I don't know why they are black and white. You tell me. Satan must have had a hand in this. Rape is a tool of the devil, and God is punishing us for this sin. It wasn't as if we were married or lovers. I don't recall having had a say in this relationship, if that's what you want to call it."

He continued, shouting, "Rape? Try and scream fuckin' rape. No one will believe you. Look at yourself. You are a pathetic piece of shit. No one would believe that anyone would rape you, least of all me. You'd be laughed out of court."

"Don't worry, I've planned this all out. Do you think I am stupid? I've had eight fucking months to think about this, and I did what I did. Those babies are safe and with a good family with kids. The family is perfect; I couldn't have planned it better. God would be proud." Angel assured him while trying to steady herself. "No one knows. No one will ever know. I am not going to tell anyone, and neither are you."

"You didn't exactly get rid of them, you stupid whore. You gave them to a family, a fucking St. Gert's family. They live right here in this fucking town. Someone will figure it out. She's a teacher, and he's a fucking lawyer. You should have had an abortion. Why didn't you?" he demanded.

"No, no abortion. I don't believe in abortion. This was the only way. Anyway, where would I have gone to have an abortion? God wouldn't allow me to have an abortion." Angel answered, horrified at even the thought of it.

He didn't let up, "Somebody will find out. This is going to ruin me. And you. You need to get rid of them or make sure that nobody, do you hear me? Nobody can link them to me. If they link them to you, I will destroy you. I don't give a rat's ass about you. You are a fucking whore, and I will not let you destroy me."

"Our lives don't have to change. I don't want anyone to know either. Can you imagine what it would do to me if people found out? It would ruin me, too! I thought about going to confession. That usually…" Angel believed that absolution was the key to heaven. The priest of her childhood had instilled that in her mind, many years ago.

He interrupted, "Confession? Fucking confession? Are you kidding? Don't even think about it. You know what blabbermouths priests are. Don't tell anyone I was here. No one, especially not one of the blowhards. Do you understand? No one."

He departed the same way he had entered her house, but even angrier. He couldn't trust her and needed to eliminate the evidence. He had tried kidnapping the babies, but that didn't work, and now the police were watching the Harte's house. Maybe he should just get rid of her. That could work. That could solve the problem.

Angel was shaking with anger, fear, and shame. How could he talk to her that way? A whore? A whore? He had called her a whore. Tears welled in her eyes and then poured down her cheeks. Damn him. Maybe he was right. Maybe she was a whore. Once, a priest had told her she was a whore. Charlie never called her a whore. Charlie had thanked her and given her special favors. And how could she be a whore if she had dedicated herself to God? Mary Magdalene had been a whore, yet Jesus loved her. She became a saint. Jesus gave her absolution. Angel needed to confess and pray for forgiveness, pray for him, pray for her sins, pray for the babies. She had never seen him as angry. He was angrier than he had been that night. She poured wine into her coffee cup, took a long drink, and lowered herself to her knees to pray. He needn't worry. She knew what she was doing.

Chapter 25

Father Matthew Hope
Tuesday

Father Matthew Hope had served as principal of St. Thomas More for 11 years. He nurtured it into one of the top academic schools in the state alongside a top-notch vice principal who was responsible for all things academic. That allowed him to enjoy the students stress-free. He enjoyed his tenure there. He could arrive at school at 8 a.m., work out at the gym for a couple hours, eat lunch, pat a few kids on the back, and disappear at 2 p.m., and no one would say anything. Of course, he was obligated to attend the nighttime activities, but only to show up and smile. It was much less complicated than being a pastor. He didn't have to preside over weddings or funerals. No muss, no fuss. School was dismissed for the summer and holidays, and he took full advantage. It was a fantastic job.

Father Hope was assigned to St. Gertrude's, but he didn't have to recite Mass, except in the case of an emergency or vacation and those times seldom interrupted his daily routine. The pastor, Father Rene Leclerq, was a workaholic and did not believe in vacations. The other priest at St. Gert's, Father O'Grady, had ulcers and popped over-the-counter anti-acid pills all day long. That type of life was not for him.

Prior to the 9/11 tragedies, his life had been stress-free. But that day everything changed, especially his faith. His only brother was killed in the

Twin Tower attack, and it had taken months to recover his remains even longer for him to recover his faith. It was a horrible ordeal for him, and he had not gotten over his brother's loss easily, but in the end, he found that his trust in God was stronger than ever.

Coming from a middle-class family with strong Catholic values, Father Hope knew he wanted to serve God. He attended Mass regularly and even surprised his mother when he revealed God's calling for him to become a priest. God wanted him to do His work. After his ordination, he was assigned to a rural parish, which inundated him with work, daily Masses, fundraising, and visiting the sick. He had a hard time saying *no*, and, consequently, didn't eat right, didn't exercise, and couldn't sleep. He turned into an emotional basket case. The diocese feared he would have a nervous breakdown and leave the priesthood. So, after 20 years, the bishop transferred him to St. Gertrude's, where he worked with the various school programs and eventually landed at St. Thomas More High School. At age 50, he began lifting weights, working out, eating right, and even perfecting his job as principal. He wanted to serve God and felt he could best do that by remaining at Thomas More High School.

It was after lunch when Father Leclerq phoned from the school parking lot interrupting Father Hope's trip to the gym. Father Leclerq called before he walked into the school in case Father Hope was out. His back ached, and he didn't want to walk any farther than he had to.

"Matt, Rene here. I need to talk to you. Can you break free for a few minutes? I'm in the parking lot."

"Absolutely, I am setting out to the gym to stretch these muscles. They get cranky when I don't use them." He hadn't been to the gym since the day before.

The principal's office was undersized and filled with trophy paraphernalia from the past 11 years. There were three scarred filing cabinets and a desk piled high with reports. Centered on his desk were a personal weightlifting trophy and a clock with a metal tag reading: "TM's #1 Iron Man," which had been given to him by the senior class a few years ago. Father Matt shifted some files and a stack of mail to the floor making room for Rene to sit down. Three minutes later, the two were seated, Rene with coffee and Matt with a bottle of mineral water.

Father Hope started, "What's up?"

"You missed the bishop's meeting this week. He assigned me as the priest representative for TM. I wanted to tell you face-to-face. We can be a great team," Father Leclerq said.

Father Hope's first thought was that this was not good news and would undoubtedly interrupt his life. What he answered was, "Yeah, I could use some advice now and then. None of the priests ever show up to the school. Maybe you can get them here." Rene was many years younger than he was, and Matt didn't like the idea of getting advice from this workaholic weirdo.

Rene gave his version of the Monday meeting, "At our Monday meeting that you missed, we discussed TM at length. The consensus is that we need to spend more time out here as a pastoral team. You've been here for a while, and although you are doing a good job, we all think that a little fresh blood would improve the situation. I'll show up from time to time to see if you need anything. The vicar general wants me to come out at least weekly." His version was not exactly what happened.

"Wow, weekly? I appreciate it. I know you are busy. Are you positive you have time to come out weekly? It might be a bit of an overkill," Matt stated blandly. With more enthusiasm he continued, "I'm on my way to the gym. Want to go?" Father Hope wished this conversation to end. He knew that it had been years, if ever, since Rene had pumped any iron. His body was that of an old man, fat and out of shape. He was a good candidate for a knee or hip replacement before he was fifty.

"No, not today. I've been feeling a little under the weather. I'll take a rain check. I do need to get back in shape," he patted his over-the-belt stomach. "I saw a bumper sticker the other day that read, 'Always marry a fat man.

He'll keep you warm in the winter and give you shade in the summer.' That's my motto. But then, I'm not getting married, am I?"

The Iron Man rose and looked at his watch. It was time for Leclerq to leave. Time was wasting.

Rene continued, "I do have something else. I haven't talked to you since you missed the bishop's meeting," he reminded Matt for the third time.

"We had graduation, and it is a hectic time of the year. I had things to do on Monday that were more important than the weekly drone." Father Hope, like most of the priests, was disrespectful of the bishop's meetings.

Father Leclerq added, "This wasn't on the bishop's agenda, but I wanted to tell you about a set of twins that were found at St. Gert's at the 5 o'clock Mass. Newborns, a boy and girl, one African American and one Anglo. Any ideas? Did you have any pregnant girls at TM who might have wanted to ditch a baby?"

"I heard about it. Are you kidding though? The babies were left at the Wrinkle Mass?" These Mass goers were very faithful, but they were old. "I am almost certain we didn't have any pregnant girls this year. Junie May Layne called earlier wondering the same thing. I'll ask the counselors though." Principal Hope prided himself on knowing the students' names and lineages, but he didn't pay much attention to what was happening with them. "The counselors went out for a caffeine fix. They should be back shortly. I'll check and get back to you." He was getting itchy to pump some iron.

Chapter 26

Bishop Connor Llewellyn
Tuesday

The diocesan populace considered Bishop Connor Llewellyn the "Mr. Nice Guy" of the parish. He clearly had a sense of humor and genuinely enjoyed people. This played well into his social and after-work life as Catholic and non-Catholics alike sought him out for regular evening speaking engagements. This worked beautifully for his schedule, as golfing, skiing, and fishing filled his days.

He was satisfied with his life. Boasting a golf handicap of eight, he golfed daily with a regular group of city leaders, including the mayor, a CEO of a technology company, and a couple attorneys. His conviviality made him popular among most of the golfers in the area. Although portly, he enjoyed the slopes, and when the snow flew, he frittered away many sunny winter days on the surrounding ski hills. Sometimes he skied and golfed on the same day. He loved fishing and was one of those who could always catch a fish. He didn't enjoy eating fish, and he gave them away to his dinner hosts, of which he had many.

Being the bishop caused no stress to Connor. His diocese was one of the largest dioceses area-wise, but one of the smallest people-wise. With the state's heavy Mormon population, little controversy came to light. He knew that Ralph Loren, his second in command, had his eyes on the bishop's ring.

Ralph would do anything the bishop told him to do, especially the dirty work. At age 65, Connor Llewellyn had done everything in life that he had wanted. He could retire at any time but enjoyed the office of bishop and thought he would wait a few years.

Bishop Llewellyn waited on Ralph this morning. He was late, as usual, although he normally didn't keep the bishop waiting long. He leaned back in his chair, closed his eyes, and uttered a silent thanksgiving for all his blessings.

Bishop Con became a priest because his mother had expected him to. She attended Mass daily and prayed for his soul every day of his life. She died during the Carter administration, but he was sure she still recited daily prayers for him. She repeated one novena after another during his teenage years. She laughed to her friends, "My boy didn't have a chance. The Blessed Virgin was after his soul; I made sure she got it."

Connor Llewellyn answered his mother's prayers when he was 17, deciding to become a priest. He matriculated at the local college and immediately applied to the seminary. Between his mother's novenas and the cost of college, he had no other choice. During those years, he had one brief affair and a few one-night stands, but he went to confession immediately afterward erasing the sins. God forgave him and gave him immediate absolution.

He accelerated his college classes and received his doctorate at age 28, a couple years after his ordination. He was content on this path, living in Los Angeles where he taught history and coached football at the Bishop Dunne High School. He taught and coached for four years before his appointment to a parish as the pastor and cherished almost every aspect of the job.

The reassignment, though, caught him off guard. The school's principal, who was also a priest, was accused of pedophilia creating a menacing scandal. Rather than close the school, the local bishop relocated all three of the priests who worked at the school. The pedophilic principal was transferred to the diocesan office in Santa Ana, where he was placed in charge of youth programs. The religion teacher-priest was shuffled to a small parish in northern California, while Father Connor Llewellyn was assigned to a large inner-city parish in Los Angeles.

While he was associate pastor at the inner-city parish, Father Connor Llewellyn met the only woman who turned his eye. She was a 24-year-old half-Haitian beauty with long legs and a welcoming smile. He came across her at the café where she worked. She did everything: waited and bussed tables, cooked, and conversed with the customers. The sparks flew the first time they met, and he eagerly returned the next day. With every breakfast or lunch at the cafe, the sparks flashed brighter and stronger. He loved so much about her but found that neither thought it important to share much about themselves. He did not tell her that he was a priest, and she only knew him by his nickname. The truth would have muddied the waters. Their affair lasted six months to the day, and without notice, she was gone. But it was just as well. Mama had continued to pray novenas, and never would have understood. After she left, he never saw or heard from her again. After 30 odd years, he was still aroused at the thought of her.

***

Ralph Loren entered with his arms full of papers. He seated himself across from the bishop and launched into their conversation. "How are you this morning, Bishop? It is glorious out there. Blue skies and warm weather. Nice day for golf, don't you think?" The bishop smiled. His tee time was at 1 p.m., and he had a golf lesson scheduled right after their conversation. He was playing with a couple of high rollers today and wanted to be sure that his short game was on.

Loren continued, "I'm working on a couple things that need your approval. First, the finance council wants to kick off a capital campaign next year. They are considering a master plan for building projects and think we need a committee to spearhead it."

"How much are they looking for?" the bishop wondered aloud.

"Oh, $20 mil or so. Enough for a down payment on a couple new parish projects. They want to buy some land to hold in reserve. The cost of land is rising, and our financial gurus recommend that we buy now. We'll have to jump through some planning and zoning regulations, but they think that we can get some exemptions. It would be a real feather in your cap to have a couple new buildings and additional plans drawn up during your tenure. How does Bishop Llewellyn Catholic Community Center ring with you? What do you think?" Ralph Loren knew how to feed the bishop's ego.

"You tell me, Ralph. You sat in on the meeting. Is it a good idea?"

Ralph answered, "Yes, it is solid, and the time is right. The finance council is ready to go. If you approve, I'll give them the nod."

The bishop assented, "Okay by me. Keep me apprised of what is happening. I don't like being out of the loop. I don't know a lot about land use laws and facilities, but they don't need to know that. Remind them that I am following what they do very closely. What else? Anything on those twins who were found?"

"Not much. They're with a family from St. Gert's. Rene informed me that they are rumored to belong to the teacher's kid. The same teacher who reported finding them. His version is that she is covering up for her daughter and blaming it on someone else. For your information, their names are Marie and Louis but no last names. We don't know where they came from. No news is good news though. I mean, the newspapers haven't picked it up yet. Rene tells me there are rumors galore. It's bound to hit the papers sometime soon. Do you have a plan?" Ralph Loren already knew the answer, but he asked anyway.

The bishop's brain flashed to the thought of Marie from long ago. What a beauty she was. He said, "I knew a Marie once. She was… No, no. I don't have a plan. That's Rene's job, but you should help him out. It will look bad for the diocese no matter what happens. Don't fuck it up, Ralph."

"Not a chance," Ralph answered.

Chapter 27

Gwen
Tuesday

Gwen was wearing down. She had forgotten how much work it was to take care of babies. Andy and Michael were a year apart, but having two at once, plus three children of her own, not to mention being a decade older, changed things. The sleepless nights certainly weren't helping. It was a tough job, the diapers, the bottles, changing the babies, then repeat. Nevertheless, when they gurgled or half-smiled or clasped her finger, it was worth every effort.

The rumor of April being pregnant was scary. Gossip like this could follow her for a long time, affect her friendships, her chance at scholarships, her attitude toward TM. Gwen wanted to be sure that she knew all the facts before she called Father Hope. This was Tuesday, and the police had not reported any progress in the case, including finding the mother, the break-in, or the mystery calls.

Gwen called Father Hope immediately after lunch. April's tears had mostly stopped. Andy and Michael continued patrolling the perimeter, punctuated with popsicles from the freezer. The babies slept intermittently. Clancy dragged himself home for a peanut butter and jelly sandwich and a brief nap before returning to his office. Detective Maggie Monroe called and checked in, nothing new on their end, though. The time was right to call the school. Gwen knew that Father Hope usually left for the gym by 2 p.m.

"Hello, Father Hope, it's Gwen Harte here."

Father Hope quickly replied, "Oh, Gwen. It's good to hear from you. I never had the opportunity to congratulate you on the Teacher-of-the-Year award. The students really like you. You aren't ready to come back to school yet, are you?"

"No way, José," Gwen laughed. "I am rebounding from that last set of compositions I graded. Besides that, I'm not doing much. Basically, I'm just staying home this summer, supervising the summer writing project, and watching kids. That brings me to why I called. I don't know if you heard this, but the rumor mill is going crazy. I stumbled across a set of twins at Mass at St. Gert's last Saturday evening. I mean, I almost literally stumbled. I know that sounds strange, but I found them under the kneelers. They are a boy and a girl, newborns." Gwen had related the story several times and feared that he would ask the same questions that everyone else had, but he needed to know.

Father Hope responded, "You found the twins? Father Leclerq came by and told me about them, but he didn't indicate that you were the one who found them. Do you still have them? I also had a strange phone call from Junie May Layne asking about pregnant girls at TM. She supports TM big time, but I don't appreciate her asking questions about our students. Maybe a TM student had the babies. I don't know. Father Rene also mentioned that one is African American and one is Anglo. How does that work?"

Gwen countered, "Yes, we have them. I must say that it has been an interesting couple of days. The babies keep us busy to say the least. Besides the endless diapers, bottles, feedings, and phone calls, we have had two mystery phone calls, one of which was threatening, and then came a break-in. Someone tried to kidnap the babies. April did some research on the Internet and learned that having twins of different races is very rare but possible. I can give you the technical explanation, but you probably don't want to hear it." She offered a silent prayer that he would not assign her to teach biology next year.

"Whoa, you said you weren't doing much this summer. It sounds like you are having a very busy summer, indeed. I'm sorry, but I don't know anything about that baby stuff. Is there something TM can do to help?" Father Hope was a priest she enjoyed, considerate and polite. She valued their working relationship.

She relayed the rumor to him, "As a matter of fact, there is. We are dealing with the TM gossip mill. Apparently, someone started a rumor that April is the mother and that we are covering it up. Her friend, Audrey, phoned to tell her that you knew and were going to expel her. She is scared to death."

Father Hope paused before he spoke. "Audrey? Audrey who? Grimes? April? No, I didn't hear anything about April. I learned of the babies this morning. That was through Father Rene Leclerq and from my brief conversation with Junie May. But April's name wasn't mentioned. They aren't hers, are they?"

The Mother Bear reflex was springing into action. Gwen would protect her offspring with all her being. "Of course not. I found them as I said. April was visiting her grandmother on Saturday night. With her brothers. I found them at St. Gert's. During Mass."

"Okay," he reacted slowly. "That sounds reasonable. I don't know about the rumor, but I'll check with the counselors. They usually know everything that is going on."

Gwen elaborated, "Can you stop this rumor? If Junie May knows about this rumor, you can be sure that others will know, too. You and I both know how the rumor mill operates at TM. One nasty little comment can spread like wildfire through the entire student body, faculty, and Catholic community. It hasn't been easy for April to make friends at TM, possibly because her mom teaches there. I don't want her to have other problems. Remember some of the rumors this spring? Holy mackerel. The students gossip about everything, kind and unkind, true and untrue."

"Hey, calm down. No need to get upset. The students like you, Gwen. How could April have problems making friends?" Father Hope queried. "Are you getting any help from the police? They should be involved. While the church is a sanctuary for leaving unwanted babies, we can be sure that the mother needs some help. Do you know Jack Shetland? He's a cop and goes to St. Gert's and could be of help."

"Yes, I've met Jack, he's working with the other lady cop, Maggie Monroe. They know a lot, but so far, haven't been of any help, My relationship with my students has nothing to do with April. Being the daughter of a teacher doesn't necessarily make her popular with other students." Gwen shook her head to herself and thought *Note to self: Another reason priests should marry. They don't have a clue about relationships.* She continued without asserting her thought, "I don't know why, except the cliques are powerful and out of control. I want to make sure that April's reputation isn't damaged. Will you help?"

Father Hope counseled her, "Of course. I don't believe it is as bad as you think it is. I haven't heard anything, and I'm sure I would hear the rumor if it were out there. Did you call Audrey's mother?" That was a good suggestion. Gwen hadn't thought of that.

"No, I haven't. Thanks for the suggestion, Father. I'll call her right after I get off the phone with you. I appreciate your support. We're trying to do the right thing here. God somehow gave us these babies to tend to for a couple weeks, until we find their mother, and my kids can't suffer because of it," Gwen stated.

"Don't worry, I am here for you. Keep me posted. If I can do something, let me know." He signed off, probably on his way to the gym. The Iron Man continued to earn his nickname.

Gwen called Audrey's mother, but there was no answer.

Maggie and Jack had made no progress on Tuesday, but they stopped at the Harte residence before going home as a courtesy check. "Anything new?" Maggie asked. "We've asked the night staff to keep an eye on your house tonight. Don't be shy about calling if something happens, even if it is in the middle of the night. We want you to be safe."

On Tuesday night, the Harte's took extra precautions, locking the doors and windows and leaving the lights on outside. Andy and Michael created some homemade noise detectors out of crinkled newspaper and spread it in front of the doors and window. They probably wouldn't work, but they delighted in crumpling newspapers and strategically placing them all over the house.

Gwen considered sleeping on the couch, as she knew her sleep would be fitful, but Clancy wouldn't have it. "Sleep in the bed," he directed, "the babies will be all right. You won't get any rest at all on the couch." Nevertheless, reminiscent of Hawley, he placed the pistol next to his pillow. The 11 years in Hawley presented an irony to them. They left their doors and windows wide open day and night, but always positioned a pistol in the car or next to the bed. It didn't make sense. Having a loaded pistol in the bedroom was normal in Hawley; Gwen hoped it wouldn't become normal here.

Clancy and Gwen fed the babies and drifted in and out of sleep, half listening for noises in the night. Gwen sleepily rallied to feed Marie and Louis a couple times before the doorbell rang at 3:30 a.m. Clancy greeted Smith and Weston with his Smith and Wesson.

"Sorry to wake you, but the detective asked us to keep an eye out for anything unusual at or near your house. We drove by an hour ago and noticed a person cutting through your yard from the alley. We tried to catch him, but he disappeared a couple blocks from here. Did you see or hear anything?" Ben Smith was the spokesperson.

"No, come in, please," Clancy invited the officers. "No, I didn't see or hear anything. Did you Gwen?"

Gwen balanced both babies, one on each arm. She agreed, "No, I have been up and down all night tending the babies, but I heard nothing. They are safe and sound. You didn't find anyone?"

Patrolman Smith answered, "No, he was gone before we could catch him. We'll keep a close eye on your place for the next couple hours. Sorry to wake you. Good night." With that, they were out the door.

Chapter 28

Maggie and Brick
Wednesday morning

"Are you okay?" Maggie asked Brick. She was nearly ready to go to work and he was still in bed, which was rare. Brick had always been a bundle of energy and with the diagnosis from exposure to the burn pits, he done a complete turnaround. His treatments at the VA seemed to help, but his energy level vacillated from low to really low. Sometimes they would bounce up to a high or nearly high, but today looked like it was going to be a really low day. She called the VA emergency number and requested an ambulance and they arrived within minutes.

She called Jack and said she would be a little late, giving her time to accompany Brick to the VA hospital. It would be a day of waiting and testing and Brick told her to leave.

"Go to work and take care of those babies. They are important. You could be waiting around all day, but I'll call you after I see the doctors," Brick told her as he rolled over to go back to sleep.

"Call me, don't forget." She kissed him good-bye but he was already asleep.

Chapter 29

Father Paul
Wednesday Morning

Paul McGraeth's vision for this life was to be a bishop. He punched all the right buttons and was sure to keep on the path that would lead him there. He enjoyed the finest. He decorated his home in greys and blacks, very chic and modern. He purchased Thomas Kinkade paintings of quaint villages. He placed mirrors and ferns in baskets throughout. He wallpapered the entryways and installed new track lighting to add panache without ostentation. On the exterior, he mounted a statue of St. Paul with a birdbath fountain complete with climbing ivy on the brick walls. An elderly woman volunteered her time to maintain the flower garden all summer. She kept it weed-free and gave the appearance that he had a professional gardener.

Father Paul became a priest for three reasons. He loved to serve God. No question about it. God hadn't expected very much of him in return. Secondly, he hoped to determine his sexuality dilemma. Was he gay, heterosexual, or bisexual? He didn't know. If the church required abstinence, he thought he could control this sexual exceptionality, as he called it. That hadn't worked out very well. The third reason he became a priest was the most important. As a young boy, he met a cardinal, decked out in his red and black. Paul thought he was the grandest, most attractive person on Earth. He was in awe of the grandeur, the pomp and circumstance, the staff, the red beanie, and the ring. Most of all, the ring. He aspired to be a bishop, but a cardinal was even better. He still had to punch the bishop ticket. A cardinal ring was just one punch away.

Two dioceses had considered him for the bishopric. Neither had worked out. His colleagues advised that he was too young. He applied for the vicar general position in this diocese but had been beaten out by Ralph Loren. The next open bishop position in the west was in Fairbanks, Alaska, the remotest diocese of all. In Fairbanks, he could have the best of all worlds, the ring, a decent salary, a house and car, utilities, insurance, food, everything. He hoped Fairbanks would have ample internet service, as it had grown to be one of his passions. The downside was the God-awful weather: short, cold days and interminable nights. That's why he would create a generous travel budget.

His confusion with his sexuality created turmoil within himself, but he had preserved his secret all these years. He had enjoyed a couple of flings while taking ocean cruises, but they were insignificant. He couldn't even recall their names.

Paul wanted out. He had to get out and away from all these problems. The diocese had given him limited staff and, God bless Ralph Loren, the Social Justice Committee. Prostate cancer was also on his mind, and he felt everything crashing down at once. This was grunt work, and he needed a change. He had been growing pessimistic and recognized an onset of depression. He thought about popping a few Valium every now and again or some other sort of chemical stimulation, but drugs, legal or not, meant that someone knew. The damned pharmacists probably blabbed as much as priests did. Some days he reveled in his position and status as a priest. On his other days, he despised that he was ever born. *There is a time for abortion*, he had thought to himself. *If I had been aborted, my life would be simple.* The fact that that statement made no sense did not matter to Paul during these times, which reminded him that he needed to call his brother in Anchorage.

Paul had not been on positive footing with his family since he admitted his sexual exceptionality. His parents avoided him, which was okay by him. They were in their eighties and lived in Florida. They had their own lives, golfing and morning strolls. Probably shuffleboard, too. They bragged on Peter, his younger brother, who was also a priest. Peter allied with his parents in rejecting Paul when he revealed his bisexuality. A few years later Peter privately disclosed his own homosexuality to Paul. No one else knew. The two brothers formed a pact not to tell their parents about Peter's sexual orientation, fearing that the revelation would destroy them. As far as Paul knew, they both had honored their pledges. Since then, Peter had become the vicar general of Anchorage. Paul was certain that he would do anything to keep people from knowing he was gay and now it was time to call in the chips. It was dirty pool, but he'd do whatever he needed to do to become a bishop. Paul needed help to get the Fairbanks appointment, and he knew Peter would help him.

Paul settled in at his desk to consider his options. This parish was the sewer of parishes. The people were old, and most of them smelled. He held funerals nearly every week and baptisms that were requested by grandparents. The millennials or Gen Xers frequented one of the other, newer parishes. Desperate needs called for desperate plans. And he was desperate.

He reflected on his deacons. Two deacons assisted him. Both were retired. They were pleasant enough but seldom available. They played golf nearly as much as the bishop and were hardly ever available for church business. When the weather was poor, they played gin. When they did show up, they wanted to run the show and do what they wanted, not what he wanted them to do. He had to put them in their place several times.

Paul brooded about the women who worked in the parish. They, too, were ancient goodie-goodies, RFs who had been serving the church forever. They gave away parish money to so-called charity cases, money he earned from his excellent Sunday morning sermons. He had other uses for the money, not for those who claimed need. He could increase his travel budget or redecorate the rectory. Those women should get real jobs. He didn't have any nuns currently, but he had hated them when they were around. They nosed into his business and didn't respect his privacy. He felt like he was the Rodney Dangerfield of the church. They gave him no respect. They didn't seem to comprehend that he, after all, was their pastor. He was their shepherd. He was the one who would make decisions. Not them. God had chosen the male gender to be priests, not females. God could have chosen women to be his disciples, to be the church foundation, but He hadn't. God had chosen men. They should listen to him. Good riddance, he thought when he was able to get to try another parish.

He reached into the back of his desk drawer and pulled out the numbers of his brother in Anchorage. He had the diocese number, the home number, and a cell number. It was June, and the days would be long in Alaska. He took a deep breath. He would try the home number first. Cell numbers could be traced.

Paul dialed the number. No answer. Damn. He must be at work. He preferred to call Peter at home. Too many people could be in his office. Yet, it was an emergency. He tried the diocese.

"Diocese of Anchorage, Pearl speaking."

"Pearl, could you please find Father McGraeth for me? Thanks."

"Just a moment, please. I'm sure he is here somewhere." She placed Paul on hold with some jazz playing in the background.

He waited a few seconds before hearing Peter's familiar voice. "Vicar General Peter McGraeth speaking. How may I help you?"

"Hey, Peter, it's your long-lost brother, Paul. How the hell are you?"

"Paul? Is that you? It's been a long time. What are you up to? It is good hearing your voice." They had always gotten along except for that brief time between when Paul admitted his sexual exceptionality and Peter admitted his sexual orientation.

Paul answered jovially, "Oh, five-foot-eleven and about 175 pounds. I'm looking good as usual. Are you gray yet?" They both had black hair and teased each other about who would be gray first.

Peter countered, "Not a hair on my head is gray. It's as black as the ace of spades. How have you been?"

Paul teased, "Liar. You're gray, aren't you? Every fuckin' hair on your head, I'll bet. Or you're bald. Which is it, you liar?" They had not seen each other in over 15 years.

"You're right, I'm mostly gray, but it makes me look distinguished." Peter grew serious. "Is everything okay? I mean, are Mom and Pop…are they okay?"

Paul retorted, "How the hell do I know? They disowned me, their faggot son, remember? I never hear from them. The last I knew they were in Florida, spending our inheritance." Paul had never quite gotten over their throwing him out of the house. He continued, "I need a favor. It's a big one. I'm ministering at Holy Father's and going nowhere. I'm stuck in a pitiful parish of thankless parishioners without any help. The bishop is an asshole and piles too much work on me. You remember that I have always wanted to be a bishop, and the position in Fairbanks is open. Can you get my name to the powers? I'd love to see some white smoke coming my way." He was referring to the practice of selecting a pope: Black smoke was released if no pope was selected that day, and white smoke was released if the cardinals had chosen a pope.

Peter answered quickly, "Whoa, that's a big order. I don't know if I can do it. The committee has already convened twice and has a couple of guys in mind. They haven't chosen anyone yet, but I don't know if I can help. Fairbanks is not anyone's first choice. It is dark 90 percent of the time in the winter and light 90 percent of the time in the summer. The winters suck, and the summers aren't much better. Forget about getting a tan. The best thing is the Aurora Borealis. Are you sure? Would you really want to live in Fairbanks? Have you ever been there?"

"I've been to Alaska, but not Fairbanks," Paul informed him, as he silently thought of the cruises. "I went to Juneau, Sitka, and Ketchikan once on a cruise. Lots of rain, of course, but I can live anywhere. Once I am appointed, I can search for a warmer position. Getting the first appointment is the tough one. Can you help me, Pepe?"

"I don't know," Peter answered. "I'll make some phone calls for you but no guarantees. Can you email me some info to have something concrete to show them? I know the bishops on the committee, but I need to make sure that I give them the right scoop."

Eagerly, Paul agreed, "Sure thing, Buddy. I'll send it later today. You want a resumé and some reference things? Would that do? I have it all on my computer. I want to update it a bit though."

They visited a while longer and hung up. "Maybe I won't have to pull out the big guns," Paul thought aloud. "Maybe he can do it without me mentioning his being gay."

Chapter 30

Gwen

Wednesday Morning

Gwen was exhausted. They had cared for the babies for three days, but it felt like three weeks, and she was worn out. After the police had left, she couldn't sleep and rose to look at Marie and Louis. She peeked in at her own still-sleeping babies. All three of them. What had she gotten them into?

She hadn't heard back from Father Hope. Health and Welfare was apparently incommunicado as Violet had gone on vacation and hadn't bothered to inform the Hartes. The police officers were interested, but she knew they worked nights and didn't devote much time to finding the mother of the babies. Detective Maggie and Officer Jack were undoubtedly her best resources, but they hadn't uncovered any new information. Detective Maggie had called every day but had nothing new to say. Father Leclerq called but also had little to say. Junie May continued her daily calls promising that she would not divulge any information to anyone, but she would tell Gwen any rumors that she heard. Gwen crossed her fingers that she was telling the truth.

Gwen felt fortunate to have the priests involved. They were good men who cared for the parishioners and strived toward positive solutions to problems. When problems arose, priests were excellent resources, she believed. Before all this, Gwen thought the move to Basin had been mostly positive. Clancy's practice was growing, and Gwen enjoyed teaching at TM. Good school. Good teachers. Good things happening. Too bad that this riddle created such turmoil for so many people.

Everyone is asleep, Gwen thought. Uninterrupted Internet time. She logged on and typed in "superfecundation" and "superfetation." Between the two, holy cow, there were over 65,000 hits. She browsed through several of the sites, which reinforced what April had found. There could be two fathers if the conditions of conception were right. Or the parents could be of different races. Both were rare. She checked her email. She found a few ads and a message from the calculus teacher congratulating her on her new role as super parent.

She returned to Google and wove her way to the blog site that she had instructed her students to use. It was a writing site where people composed essays and opinions on a myriad of events. This website encouraged good writing practices with immediate feedback from their peers. She linked it to the school website and could monitor it easily. It was open to other students, parents, administrators, and the priests of the diocese. She paired her students with kids she knew from Hawley. They were soon entertaining each other with information about their schools and practicing their composition skills. Her incoming seniors were to write about Americana over the summer. It was time to verify that her students were fulfilling their summer writing projects. Some were. That was good news. She would have to remind the rest. A call to their parents would do the trick.

She scanned the blog site regularly to monitor the writings and check for mischief among her students. She didn't read everything but tried to read and respond to some writing each day. Occasionally parents or teachers posted items, something she saw as a great enhancement to the website. Today she noted a blog with the subject of *Twins,* which caught her eye. She double clicked on it. It was five lines long about a birth experience. It focused on giving birth to twins of different races and was signed *Angel Eyes.* It was a short paragraph with no questions or opinions. She thought about who had access to the blog site. A student? A teacher? Who else? She would mention it to Maggie the next time she saw her. She was about to answer when Marie and Louis screamed for breakfast. She could check it out later.

Everybody rallied as the babies shrieked. Two babies could certainly wreak havoc on a household schedule. She picked up the babies, fed them, and changed them while Michael and Andy set out the Cheerios, and April made orange juice from frozen concentrate. Clancy started the toast and soon breakfast was on the table. "I wonder what today will hold," Gwen speculated aloud. "We have had more than our share of excitement in the past few days."

Chapter 31

Father Rene
Wednesday Morning

Father Rene cleared his morning agenda. He had already recited Mass to the few Religious Fanatics who attended the early morning service and drank a cup of coffee with the custodian. He needed to go to the hospital to see a parishioner and make a couple phone calls to some ailing widows. But other than that, he was free. It would be a good day to spend at Thomas More High School.

Father Rene Leclerq phoned the mother of all gossip, Junie May Layne. He usually avoided calling her because she was prone to endless chattering. Today he needed information, and she was the most likely person to have it. "Junie May, it's Father Rene. How are you?"

"Good morning, Father Rene. I'm fine. I was about to phone you. Did you find out about the Harte girl?" Junie May's curiosity was getting the best of her but didn't add her usual 20 questions/20 answers. Her rapid-fire drawl remained in effect.

Father Rene inquired directly, "Are you quite certain about the Harte girl and the twins? Do you think she is the mother?"

Junie May reacted without a pause, "Yes, I am quite sure. Why else would Gwen Harte agree to take them as foster children? She has enough to do with her job and her own children. If I were her, I wouldn't take them.

She tied herself down for the summer for no reason at all. No one does that. No one. April must be the mother. They are not *our* kind of people. They're from Hawley, wherever that is. I've never even heard of it. Everybody says April gained weight this spring and absented herself at the end of school. Of course, Gwen wouldn't say, but my humble opinion is that little Miss April Harte was getting ready to give birth to these babies."

"Wouldn't her mother have taken her to the doctor?" Father Rene probed. "That would be the sensible thing to do."

"Sensible, perhaps, but not if she is covering it up. No one is that charitable. Two babies of different color. No one is that charitable," Junie May repeated. "Mark my words, Father, April Harte is the mother of these twins. I don't know who the father is, but obviously, he must be African American. We don't have any of those people at TM. The police claim they are investigating, but if you ask me, her lawyer husband paid them off. The Hartes aren't from around here. They aren't TM type of people."

Junie May was starting to repeat herself. Father Rene thanked her and hung up. Junie May would not be the only one who thought this way. He needed to make his point with Father Hope that he was the boss and this information would factor into doing exactly that.

Chapter 32

Father Josey
Wednesday Morning

Father Josey rose early and tuned in to watch the CEO of GrayBonePhone7 Technology, Denton Dublinsky, ring the opening bell on CNN. A brief blurb announced GrayBonePhone7's surprising continuous ascent, followed by a report on the Middle East. Josey flipped the TV off and his computer on. A couple of things ruled his docket today: a finance council meeting, a baptism information session, and a visit to the local hospital. With those completed, he could spend his time watching his portfolio. He could earn some money today. He looked at his brokerage account online: $200,000. It was there, the credit card company had made the deposit. Wonderful! He had never had that kind of money in the bank. He looked at it and fantasized.

He inspected his online listings. GrayBonePhone7 was climbing again. It closed yesterday at $52 and now, at 10 a.m., was at $57. He checked the chat room and the early morning reports. The major investment companies had good things to say about GrayBonePhone7. DBLUP wasn't online this morning, but he was sure to approve. He couldn't miss.

"Strike while the iron is hot," he murmured to himself. He put his hand on his shoulder. Perfect.

Click. Click. Click. He now owned 3,500 shares, plus the 700 he bought for himself earlier in the week. Adding in the 210 shares Our Lady owned totaled 4,410 shares in all. He thought aloud, "I'll let it work all day Friday and Monday and then pull the $200,000 and the church's 210 shares out on Monday afternoon. Marcy will be back to work on Tuesday." This is a perfect plan. A perfect plan for a perfect, I mean *nearly perfect* priest. Maybe he had learned more in his finance classes than his professors thought.

Josey slipped into his blacks and headed out to the finance meeting at the diocese. Ralph Loren had already taken his place in the chairman's seat when Josey walked into the room for the meeting. He hadn't known the vicar general very long and wanted to be on familiar terms with him. The other priests informed him of the VG's power over the bishop. He wouldn't mind the VG knowing how he was doing with his parish dollars. If he could increase the parish coffers, it would be a real feather in his cap and maybe he could become VG someday. Perfect.

"Josey, how goes the battle? How do you like your first parish?" The vicar general always acted happy to see him. He was a real gentleman.

"It's good," Josey answered enthusiastically. "The people are amicable, and they volunteer for everything. I have a wonderful staff. The administrative assistant really runs the parish. I don't have much…" He interrupted himself saying, "I mean, she is easy to direct. Whatever I tell her to do, she does. Without question."

The vicar general surprised Josey with his next comment. "Yes, I know Marcy. If I were going to pick a woman to screw, she would be the one. She is one fine-looking woman. She and I matriculated in college together. We were friends long before she worked at Our Lady. She is wonderful, generous, faithful, and kind, all the Boy Scout qualities. She is easy on the eyes, too. One of the better-looking secretaries on the Baywatch scale. In this business, you must appreciate the good ones. You could have inherited one of those true-blue faithful women who look like cafeteria ladies from grade school. Marcy is the exception. Treat her kindly, my friend. You got the best."

Josey had trouble picturing the vicar general screwing Marcy, although he had romanticized an affair with her himself. The vicar general presented himself as a righteous man. Josey responded, "She's been under the weather a bit and has complained that she's gained a few pounds. She took some time off this week, and I hope that she feels better when she gets back. She's a pretty one, alright, but besides that, she is a good administrative assistant. She knows what she is doing and makes my job easy. I guess I haven't seen the other churches' secretaries. Anyway, I have been working on my budget quite a bit." Josey hoped that the VG would ask him what he was doing with the budget. He was dying to tell him.

The other members of the committee came in, and the meeting started. There were eight men on the committee, all local businesspeople. The VG's administrative assistant took notes and presided over the ambiance with coffee, donuts, and a fruit plate. The vicar general suggested that Josey lead the prayer. He gave thanks for their committees and the wise decisions they would make.

Chapter 33

Father Matthew Hope
Wednesday Morning

Father Hope arrived at work late on Wednesday morning. "No need putting in overtime during the summer," he mused. "I'll show up at 10 o'clock, head out to the gym at 10:30, and be back by noon. Plenty of time to do everything that I need to do today." He wore Nike shorts and a gray TM t-shirt. He wouldn't have to change.

At 10:15 a.m., the phone rang. "Father Hope, it's Junie May. I have learned the most terrible thing. I am glad you are there. I thought you might be going to work out this morning, but I guess not. One of your girls, a TM girl, gave birth to twin babies last weekend. I can't believe that it would happen. She isn't married, and she gave birth to twins. And worst of all, one is an African American baby, and the other one is white. I am reluctant to tell you who, but for the sake of TM, I must tell you. We can't let this type of thing happen at Thomas More. If it does, we won't continue to get the best and the brightest into our school. And you'll never guess who it is. It is April Harte. Her mother is your English teacher. I don't know who the father is though. I saw the twins on Monday. They are dahl-ing, but April acted as if she didn't know a thing about it, making it obvious that her mother is covering up for her. Can you believe it?"

"I heard about the babies but don't know who the mother or father might be. Where did you hear this, and how do you know it is true? It might be idle gossip." Father Hope never liked hearing from Junie May. He yawned and stretched his legs while he talked to her.

Junie May continued her rant, "Father Matthew, I can't divulge my sources. I would never gossip. But my information comes from a reliable source, a very reliable source, you understand. I can't believe that this would happen. If she goes to school at TM, our patrons, especially the moneyed ones, will fade away. This type of thing didn't happen when I went to TM. Only the best families sent their children to TM. I was the senior class treasurer and homecoming queen runner-up, and I knew everybody then and now. I know that this type of thing did not happen when I was in school."

"I need a source, Junie May. Who told you that April was the mother? Gwendolyn Harte? I don't deal in rumors. I agree that if April is the mother, she needs to be disciplined. I will not accuse her before this rumor is verified. Can you give me some specifics?" Father Hope continued to try to coax the truth out of her.

"No, my lips are sealed. I can't say anymore. What I will say is that you need to ask Father Rene Leclerq. He knows. You priests can talk to each other. You must have a priest code or something. He'll tell you. He knows the truth." Junie May was determined not to divulge her sources.

"I hope that you won't carry this further," Father Hope advised her. "We priests will attend to it."

They signed off. Father Hope sorted through the mail of the usual deluge of catalogs and advertisements and then went to the local athletic club. He would deal with this later.

***

He did an extra set of weights on Wednesday morning before returning to school. He then invited the counselors into his office to consult with them about April.

The counselors for the 700 students at Saint Thomas More High School were always eager to please students and staff and tried very hard to present a positive image about TM to parents who stopped by. They had worked at TM for many years and enjoyed the environment, mostly calm with an occasional storm of student-on-student attacks in the locker room. The counselors lived by their creed and were in counseling themselves. For that reason, Father Hope seldom sought their advice. Counselors who needed counseling themselves didn't ring right with him.

"I received a phone call this morning from Junie May Layne," he began.

"Oh, that gossip, you can't believe anything she says," Candace Bratt, the senior counselor responded. Candace was tall, too thin, blonde, and recently divorced. She looked younger than her 45 years. She had begun lifting weights, and Father Hope had noticed that she was looking fitter, and he wondered if she was anorexic. Perhaps that was why she was in counseling. "Junie May can spin black to white in a flash. She uses the same counselor that I do. Her sessions fall on Tuesday and Thursday and mine, on Monday and Wednesday. Thankfully, we miss each other."

"Junie May claims that April Harte was pregnant this year and gave birth to the twins who were born this past weekend. You think there is any truth to it?" He was hoping they would say no.

"I don't know, but I doubt it." Candace began slowly. "April is kind of quiet and doesn't have very many friends. She didn't look pregnant. I met with her after Spring Break. No students fed me any gossip about it. Junie May might be fabricating this tale."

Her co-worker, Sharon Rogers, agreed. "No, not April. She's not that kind of girl. She is a straight arrow, and Gwen has a good handle on her activities. She knows where and with whom she goes. She's bright and a good person. I don't think she was pregnant."

Sharon, the shorter of the pair, was younger than Candace, but looked older. She was in an unhappy marriage but, being Catholic, was determined to stick it out. She attended marriage counseling without her husband trying to salvage her marriage. Sharon's opinions seldom varied from Candace.

Father Hope sighed. "I was pretty sure that you would say that. I didn't think that she was pregnant. Gwen called earlier complaining about this rumor and wanted me to stop it. I wish I knew where the rumor began."

"Good luck, Boss," they chimed together and left.

"I guess I'd better call Gwen," he mumbled half to himself and half to no one in particular.

He retrieved a bottle of Evian from his refrigerator, and at 1:45 Father Hope dialed the phone. He hated to call Gwen as she had her hands full, but he promised her he would call her if he caught wind of the rumor. The phone rang several times before Gwen answered, "Hello."

"Gwen, it's Father Hope. I don't want to pull you away from something important. I can call back later." He didn't want to tell her about the conversation with Junie May.

"No, Father, I can talk. They are both asleep, thank heaven. They usually alternate waking and sleeping. When one goes to sleep, the other wakes up. It's a vicious cycle. Both babies were lying on the couch when the phone rang. They don't move around much yet, but I wanted to transfer them to the crib before I answered the phone. I can talk. It's a good time."

He started tentatively, "I didn't want to call you, but I promised. I had a phone call with some ugly gossip about April, I'm sorry to tell you."

Gwen uttered a little yelp. "Who called you? What kind of rumor? What phone call? Who told you?"

"The rumor is what you told me: that April is the mother of the babies, and your family is covering it up."

"What? What are you talking about? I can't believe this. We are trying to do the Christian thing here with these babies and now these accusations of a lie and a cover-up. Don't people have anything better to do with their time than gossip?" Gwen was furious. "Who told you?" He didn't say the name *Junie May*, but she had her suspicion.

"I can't say. I am trying to stop it. I wanted to tell you that the rumor is out there. I'll do my best." Father Hope had no idea how he was going to stop this rumor, but he didn't say anything to Gwen. "Keep your chin up. I'll be in touch with you tomorrow."

Chapter 34

Father Rene Leclerq
Wednesday Morning

Father Hope hung up the phone and finished his bottled water. "That wasn't too bad," he thought aloud. He dialed Father Leclerq's number. "Rene, it's Matt Hope."

"You didn't go to the fitness center this morning?" Rene asked. "I am on my way over to see you."

"I went earlier this morning. One of these days, you should join me."

"Yeah, sure, maybe one of these days," Rene answered, while thinking that it wasn't in the realm of possibility. He couldn't imagine himself at the gym. Everyone would laugh at him. Getting him to the gym would take a miracle from the Virgin.

Father Hope wasn't listening to him and took the offensive. "I thought we might talk a bit. What is it that you want to do at TM High School? Advise me? Run the show? Teach religion? Now, that's a good gig. You teach five hours a day, go to work at 8, and are off by 3, with an hour off for lunch. You get a pass to all the football games, and you'll get every summer off. You have no Lenten lunacy and no frantic Christmas Masses. And you get time-and-a half-off for good behavior. You can't beat it. Interested? I can always use a good theology teacher. Lay people don't understand the Scriptures the way that priests do." He continued his sales pitch, "We have a woman theology teacher, can you imagine? God would turn over in His grave. If He had one, that is." Like most priests, Matthew Hope tolerated women in the church, but didn't respect them. His calling was a good ol' boys' club and probably always would be.

Rene didn't respond to the job offer. "I want to talk about the twins. The ones that that woman found at Mass. The Harte woman, the ones that belong to the Harte girl. She's the mother. I have it on good authority."

Father Hope was incredulous saying, "I don't think so. Did someone see her give birth? I can't believe she's the mother. I talked to the counselors who were also in agreement that April is not the mother. Where did you get this information? Junie May Layne? She is such a gossip, Rene. Don't believe her. She is not a source of 'good authority.'"

Rene paused considering how to respond. All the priests knew of Junie May's gossip patterns, and Matt Hope nailed it. "Never mind who my source is. She came to me in confession making it off limits." Rene was lying, but he knew that Matt wouldn't confront him if he told him he obtained the information during a confession. "I think we both know what needs to be done. You need to dismiss Miss Harte from TM. This scandal will ruin TM and could come back to haunt you and me if it isn't handled correctly. I mean dismiss her at once."

"I don't want to dismiss her. Dammit, Rene, she is a lovely girl. This will ruin her chances for college. It will damage her reputation and destroy her emotionally. She's not the mother. Your source is lying." Matthew Hope was not often aggressive but was now. "You are wrong, Rene. Dead wrong."

"Have you talked to her?" Father Rene demanded.

Father Hope answered quickly, "No, I talked with Gwen, her mom, but not April."

"You need to talk to her and then expel her from school. What's so hard about this, Matt?" Father Rene continued, growing louder. "Just get rid of her."

"What if she denies it?" Father Hope didn't want to confront her.

Rene was matter of fact, "Mrs. Harte is lying. You might as well face it. Of course, she would lie. Why would she tell the truth? She has everything to lose and nothing to gain. If we don't handle this correctly, meaning expel her from TM immediately, we will lose our big supporters. You have enough trouble with your finances. You don't need your perennial donors pulling out, too."

What Rene reported was true. The finances at TM were tenuous. People didn't want to have a tuition increase, yet teachers always requested higher salaries. It was a constant battle, yet Father Hope wasn't about to let Rene win this battle, "Is that what this is about? Money? I can't believe this is about money. Who is your source, Rene?"

Father Rene answered, "I told you. I can't say. Trust me on this one, Matt. Trust me, because I know what I'm doing."

"I don't think so," Matt Hope articulated.

"The bottom line is that you work for me now," Father Rene asserted. "If you like your cushy life here at TM, you need to obey me. I'll replace you with O'Grady in a heartbeat. You can take care of the finances at St. Gert's, do all the Masses, and start shoveling Rolaids down your throat. And I guarantee you won't get gym time." Rene knew that gym time was important to the Iron Man.

Father Hope could not believe his ears. He knew that Rene was vindictive but did not expect this much anger. Matt assumed he would be at TM until he retired. He liked his life, short days, time for himself, summers off. It was a great job.

Rene was younger than many of the priests, but far more uncompromising. He had built a track record with principals. If they weren't to his liking, he erased them from his slate. He loathed women in leadership, especially women principals. At his prior parishes, he fired them within a month of his arrival. He had also eradicated some men, but Matt had no idea he was on Rene's hit list.

Father Hope decided to go a different direction to get Rene out of the picture, "Perhaps we should talk to a third party, Rene. Another priest, the VG, the bishop?"

Rene retorted, "Hey, don't you get it? This is my call. I'm in charge of diocesan education. I'm your boss at both St. Gert's and TM. You don't get a vote. Get rid of her. I am going out of town tomorrow, and when I return, she'd better be gone. Get rid of that girl. Today."

Father Hope argued, "No, Rene. This is my call. I'm the principal. I call the shots. Don't mess with me, Rene. As far as the counselors and I know, she wasn't even seeing anyone."

"You and I both know that you don't need a boyfriend to get pregnant," Father Rene screamed over the phone.

They hung up. Father Matthew Hope sat back in his chair pondering what to do. "Rene is a dangerous man. He needs to be gone."

Chapter 35

Father JP Shannon
Wednesday Afternoon

Father JP Shannon didn't get involved with parish business much. His religion started and finished on the 1st and 18th holes. Today, though, he had played with Junie Mae's husband, Reggie Layne, and this required a call to Rene.

"Rene, this is JP. Got a minute?"

Father Rene answered, "Sure, JP, anything for our number one fundraiser. What do you need? New golf balls or new head covers?" Rene hoped that JP didn't hear the sarcasm in his voice.

"No, nothing like that. I needed to call you about those babies. Did you figure out who the mother is? I did. She's in your parish," Father Shannon stated.

Rene answered feigning ignorance, "Really? Since they were found at St. Gert's, I sort of assumed they belonged to someone at St. Gert's." Rene remembered that JP wasn't known for his rocket science brain.

"The word on the street is that they belong to one of the TM teacher's kids. The one who teaches English at TM, Mrs. Harden, I think her name is Hard-on, something like that." Father Shannon smirked at his own comment.

"Harte," Father Rene corrected.

Shannon continued, "Yeah, yeah, Harte. Do you know her?"

Father Rene admitted that he did. "Yeah, we've met. She is the one who found the babies, and they're at her house. I visited her right after she found them."

Father Shannon answered, "Found the babies, my ass. They're her daughter's. She put them there. That's clear. You need to do something, Rene. You're in charge of that school. My advice is to get rid of her. I mean the daughter. Maybe the mother, too. They'll make the school look bad. We look bad enough with all this pedophilia crap going on. Our diocese has escaped so far, but this could open us up to a lot of scrutiny. All we need is to have our teachers, or even worse, our students, with illegitimate children. It sends a bad message to the parishioners, the donors, and the old money that we can't do without. They'll think everybody is screwing everybody, and the money will dry up. That would be bad news for Thomas More. Back in my day, we would meet her at the door and kick her sweet little ass back home. If she was a good-looking piece of ass, we might fuck her before we ousted her. She'd never dare say it was a priest. I suppose there are rules about that type of thing now."

Father Rene answered, "You know better than that. Things have changed a little, JP, but I'm working on it. I heard that it was the Harte girl and talked to the Iron Man about expelling her, but I don't think he has done it yet. I'll keep on it. Why don't you call him, too? He isn't keen on expelling her. I think he has a soft heart for the low-life cases and doesn't want to do it. A call from you might kick his reluctant butt into action." Rene could use some help dealing with Father Hope.

"Yeah, sure. I can do that. He's a hard one to catch. He's always pumping iron. When's a good time to call him?" Father Shannon agreed reluctantly, knowing his own tee times caused him to be as difficult to catch as the Iron Man.

"You can probably catch him tomorrow. He goes to work at TM before going to work on body beautiful," Rene answered.

Father Shannon announced, "I already have an early tee time, but I'll see if I can catch him later."

Chapter 36

Angel
Wednesday Afternoon

Angel took the afternoon off. She had a headache and didn't want to go to work. She seldom took days off, but she was sure no one would miss her. Her breasts were still hurting, and she felt sad, sadder than she had been for a long time. Post-partum depression perhaps. WebMD discussed it, and she decided that's what it was, as she had all the symptoms. She told her coworkers that she was going out of town for the next few days but actually made plans to hide out in her house. She needed to rest.

She was surprised at how much she missed the babies. She thought that they would be out-of-sight, out-of-mind, but that wasn't so. They remained in her heart and in her mind. They were children of God, and she wanted them baptized.

She thought about her own childhood and the drunken stories that Charlie had told her. She had existed all these years without knowing about her parents. Her father left before she was born, and her mother ran away with a cook. Some years ago, she had engaged an adoption investigation firm to search for them. There were a couple of leads that emerged, but they fell through. She gave up after a few hopeless months and concluded that they had simply abandoned her. When her stepfather died, she felt like he had abandoned her, too. It was something she would never get over.

Thinking about Charlie, Angel recalled something that she had forgotten years ago. One night, after Charlie had finished off a 12-pack of beer, he was mumbling something about her mom being half Haitian. She didn't pay much attention to it and thought it was the alcohol talking, especially because she was fair skinned. But the more she thought about it, she wondered if maybe it was true and that is why one of the babies was dark. She could check that on the Web.

***

Angel's college days had been demanding. With no money and no scholarships, she solicited the church for help. They provided a mere pittance, a few hundred dollars a semester. She had no choice except to work at night to be able to attend daytime classes. The only available jobs were in security, but as a woman, she could not get hired. She took some classes in self-defense, cut her hair short, and dressed like a man for the interview. She got a job as a night security guard at the mall and worked security at various events. Her masculine appearance guaranteed her safety, gave her authority and clout. People didn't talk back to her. The job was the pits but paid the bills. Her schedule gave her plenty of time for prayer.

Angel attended school in the mornings, slept in the afternoon, and worked at night. To save time and money, she simply wore men's clothes every day. She had no time for a social life, which was fine with her since she had no friends and didn't trust anyone. Everyone in her life abandoned her. Why seek added pain?

Angel went to bed early on Wednesday night. She drank her usual three glasses of wine plus another to help her sleep. She took a handful of pain relievers for her headache. In addition, she popped a few over-the-counter sleeping tablets. That would help her sleep for sure.

She recited her prayers for the babies and the Harte family. She prayed the babies would be happy and healthy and then drifted off to sleep.

Chapter 37

Detective Maggie Monroe
Wednesday afternoon

Maggie had worked in the office all morning, researching and making phone calls. She had read the report about the break-ins that the two Bens had covered the night before and was waiting for them to come back on duty, when she got a call from Brick.

"Hi Maggie, I'm home. The VA brought me. Those volunteers are amazing. I'm fine. They gave me some miracle drug, one of those 'take two and call me in the morning' type drugs and I immediately felt better. And they sent me home. I didn't want to interrupt your abandoned baby case, so I just had the volunteers bring me back home. I'm fine. They had me skip PT today but I'll have to go in tomorrow. I've already arranged transportation. So, how are those babies doing? You got any leads about their parents."

Maggie was amazed. This morning, he couldn't stand up and now he was doing a proverbial jig. "That's great. Maybe they should give you that drug for daily use."

"No, we don't have any leads yet. We're still trying to get info from the church and it's slow going. Remember how the Diocese dragged their feet when Fitzwater was murdered. It's no better now. You'd think they'd learn. I'll be home soon, don't overdo. How about I bring Chinese food for dinner, then neither of us has to cook? Gotta go, love you." It looked like Brick would have a good day.

Chapter 38

An Intruder
Early Thursday Morning

Total blackness in Basin didn't occur until late during June. He went to bed early and set the alarm for 2 a.m. When he roused, it was dark, cool, no clouds, and no wind with a sliver of a moon. "She ought to have finished her wine by now," he thought. He felt sad, but this had to end.

He prided himself in knowing right from wrong. His moral compass said that this was not right, yet he hated her for who she had become. He hated her for the fraud she committed on God and the church. He hated her for the fraud she committed against him. He hated her for everything. She caused too many people too much pain. If only they knew her secret.

He had spent the last three nights carefully considering his options. "There is no other way. Too much is at stake. I'm doing her a favor. I'm doing God a favor. Perhaps God made a mistake. She is a waste of good air. There is no other way." He quickly dressed in black Levi's, black Nike running shoes, and a black hooded sweatshirt. He skirted down the back alleys alternately jogging and walking and quickly covered the three miles to her house. He crept close to the shrubs and saw no one except a few alley cats prowling for scraps. He wore a baseball cap low on his face with surgical gloves and his father's pistol jammed in his pocket.

His father presented him with the handgun as a teenager long before he went to college. He never used it, except for waving at Mormon missionaries when they knocked at his door. He often bragged to his fraternity friends, "If you want to get rid of the goddamn missionaries, wave a gun at them. They'll think you're crazy, and it scares the hell out of them. They won't be back." His father advised him to clean it weekly, and he oiled it religiously every Saturday night, as he had been instructed.

He had thought this through. Enter the house, fire the pistol once, twice to be sure, and leave. His pistol held two bullets. Use them both. Be sure to use a pillow to muffle the shots. No one would see him. No one would know. He planned carefully, considering each step of the way. Earlier in the day, he checked to see where the furniture was. Counted the steps to her room. God, the filth. He hated her for her filth, too. He had checked the doors to see if they squeaked. He looked in the basement, all of the closets, and even the God-awful, filled-to-the-brim cupboards. All he needed to do was fire the pistol through the pillow and leave. No problem. It would all be over soon.

He thought about Angel. She looked like hell. The babies, the birth, the secrecy, the evil. They had taken a toll on her. Her pain was about to be over. He was doing her a favor. This was the right thing to do. She was a tool of the devil. God was on his side. He, too, hated her for being a tool of the devil.

He positioned himself inside the fence and surveyed the neighborhood. He listened for any sounds. It was quiet. No cars. No walkers. No dogs. He put on the gloves and tested the door. Unlocked. He looked in the window. A gentle flickering of candlelight but no movement. He entered the house. Predictably, the wine bottle was empty. It had been unopened when he was there earlier. Good. She shouldn't hear him. The ghostly candlelight gave him enough light to maneuver around the furniture.

He thought of the old comedy, Cary Grant in *Arsenic and Old Lace*. He starred in the play during high school. "Ah, ah, ah," the old ladies warned Mortimer as he was about to down a glass of wine. Shaking his head, he refocused on the mission.

He entered her bedroom and observed her for a few seconds. She was lying on her back, mouth agape, a gentle snore accompanying her regular breathing. Two candles burned at the foot of her bed. She was nude covered by a sheet with a swollen breast and one leg protruding. A blue terry robe lay across the end of the bed. He heard nothing and saw no movement. The cats must be outside.

He crept silently to the bed, and without giving it a moment's thought, he shot her, first through the throat and then through the temple. He used a pillow to muffle the noise, but he couldn't be sure that no one heard. He felt anger, sadness, remorse, and fear. What if he was wrong? Perhaps he was wrong. Would he have to face God on this one? He would go to confession and ask for absolution. That would work.

He gazed at the candles, glanced at her, and panicked. Blood oozed from her throat onto her bedding. His mind raced with questions: *What if they trace the pistol? Who knew that he had a pistol? What if they link it to him? What if he was wrong? Can they trace the gun?* He had forgotten that the police could trace guns. *Shit*, he thought. *Shit*.

The candlelight flicked his mind to another channel. *If she is burned, they can't trace my gun. I'll make doubly sure,* he thought to himself. He stole quickly through the house, gathering up additional candles and lighting them. "This house is worth a fortune. What a waste," he brooded as he lit them. "What a fucking waste." He ignited candles in every bedroom, bathroom, the kitchen, and the living room, gave them a gentle nudge, and watched them grow from flicker to flame to blaze. As soon as the incineration began, he left through the back door. He heard a cat's meow as he shut the door.

At 3:30 in the morning, Angel's house was fully ablaze. It burned for nearly 30 minutes before the fire department received a call. When the firefighters arrived, the structure's dry wood was completely engulfed in flames. There was little to do except watch it burn.

Thursday morning headlines read: *Catholic Rectory Consumed by Fire.*

Chapter 39

Bishop Connor Llewellyn
Thursday

The Thursday morning headlines shocked the town. Fires were rare, and few fire-related deaths had occurred in the past 20 years. The fire department initiated its investigation early Thursday morning. The house was situated in the historical district and was considered a time-honored gem of Basin. Its original façade meant that it was subject to rapid and thorough burning. They found one person, a few pieces of charred furniture, and two cats. They planned to investigate it as arson.

The bishop and the vicar general drove over to the St. Gertrude's rectory to view the smoldering remains of the rectory. Father Rene Leclerq had purchased it long before the prices of houses began to soar. Neither had heard from Father Leclerq, and they immediately called a meeting of the priests of the diocese. Vicar General Ralph Loren informed his administrative assistant, "The bishop wants all priests at this meeting at 10 a.m. All priests and no excuses." She began her calls.

The St. Gert's community, led by Junie May Layne, leaped into action. She organized prayer services, vigils, prayer trees, and fundraisers to offset the loss. She wasn't the only one jumping to conclusions, Fathers Hope and O'Grady recited a special Mass for the victim, whom they assumed to be Father Rene Leclerq; however, the police had still not made a positive identification of the victim. The bishop unexpectedly joined them in the Mass and declared it a diocesan tragedy. He announced that the diocesan flags would be lowered to half-staff. He called his friend, the mayor, to confirm his Friday golf date and to request that the city flags be lowered.

All priests except Father Rene Leclerq arrived on time. They all wore their blacks with white collars, which was standard formal dress for priests. Ralph Loren led the meeting, "Gentlemen, we have a tragedy. I guess it takes a fire and a death to get you all here. Thank you for coming on such short notice. Let's begin with a prayer. Bishop Con, would you pray for us?"

Bishop Con was quick to pray, "Dear Heavenly Father, You've brought us together to try to help us create harmony in this time of need. We pray that You will help us come to a consensus as to how to deal with this tragedy. Grant peace to the soul of the victim. In the name of the Father, Son, and Holy Spirit. Amen."

"Thank you, Bishop. The reporters are already hovering around the diocese today. Let's get our ducks in a row," Ralph proclaimed. He spoke quickly, mincing no words. "I've been in touch with the insurance company, and our insurance is solid. We shouldn't have any problem recouping the house equity. That house was worth a mint. Let's hope the insurance company will pay the full value. Does anybody know about Rene? Has anyone heard from him?"

Father O'Grady said, "We know there was a person in the house, but it can't be Rene, because he told me that he was going out of town and would be gone from Wednesday afternoon through Friday. It's unusual for him to be gone, but that's what he told me."

Vicar General Ralph Loren snapped back, "You mean that Rene is out of town? Where did he go? Did he tell you that?"

Father O'Grady answered quickly, "He called a day or so ago. I wasn't really paying attention, but he wanted me to recite daily Mass on Thursday and Friday mornings, because he was leaving town for a couple of days. I can't remember if he said where he was going."

"He really left town?" the bishop repeated.

"Nobody's assuming anything," Ralph declared. "All we know is that he isn't here. We know for sure that a person was in the house. If Rene is out of town, it can't be him. And that's a relief. But if the person in the house wasn't Rene, who was it?"

The bishop continued, "I don't know what to think. What do you all think? How about you, Matt? He was excited about the Thomas More committee assignment. Did you talk to him yesterday?"

Father Hope said, "Yes, he called about noon yesterday. He made some noise about those twins found in St. Gert's last week. He ordered me to fire a teacher. He thinks the twins are her daughter's babies. He was very irrational and stated that he would be gone today. He didn't say anything about Friday."

JP spoke, "I talked to him yesterday. He didn't say anything to me about being gone."

Father O'Grady opened a new package of antacids and passed them around.

Ralph asked, "Anybody else talk to Rene yesterday?"

The men were quiet for a moment before the bishop spoke. "Let's go over what we know and what we don't know. My main concern is the press. What we know is that Rene talked to the two of you yesterday, and he told you that he was going out of town. If he went out of town, we can be sure that the deceased isn't Rene, right? The police have not released any identification, so we shouldn't jump to conclusions."

The priests all looked at each other and nodded at the bishop as he continued, "He was working on the issue of those damn twins who were abandoned in the church. Other than that, he was performing normal duties. Is it possible that the babies were related to this fire?"

Paul McGraeth reacted quickly, "How would that work? No, they can't be related. The babies were found last week, and the fire was last night. So, that's unlikely. Two isolated incidents. Let's not try to make something out of nothing."

Ralph voiced his plan, "We aren't much better off than we were to begin with. The press is going to deluge us with questions, and we need to be firm on our answers. The police, too, if they show up, and I'm sure they will. I have a plan, and everyone must follow it. I will put it in memo form. I want us solid in our statement to the press." He wrote as he talked.

"First, we are grieving at this tragedy. It is unbelievable that this could have happened in our diocese."

"Second, we are doing everything possible to find out about the victim and his or her family. It is at these times that we trust in the Lord for guidance."

JP interrupted. "Whoa, *her*? What's with *her*? We don't want to have a '*her*' in the rectory. If it was a '*her*,' she was an intruder."

"You are right, JP. Thanks," Ralph Loren continued. "I will leave the second point out. That is probably a good idea," He scratched it out and continued to write.

"Third, or rather second, we will cooperate with the police and fire departments in every way to determine the cause of this tragedy. We ask God's blessings on the diocese and the city. And the first responders, of course."

Ralph looked around at the group, half thinking aloud and half taking control. "If you have any reporters or police coming your way, send them to the diocese. I will be the central contact point. I'll do the damage control. Does anyone know anything else?" No one answered.

The bishop looked at Ralph and thanked God for His blessings. *Thank God for Ralph Loren,* he thought to himself as he had done many times before. The bishop closed with three Hail Mary's for the victim.

Chapter 40

Detective Maggie Monroe
Thursday morning

Maggie was up early, awakened by sirens blasting by their house while it was still dark. Three engines, a three-alarm fire, followed by an ambulance. Brick had had a good night's sleep. That drug was amazing. We want more, she thought. She dressed quickly, leaving the coffee on for Brick, kissed him good-bye as he slept, and headed to work.

Chief Tucker met her at the door of the station. "Maggie, I'm glad you are here, and I hope you brought your investigator's cap. There's been a fire on the other side of town, one of those old houses, and it's burning like a sun-of-a-gun. It belonged to some minister, a Catholic priest, I think, but I'm not sure if he owned it or the church did. I sent a couple police officers over, but I want you and Jack to go. I'm making you the lead person on this one," he said. "You aren't making much progress on finding the parents of those twins, so this will take priority and maybe you'll do better on a house fire than those babies. I want you and Jack to head down to that house and see what you can see. I called him a few minutes ago, and he'll be here shortly. The police officers who answered the call are still there, Ben and Ben, you've met them already, but we are short-handed, so you and Jack are it. They go off shift as soon as you get there. I've been thinking, both of these deal with the Catholic church, maybe somehow, they are tied together. But prepare yourself, a person died, burned up, so it won't be a pretty sight. Are you up for it?"

Maggie was taken aback. *Take the lead*? "Of course, I can do it. It won't be the first fire I've investigated. Arson?" She was thinking of the time the Barrier brothel caught on fire, rousting out partially clothed men and women in a sort of circus scene. "We're on it, but how do you think they tie together, and do you know the name of the victim?"

"No, no name yet, because he hasn't been identified. I'm not sure how they tie together, just a hunch, but if my hunch is right, you'll figure it out. Jack has good instincts, so use him. At least you'll see our department at work, even though it'll only be the two patrolmen and you and Jack," the chief continued. "The fire marshal, Dolan, is a good person to meet, too. He helps us out from time to time. He's already called me and is at the scene. By the way, here is your badge, FedEx dropped it off last night, and you should pick out a pistol from the weapon's locker. I doubt you'll need it, but it's good to have it when something like this happens. I wonder what's taking Jack so long?" Maggie pinned her badge on, and she checked out the weapon locker while she was waiting. She was feeling a little better, somewhat validated. Two cases, maybe tied together, maybe not.

She found a couple weapons that she liked, a Smith & Wesson .38 revolver, Airweight, two-inch barrel, or a Sig P320, 9mm, with a smaller hand grip. She was used to the Smith & Wesson, it fit in her hand and the holster sewn into her blazer. She would fire it at the range tomorrow for her qualification record with the police department, but it was fine to carry for today. She had just finished signing the necessary papers when Jack appeared.

She said, "Time to go, Jack. There's been a house fire, one of those 19th century homes across town. The chief put me in charge of the investigation, so let's go. The fire department has things under control, but if this town is like any others, people will be walking all over the evidence. The two Bens are already there, but we need to go now."

"Chief called me before I finished my coffee. Was anybody hurt?" Jack asked as they headed out the door. He was armed with his usual police paraphernalia and looked scary as ever.

"Yes, a priest lived there, and somebody was in the house and died. The chief warned me, and I'll warn you. Burned bodies can be grisly," Maggie said. She was an experienced investigator, but Jack had not shared his history. The chief said he had good instincts; this would be a good opportunity to check them out. She knew he had been at the PPD for a couple years, but in what capacity? She was unsure.

She smiled to herself. This was her first big case in Basin, and it would be critical for her to prove herself. "You drive," she said to Jack. "I'm not sure where we are going."

Jack answered, "Me either, exactly, but we'll find it. Looks like we just need to follow the smoke. Five or ten minutes, I think." They could see some wisps of smoke from the police station parking lot. Jack turned on his lights and sirens and peeled out. "Hang on."

Jack wasn't afraid of speed, and they arrived in four minutes flat. Two of the three firetrucks had already left, and the third one was cleaning up. A small crowd of neighbors, mostly still wearing pajamas, milled around, watching the emergency vehicles do their work. A truck, labeled, "Fire Marshal," sat across the street. Jack parked next to the fire marshal's rig, and they stepped out of the cruiser.

The fire marshal greeted Jack, and Maggie introduced herself. "I'm Detective Maggie Monroe, the new investigator with the department, but most people just call me Maggie," she said as she shook Dolan's hand. "The chief assigned Jack and me to the case and put me in charge." She wanted to make it clear that she, not Jack, was responsible for the investigation.

Dolan shook her hand and grinned. "I heard he hired a woman, and I'm glad. The good ol' boys' club has existed far too long and needs to be broken up. I'm glad to meet you, Maggie."

She already liked Tom Dolan. "Thanks, do you have anything to tell us?" Maggie asked.

"A priest lived in the house, Father Leclerq. I think he was assigned to St. Gertrude's which is a few blocks from here. According to the neighbors, he was home, but he was a real loner, and nobody had seen him recently. The body has been sent to the morgue where they'll try to verify if it was him or someone else."

Maggie and Jack both looked at him with surprise. She said, "Father Leclerq? Did you say Leclerq? He's the same priest we are working on in another case. The chief suggested the two cases were related, and by golly, I think they are."

Chapter 41

Father Paul McGraeth
Thursday Morning

Father Paul took a nap when he returned from the bishop's meeting. He had played with his computer for a while, finally falling into a deep sleep. He roused at 8 a.m. and read the headlines in the paper. Morning Mass was followed by the meeting at 10 a.m. By 11 o'clock, he was exhausted.

When he rallied, he continued working on his resumé. It was impressive to say the least. He served God in several parishes that loved him. He managed finance committees, spirituality committees, social justice committees, personnel committees, and had begun a charity for the homeless in Milwaukee. He presented workshops at Catholic conferences, especially on the subject of "The Freedom of a Moral Life." Once a parish heard him, they invited him back. He was entertaining and sincere. He was loved everywhere he went.

During the cruise stage of his priesthood, Father Paul visited the diocesan offices and parishes in every port and interacted with dozens of priests, bishops, archbishops, and cardinals. He remembered them on his Christmas card list and sent bottles of wine to the cardinals every year. He hoped that his generosity would remind them of his excellence and virtuosity. He had cultivated many friendships, and now, when he needed to call in his chips, they would be available. He used email and social media to garner those relationships.

Paul received his bachelor's degree from a state college and graduated summa cum laude. He excelled in his seminary studies and attended school in Rome for two years. When he returned to the United States, he was assigned to Milwaukee and remained there for ten years before transferring to the Pacific Northwest. When he became the pastor of a mostly Spanish-speaking parish, the diocese sent him to Colombia to sharpen his Spanish language and cultural skills. He remained there a year, and upon his return, became pastor at Clarksburg where he met Mark. After Clarksburg, he was promoted to Holy Fathers, which had been the tiara of parishes at one time. Unfortunately, as Basin expanded and new parishes were built, Holy Fathers dwindled and became the urban blight challenge of the diocese.

His resumé looked good. No, it looked great. He accomplished much in his life and now he wanted to relax and let others do things for him. It was only fair. He owned a replica of a bishop's ring, which was housed in his desk. He extracted it from the drawer and placed it on his finger admiring its glossy finish. "I'm finally going to get it," he murmured aloud. He smiled at his good fortune.

He sent the resumé to his brother in Anchorage and called him to be sure that he received it. Anchorage email was not always dependable, so he had to be sure that it arrived.

"Diocese of Anchorage, Pearl speaking."

"Pearl, is the Vicar General there? I'd like to speak with him, please," Father Paul asked.

"Just a minute, please."

Peter McGraeth came on the phone, "Vicar General speaking. How may I help you?"

"Hey, bro. How goes it?"

"Paul. Good to hear from you. What's up?"

Paul said, "I called to tell you that I emailed you my resumé and want to be sure that it arrived. I am ready, willing, and able to go to Fairbanks. Any word on other candidates yet?"

"Great, I haven't seen it yet. Hold on while I check my computer," Peter pressed the hold button, and some jazz played in Paul's ear.

Peter came back on the phone, "It's here, no problem. I talked with a couple of the bishops on the screening committee. They don't have anyone they like. Of course, the final decision is from Rome, but the Holy See always takes the recommendation of the Archdiocese Committee."

"Who is on the committee?" Paul wanted to know.

Peter responded, "Our bishop is the chair. There are other bishops from Seattle, Portland, and San Francisco, and a cardinal from Denver. It's a given that they will take the recommendations from the local screening committee and decide before turning it over to the pope. He gets to make the final call. Do you have any connections?"

"I know the bishops from Seattle and San Francisco, but not the one from Portland. I haven't met your bishop, but I trust you'll talk to him. What does he drink, wine or whiskey? I'll send him a little gift," Paul requested.

"Whiskey, Maker's Mark, I'll buy a bottle and send it to him with your name on it. Consider it done," Peter announced. "I'll look over your resumé, and if I need to add to it, I will. You've had a lot of successes, so adding a couple won't be a big deal. Of course, I won't tell him that you used to throw the ping pong paddle at me after I slammed the last point. They probably don't want someone with your temper."

Paul breathed a silent sigh of relief thinking, *You are so fortunate that you cooperated. You have no idea of the fury I could wreak on you.* Instead, he said, "Thanks a lot, little brother. I owe you one. The old folks in Florida will be thrilled if I get this appointment. Their faggot son becomes a bishop. They'll never believe it."

Chapter 42

Father Josey
Thursday

Josey was quiet as he left the meeting. He hadn't known Rene. What he knew of him wasn't positive. From what he understood through the priest hot line, Rene was sort of a prick, bossy, and always wanted things his way. Nevertheless, he felt sorry for him, assuming, of course, that he was the victim.

He stopped at the diocesan mailroom and picked up the mail for the Finance Council. Not too much. A couple bills and some junk mail.

Josey rushed back to Our Lady. He couldn't help but think about the stock market and his success. He knew that he should be thinking about Father Rene, but Thursday and Friday were big days for GrayBonePhone7. He wanted to verify that everything was falling into place.

He keyed in his password to recheck his portfolio. He owned over 4,400 shares with a total investment of $233,800. The current value of $61.75 or $271,700, meant nearly $40,000 profit. He would repay the $200,000 to MasterCard and the rest was his and Our Lady's. Hallelujah. God is good.

Josey checked to see if DBLUP was online. He was. He wanted to crow a bit of his good fortune. "Nearly 40k profit," he typed. "Nearly 40k!"

DBLUP typed back, "Too bad u didn't buy some on margin. U could have doubled it."

Tap, tap, tap, tap. "Margin? What r u talking about?" Margin, of course. Josey learned about margin in his finance classes, but it had escaped his memory. "R there rules?" Josey typed into the text box.

"Not really. Margin is ur buying power. If u have $100 cash, u can invest $200, i.e., $100 on margin. If u have $5K cash, u can invest $10K with $5k on margin. It is prty simple. How do u think all those nerds made fortunes on the tech stocks? Margin. Sure, there's a little interest, but what the hell, as long as it is going up, who cares?" DBLUP answered.

"And $100K would mean i could invest $200K? Is that what it means? Is there a limt?" Josey typed.

"No limt as far as i know," DBLUP texted. "I do it all the time. It's good, safe, easy. Say buying on margin when u buy. No prob. And 'member, they're gonna split. I'm sure of it."

They chatted a few more minutes and signed off. Frustrated, Josey started to beat himself up mentally, "What was I thinking? The split is a sure thing, and I could have doubled my money. It is probably too late to do it now."

He returned to the stock reports. All the major investment firms predicted that GrayBonePhone7 would split late today and immediately bounce back. They called it the Rubber Band Stock. He would pull out on Monday afternoon or Tuesday morning at the latest. At $61.75, a split would drop the price to under $30, but when it bounced back, as they predicted, he could make $10-$20 profit per share. Per share. He had 4,410 shares, meaning nearly 9,000 shares with a split. That meant nearly $90,000 in profit. In addition to what he had already earned. The numbers were getting too big, but even the conservative firms were speculating a split. Conservative estimates. By Monday, it could be $75 or $100.

Josey started chattering to himself, "Things are moving too fast. I need to think." He pulled out a yellow pad and pocket calculator and wrote down some figures, speaking aloud as he mulled over his dilemma, "A week ago Our Lady had $7,500, and I had $26K. Now we have over $300K between us. Of course, I must repay the MasterCard loan. That goes without saying. That means over $100,000 profit. $100,000. Do I dare? I'd be a fool not to. The building fund for Our Lady was invested in a CD and worth $15,000 and change. I can withdraw it and pay a small penalty. That would be good, too." He had gotten lost in his computations, but that was because the numbers were growing too fast. He couldn't lose. He would pay the penalty out of his own pocket. That would be a good donation to Our Lady. Click. Click. He transferred the money to his account.

While he waited for the transfer confirmation, he picked up the Diocesan Finance Council's mail and thumbed through it. A bill from the auditor for $15,000. God, they charge a lot. A bill from the office supply store $45.85 for some paper products, paper clips, and correction fluid. There were also a couple of ads from software companies for financial software and three credit card ads. The usual. *The diocese gets the same mail that I get,* he thought to himself.

He sat down at his computer to type in his stock order using margin. *I've never done this before,* he thought. *I need to do it right.* He leaned back and studied the screen. He punched in the numbers and purchased another 250 shares, bringing his total to 4,660 shares. Amazing. He sat back and watched the numbers move upward as he purchased his shares.

He glanced at the pile of mail on his desk noting three credit card offers. Another $150K? Divine intervention, God must be intervening. I have never seen as many free credit cards offered in a week. These numbers are rolling fantastically.

By 1 p.m. he had notified the credit card companies that he had accepted their offers. They deposited $150,000 into his checking account. By 2:15, he had invested this $150,000, plus $150,000 on margin. The price was $65 per share. With the click of his mouse, he now had a total of 9,025 shares of GrayBonePhone7 Technology. He would pay it back on Monday. Just to be safe.

They split at 3:05. He owned 18,050 shares of GrayBonePhone7! Josey started humming his theme song, the Mac Davis hit, "Lord, it's hard to be humble when you're perfect in every way." He kept his fingers crossed for luck.

Chapter 43

Gwen
Thursday Morning

The news and rumors struck the Harte family hard. Although they had not been acquainted with Father Leclerq for very long and had no personal relationship with him, he was a priest, their priest. He had visited them the day after the babies were found. His sermons lacked inspiration, and he had been of little help with the twins. April's moniker, Father Lacking-in-Charisma, stuck in Gwen's mind as she thought about him. Nevertheless, as Catholics and members of the Catholic community, they supported the priests. The unwritten Catholic code held that it was unacceptable to criticize a priest to anyone, especially an outsider, a non-Catholic.

After four days of marathon diapers, feedings, and countless loads of laundry, punctuated with gurgles and finger grasps, the Harte family had fallen head over heels in love with Marie and Louis. Each had a unique personality: Marie was larger with an outgoing personality, and Louis was detached, but his eyes tried to focus when they talked to him. Louis was always hungry, and Marie always needed a new diaper. They were rapidly becoming an integral part of their family.

The babies finally fell asleep, and Gwen thought about the blog she had seen a few days ago on the Internet. She keyed in her password and once again wove her way through a myriad of Internet sites. Where had she seen that one? There are so many blogs. She persisted until she found the subject "Twins that aren't twins." A few bloggers commented on the site originated by *Angel Eyes*, but mostly pejorative ones. Some had racial slurs. How could people be so crass? She reread the original entry...

Two babies born at the same time, but one black, one white. Twins? God is punishing me for my sins. The Almighty tempted me, as the serpent tempted Eve. The babies are of the devil. Their father told me that, and he's right. It was my fault. I should never have allowed myself to be raped. My fault that the devil was tempted. I must repent, repent of my sins, repent for the babies, repent for the father. I am sorry for my sins. Let this serve as my confession to God. Angel Eyes

The responses, in part, read:

One black, one white...not twins. Can't be. You must be nuts.

Rape is not your fault. Go see the police.

Devil babies. Sounds like devil worship. Voodoo, if you ask me.

Get some help, Girl.

Praying for you. Keep the faith.

Angel Eyes responded, *I have made my confession. Marie and Louis are now children of God. Let God be with them throughout all their days. Angel Eyes*

There were no responses to this blog.

Gwen felt sure she had found the mother, but how can Gwen identify *Angel Eyes*? She typed a response:

Are you OK? What a terrible ordeal for you. God will forgive you. Would you contact me? My phone number is..."

Gwen deleted the last sentence. It was a bad idea to put your phone number on the Internet. How could she have Angel Eyes contact her? She debated whether to call Maggie, thinking the police might scare her off and decided to see if the writer would answer before contacting Maggie and Jack. She hit send with the first four sentences signing herself with a simple G. Gwen hoped she would respond to her post.

Chapter 44

Detective Maggie Monroe
Thursday

Gwen fed one baby or the other almost constantly, and it was once again in the middle of feeding time when Detective Maggie and Officer Shetland rang the doorbell. Maggie started, "We've been working your case, and so far, we have come up cold. We came by to see if you had any other calls or have thought of anything else that might help us." Gwen held Louis and rocked Marie with her free hand. She invited them to sit down. Maggie sat and Jack remained standing.

Gwen answered quickly, "Nothing that might help find the mother, besides the note from Angel Eyes that I mentioned. The gossip mill is spreading the rumor that these babies belong to our daughter. I don't know why people are cruel, but there are those who like nothing better than to hurt other people. Thankfully, we had no other calls or people breaking in. A very welcome peaceful night allowed us to sleep a few hours. This morning's headlines were shocking, though, about Father Leclerq's house burning down. Was Father inside?"

Maggie answered, "The arson team is investigating it, and they haven't released any new information. The victim's name is unknown, but we assume it was Father Leclerq. No one knows until there is an autopsy."

"Really? Oh, my gosh, an autopsy. Hasn't anyone heard from him?" As quickly as the barrage of questions came to her, she asked the officers, "Who does an autopsy? The coroner? The hospital? The police department? Where do they do them? Here in Basin? Do you know how old the person is...was? When will that be?" Playing 20 questions had Gwen sounding a little like Junie May. God forbid that she mirrors that woman in any way.

Maggie responded, "I dunno, maybe today or tomorrow. Autopsies are performed in almost all unnatural deaths. We have not determined whether it was natural or unnatural. The fire destroyed the house. It happened before light this morning, and by the time the fire department arrived on the scene, it was completely engulfed in flames. We drove by this morning on our way here. A real tragedy, a gorgeous old house in Southside. They say that when the yuppies discovered those houses a few years ago, the prices escalated. Insurance probably won't pay diddly squat toward its real value."

Jack added, "Our objective in coming by is to discuss your, that is, the babies' case, Ma'am. No fingerprints showed up on the window from the break in. He must have been wearing gloves. The two phone calls, the baby blanket, and the rosaries are all we have to help us."

"Have you recalled anything else about the callers' voices?" Maggie asked.

"No, nothing that might help," Gwen answered. "I've rolled it over in my mind time and again, and I am sure that the first and second callers were not the same person, their voices didn't sound the same. I don't know if I've heard the voices before. Sometimes something flashes through my brain that I had heard before, but I can't drag the information out. I don't think I know them. I wish I could be more help."

Michael and Andy raced in from outside and interrupted her answer. Michael backed up as soon as he saw Officer Shetland's towering figure, but Andy spoke for both saying, "Hello officers. Did you find him yet, the guy in the baseball cap who was driving the car?"

Jack responded, "That's a negative, men. We're still looking. If you fellows see any strangers, be sure to tell your mom to give us a call." The boys nodded and headed to the kitchen for something to munch on.

Maggie thought aloud, "So, if we can't distinguish the voices, all that we have to go on are the blankets, the rosaries, and the babies…and maybe the blog. So, let's talk this through. First, the blankets. Have you ever seen this type before?"

Gwen replied, "No, they look like plain old military issue wool blankets. Army issue, except they are blue. Does the Army issue blue ones? I know for a fact that the Marines don't use blue, rather army green, but maybe the other services do."

"Good suggestion, we'll call out to the Air Force Base. Do you have any other ideas?" Maggie asked, writing as she spoke. Gwen shook her head.

Maggie asked, "Okay, what about the rosaries? I'm not Catholic and don't know anything about rosaries. Who has them and how do you get them?"

Gwen gave as much information as she could. "I don't know much. Almost every Catholic has them, but I don't know if, well, besides the faithful Catholics, who actually uses them. You should ask a priest. He could probably give you better information than I can. You can buy them anywhere, but Edna Bilbaostrigo told me that this type is rare, the kind with the little wire wraps on them. She seems to know a lot about rosaries and other kinds of religious symbols. The beads on most rosaries are looped together with wire hooks. There are a couple of religious gift shops in town. You could try them. Edna's daughter, Junie May, thinks you could get them over the Internet. I'm a convert, so this is all new to me."

"Is that Junie May Layne, Ma'am?" Jack asked.

"Yes, how are you acquainted with her?" Gwen responded, surprised.

Officer Jack answered, "Ma'am, she is in the middle of a lot of things. She's a friend of my mother, and I hear church-related gossip through my mother. We're members at St. Gertrude's. It seems that every time something arises involving a Catholic, Junie May's name comes up, I wonder how she got involved with this?"

Maggie looked up from her note taking but didn't say anything. She had never met Junie May, but it's always good to know the source of tales, whether gossip or facts. "Jack, maybe we should discuss the church gossip later. I want to know what, if anything, you've heard but gossip is gossip. Sometimes gossip will lead us where we need to go, and with this case, we've got nothing, so I want to know what you've heard."

Jack nodded and said, "Yes, Ma'am." He turned toward the door, ready to leave.

Gwen was a little confused and looked from one to the other, then suggested. "Maybe she got it from her father, Frank Bilbaostrigo. He was in the church when I discovered the babies. He helped me put them into the car to take them to the hospital. You should speak with him."

Jack answered, "Yes, Ma'am. We'll see him today. The only other evidence we have then, Ma'am, is your set of twins. Who is their mother? DNA testing costs a great deal and probably won't prove anything, especially if the mother is a young teenage girl." He looked at Maggie and did an about-face and headed to the door, opening it and stepping outside.

Maggie stared behind him, then followed him to the door. "Teenage girl? What teenage girl? Do you know something, Jack?" Detective Maggie said.

"Not really, just rumors, I'm sure they are untrue. My mother," Jack mumbled. He was almost to their car.

Gwen had moved to the front steps as the two began to leave. "What's going on? Jack? Maggie?"

Maggie's face grew dark, but she decided not to question him in front of Gwen. Too many things were lining up, causing her to have a nagging doubt. She turned back toward Gwen, excused herself, and was out the door before Gwen could put Louis back in the crib. Maggie called over her shoulder,

"We will be back in touch, Gwen. In the meantime, let us know if you have any more trouble."

Jack was already behind the wheel and pulling away from the house. "My mother, Maggie, she's the one who told me about teenaged girls. Junie May told her that April had a baby last week. I gotta go talk to my mom."

Chapter 45

Father Matthew Hope
Thursday

Father Matthew Hope was of two minds as to how he should react to Rene Leclerq's death, if indeed he was dead. He disliked him and thought little of his methods and personality, yet he was a priest, one of God's chosen. Because Rene chaired the Board of Directors, Father Hope presumed that the school should do something, but he didn't know what. He would ask his administrative assistant. She'd know.

Father Hope postponed calling April. It would be painful, and he didn't need it. After all, it wasn't his responsibility. She had a mother. If April had been the one to give birth to the twins, it was her parents' fault and responsibility. If she hadn't, they could take care of it anyway. It wasn't his problem, although he decided to make a house call on the Hartes to check on the twins. He showered and redressed into his blacks, placed his black TM baseball cap on his head, and drove to the Harte's house.

It was late in the day when he pressed the doorbell and peered through the open glass storm door. Gwen met him with Marie in her arms. "Hi, Gwen, I hope you don't mind, I thought I would stop over to see your babies. It isn't every day that my favorite English teacher gets a visit from the stork," he commented, laughing.

"Oh, Father, thanks for coming," Gwen greeted him. "Please excuse the mess, babies take a lot of time, and I seem to have a lot of visitors and non-stop phone calls. The news about Father Leclerq, I can't stop thinking about him. Is it true? Was he in the house when it burned? The rumors are flying, first I heard he was out of town; then I heard that he was killed. Which is it? He was my pastor. I can't imagine how he burned his house down. You knew him, didn't you?"

Father Hope assured her, "Yes, it's frightening. I didn't really know him well. Besides my duties at TM, I am also attached to St. Gert's, and work as a substitute priest when needed, but I didn't work with him much. I barely knew him." He continued to ramble on, "I landed here about 12 years ago, but Rene came a couple years ago. He's a workaholic, no rest for the wicked, himself or anyone else either. Last week, he took over as the chair of the TM School Board. He showed up a couple days ago to pontificate about how we should do things. He and I didn't agree on some things, probably most things, except, of course, faith and the Catholic Church. We met at the diocese occasionally but didn't socialize. He came over to TM when he needed something, but being on the school board, he probably would have been there a lot. It's strange because I just talked to him yesterday." He silently chastised himself for telling Gwen about his reservations and broken the cardinal rule about not speaking ill of fellow priests. He recalled his conversation with Rene about expelling April and firing Gwen but didn't share that with her. "How is your summer going with these new additions to your family?"

Gwen was surprised that Father Hope spoke so freely. "The police showed up today again. I think they've got something going, but they are tight-lipped about it. That lady cop, Maggie and her partner, Jack Shetland, you know him, I think.

"My summer? Oh yeah, so far, it's been full of surprises. The kids have been great, but my summer plans for rest and relaxation and getting caught up on my chores took a nosedive. I still have boxes in the garage from our move a year ago, meaning either garage sale or reorganizing. Do you remember Robert Burns and 'the best laid schemes of mice and men often go awry' That would be me this summer." As an English teacher, Gwen knew this passage, but the literary allusion was lost on Father Hope.

Father Hope wrinkled his brow at her comment, and countered, "Sure, Burns, I've heard of him. What a guy." His idea of literature was a bodybuilding magazine.

Gwen grimaced at his lack of literary acuity but didn't say anything. What a guy, indeed. "The babies are right here. It is a joy to care for them, although they are exhausting me. I need a vacation from this vacation. Would you like to hold one?" she offered, passing Marie to him. Marie opened her eyes, as if on cue and blinked slowly at him. "Isn't she a charmer? I can see her now, 17 years old and beguiling the football team at the homecoming dance. You and I will probably be hanging around TM with our canes and walkers." Father Hope was in his late forties but considered himself as fit as a 25-year-old; he frowned at the thought of himself with a walker or cane.

"And here is Louis," Gwen said, cradling Louis in her arms. "He is smaller but thriving. He is always starving; he hasn't turned down a drop since he arrived."

Father Hope fixed his eyes on Louis for a moment and gazed awkwardly at the bundle in his arms. "I can't imagine taking care of two babies. How are you managing? Where is April? Is she helping you?"

"She has been an enormous help. She took the night shift last night and is sleeping late today. You know teenagers. They like to stay up all night and veg during the day. Fortunately, I think she realizes how difficult it is to care for babies, and it will be a long time before she makes me a grandma."

Father Hope sat in the rocker with Marie on his lap. He hadn't held a baby in a long time and felt uncomfortable. His biceps bulged as the baby stirred. "Have the police been able to find any clues, any leads as to whom the mother is?"

Gwen exclaimed, "No, no leads. The police haven't shared anything either, if they have something else, so it's a big zero. Nothing. Personally, I think the rosaries are a dead end. They originally generated a flurry of hope, but nothing has evolved yet. The blanket had been torn in half and was a heavy blue wool scratchy thing, like an Army blanket, except it is blue. The police are checking it out."

Father Hope said, "I am curious about the blanket. Blue wool, you say?"

"Yes, they are blue wool, kind of scratchy. Dirty. Someone cut a blanket in half and bundled them up," Gwen answered.

Father Hope continued, "Not much to go on. These little tykes don't have much going for them, do they? What have you unveiled regarding the racial issue?"

"April researched on the Internet about black and white twins, but we don't know anything except what I mentioned before. And then there are the blogs." Gwen related the story of the blog hit from Angel Eyes. "I don't know how to deal with this. Maybe the school tech guy can help me find the author. The beauty of my blog site is that it is unidentifiable. People can write without inhibitions, but that's also a curse. April and I have done extensive research, but we were unable to find anything about Angel Eyes, true or false. We've come across some real nastiness with the rumor mills out there though. Speaking of which, did you find out who started those rumors about April?"

This was the question Father Hope dreaded and intended to avoid. "No, I don't know who started it, but unfortunately, it is going strong. In addition, I don't know anything about blogs...sounds like some sort of disease, but my technology expertise stops with plugging in a perfectly good typewriter. I probably need to talk to April to learn her version of the story. Do you think she will talk to me?"

"She'll talk to you, but there is nothing to these horrible rumors. Should I wake her, and you can talk to her now?" Gwen wanted to get to the bottom of this rumor and get back to normal.

"No, let's wait. I'll visit her on Monday. There is no need upsetting her over the weekend." Father Hope returned Marie to Gwen's arms, said goodbye, and headed out the front door. Time to go to the gym.

Chapter 46

Detective Maggie Monroe
Friday

The police finally officially announced that the fire had taken a victim, although they didn't have a positive identification. The local parishes maintained all-night vigils with parishioners praying for an hour at a time for the victim. The bishop appeared at all four parishes as a symbol of sympathy and benevolence. Early Friday morning, Detective Maggie Monroe, Officer Jack Shetland, and the fire marshal, Bob Dolan, visited the diocese. While the bishop prayed for the victims at Mass, Vicar General Ralph Loren contended with the police.

"Good morning, officers, God bless you on this fine June morning. May I offer you some coffee and a Krispy Kreme donut?" Friday mornings meant Krispy Kremes at the diocese. There was no Krispy Kreme bakery nearby, but there was one next to the Nevada State Capitol and a local entrepreneur made a donut run to Carson City every Thursday night and sold donuts at a premium to local businesses. The diocesan employees loved their Friday morning Krispy Kremes.

Jack stood at parade rest while Maggie did the talking. "No, thanks, we already had ours at the station before we came out. They arrived early and were gone in a flash. I had never had Krispy Kremes before moving here, and God should bless the person who drives to Carson City to get them." The entrepreneur's name remained a secret, but numerous street-side vendors throughout the city hocked the donuts each weekend. The whole city wondered who made all these trips and raked in all that money.

The vicar general was very amiable this morning and smiled at her comments. "Thank you for your prayer request, Ms. Monroe. That's a good prayer, even though it is for Krispy Kremes, but I know many people in Basin agree with you," he gave out a little laugh, "and I'll remember it this afternoon. What have you learned about the victim? Did you find out who it is?"

"I'm Maggie, I prefer you call me Maggie," she said, wanting to put the vicar general at ease. "We don't know much, but what we do know is that the victim was a woman. The autopsy reports that she was shot first before the house caught on fire. It wasn't pretty."

After a long silence, the vicar general finally spoke, "A woman...in the rectory? That, that can't be. I mean, thank God it was not Father Leclerq, but who could she have been?" Ralph breathed a silent sigh of relief. The news momentarily lessened the VG's grief, but now he had to contend with the critical issue of a dead woman in the rectory, plus Father Leclerq was still missing. Was this good news or bad? For sure, it was the beginning of a media nightmare for the diocese.

Jack responded, "The body was very badly burned, and not much remained to identify. We autopsied the remains yesterday afternoon, and it revealed that she was shot in bed, probably while asleep. Her system contained a bit of alcohol, but no smoke in her lungs verifying that she died before she was burned. We don't know who she was. She could have been anybody, but nobody has been reported missing recently. We hope that Father Leclerq might know her. Have you been able to reach him?"

The vicar general presented his answer quickly, "No, he told a couple people that he was going to be gone for a couple days but didn't say where he was going. He is very predictable, and Father O'Grady expects him back today, or tomorrow at the latest. He never misses Mass. He is a real workaholic, but I'm not worried about him. Anyway, back to the woman. Could she have been a street person?"

Maggie responded, "That's a possibility, I suppose. We don't know who she is. While she slept in the bedroom, somebody shot her, and set the house on fire. And now, Father Leclerq seems to be missing, too. Does Father Leclerq have any family, maybe a sister who was staying with him? Or a lover? What can you tell us?"

Loren hesitated before answering, then smiled and shook his head. "Lover? Ha. You've obviously never met Father Rene. He avoids women, and I can say with a great deal of certainty that she was not Rene's lover. Now, as for a sister, I don't know. He's never mentioned any family, but... we'll do some checking. We'll do what we can to help you." The VG had no intention of revealing Rene's background to the police, but they would never know that. Priests' personnel files were private, and as long as he remained VG, they would stay that way. As far as he was concerned, the less the police knew, the better.

Jack responded, "Two cats also died in the fire, Sir. Did Father Leclerq have cats? They might have belonged to the woman."

"Yes, Rene had a couple cats," Vicar General Loren reminisced. "He used to talk about Shah and Pshaw, S-H-A-H and P-S-H-A-W, sort of a play on words. He named one after the Shah of Iran and didn't want to remember another name, so he named the other one Pshaw, with a 'P.' That's Rene for you. He didn't want to remember two names, as the cats didn't listen to him anyway. I think they were Persians, but I never saw them. Father Leclerq is a loner. Everything's a secret with him."

Maggie responded, "We need to speak with Father Leclerq. He surely will be able to shed some light on who the woman was and why she died in his house. Did you learn where he is?"

Lights, bells, and whistles went off in the VG's head, and his face hardened. Is Rene a suspect in this shooting? Did he kill this woman? Rene is eccentric, but could he be a murderer? He didn't think so. He paused before he spoke and enunciated the response he had written and memorized earlier slowly and deliberately. "We are unsure where Father Leclerq is right now. We will cooperate with you in every way to determine the cause of this tragedy. We are praying for the victim, law enforcement, and for our city. Thank you for coming, and God bless you." He did not want to give the police any additional information. He stood and moved toward the door, confirming that he was finished with the conversation.

Maggie looked up at him, wondering. His answer sounded so canned that Maggie's ears stood up, and she felt a chill run down her spine. Something was off. She rose to leave, and stepped closer to the VG, "We'll be back."

Dolan looked at Maggie with a question mark on his face and stood to leave, and Jack Shetland snapped to attention as the VG opened the door. They had gained little, if any, new information, but the VG made all three of them think something was wrong. When they were outside, Jack spoke up first, "Wow. Was that a cool reception or what?"

Maggie agreed, "Whew, that wasn't cool; it was downright cold, ice cubes in spades. Do we have some duplicity here? Loren reported they would cooperate, but he sure hustled us off. Do you suppose he knows something about either Leclerq or the woman? As an outside chance, let's process Leclerq's name through the NCIC computer to see what comes up. Let's also process the VG's name. Ralph Loren."

Bob Dolan answered, "You go ahead and do that. I'm thinking of the questions he didn't ask, like how did the fire start or who shot her? What he didn't ask might be more important than what he did ask. I'm going back over to the house to see what other information we can find. I'll talk to you later."

Maggie had a bit of experience with the Catholic Church and although she bore no bias, she had noticed priests enter the priesthood for a variety of reasons. Most of them have the love of God in there somewhere, but they admit to many other reasons: to escape an unhappy family life, to gain an education, to avoid other types of work, to achieve status, to fulfill their mother's expectations, to travel, and, of course, the unmentionable, to escape sexual dysfunction, such as pedophilia. Maggie had known ministers in other faiths and she supposed some became ministers for reasons other than the love of God. Some probably had ulterior motives, but it wasn't widespread, obvious, or admitted. Other faiths encouraged marriage, and their wives or husbands and children perhaps kept them balanced. However, in these positions as faith leaders, trust and moral authority, temptations of the flesh and money creep in and the most vulnerable suffer regardless of the organization. She had a feeling in the pit of her stomach that the stonewalling by the vicar was a cover-up or at least a clumsy attempt at bluffing.

Chapter 47

Bishop Connor Llewellyn
Friday

The bishop and the vicar general almost stepped on each other as they crossed the common waiting room to enter the other's office. They entered the bishop's office and shut the door, pushing it twice to make sure it was soundly closed.

"What did they want?" Bishop Con hissed at Ralph.

Ralph Loren spoke rapidly to the bishop, "Both good news and bad news. The good news is that the victim was not Rene. The bad news is that it was a woman."

"You must be kidding. What woman? A woman in Rene's house?" The bishop was incredulous.

Loren continued, "The police probed a bit asking routine questions. What did we know? Where was Rene? Who did we think the woman might be? She was shot before the house burned, but they didn't expand, and I didn't ask. From their tone I suspect that they think Rene had something to do with this murder. It wasn't what they said, rather what they didn't say. Don't worry. I sent them packing."

The bishop took a bottle of water from his refrigerator. He guzzled a half bottle before he offered, "Are any of them Catholic? We could call their pastors and have him talk to them. This is something that needs to stay in house, which means nobody talks about it, and we must find Rene. And we must know about that woman, whoever she is, before the police find out about her. As soon as the police find out, the media will be all over it. Do they have any idea who the woman is?"

"No idea at all. The cops' names were Monroe, Shetland, and Dolan. No tell-tale Catholic names in those," Ralph answered.

"I can't imagine Rene with a woman. That's a laugh. He's not that type. And I don't think he is screwing a man. Now, if it was Shannon, McGraeth, or that new kid, Josey, I would believe it, but not Rene. No way. Not Rene. Maybe the woman was his sister. Did he have a sister? Maybe O'Grady knows more than he's saying. Maybe it was a fucking family reunion." The bishop seldom offered profanity, but the idea of Rene with a woman aroused his attention. "I've canceled my golf game. I am here for the rest of the day."

"Okay," Ralph started, "here's what we are going to do. You call St. Gert's and find out about his family. Sisters, brothers, parents, that type of thing. Tell the office staff not to talk to the media or police or anyone, they should refer them back to me. Make sure they understand 'no one.' If they don't have anything on him, call Holy Mount Seminary to see what they have. Was he at other dioceses before he came here? Find that out, too. Somebody knows something, we must get to it before the police go any farther. That one police officer, the detective, I think her name was Maggie Monroe, is really snoopy. Meanwhile, I'll talk with the Iron Man and O'Grady. That's quite a pair: the Iron Man and his constant muscle flexing and Father Ulcer with his lifetime supply of antacids. God, how did we ever get these priests?"

The bishop looked at him and nodded. "I'll call the others. This could be bad, very bad."

Chapter 48

Gwen
Friday

It was Friday, and the Hartes had tended the babies for almost a week with no progress toward finding their mother or father. They had found nothing, no leads, no clues, and the chances of finding the parents diminished with each day. Clancy reminded her often that the wheels of justice move slowly. Gwen couldn't help but think that the wheels weren't only slow, but frozen.

Gwen was impatient, they seemed at a standstill with the Case of the Missing Twins, as Andy called it, so decided to review what she herself knew. The house was quiet, April had gone to the grocery store, the boys were patrolling the neighborhood for suspicious people, and the babies were asleep. She poured herself a cup of coffee and retrieved her stack of lined 4x6 note cards that she used to keep track of things. Clue cards, she called them. She had drawn a line down each card, labeling each column into "known" and "unknown." It was a tactic she had used with her students when she taught them character development for their Advanced Placement Composition class. As she thumbed through the cards, she realized that she didn't know much and hoped that she could talk to Maggie soon.

Murder in the Diocese

The doorbell rang. "Oh, great," she said to herself, "just when I think I have peace and quiet, Junie May shows up." She slipped on her sandals to answer the door.

It wasn't Junie May after all, it was Detective Maggie, her wish had come true. "Good morning, Gwen, do you have a few minutes to talk?"

"Of course, Maggie, I was just thinking of you. Whenever you and Jack come by, there seems to be a lot of disruption, especially when the boys see him. For some reason, he fascinates them. Would you like something to drink? Water or coffee?"

"Yes, he's good with kids. Coffee sounds heavenly, the boys at the station don't know anything about a good cup of coffee, and I'll bet you do," Maggie answered. "When I was sheriff in Barrier, I grew to appreciate a good cup of coffee. My husband, Brick, is the supreme coffee brewer. He's ill now, so I'm on my own, and I'm not so great at coffee brewing either."

"I'm sorry your husband is ill. Is it serious?" Gwen asked.

"Yes, you might say that. We moved here so that he could be seen at the VA. He was always as healthy as a horse, then one day he wasn't," Maggie said. "The VA has been wonderful, but they are still trying to figure out his mystery illnesses. But he's not the reason I'm here."

"Sure, I understand, you are here about the babies. But I'm also curious about what's happening with Father Leclerq. We attend St. Gert's, and he is our priest," Gwen said. "First, though have you made any progress about the babies yet? I just started rethinking everything to see if we have inadvertently left anything out. I'm sure you have a better way to decipher clues, but this is what I am doing." She showed Maggie her cards, the clue cards.

The boys burst through the door, "Mom, we saw Maggie's police car here. Can we help? I've always wanted to be a detective. I could be like James Bond. I'm Harte, Andy Harte. I like my milkshakes shaken not stirred," Andy joked. "Can we help? Maybe we can help you find the mother."

Gwen started to send the boys outside, but Maggie interrupted, "That would be great," she responded, "I'm interested in what you are seeing when you patrol the neighborhood."

The boys sat down on the couch and Andy answered first. "Mostly we see people just driving around, but once we saw a guy with a black hoodie who circled the block twice. We were going to stop him, but he left when he saw us watching him. Then we saw him the next day, too."

"Did you notice anything else?" Maggie asked.

Andy answered, "No, just the hoodie. But when he drove away, something flashed. I don't know what. Maybe he wore glasses or something. Michael thought it was in his hand, maybe a gun or knife, but I don't think so."

Michael nodded, "It might have been a gun, but I didn't see it, and he didn't shoot at us."

Gwen said, "A gun? Good grief, why didn't you tell me? If he comes around again, tell me right away. Don't get anywhere near him! If you see something, tell me, and I'll call Maggie."

Gwen wasn't sure about them helping, but she thought since they were there, they wouldn't be any worse off than they were right then. She explained to the detective what they were doing and held up the first card, "Okay, first clue...blue blankets. What do we know about them?"

"Blankets? What blankets? What are you talking about?" Maggie demanded.

"You know, the ones the babies had on when Mom found them," Michael answered. They are blue, scratchy, yucky with cat hair on them. They look like our camping blankets, but ours are green."

"I don't know anything about blankets. I haven't seen them. What are you talking about?" Maggie said again.

Gwen hit the side of her head with her hand, "Oh, I guess I forgot mention them to you. I've repeated the story so many times that I am starting to lose track. We still have the blankets if you'd like to see them."

"I guess I am not sure what you mean." Maggie said. "We have the blankets you had at the hospital, the whitish ones, the baby blankets. They had put them in the trash, but luckily, we could retrieve them because the trash was still there. We never saw any blue ones."

"The blankets they arrived in," Gwen said. "When I found the babies, they were wrapped in these military style blankets. Blue, wool. Very rough and itchy. They aren't made for babies, that's for sure, but maybe this is something that will help."

Andy interrupted, "And they had cat hair all over them."

"Cat hair? Are you sure?" Detective Maggie exclaimed, arching her eyebrows.

Gwen answered, "I didn't notice any cat hair. I noticed that they were filthy. They're like the bivouac blankets that their dad and I got in the Marines."

"Yes, there was cat hair. It was longish, kind of white and silky. Don't you remember, Mom?" Michael was certain. "I tried to pull it off, but it stuck to my fingers. There was a lot. Do you want to see the blankets? They are outside."

Michael darted to the door and went outside, but the blankets weren't where they had left them.

"Look in the laundry room," Gwen said, "I put them in there, but I spilled water on one of them this morning. Bring the dry one and put the damp one on the washer to dry."

"Oh, no, no. Please don't wash it or put it in the dryer because it will remove evidence," Maggie said.

He returned in a flash and handed a blanket to Maggie. Sure enough, cat hair clung to the blanket. Perhaps it was angora, long, loose, and silky, and slipped easily through her fingers. "I haven't seen the blanket, and there is nothing about the blanket in the notes. I wonder why." Maggie pulled out her notebook and wrote "cat hair," then asked, "What else can you see on this blanket?"

Andy continued, "There is some stuff that is stuck to it, too, like paste or glue. Look, it peels off. Maybe it's candle drippings. The candles at church drip, and it's hard to get off the altar cloth. I had to clean it once when I had to be an altar boy in Hawley."

"Wax? Candles?" Maggie smiled, amazed. "You guys are great detectives." She wrote in her notebook again and said, "I'll have it checked out. Do you have a plastic bag I can put it in? Let's keep going, Now, what don't we know about the blanket?"

"We don't know where it came from or how old it is or where it was bought or who it belongs to," Andy told Maggie.

This time it was Michael's turn, "We could call the military surplus store to see if they sell them."

"Great idea, I'm going to do that right now," Maggie pulled out her cell phone and checked the number and dialed.

When the clerk answered, Maggie stated, "I am trying to track down a blanket, navy blue woolen, military issue type. Do you sell them, or can you tell me where I can buy one?"

Maggie took notes as the clerk on the phone spoke, "Yes, we carry the woolen blankets. We have Army green and a few navy-blue ones. They are $29.95."

"Which service uses the blue ones?" Maggie asked.

"I am not sure, but I think the Navy had them in the past, and the Air Force has them now. The green ones are popular, but I think the blue ones are more attractive," the clerk stated.

"Anyone else?" Maggie continued.

"Not that I know of." Short and sweet. Maggie didn't know if this was good information or not, but she recorded the information from her conversation in her notebook.

Gwen picked up her next clue card, which dealt with the phone calls. She read them aloud. "I think the first call was the mother pleading, 'I want them to be okay. Take good care of them, please. When you get them from the hospital, safeguard them as your own children. Tell them that I love them. I named them Marie and Louis. Raise them with God, Mrs. Harte.'"

Luckily, Gwen had recorded the call verbatim immediately after the original phone call. The mother obviously knew that she had the babies, which might have meant she had observed Gwen carrying them from the church or someone else had told her of it. They knew that she wanted them to be okay. She didn't merely drop them off and disappear. She cared enough to observe who took them. Had she been in the church?

The second phone message was very brief: *They are the devil's own. Give them back to God.* "Nothing else."

Maggie was thinking aloud. "Do you think the second call was from the father?"

Gwen answered, "I'm not sure. Both voices were scratchy, but it could have been the phone. Both calls were labeled 'restricted,' but that doesn't really mean anything. I get restricted calls all the time. Even from the church."

Andy added, "We studied about the devil in theology class at St. Gert's. Maybe the mother was my teacher."

"Don't be stupid, Andy," Michael answered. "Your teacher was not going to have a baby."

"Michael's right, Andy, don't spread rumors," Gwen had had enough of rumors.

Maggie had thoughts about the calls, but didn't share them, "Okay, here's the last question, what about the names? What information can we gather from the names of the babies, Marie and Louis?"

"Maybe they are the mother's and father's names," Gwen suggested. "Marie and Louis what? That's the question. I don't think we know anybody named Marie or Louis, especially not at church."

Maggie expanded, "That's a good suggestion, but I wonder if the mother and father were married. It could be the mother's parents' names or the father's parents' names if they weren't married. On the other hand, they might be names that the mother likes. On the third hand, friends of hers or her grandparents. Who knows? That one has a whole lot of unknowns."

"I'm out of ideas," Gwen said, but Michael reminded her of the car that drove by. "Don't forget, Mom, we think that was the guy who tried to steal the babies. He was scary looking and drove by real slow."

"Really slowly," Gwen corrected him. Being an English teacher meant the constant correction of her children's grammar and vocabulary.

"Yeah, really slowly. He drove really slowly," Michael voiced, rolling his eyes.

"Describe the car again," Maggie requested.

Michael repeated, "It had writing on the door, like a pizza delivery car. Except it was a black SUV. It didn't have the thing on top. And the guy had a baseball cap on."

Maggie wrote in her notebook, "Man with baseball cap. Car with writing on the door. Nothing on top." This was sketchy information if it was information at all.

On the next card, Gwen recorded "blog." She explained blogs to the boys and wrote down what she remembered of the blog ending with "Angel Eyes." She should have printed it out. Maggie was curious. She had never heard of these kinds of blogs, and the idea that someone would randomly write about personal things seemed odd. Nevertheless, she took the information, and Gwen shared the website with her so she could have a look for herself.

"We have another clue, Mom. The babies are of different races. One black. One white. Isn't that a clue?" Michael pressed.

"Yes, it is, Michael. Indeed, it is. That means that someone in the family was African American or had African American heritage. It could have been the father or the mother or one of their parents or a second father. That narrows it down. We don't have a suspect, African American or not." She wrote down on the card, "Races of twins."

Maggie was happy, this trip had been profitable, the blankets, the blog site, and man who the boys had seen. Nothing was certain, but she felt that this information would bring them closer.

Chapter 49

Father Josey
Friday

Father Josey recited Mass alone on Friday morning. The usual handful of RFs hadn't appeared. He supposed that they would attend the memorial Mass at St. Gert's. He called upon God to watch over his computer pursuits, the money that he had invested on behalf of the diocese, his parish, and himself. The first reading was from Genesis, "Be fruitful and multiply and replenish the earth." Was this a sign from God? "Be fruitful and multiply. Oh, God. Yes, please," he prayed. His day trading ventures might not have been God's exact intention, but he was sure that God knew what he meant.

After Mass, he turned his computer on. He checked his bank account through on-line banking and breathed a sigh of relief that the prices were rising. The split had set the closing price at $31. That grew to $34 by 9 o'clock. "Okay, be fruitful and multiply. Lord, it's hard to be humble," he repeated aloud.

He recalled from his college classes that having all one's eggs in one basket was risky, but it was only until Monday. Marcy would return on Tuesday. On Monday afternoon, he would pull out the $350,000 from the MasterCard loans, repay the margin, and have a couple hundred thousand left over. He would keep 75 percent of whatever he profited for himself and turn the other 25 percent over to Our Lady of Perpetual Tears.

In addition, he would donate 20 percent of his profit to the church. That was fair. Be fruitful and multiply.

Chapter 50

Father Paul McGraeth
Friday

Anchorage's Vicar General Peter McGraeth called his brother early on Friday morning. "Good news, Brother Paul. Very good news. The bishop likes your resumé. He was very impressed and forwarded it to San Francisco, Seattle, Portland, and Chicago. It is a matter of time. They meet next Tuesday in Seattle. You might get the smoke after all. And the Maker's Mark hit the spot. You're in, Bro."

"So soon? I hadn't expected it this soon." Paul McGraeth could not have been happier. Privately he thought, *I want to get the hell out of this town as soon as I can.*

"You remember how Mother Church works, Paul. Slowly. It takes time, and time is what Mother Church has more of than anyone else. You can get the nod from the bishops, but it will take a while to have Rome affirm you. Be patient, mi hermano. My bishop here in Anchorage will do what he can to expedite your selection."

"You know, Pepe, I am due for a vacation. Why don't I come north, and we can go fishing while we wait? What do you think?"

Vicar General Peter McGraeth was excited, "Now, that sounds like a plan. Bring your pole. The salmon are running. How soon can you get here?"

Chapter 51

Maggie and Brick
Saturday

Maggie had been working with the Basin police for a week, and was ready for a weekend. As sheriff, she had few days off, as her office only had KG, Brick and her to do the crook-catching. But now, she was part of a larger team and this allowed for a weekend breaks, although it seemed to break her continuity in her cases.

The chief seemed to appreciate her a little more, actually smiling when he saw her. She was glad for the work and even happier that Brick seemed a lot better, at least for the time being.

They went on a long walk, talked, went out to dinner at a local steakhouse, and made love. It was nearly like old times. His skin color, which had turned grayish before, now was better and he looked healthier. They called their kids to tell them the good news. They knew his progress could fade away, but it had been a good week and Brick wanted to tell them about it.

Maggie was getting a feel for the city of Basin, and felt like she was contributing. She hadn't caught any crooks, but she was working on it.

Chapter 52

Bishop Connor Llewellyn
Sunday

Father Rene Leclerq never missed Mass, but he did not appear for the Masses on Saturday or Sunday. Father Hope served the two Saturday night Masses. Fathers O'Grady and Loren officiated at three of the four on Sunday with the bishop celebrating the final Mass. The bishop delivered a charming homily that was interspersed with inspirational and entertaining stories. The flock adored him, and he delighted in their delight.

After everyone finally departed, Bishop Llewellyn entered Rene's office to store the robes that he had borrowed. He hung them up and swept his eyes over the filth and clutter in Rene's office. Aloud he growled, "What a mess. I must remind the priests about the example they set with orderliness. Or encourage them to hire a housekeeper." Money was always tight, and priests often conned parishioners into cleaning their offices, which meant that it was done piecemeal, *mas o menos, mas menos que mas*. "More or less, more less than more" was a common statement among the priests of the diocese when they solicited help with something.

The bishop had freed up his afternoon. He had promised Ralph that he would search for information on Rene's family and decided to start his search in Rene's office.

He selected a Diet Coke from Rene's mini-refrigerator and deposited a quarter on a dish sitting on top of the refrigerator. He popped the tab on the can, took a sip, and sank down into the chair facing Rene's desk. He closed his eyes for a few minutes, recited a Hail Mary for Rene and the fire victim. It wasn't like Rene to be absent for this long, and the bishop was worried. Parishioners were asking questions for which he had no answers. He opened his eyes and gazed at the disorganized desk in front of him. "I wonder if there is anything in this mess that will give a hint." He got up, walked around to Rene's chair, and sat down. The rickety oak chair nearly toppled with his corpulence, and he grabbed the desk to keep from falling. *He needs a new chair*, the bishop thought, never once occurring to him that perhaps he needed to lose a few pounds.

He leafed through the papers strewn around his desk, which included mail with the usual drivel: newsletters, magazines, bills, and credit card offers. It was piled high with miscellany: a yellow pad with a hand-written list on it and a phone number. An empty bag of Cheetos and an unopened package of black licorice. A desk calendar dated February 6 and list of things labeled *To Do* that was too long for any reasonable person to do in the confines of a lifetime. It did not include "clean my office." Rene was a workaholic, and a dirty one to boot.

The bishop tugged on the center desk drawer, which grated as it opened. "My God," he thought aloud. "Has he never cleaned a drawer?" It was jammed full, front to back. The bishop stared in awe at the array of junk, calculators, combs, staples, 14 or 15 rosaries, at least that many Catholic lapel pins and crosses, paper clips, tape, pens, pencils, change, stamps, you name it. *Rene is a pack rat. If I ever need any office supplies, I know who to see. I need to find some clues. I wish I knew what I should be looking for, but maybe I'll know it when I see it*. He pulled out a pad of paper with a list of names. They were listed one under each other separated by a line down the center of the paper. On one side of the paper, there were the names Chris, Angelica, Louise, Marie, Luisa Maria, Christina Marie, Renee, and on the other side of the paper were Louis, Charles, Paul. He shook his head, *Catholics. They always name their daughters after Mary or Chris.* Probably a good 25 percent of the Catholics had either Mary or Chris in their first or middle names. He laid it aside. It was obviously a list of parish workers for one of Rene's many projects. A few other pieces of paper contained names, numbers, or addresses with nothing making much sense. With much effort he jostled the contents of the drawer to shut it and reached for the filing cabinet. "I can't wait to see what this looks like."

The left-hand drawer contained junk filled with who knows what. It looked as if Rene had recently cleaned off his desk and dumped it in the drawer. He inspected the top layer, which included papers, unopened mail, pens, and office tools, and then decided to try a different drawer.

The next drawer yielded some organization with manila file folders filling the drawer. Some folders had typed labels while others were scrawled in a felt tip pen. He ran his fingers over the labels: *A* through *M* were mostly alphabetized. His fingers stopped on the *Leclerq* folder, and he pulled it from its position. It mostly held college and seminary transcripts plus his appointment letter to St. Gert's. He scanned the list of courses and grades that seemed average, he thought, and returned it to the drawer. Other than Rene's name, it held no information that might indicate his family. The transcripts listed no names or addresses except California as his state of residence. He continued his journey through the drawer and stopped at the folder named *Hope*. He reviewed it out of curiosity. Transcripts again showing above average grades. No surprise here. Hope's major had been physical education. An evaluation form on Matthew Hope, signed by Rene, had been completed last week. It wasn't positive, and the bishop noticed that it had not been signed by Father Hope. He wondered if Father Hope had seen it. Sloppy way to do business. He would ask Ralph to talk to Rene about it. He closed that folder and put it back in the drawer.

The third drawer held *N* through *Z*, but there wasn't much past *T*. The St. Gert's folder was several inches thick. Probably everything that didn't have another place went into that folder. In the middle of the drawer, near the *P* section, one folder stuck out. It wasn't a folder, rather a manila envelope, labeled with *Personal* scrawled in felt tip marker. The partially affixed metal clasp caught on the next folder when he pulled it out of the drawer. The envelope was bulky, worn, and taped shut. "Maybe this will tell something about Rene's family. I hate to open it, but since we can't find Rene, we have to try to find his family." He peeled off the tape, opened the clasp, and began to remove the contents.

Bishop Llewellyn moved to a sturdier chair. The packet held only a dozen or so documents, fewer than he originally thought. This could be the file he was looking for. It seemed to have some background, some phone numbers, and hopefully, some personal information. He sorted through the pile of papers one by one. The first document was a birth certificate for Rene Leclerq, born 37 years ago, an August baby, Virgo. Not that any priest paid attention to astrological signs. He continued leafing through the folder. A baptism certificate, a passport, a paid-off loan application for his college, a confirmation certificate, a social security card, and a copy of his social security card. There were a couple of surplus passport photos, an insurance policy, and the results of blood work from a few years ago showing high cholesterol. *He should go on a diet.* A postcard and letters in envelopes rounded out the contents. He didn't see an address for Rene's parents. He continued through the pile. The next sheet of paper was a copy of an application from a birth registry agency called Right Birth, one of the companies that searches for parents of adopted children. "Right Birth. I've heard of them and that might explain some things." He scanned the form.

Name: Rene Leclerq
Place of birth: Los Angeles, California
Address: 1842 Los Ducos Street

What a coincidence, Los Ducos was two streets south of Olva Street. And the Rendezvous Diner where he had met Marie. It's probably all changed now, he mused.

"Amazing. What a coincidence," Bishop Con murmured aloud. "I wonder if he ever ate at the Rendezvous. I will have to ask him when he gets back. I wonder if it is still there." Great food, but it was the server who he remembered. Marie. He had known Marie in 1965. What pleasant remembrances this form was bringing back. She loved the Beatles and Elvis. They had seen *To Russia with Love* together at the local theatre. They spent Christmas Eve together. Oh, my. He smiled and quickly read the rest of the form.

Date of birth: September 12, 1966
Sex: Female
Mother: Marie Leclerq, no known address
Occupation: Waitress
Father: Lou Last Name Unknown, no known address
Occupation: Unknown

He stopped and eyed back to *Sex: female*. He read it aloud. "Female. No, that can't be right. He must have written it wrong; he must have written his mother's sex. That doesn't make sense either, of course all mothers are female. Female. Female? Marie, Marie Leclerq. Could it be? I never knew Marie's last name. She was French Haitian from a little village named Rendevie. That was why she worked at the Rendezvous Diner. It reminded her of home. Oh, my God. Oh, my God. *Father: Lou Last Name Unknown*. That can't be. That can't be." In those days, the bishop was known as Lew. He formalized his name to Connor when he became a priest. He told Marie that his name was Lew. She might have thought it was Lou. She called him "Louis" with her French accent. He looked again at the birthday and recalled that Christmas Eve nine months earlier than Rene's birth date. Oh, my God.

The bishop's mind was on fast forward. *Rene is her child, but that's impossible. Impossible. God would not have done this to me. No, Rene is my son? He can't be my son. It says female. Rene is my daughter. But Rene's a priest. He can't be a woman. Marie and I only made love a few times. She could not have become pregnant. Impossible. Impossible.*

The bishop remained inert for the next 30 minutes, reading and rereading the form. He tried to recall her last name. She never told him. He knew that she was French Haitian. His mind raced as he tried to decipher his fears. *We had only been together a few times before she disappeared in 1966. I was young. Twenty-eight years old. She was younger. I can't jump to conclusions. My God, this can't be true.*

He had been in Rene's office for nearly an hour when the phone rang. "Bishop, it's me, Ralph. I didn't know where you were and thought you might have disappeared too."

The bishop didn't say anything.

"Bishop, are you there? Bishop? Did some talkative parishioner capture you? Or did Junie May Layne stop you to talk your ear off." He drawled the "Junie May." "When are you returning to the diocese?"

The bishop snapped, "I'm coming back now, Ralph. Oh, Ralph. I've got to see you. I'll be back to the office in 15 minutes. Wait for me."

The bishop drove his black Lexus back to the diocese with the manila envelope in hand. Despite the perfect 75-degree temperature, he was in a fog. He was unsure of where to go, who to tell or not to tell, and how to unravel this situation. He thought of Marie. Marie, his one love. He loved her beyond how he loved God.

He let himself into his office through the back door. He didn't want to see anyone today except Ralph. Ralph would fix it. Ralph always fixed things. That was his job.

"What's up?" Ralph Loren queried, puzzling at the bishop's sober demeanor. "Did you find anything in Rene's office? I took a chance that you would be there."

"You've got to look at this. And listen to my confession. You must fix this, Ralph. You've got to fix it."

"I can fix anything, Bishop Con," Ralph told the bishop, "Almost anything. Did you find Rene's parents?"

Bishop Con slowly shook his head and began to talk while handing him document after document: the birth certificate reading *female,* the Baptism certificate reading *female,* the college loan application with *Miss* checked, and the form from Right Birth, depicting Rene's family history. Bishop Con related his story and made confession to Ralph, and Ralph absolved him of the sin. When they finished with all the documents, Bishop Con was in tears. Ralph was stunned.

"What have I done? One indiscretion. One. I am a priest, a bishop. I can't have a child. And Rene. My God, Rene. He can't be my son. He's a woman. How can he be my son?"

"Stay calm, Bishop, we can fix this. You are a bishop, but you are also a man and entitled to mistakes. You made a mistake. God heard your confession and gave you absolution. Now we must fix it, and no one needs to know. I need some time to figure this out. You can't talk to anyone. Go home, stay there, and do not come to work tomorrow. I'll tell people you are sick. You are sick, sick with grief. Over Rene. They'll believe me. Go home now and stay there, including no golf." Ralph led the bishop out of the building and put him in his Lexus. "Home, nowhere else. Do you hear me?"

The bishop bemoaned, "Yes, Ralph, I'll go home. I have nowhere else to go. I am ruined. Please fix it, Ralph. Fix it."

Vicar General Ralph Loren spent the rest of the day in his office, thinking, praying, scheming.

Chapter 53

St. Gertrude's Parish Office
Monday

Detective Maggie and Officer Jack arrived at the St. Gert's parish office early Monday morning. They found their way to the office where the administrative assistant was tidying up her desk for the week's work.

Maggie introduced herself and asked, "Any word from Father Leclerq yet? Did he show up for the Masses this weekend?"

"Not for the one that I attended, and I haven't seen him this morning. He hasn't called in. Would you like coffee? I just started brewing it," she responded.

"No, thanks. Do you mind if we look in his office? Maybe we can find something that would help. Specifically, we are looking for any information regarding his family," Maggie said, moving her eyes across the office, taking in the many pictures hanging from the wall.

"He never mentioned family, but he didn't say much about much," the admin-assistant frowned as she spoke. "Well, I guess it would be okay to look in his office, but it's a mess and please don't touch anything. He never lets me touch anything. He says it is all personal. Father Rene needs a class in cleaning if you ask me. I told him one time that cleanliness was next to godliness, but he told me to mind my own business."

The two police officers entered the office and were shocked at the clutter the room held. They didn't touch anything but took stock of his desktop, bookshelves, and open filing cabinet. Jack snapped a few pictures while Maggie wrote down the phone numbers that lay atop his desk. After about ten minutes, they left, thanking the receptionist. "We didn't touch anything, we only looked around. Call us if he calls in, would you?" Jack handed her a business card. "You can reach either of us."

Maggie and Jack returned to the office and checked the reverse telephone directory to identify the numbers that Maggie had copied from the papers on Father Leclerq's desk. They had to locate the family, if any existed. The first number was for Holy Father's rectory, followed by numbers for Junie May Layne, the local hospital, and the diocese. Another dead end.

Chapter 54

Gwen
Monday

The weekend passed without further incident. On Saturday evening, the Hartes celebrated Louis and Marie's one-week birthday with cake and ice cream. Andy and Michael rigged streamers throughout the house. April bought them a mobile for the crib; Michael and Andy pooled their money and bought a football for Louis and a doll for Marie. The boys borrowed the new football and spent the afternoon outside.

No mystery callers had contacted the Hartes since Tuesday, and apparently neither Health and Welfare, the police, nor the church had made progress in finding the parents. The Catholic community remained in shock over a woman's death in the rectory. Father Leclerq disappeared when his house burned. There were rumors, rumors, and more rumors.

Junie May Layne was in her glory. As one of those people who enjoys being the bearer of bad news, she was determined to bring Gwen, April, and the babies into the gossip huddle.

"Good morning, Gwennie. Junie May here," she chimed in a sing-song voice. No one had ever called her Gwennie, Gwen grimaced but didn't say anything. "How are you and those dahl-ing babies?" Her drawl was quite pronounced this morning. "I can't go a day without finding out how they are. Do we know who the mother is yet? I haven't heard much out in the community, but I am praying for them. I put their names on the prayer tree. Are you a member of the prayer tree? You can get on it by calling Mary Elizabeth. She'll put you on. Do you have her number?"

"Oh, good morning, Junie May. What a surprise to hear from you." It wasn't a surprise at all. She had called Gwen at least once a day since the babies arrived at the Harte home. Gwen didn't know how to answer her questions as she blurted out so many at once, so mostly she ignored them.

Junie May continued her palaver, "How is April? I heard she was sick. I hope it isn't anything serious. Young girls can get all kinds of things. Some have trouble with their periods and all that as they enter womanhood. Is April having trouble with her periods?"

Why would Junie May ask about April's periods? She answered guardedly, "April is fine. She has a few allergies, mostly to house cleaning dust and teenage burnout. Too many things going on and not wanting to let go, but she's fine."

Junie May continued without a breath, "I'm sure she is. Does she have a boyfriend? She is such a dahl-ing girl. Pretty, athletic, and smart. She must have boys flocking around her at TM. She is dahl-ing. Father Hope adores her. He says she is one of the nicest girls in the school. Father Hope doesn't give out compliments like candy. He wouldn't divulge anything unless he adored her. Does she have a boyfriend?"

Junie May Layne's conversation about April riled Gwen. What is it with her today? What does she want? She usually chatters, but her chatter is about April today. First, her periods and now, her boyfriends. "No, April doesn't have a boyfriend. She has lots of friends, both boys and girls." Gwen thought she might try to get some information about Father Leclerq from the Mother of All Gossip. "What do you hear about Father Leclerq? Has he returned?"

Junie May answered, "No, isn't this the strangest thing? He disappeared at the same time that the dead woman was found in his bed. They don't know who she is either. I'm sure she was an intruder. Shameful, intruding into the life of our holy priest. I guess the police didn't work on it over the weekend, but I went to Mass on Sunday morning and didn't get any new information. Father O'Grady recited the Mass I attended, and he's either not talking or doesn't know anything. I'm headed over to see him now. Have you heard anything?"

"No, Junie May, not me," Gwen responded. "I don't hear anything about anything. We didn't get to Mass yesterday. The babies are still too young to be out in public. Sorry, I need to go. The babies want something to eat." That was always a good excuse to use to get rid of Junie May. "I'll talk to you later. Bye."

Chapter 55

Father Josey
Monday

Josey got up early to run two extra miles at 5 a.m. He spent a restless night worrying about GrayBonePhone7. His good angel and his bad angel wrestled each other atop the PERFECT tattoo on his shoulder. How could he be perfect if he made a mistake by investing in GrayBonePhone7? On the other hand, how could he be perfect if he hadn't taken this opportunity? The bishop and the vicar general were always talking about money. Money drove success, even in the church. He had good advice, at least it was as good as he could expect. The stock brokerages used analysts, and DBLUP was an analyst. One analyst was as good as the next.

His morning run cleared his head allowing him to get on with his work. His schedule was full today. There was a memorial Mass for that dead woman. She was still unidentified as far as he knew. All priests were *asked* to attend. Being asked by Ralph Loren meant required. He should clean the office before Marcy returned. She always kept things tidy, and he let things go while she was gone. He needed to call his youngest sister because she was having marital problems. He needed to monitor his stocks. He had a lot riding on today's events. Today was the day. He would pull all the money out before 3 p.m.

When he returned from his run, he tuned in to NBC to see what had transpired overnight, nationally and locally. The usual: a bus accident in Virginia, problems in the mayor's office, a speech by the president's press secretary, and a volcano that was about to erupt. In the business world, things seemed stable. Digitoma was having difficulty. They might go under. Thank God that he had gotten rid of it.

He flipped on his computer and checked the opening numbers. After the split on Thursday, they had remained static, up a few cents, down a few cents. "Go up, young man, go up," he urged his stocks. "Be fruitful and multiply. Let's hit $50 today. What do you say?" He entered the chat room looking for DBLUP, but he wasn't online yet. A couple others were talking about Digitoma and their losses there. *Fools,* he thought. *You should have done what I did. GrayBonePhone7 is where it's at.*

Father Josey served his daily Mass and started out to St. Gert's for the memorial service. "I'll be right back, Sweetheart," he whispered to his computer as he patted the monitor. "Don't go away."

Chapter 56

Vicar General Ralph Loren
Monday

Ralph Loren remained in the diocesan office all night figuring out what to do. He intermittently dozed on his couch, but not for long. It was essential to protect the bishop. The bishop's reputation was critical for his own power play. If the bishop went down, he went down. If the bishop lost his power, Ralph would never have the bishop's ring, beanie, or the staff. That was a given. Paul McGraeth was waiting in the wings for his job and his power. He couldn't let that happen. He had to protect the bishop at all costs.

The issues at hand were damning. If Rene were a woman, as the birth certificate indicated, it was likely that she was the victim in the fire. That would bring countless inquiries to the diocese with damaging headlines about St. Gert's, Rene, the diocese, and the bishop. And him. An inquisition of this nature would suck Ralph Loren into a spinning abyss, which undoubtedly would destroy his pristine reputation. No clean and clear reputation, no beanie, no ring. It was as simple as that.

On the other hand, if Rene is a man, he had flown the coop. God damn him. Where was he? Did he kill this woman? Did he know this woman? Did he know who killed this woman? And what about the birth certificate? Falsified? Maybe Rene wasn't involved at all, which would mean the church wasn't involved. He had known Rene was trouble from the first time he met him.

But if Rene were a woman, she had been ordained a priest illegally. All the works, the sacraments, the committees, and the acts were invalid. How many marriages and baptisms would have to be repeated? How many frigging souls had Rene sent off with last rites that were now invalid in limbo or hell or somewhere in between? And confessions, which were sacraments heard by priests and priests alone. If Rene were a woman, she had probably blabbed those juicy items. The church did not authorize women to perform these sacraments, and they would be void. Ralph could cover up some things to the parishes and the news media. Maybe even the police if that became necessary. But Ralph couldn't cover these acts up to God. God would have to deal with Rene in her own right. However, it would be Ralph's responsibility to cover them up to the Catholic community and to the rest of the world.

The bishop thinks that Rene is his child, son, daughter, whatever. How could that have happened? God would absolve the bishop of any indiscretions, but Ralph needed the accusations to go away.

Rene had to be a man. That was for damn sure. If Rene were a man, the diocese would have to deal with the priest leaving. Ralph would make damn sure that Rene was a man. No one suspected that Rene was a woman. There was no proof. Only the bishop's inane ramblings, and those could be explained. Perhaps the bishop needed a nice, long vacation, too. After all, he was an old man. Ralph might be able to prove that he was crazy or maybe hallucinating. And, as for Rene, he had disappeared, that's all. He disappeared, not unlike other priests or lay people. It wasn't that hard to have a person disappear. He had done it before, three child molester priests, two lesbian nuns, and a partridge in a pear tree. Ralph could make Rene disappear permanently. The bishop, too, for that matter. Easy.

Chapter 57

Father Josey
Monday

Father Josey Zabalapeda returned from the memorial Mass before noon. All priests had been there, except Rene. God only knows where he is.

He looked around his office and decided to organize it before he looked at his stocks. He couldn't spend all his time day trading. Once he sat down, he was not likely to get his other chores done. He finished that task before 1 p.m. How did Marcy keep things neat and tidy?

He turned on his computer and logged in. "We want 50. We want 50," he chanted to himself. "We want 50. Sixty would be sexy, but 50 would be nifty."

The computer took forever to click through the menus. Why was it booting up so slowly? When he cashed in his stocks, he would purchase a new high-speed computer. Finally, it clicked onto his page. He couldn't believe it. It must be wrong. What was going on?

GrayBonePhone7 was reading $13, which was less than the split price. Way less than the split price of $31. Maybe the computer readout was wrong and reversed the numbers. Thirteen to 31. That must be it. Reversed. The editors would catch it in a minute. He hit *reload* on his computer screen and shook the monitor.

He lurched over to the TV and flipped to a business channel. The anchor was reading the list of stock ups and downs. GrayBonePhone7 had taken a sudden downturn. The GrayBonePhone7 CEO, Denton U. Dublinsky, had been arrested on the grounds of stock manipulation with a pump and dump scam. GrayBonePhone7 had been showing progress by itself. However, in the ebb and flow of the marketplace, it seemed that Mr. Dublinsky interfered with that natural course of events for his corporation. He leaked to various day trading chat rooms that GrayBonePhone7 was on the verge of introducing a new telecommunication technology. As he pumped, he drove the stock prices up and induced a split. Immediately before the split, he dumped and sold all his GrayBonePhone7 stocks. He utilized several different day traders' chat rooms to leak phony information about his corporation, encouraging unsuspecting day traders to buy his stocks. His code name DBLUP was a clever take on his last name. The SEC cops charged him with market manipulation, and he would likely be spending time in jail...without a computer.

Josey stood up and immediately sat down again. He smashed one hand against his desk and grabbed his keyboard with the other. He hit reload twice and stared wide-eyed at the screen before him. GrayBonePhone7 was plummeting. In those few minutes it fell to $8. Then $7. Oh, God.

Josey quickly typed in his password to enter his account. How could he get the money out? He should be able to cancel his stock dealings. He checked all the menus and couldn't find anything that would allow him to cancel his stock purchases. He typed into the search box: Change Order and a list of options came up, but none were retroactive. He typed in Retroactive Change Order. Nothing. He typed in: Changed my mind. Nothing. Mistake: Nothing.

In those few minutes, GrayBonePhone7 plunged to $3 a share. Even with his 18,050 shares, he owned only $54,150 worth of stock. How could this have happened? He had prayed each day and listened to God. God spoke to Josey during Mass, "Be fruitful and multiply," and he had. God would not destroy his perfect plan.

Before the day was out GrayBonePhone7 Technology was worth less than $1.00 a share. It closed at 63 cents. His 18,050 shares were worth just over $11,000. What would he do?

Chapter 58

Vicar General Ralph Loren
Monday

St. Joseph Retreat Center was a center used by various dioceses to counsel priests who had victimized children or other parishioners. In addition to being in a normal 12-step treatment program, residents were forbidden to talk to each other except during their group counseling. Originally, it had been a Trappist monastery and speaking aloud was completely forbidden, but as monasteries diminished in numbers, it evolved into a retreat center to stay afloat financially. Through the years, they added a 12-step program and other popular therapies for dealing with problematic clergymen and were able to keep the facility full. St. Joseph's Retreat Center assigned a nickname to each participant allowing their real names to remain unknown to the other patients. They advised against patients discussing their past indiscretions even within the confines of group therapy, guaranteeing complete privacy especially since HIPAA laws also forbade caretakers to release private information. Telling his parishioners that Rene was at a priest retreat like St. Joseph's was the perfect cover-up for his disappearance.

Ralph connived to tell the parishioners that Rene collapsed from working too hard and that he was going on retreat for a few months. Everyone knew Rene worked too hard, making the cover story believable. The diocese would assign Father O'Grady to be the pastor, assisted by Father

Hope. Some other rookie priest would join them soon and the parish would once again have enough priests to keep the parish happy. He would ask the faithful to pray for the return of good health to Father Rene Leclerq. Maybe some novenas, too. If he found the right new priest, it wouldn't be long until the entire parish forgot about the good Father Leclerq.

Chapter 59

Father Josey
Monday

Josey decided to cut his losses. He had invested $26,000 of his own and $7,800 of Our Lady's money, plus the building fund of $15,000. If he turned over the entire $11,000 to Our Lady, the parish might not realize that his investment went south. He would replace the building fund money a little at a time. No construction was planned yet. It should be okay. He had lost everything, but that was okay. Not exactly okay, but it would have to do.

As for the credit cards, he would call MBNA and Citibank and tell them what happened. He knew they would understand. He had charged $100,000 for himself, $100,000 for Our Lady of Perpetual Tears, and $150,000 for the diocese. It was $350,000, but they were big corporations with lots of money. They would not miss this paltry amount of money. After he explained to them what had happened, he would tell them he was a priest, and they would believe him.

Priests get special privileges. Everybody knew that. You needed to know the right people. Get a speeding ticket? The mayor or the ombudsman will fix it. Need to buy a car but not qualify for the loan? Ask your friendly banker, and he will get you a loan and qualify you for a better car at a reduced rate. Want to go on a cruise? Call the cruise line, and they'd be happy to take you free. They might even set you up with a line of credit for the casino. Need to do better on an entrance exam? Ask the dean to turn his head. Need an abortion for your administrative assistant? Ask the right people. Josey had seen all of these happen in his brief tenure as a priest. You had to know the right person. The right people were available in every parish.

Despite his tattoo, Josey knew he wasn't perfect, but he knew that honesty and integrity reigned high in his list of values. Be honest, tell the truth, and flash the white collar. They would come around. Credit card companies have lots of money. These giant corporations could write this off for the church, and it wouldn't be a wrinkle in their financial statement. They advertised: *Use our credit to solve your credit.* Their suggestion. Their idea. They could deduct it from their taxes. Use a charity. Giving money to the church was a charity. It could be a tax credit. At least it would be a deduction. He reached over and pulled one of his old finance books from the bookshelf. He looked up charitable giving. There was a whole chapter about it.

Margin was different. He wasn't sure about margin. He hadn't understood margin when he was in college, or maybe he had skipped class those days. He looked it up in the glossary, and it read: *Margin Call. The recall of money borrowed on margin in a stock purchase.* He wasn't sure what that meant. How can they recall the money? He didn't receive any money. It was a paper chase. He wasn't sure of exactly how much money he had used on his margin, but he thought it was $350,000 plus $33,800 equaling $388,800. This could be a problem, but he was certain that if he invested it through an upscale market company, they too would write it off as a charity. He was positive. But as a day trader, he wasn't sure. He needed to talk to DBLUP, he would know. But DBLUP was in jail.

Chapter 60

Father Paul McGraeth
Monday Afternoon

Paul made a reservation for his flight to Alaska. He would leave for vacation on the late-night red-eye flight on Tuesday night and fish for a couple weeks with his brother. This would give the Holy See plenty of time to light the fire for the white smoke.

If all went according to his schedule, the committee would send his name to Rome in late June before he ended his fishing trip. He would then stay with his brother for a couple months before being installed as Bishop of Fairbanks in September. He would not return to the continental U.S. at all. He would box up his belongings tonight, and the diocese would pay to have them shipped up to Fairbanks when he got the call. It was a good plan.

He would suffer through the bad weather and dark days of December and the Christmas season, but in January, he would take two cruises in the Caribbean, offering his services as the cruise priest. In February, he would give himself a sabbatical and attend the Bishop's Conference in Phoenix and link it to a vacation in Cabo. He would suffer a month of cold and work in March, but in April, he would make a surprise visit to his parents in Florida and work on his tan. They disowned him once, but now that he was a bishop, they wouldn't dare put him out of their house. He could tolerate

Fairbanks in the summers with the good fishing and great weather. Things were looking up.

Chapter 61

Junie May Layne
Monday

Junie May Layne was living a dream. All these rumors were too good to be true. She came alive with all the events and rumors. The buzz of April Harte being the mother was perfect for maintaining her status as Queen of the Rumor Mill, and now the death of the woman in the priest's house. She was in the center ring and in her glory. How much better could it get? She loved the proverbial hot potatoes that were being tossed around the diocese. After her conversation with Gwen this morning, she was positive that April was the mother of the babies. It was her God-given duty to protect Saint Thomas More High School at all costs.

Junie May donned her favorite outfit and carefully applied her makeup. She had always wanted a faculty position at Thomas More High School, and it was time to turn her hopes and dreams to reality. As she drove across town to TM High School to discuss all these things with Father Hope, she reviewed her plan. She considered Father Hope to be sort of wishy-washy. She trusted Father Rene to manage the principal, but now Father Rene was unavailable, but she could fill in as keeper of the faith. She and Father Rene had already discussed all of this, and things seem to be falling in her direction.

Everybody who mattered knew what needed to be done. At least she and Father Rene knew. If Gwen Harte left the school, Father Hope would have to find another English teacher. If she didn't quit, it was time for her to go. Whether Gwen Harte was fired or resigned was of no consequence to Junie May. TMHS did not need people like the Hartes at the school. The priests agreed that April was the mother of the twins and that Gwen lied when she took in those babies. Lying to a priest was a capital sin, she thought. Junie May hadn't taught school in a long time, but maybe she could fill in. Junie May Layne, Saint Thomas More High School English teacher and cheerleading coach. She could live with that. She could involve herself with the events at TM. Being former class treasurer was like icing on a birthday cake, she was sure she was a shoe-in.

Father Hope sat at his desk signing acceptance letters for incoming first-year students. Surprised to see her, he rose when she came in. He grimaced, then smiled. She usually called before she dropped by.

Junie May began her monologue, "Father Hope, how are you today? I thought there was a chance that I'd miss you if you were working out. Maybe you went earlier or maybe you are going later. It makes no difference to me, you understand. You are an outstanding influence on our young people, a real model for these students, reminding them to keep their bodies in good shape. Look at me. I should follow your example, too. I should purchase a membership to a health club and learn how to use those machines. Maybe you could show me sometime. They look frightening." She jiggled as she sat down.

"I know that it makes you feel better. How are you, Junie May?" he regretted the question the minute he voiced it.

"Funny you should ask. I'm fine. I've been to the doctor a few times this spring, little things, mostly girl stuff. I won't go into details. The doctors put me on some different types of medicine. I don't know what they are, but I feel better. They suggested that I had depression and put me on an anti-depressant to take the edge off. I stayed on it a few weeks but decided

I didn't want the health risks. You know, what they advertise on TV: liver, kidney, heart damage. The cure is worse than the disease. Don't you think so, Father Hope? Nevertheless, it is nice to have that other little pill take the edge off."

Father Hope was uncomfortable with her monologue of her health issues and wanted to change the subject. "What's on your mind today, Junie May? TM is across town from your house. You didn't drive all the way out here to chitchat about being fit, did you? Maybe you want to give us a donation?"

Junie May did not beat around the bush, "No, not exactly. I came out to see what you are doing about Gwendolyn Harte and her daughter and the babies that Little Miss April Harte gave birth to. Before he disappeared, Father Rene spoke to my husband and me. It was our understanding that you would dismiss the Harte girl and her mother from TM. Everybody, the entire Catholic community, agrees with us. I've had a lot of phone calls, and everybody I've talked to says the same thing. She needs to be gone from TM. They are simply not our type of people. What's important here is St. Thomas More High School, not some virtueless foreigners from Hawley, wherever that is. Did you dismiss April, and is her mother going to quit, or are you going to fire her?"

Father Hope retorted, "Junie May, stop. You are aware that I can't discuss students or personnel with you. This whole thing is gossip. I know that you would never spread idle gossip, but this is exactly what it is. Father Rene and I will compare notes when he returns. He and I will decide what is the truth, and we will deal with it. I'm going to put it bluntly: This is an issue for us and not you."

Junie May was not about to accept his answer. "What if he never gets back? What if he up and left St. Gert's? It is our duty to take care of TM and its academic and social reputation. I tell you—you need to get rid of her. Get rid of them. I know you are dismayed at the idea of hiring a new English teacher at this late date, but I would be happy to fill in for a few weeks until you can find the right person for the job. Gwendolyn Harte is not the right person, and that April girl is nothing but trouble. You can see that by looking at her. She was overweight and now has babies. Babies, at age 15. Shameful. If you are going to remain silent, I'm going straight to Bishop Con."

Junie May had been trying to get hired at TM for years, and Father Hope recognized her ploy, but did not expect her audacity in this matter. He was rankled. "You don't need to see the bishop. I'll see him. Junie May, this is none of your business. Father Rene and I will take care of it when he gets back."

Junie May rose in anger, "I'm not going to remain silent on this, Father Hope. I have an investment in TM. I attended this school and have influence. I don't want TM to develop this type of reputation. I'm not taking a back seat here. I'm not. Either you take care of this, or I will. I will not be quiet. No, I won't." She left in a huff.

Father Hope paced his office for a few minutes. He was angry at Junie May's insistence that April was the mother and that both Gwen and April leave TM. And as for her *filling in* as English teacher: "Over my dead body," he thought aloud. "Over my dead body."

If Rene were dead, the bishop would assign a more congenial priest as chair of the board. Father Hope would be able to work with him. The new appointment would probably not occur until fall, long after contracts were out, and the students were in school. On the other hand, if Rene were alive, he would have to deal with him and his assignment at the school. He didn't want Rene to be dead, but his life would be a lot easier if he were.

Father Matthew Hope decided to pay another visit to Gwen and the babies. He had put off telling her about Rene's ultimatum, but Junie May's conversation worried him. If Junie May took this issue to the bishop, as she was sure to do, the bishop would fold on it. Bishop Con was a weak man and would be overpowered by this former runner-up-to-homecoming-queen dynamo. He needed to speak with Gwen first, followed by a visit to the vicar general to verify that the bishop would see things his way. He hoped that

Gwen would be able to handle what he had to tell her. He finished signing the letters, reattached his collar, and drove over to the Harte residence.

Chapter 62

Gwen
Monday

Twenty minutes later, April answered Father Hope's knock at their door. He greeted her with, "April, it's good to see you. How are you? How is your summer vacation?"

"Oh, Father Hope, I didn't know you were coming by. I'm fine. Vacation is okay. I don't get to see my friends enough, but I get to sleep in every morning, and that's great. It's been fun helping with the twins. I didn't think I would like to have them around, but they are fun, a lot of work, but fun. Speaking of sleeping late, my friends and I would like to have school start at 10 a.m. instead of 8 a.m. How about it, Father?"

He laughed, "No, sorry. 8 a.m. again this coming year. Let's see now, you will be a sophomore this year, right?"

April showed him into the living room, "Bummer. It never hurts to ask. No, I'll be a junior. I can't believe that in two years I will graduate and go off to college. Where do you think I should go?" April asked.

"I went to Gonzaga. It's a good school. It's not too far from home, and it's not too big. The Zags play a decent game of basketball and have played in March Madness a few times. You would love it there. Have you been up there to visit? Lots of TM students go to Gonzaga," Father Hope answered as he sat down.

"Yeah, we went to a basketball game at Gonzaga when we lived in Hawley," April answered. "I didn't look at it like a potential college because I was in the seventh grade at the time, but it was pretty. The students seemed nice. The cheerleaders were awesome. My counselor, Mrs. Bratt, suggested that I go to Gonzaga or Portland State. I plan to study English, followed by Law School, but I can study English anywhere. My dad went to the University of Florida Law School, the Gators. I might look there. It's big, though, but they have a lot of sororities. My dad teased that I should be a Tri-Delt, so I would only have to learn one Greek letter. He's always teasing me." When she realized she was rambling, she excused herself. "Anyway, let me go get my mom. She's pulling weeds in the garden." April went outside to find her mother.

Marie and Louis were sound asleep in their crib. Father Hope thought they had grown since he saw them on Thursday. They looked a little more like babies and less like monkeys. *I wonder what kind of father I would have been. I never thought about it, but I'd bet I would have been a good one. We would have played football. Lots of football. It's a great way to build confidence in kids*, he thought. "Of course, not for little girls," he murmured, looking at Marie.

Gwen came through the door wiping her wet hands on a towel. "I didn't know you were coming, or I would have been cleaned up. Yard work never ends. Would you like something to drink?" Before he could answer, she asked April to bring Father Hope a bottle of water. "I know he doesn't drink coffee."

April exited. "I'll bring one for you, too, Mom."

Father Hope began, "Your summer has been anything but relaxing. How are you getting along? With the babies and all? I can imagine they are keeping you pretty busy."

Gwen nodded slowly and replied, "We seem to be getting along okay. The police haven't made any progress toward finding the parents, either the mother or father. The boys and I have been trying our hand at our own investigation, but it hasn't reaped any benefits either."

"Have you found out anything at all?" He wanted to avoid the subject of April as the babies' mother for as long as possible.

The index cards that she had shared with Maggie were lying on the coffee table. She picked them up and handed them to Father Hope. "This is what we have. I'm afraid it isn't much."

Father Hope leafed through the cards saying, "Rosaries means Catholic. That narrows it down to a few billion. Not much to go on." He turned over the next card reading, "Blankets. Blue wool with cat hair."

Gwen reached over the back of the couch and pulled out the remaining blanket. "This is one of the blankets. The blanket had been cut in half. We gave one to the police but kept the other. The detective called the Army-Navy store, but they weren't much help. The cat hair was Andy's observation. I hadn't paid any attention, but he noticed quite a lot of fine cat hair on the blankets."

Father Hope picked up the blanket and looked at it, noting the cat hair. He rubbed it between his fingers. "I have a blanket identical to this. I got it when I was in Holy Mount Seminary. They gave them to us as a part of EPP, Early Preparatory Program, to get us ready for sacrifice. The dorms didn't have much heat, and they removed most of our earthly possessions. We were allowed a few basics: sheets, a pillow, and one of these blankets. Almost like prison. They are warm, but I'm allergic to wool. I never used it much. It made me sneeze, so they gave me a different one. Most of us used them, though, because they were so warm." April returned with bottles of water and went to check on the boys. "I still have that blanket. It's in my closet."

Gwen gazed after April, "They gave these out at the seminary? Did all priests get one? We only thought of the military, not of the seminary."

"Yeah, at least they gave them out at Holy Mount Seminary when I attended. As far as I know, they were standard issue at all the seminaries. You know the church. Buy in bulk to save a buck. Most of us here still have them. I kept mine in case the heat goes off. A sneeze is better than a freeze." He smiled at his little rhyme.

He turned to the next card. The phone calls. "It was good thinking to write these down, but I don't see anything that makes any sense. The second call makes no sense. *They are the devil's own, give them back to God.* That's weird. Who would say that?"

"This whole thing is weird if you ask me. Abandoning these lovely babies in church and calling with messages. It's all weird," Gwen responded.

The next card dealt with the names of the babies: Louis and Marie. "I am sure this is a clue. We tried to think about why the mother named them Marie and Louis. They are rather old-fashioned names. The girls today are being named Tiffany and Brittany with multiple spellings. Parents use the letter 'i' instead of 'e' and 'q' for the letter 'c.' Letters added, or letters eliminated. The names Marie and Louis are lovely, but they are an anachronism." The minute Gwen used the word *anachronism*, she knew she lost Father Hope. "Out of step with our times," she clarified.

"I wouldn't know about that; I've never named a baby. Marie and Louis are nice names. I have an Aunt Marie, and a friend of my father was named Louis."

"Exactly," Gwen agreed, "older, out of date names. Not for today's kids."

He flipped to the next card, "Pizza delivery car without the dome. Guy with a baseball cap on. That cuts it down to half of the population. Everybody wears a baseball cap in Basin. Too bad it wasn't a fedora."

Gwen smiled, "Andy and Michael saw a guy drive by slowly in a dark car the day after the break-in. It was a black SUV with a logo of some type on the door. They are convinced that he had something to do with it. I doubt it is a clue, but who knows? We'll take anything right now."

Father Hope flipped to the next card, "Race."

Gwen responded, "That's obvious, but we don't know if we are looking for people who are African American or Caucasian, or both. It isn't much of a clue, at least from this private-eye agency. The superfecundation angle puts a new spin on the parents."

Father Hope looked puzzled, and she realized he hadn't been privy to this information. She briefly explained about having parents of two different races. He seemed a bit uncomfortable about this subject, and she continued with the next clue card.

The last one read, *Blogs with Angel Eyes* as the primary point of interest. Father Hope listened to Gwen's explanation of blogs and answered, "I don't know any Angel Eyes either. God, devils, angels. Weird. I wish I could be of further help, but we are going to have to let the police deal with it." He placed the cards back on the table. "I guess I had better get to the reason for my visit. You probably don't think it was to look at your clue cards."

"No, but we are always glad to see you. What's on your mind?" Gwen asked, somewhat haltingly.

Father Hope replied slowly, "It deals with the babies. And Father Leclerq. And TM. And April. I don't know how to say this, so I'll just say it straight. Father Leclerq came to me last week and insisted that April is the mother of these babies."

"No. No. No, you don't believe that gossip, do you?" Gwen answered with another question.

Father Hope responded, "No, I don't. But since then, other people called or came by with the same accusation, Father Leclerq was insistent and told me he would fire me if I don't discharge April from the school." In truth, Junie May was the sole complainer, but she mentioned that many people knew and supported her way of thinking.

Gwen's Irish dander was rising. "What? That person is Junie May, right? And what are you even talking about? These babies aren't April's. I found them. I found them in church. In Father Leclerq's church. He was there when I found them. He called me that day and came over the next day. I told you about it. Don't you remember?"

"Yes, I remember," Father Hope assured her, "you told me that you found them, but he thinks you are lying to cover up for April. The counselors noticed that April gained weight this year and missed her final exams. They concluded that she was about to give birth to these babies." He was also stretching the truth here, but he wanted to get to the bottom of this.

"What do you want us to do? Take a lie detector test? Have I ever lied to you? Ever? Have I? Why would I lie about this? What do you want us to do, go to the doctor to verify she didn't have a baby? Would that give you the balls to defend us?" Gwen raised her voice at her boss, immediately regretting her comments. "This makes no sense."

Father Hope raised his hands to calm her, "Now, Gwen, I know you are upset. I am going to see Bishop Con after I leave here to talk to him about all this. The diocese is quite discombobulated between the death of the unknown woman and Father Rene's disappearing act. The issue with April isn't quite as serious as the other two, but in my mind, they need to address it also. Bishop Con and Vicar General Ralph Loren have their hands full. The bottom line, though, is that we want all this cleared up. We all want what's best for April, don't we?"

"It sounds to me like what you want is what's best for you and the priests," Gwen countered. "What's best for April is that you and Father Leclerq stop listening to rumors and start acting like priests, like charitable human beings, giving people the benefit of the doubt. This is unbelievable. I am going with you to see the bishop."

"You can't do that. He won't see parishioners about trivial things. If he did, he would be seeing people all day long." Father Hope was lying to Gwen, but he didn't want her hysteria to influence the bishop. If April Harte was not dismissed from TM by the time Father Leclerq returned, he was sure he would be shoveling antacids down his gullet as a priest at St. Gertrude's. "I'll talk to the bishop, and I'll call you after."

Father Hope didn't blame Gwen for being angry. In his heart, he didn't believe that the babies were April's either. With all the other issues that the bishop had on his plate right now, his timing would be poor, but he could think of no other solution. Perhaps the bishop could talk some sense into Rene, when Rene came back. If the bishop wouldn't talk to Rene, maybe the vicar general would. He was the peacemaker of the diocese. Ralph Loren could pour holy water on almost any troubled water and turn it into a placid lake.

Chapter 63

Bishop Connor Llewellyn
Monday Morning

The bishop spent the morning at home, eating, drinking coffee, pacing, and praying. Ralph Loren called to remind him to stay at home, but he was as restless as a cat and found himself pacing from room to room without purpose.

The bishop lived in a large house in an upscale neighborhood. Some would call the edifice a mansion. A wealthy parishioner donated it to the diocese when he sold his multi-million-dollar wood products corporation and moved to Portland.

The two-bedroom house sat on the 7th tee of a private golf course and was 8,000 square feet with 18-foot ceilings, 10-foot mahogany doors, fireplaces in every room, and a five-car garage. The library was 20-foot x 20-foot, walled with teak bookshelves that he filled with books he had collected through the years, and served as a showroom for the many trinkets that parishioners bestowed upon him. The two-inch thick, pale-yellow carpet was luxurious. All four bathrooms had heated toilet seats, heated towel racks, and heated tile floors. The structure was a bit opulent, but nevertheless comfortable and great for entertaining. Bishop Con did not like to display opulence. When he hosted parish workers, he entertained in parish halls, but when he hosted people of status, people of money, he opened these resplendent facilities.

With two bedrooms, one of which he used as an office, he seldom hosted overnight guests. He welcomed visitors for a meal or party, but not to spend the night. It was a perfect arrangement for the bishop. He loved to entertain, and was the life of the party, but all-night visitors were not welcome.

On Monday morning, as he sipped his coffee and dined on the Eggs Benedict that his cook prepared, his thoughts vacillated between Marie and Rene. How could Marie have done this to him? She said she loved him. Their affair was brief, and most of their time was spent eating chicken fried steak dinners at the Rendezvous Diner. They enjoyed some dates on the beach to watch the tide come in or go out, along with a few movies, cheek-to-cheek dancing, flirting, necking, nestling, and a couple of midnight trysts at a local motel on the beach. They had been discreet. At least he had been discreet. He thought she had been discreet, too. He was a priest, but she did not know that, nor about his vows of abstinence. Most priests use the don't-ask-don't-tell policy to avoid disclosing their personal habits. He knew that he loved her and had never loved anyone else. It was only Marie, no one else. Of course, he wanted sex with a few women, but they were priest-baiters, wanting to brag they had screwed a priest. Marie was different. She said she loved him. She demonstrated her love that Christmas Eve. He wondered where she was now. Did Rene have an address for Marie? Perhaps someone could clear it up.

He tried to call Ralph, but he was in a conference and could not be disturbed for the bishop or anyone else. He waited for Ralph to return his call. Half-hour later he tried again. Glenna, the diocesan administrative assistant, announced that he was unavailable. The bishop decided to drive to St. Gert's to go through Rene's office again.

When he arrived at St. Gert's, the office staff rose to greet him. The administrative assistant said, "Why, Bishop, we didn't know you were coming. Could we get you coffee, donuts? What can we do for you?" They were falling all over themselves, as usual, to impress him.

"No, I need to look for a couple things in Father Leclerq's office. You haven't heard from him, have you? No one apparently knows where he is, but we are trying to figure it out. Is Father O'Grady here?"

"No, to both questions. We're terribly worried about Father Rene. Father O'Grady is visiting Mrs. Shanahan at the hospital. They took her in last night. Stroke. He'll be back soon. Do you want me to call him on his cell phone?" the administrative assistant offered.

"No, I'll be fine. I don't need him. I just wanted to know if he was here." Bishop Llewellyn did not want to see Father O'Grady at all. In fact, he thought he would have to figure out how to get rid of him if he was there. "I'll try to find what I need and be off. I shouldn't be more than a half hour. Don't bother about me." He went into Rene's office, shut the door, and locked it. *Snoopy busybodies,* he thought to himself.

Remembering the tipsy chair, he gingerly seated himself at Rene's desk. "Dammit," he said, as the chair teetered. He opened the desk drawer again and began sifting through the junk. He found the list of names again. "I wonder who these folks are." He opened the fourth file drawer, which he missed on his previous visit. He unveiled pictures of Rene's college and seminary days. In one of the pictures, Rene stood in the front row of his class. In another, he raised his glass with the others apparently toasting the end of seminary. The bishop held the photo up to inspect it, "Rene sure looks like a guy in these photos."

He opened the closet and stepped back in disbelief. "Junk. My God, this is awful." The closet was jammed with multiple boxes stacked on top of each other without order or semblance. A hodge-podge of boxes, blankets, books, and what looked like old sweatshirts perched on the shelf above the boxes. Magazines, newspapers, and other mail items sat atop the boxes, all of which were shoved into the tight space.

"My God, this is hopeless," he said to himself as he leaned on the closet door to close it. He turned toward the bookshelf. Books on top of books filled the shelves. There were all types, mostly religious, some seminary-issued texts, and some religious classics. Many religious books looked bland and uninviting, but the priests kept them hoping to impress visitors with their erudition and to look more literate than some were. He scrutinized the shelves until he uncovered what he was hoping to find: a photo album. He sat down and opened it. A picture that was not affixed to a page fell out. The photo was in such bad shape that the people in the image would be unrecognizable to anyone who did not know them. It was torn and faded, but Bishop Lewellyn knew instantly who the woman was. It was Marie, smiling in front of the Rendezvous Diner with a baby in hand. From what he could make out, the baby wore a dress and bonnet. There was a purple date stamped on the side of the photo. It was faded, but he thought it read 1967. The baby was maybe a year old. As he tried to fill in the missing parts of this worn picture, he recalled Marie's long dark legs that extended beneath the miniskirts she wore, and how she filled out her sweaters. He thought about how her long black, wavy hair fell below her shoulders and how her beautiful smile lit up her whole face. He quickly leafed through the rest of the album and saw a brief recap of Rene's life. A couple of the photos were labeled *Angel* or *Rene* with their ages listed. The bishop thought that Angel must be a sister, although he saw no pictures of two children together. There also was a photo of a man in a Navy uniform with the name C. Crevits on the pocket. "I wonder who he is," he considered. No other pictures of Marie were in the album.

The bishop pulled out several photos and replaced the album on the shelf. He plunked down again on the rickety chair and steadied himself. He leafed through the photos several times saying aloud, "My God, how can this be?" He paused with the tattered photo of Marie.

The bishop pocketed the pictures and drove his Lexus back to the diocese thinking, *To hell with Ralph. He's the VG. I'm the bishop. I'll make the decisions around here. To hell with him.* He waddled up the stairs to his office.

Ralph's door was shut. "He's on a call," Glenna reminded. "He's been in there all day, Bishop, no visitors. He's alone. The phone has been lit up like a drunk with an open tab in the bar. He's on the phone now," she looked at the lighted phone buttons. "Are you feeling better? Is everything all right, Bishop?"

"Yes, I'm feeling ducky. Everything's just ducky," he growled at her.

Bishop Con went into his office, slammed his door, and dialed Ralph's number directly. "Ralph, we need to talk. Now. I'm in my office."

Ralph stepped out of his office and bee-lined it to the bishop's office. "You are supposed to be home, not here. I've been working on your problem all morning. I told you to stay home. Why aren't you there?"

"I'm sure you have been working on it, but I have, too. I found a picture. I went to Leclerq's office and found a damned picture. Rene is my son. Or daughter. I found a picture of Marie, the girl I told you about. She was his mother or her mother. Whichever. God, what a mess."

"You found a picture? A picture of Rene's mother? Is she the woman you had an affair with in 1965? My God, Con, a picture?"

"Yes, a picture," He snapped back. "Here it is. It is very worn and in poor condition, but I know it is her." He handed Ralph the photos he had brought with him. "Marie with a baby, 1967," he said aloud. "The baby must be Rene."

Chapter 64

Father Matthew Hope
Monday

Father Matthew Hope did not stop at the receptionist's desk when he entered the diocesan office but ascended the stairs two at a time to the throne, as some clergy called the bishop's office. It was nearly noon, and the office staff had shuffled off to lunch with their brown bags into one of the several conference rooms in the building. About ten people worked in the diocesan office, including accountants, secretaries, division leaders, and the two nuns who ran the office staff.

He met Glenna on the stairs with a brown bag in her hand. He greeted her cheerily, "Brown bagging it today? Can't you get the VG to give you a raise so that you can eat downtown? I'll talk to him."

"Oh, I wouldn't talk to him today, Honey. Something's going on. Something big. Both the bishop and the VG are as tightlipped as turkey on rye with mustard. I don't know what the problem is, but I wouldn't ask for anything today. Wait until tomorrow. The VG is abrupt to boot. The bishop looks like he has eaten a goldfish on a dill pickle cracker."

Glenna was an amiable lady who had worked at the diocese for 25 years. She was adept at using metaphors and similes. If she didn't know one, she created one to suit the situation, seldom using the same phrase twice. Sometimes they were a little crass, which always surprised people new to diocesan business. She amused her listeners and people often baited her to hear her humor. She was wise to the intense politics of the diocese and had seen people rise and fall. She was strictly business with a good sense of humor. Both were essential ingredients for her job.

"This can't wait. I must see the bishop. It has to do with those babies that the parishioner found at St. Gert's," said Father Hope.

"Oh, those poor babies. With all this hubbub about Father Rene, I had forgotten about them. Maybe all this secrecy is about those poor little orphans with no Daddy Warbucks. Maybe what you have to say will improve things. You can sure try. Toss 'em a chicken bone and see if they take it. Good luck, Padre." She continued her trip down the stairs.

Father Hope nodded at her thinking and wondered where in the world she got her sayings. "Well, here goes nothing." He admitted himself to the empty waiting room and rapped on the bishop's door.

He knocked twice before the bishop answered the door. Glenna was right. He did look rattled. His wrinkled blacks looked as if he had slept in them. His collar was unattached and donut crumbs sprinkled on his black shirt. "Bishop, I need to talk to you. Do you have time now, or should I come back in an hour?"

The bishop positioned himself in the door, "Oh, Matt, not today. I'm swamped. Ralph and I are both swamped. We have an emergency. Can you come back tomorrow or better yet at the end of the week?" The bishop looked worn. Matt looked past the bishop and noted Ralph talking on the bishop's phone.

Father Hope hinted, "It's about those babies that a teacher found at St. Gert's. It can't wait, but it shouldn't take too long."

So wrapped up in his own ordeal, he had forgotten about the babies. "Babies? What babies?" the bishop wrinkled his brow.

"The babies that a parishioner found at St. Gert's a week ago. She's a teacher at TM. Newborns, one was black, one was white. Rene mentioned them at Monday's meeting a week ago. I wasn't there, but he told me he mentioned them. Now he's got his knickers in a knot about them. I need to talk to you."

"Oh, yes, of course, now I remember. There are so many things going on around here. The babies, what were their names again?" the bishop asked.

Father Matt reminded him, "Marie and Louis. Somebody called the foster family and said their names were Marie and Louis, and that's what we call them. We don't know the last name."

The bishop's face reddened as he stared blankly at Matt. He said, "Oh, my God. Oh, my God," and closed the door in the face of Father Hope without another word.

Chapter 65

Detective Maggie Monroe
Monday

Early Monday afternoon, Maggie and Jack showed up at the Harte's residence. Gwen answered the door. "Hello, Maggie, Jack," she greeted as they crossed the threshold. "Any news of what's going on? Did you make any progress? Is there any word on Father Rene or the woman they found in his home?"

Maggie shook Gwen's hand, "Nothing new. We're still working on it. You called and said you might have something, what is it?" Maggie was in a hurry; these two cases were merging, and she needed to think it out.

Gwen had called and left them a message after Father Hope left. "Maybe something," she explained, showing them the now-dry blanket that was in a plastic bag. "I didn't find out anything else with my clue cards, but Father Matthew Hope came by. He's the principal at Saint Thomas More High School, and he offered some information. He didn't know much about the rosaries but had some information about the blankets. I don't know if it is worth anything, but he said that besides the military, seminaries like Holy Mount also issue blue woolen blankets to the students and seminarians as part of their 'humility training.' Most priests in this diocese attended Holy Mount Seminary, and they supply the students with whatever they need, including bedding, sheets, pillowcases, and blankets. When Hope attended, they issued the seminarians blue wool blankets, identical to the one the babies were wrapped in."

Maggie was scribbling madly, "That is interesting. I'll give Holy Mount a call."

Gwen handed Maggie the plastic bag. "You should have this."

The investigators eyeballed the blanket with increased interest. At the same time, they thought of the priest's house that had burned down. The fact that there were cats in the house when it burned had not been released to the public. Maggie looked at Jack, "This gives us something else to check. Let's question the bishop about seminary blankets, which seminaries distribute blankets, and which ones don't. He might advise us who to call."

"Have you already spoken with the bishop about the babies?" Gwen thought about Father Hope's comment about trivial things. "I understand it's difficult to see him. I'd like to have an audience with him myself."

Jack replied, "No, we haven't spoken with the bishop. We saw a general vicar, a Father Ralph Somebody, Lorn or something, regarding the fire and the woman who died, but the bishop wasn't available. Father Lorn stressed that he was in charge. We might pay a visit to see them since we've got two cases that involve the diocese."

Gwen corrected him, "Ralph Loren, pronounced the same, but spelled differently from the designer, Ralph Lauren, L-O-R-E-N. She spelled it out. You saw Vicar General Father Ralph Loren. Most people agree that he's the big cheese, not the bishop, but I haven't figured out all the politics of the Catholic Church. From what I understand though, it has mega-politics. Have you identified the woman in the fire? And has Father Leclerq returned?"

Jack said, "No, we are performing a DNA test on the victim, but it isn't back yet. We don't routinely do DNA tests, so it takes a while. The lab always claims to be backlogged."

"I suppose it is, but you'd think in a case like this, it wouldn't take long. Of course, you are dealing with two slow things, the long arm of the law and the shortsightedness of the church. You might be waiting until next year." She was quoting Clancy.

Gwen walked the police officers to the door as they left.

Chapter 66

Vicar General Ralph Loren
Monday

At 2 p.m., Maggie and Jack entered the diocesan office. The volunteer receptionist smiled and offered them a chair. She called Glenna who worked on the second floor to ascertain when the bishop might be available. Jack stood while Maggie sat down and picked up a colorful brochure with the headline, *Absolution: Healing the Soul,* authored by Vicar General Ralph Loren. A few minutes later Glenna descended the stairs. "The bishop is unavailable today. Sorry. You'll have to make an appointment. He is booked," she announced as she flipped through a calendar. "Hmm. It looks like he won't be able to see you before, um, until after the Fourth."

"The Fourth? The Fourth of July? Hold it. That's three weeks away. We are investigating a death, possibly a murder. We can't wait until July."

"His calendar is booked as tight as a penguin's tush. You can either take that time or not see him at all." Glenna looked up and smiled.

"How about the general vicar, Ralph Loren? We'll see him then," Jack said curtly.

"The vicar general? I don't know. I doubt it, but I don't keep his calendar. He does that himself. Phone me, and I will request that he give you an appointment. I'll get back to you with a time and date. These are very busy men, busier than a one-eyed man in a room full of strippers." The officers were surprised at this unexpected comment from the bishop's administrative assistant, but Maggie didn't like the answer and narrowed her eyes.

Maggie blurted out, "Let me get this right. You expect officers of the law to wait three weeks to see the bishop? And, you say the vicar guy *might* see us later if we call, and *if* he can fit us in? We'll see him *now,* and we'll see him *right now.*" Maggie was not about to take no for an answer. "Abandoned babies is one thing, but a murder is quite another."

"I'm sorry," Glenna responded sweetly as she turned and started her ascent. "God bless you, and have a nice day, officers. Keep a song in your heart, and don't let that bugger out."

Glenna was on step number three when Maggie said, "Ma'am. Excuse me, Ma'am. We have a couple other things." Glenna paused and turned. Maggie's face had turned red, and her words were short.

"What else can I do for you?" Glenna asked.

Jack Shetland took four strides toward her and demanded, "Ma'am, are these two gentlemen in the building?" He was on the staircase landing, and although she stood on the third step, he looked down at her.

"Yes, but they won't see you today," Glenna repeated. "They're occupied, like I told you. Time is tight here at the diocese."

Maggie didn't take her answer lightly. Maggie drew herself to her full height and stepped between them. "That may be how the church works, Ma'am, but I believe that Christ said something about render unto Caesar what is Caesar's. Miss uh, whoever you are, today we are from Caesar's office and doing business on Caesar's schedule. Tell your bosses that we are here. We want to see them now or will find use for the three pairs of handcuffs that are attached to my partner's belt. We'll serve all of you with a warrant for obstruction of justice. For you, Ma'am, and for the gentlemen upstairs." She paused for effect. "Ma'am."

Maggie pulled out her cell phone, "I have the local paper on speed-dial, and I'll make sure the TV cameras are rolling as we take them out in handcuffs. Go get your bosses. Now."

Glenna's mouth dropped as the two police officers spoke to her. How dare they talk to her like that? She was the bishop's administrative assistant. "I'll be right back," she called over her shoulder as she double-timed it up the remaining steps to the office.

In less than a minute, Glenna was back on step one. "You officers toot a mean bagpipe. The bishop and the vicar general will see you now."

Chapter 67

Bishop Connor Llewellyn
Monday

The four sat down in the bishop's office while Glenna retrieved fresh coffee. VG Ralph and Bishop Con were weary. They had been scheming and strategizing all day. For these visitors, though, they reattached their collars and appeared very formal in their blacks, although neither had shaved. The bishop began the conversation, "Would you like a Krispy Kreme? I know it is Monday, but I'll bet Glenna can rustle up a couple and warm them in the micro. Here she is. How do you like your coffee?"

"No. No, thank you," Maggie said. Officer Shetland stood with his hands clasped in front of him.

The bishop was going out of his way to endear himself to the police officers. "We want to thank you for the good work the police do and particularly have done in working on this case. You officers are wonderful, very convivial. I'll have the ladies of the church begin a novena for you this week. It's a very powerful prayer spread over nine days that works miracles. In addition, we'll try to donate to the Police Fund on behalf of the diocese. We don't have a great deal of extra money, of course, but always have something for the children. How would $5,000 be? We want to say thank you for a job well done."

Maggie saw the bishop sidestepping. A bribe? Was he offering her a bribe? She thought of the old saying, "Money talks. Bullshit walks," and ignored his comment but wrote it in her notebook and started her questions. "We are trying to identify the woman in the burned house. Do you have any knowledge of who that might have been?" she inquired.

The bishop remained silent and let Ralph do the talking. "No, we don't know who she is yet. We have spoken with the other two clergymen who are assigned to St. Gert's, Fathers Hope and O'Grady. You may have spoken with them. They are also baffled. Our best guess is that she was a transient, but we don't know who she was."

Maggie prodded, "You don't have any ideas? Do you have a list of homeless people who are quote unquote regulars and come to the church often for food and shelter?" She made quotation marks with her fingers to emphasize her question.

The bishop said, "We could make that $10,000, don't you think so, Ralph?"

Loren glanced over at the bishop and continued, "Street people drift in and out of the community and don't usually leave their names. We're pretty sure she is not a street person, but we are praying for her soul."

"Of course. You mentioned that you think she was a transient but don't think she was a street person. Is there a difference? Can you distinguish between them for us?" Maggie prodded further.

Loren back peddled, "Transient, street person, migrant, they're all about the same. It probably was a street person now that you mention it."

"Now you think it was a street person," Jack repeated, "but you don't know who, right?"

Maggie continued, "We'll come back to that another time. Okay, let's move on to Father Leclerq. We are trying to locate him. Have you heard from him, or do you know where he is?"

Father Loren cleared his throat and pronounced, "Father Leclerq is unavailable. He is incommunicado right now at a priest retreat working through some personal problems."

"Where is it? Here in Basin?" Maggie inquired. "I'm not aware of a priest retreat house in Basin. Where is it?"

The vicar general was adamant, "I can't say. He is in a private, priest retreat house."

Jack was through with the idle chatter and asserted, "I don't give a flying f..., please pardon my language, Sir. I mean, I don't care whether it is a private retreat house or not, we need a phone number and address, Sirs." The vein in Jack's forehead had turned red and pulsated as he talked.

Ralph Loren asserted, "It's not going to happen. I can't give you the address."

Maggie took over again. "Can't or won't? When will he return?"

"I can't say. He is on an extended retreat. A sabbatical," Ralph Loren repeated. "I can't and won't say anything more."

Jack looked at him crossly and lowered his voice, "Cut the crap, Father. If you know how long he will be gone, you know where he is. You need to tell us where he went. This is a criminal investigation."

"Truly, we can't say," the bishop interrupted. "You are aware that the clergy is bound not to reveal things that come to us through the confessional."

"Are you saying that he told you where he was going during a confession?" Maggie demanded. "You are full of crap."

"Yes, we are. I mean, no we're not full of crap, but he did come to confession. That's exactly what we are telling you," Ralph replied, his answers and questions were getting confused.

Frustrated, Maggie changed direction, "What can you tell us about his family?"

The bishop answered this question. "Rene was, uh, is a very private person. He did not share his personal life with anyone. We asked his administrative assistant, and she has no information, no phone numbers."

Maggie continued, "Okay, on another topic, someone abandoned two babies last week at St. Gert's. We want to know about them. What can you tell us about these babies?"

Ralph answered the question, "The twins at St. Gert's? Yes, we heard about them, poor little orphans. I can't imagine anyone leaving them in a church. We are praying for them, too. And for their parents, that they may know the right thing to do in their time of struggles."

"Okay, Fathers, when they were found, they were wrapped in blankets, blue wool, the same type that some of the seminaries issue their seminarians. What can you tell us about these blankets?"

Loren confirmed, "Most of our priests attended Holy Mount Seminary. As far as I know, the seminaries did not distribute blankets to the seminarians. It must be a rumor. People love to tell rumors about priests."

Maggie commented, "That's odd, because when we talked with Father Hope, who also attended Holy Mount, he disclosed that *all* the priests received blue wool blankets when they started seminary. Why am I hearing two different stories about blue wool blankets?"

"I can't imagine why Hope would say such a thing," Bishop Con blurted out. "He must be confused. Hope barely got through the seminary. He was a PE major in college and cut many of his seminary classes to work on 'body beautiful.' Hope doesn't know what the hell he is talking about."

Maggie smiled at his use of profanity. They were making some progress, she thought. "Do you have any employees named 'Angel?' Or something like Angel. Angelica. Angie. Or angel derivatives?"

"Probably. We have a lot of employees, and Angie is sort of a traditional Catholic name. We'll have Glenna check with personnel and get back to you," Father Loren assured them.

Maggie and Jack asked a few additional questions but appeared to be getting nowhere. As they took their leave, the bishop called after them, "We could make it $20,000 if it would help."

Chapter 68

Detective Maggie and Officer Jack
Monday

Maggie and Jack returned to the station house to go over the two cases involving the diocese. Frustrated at the lack of information, the two investigators sought the advice of their boss, Chief Tucker. Luckily, he was free, so they were able to give him their report.

Maggie began, "We've got some hanky-panky going on at the Catholic diocese. We don't know what, but we think the bishop and his lackey, the vicar general, lied to us at least three or four times during our conversation with them. We think they are covering up something, we are not sure what yet, but it's there. I can sense it. The bishop even offered to give $20,000 to the Police Fund."

Chief Tucker spoke up, "What? Twenty grand? Was he trying to bribe you? Unbelievable." He sat down and shook his head. I really hope this isn't true. I'm Catholic, and I would hate for another scandal to hit the Catholic Church. This bishop is well liked as a man of God. Now, the last bishop, Tom Chaufer, would as soon lie as tell the truth. But Bishop Con? People love him. He wouldn't do anything to damage the church. Certainly, he wouldn't lie. But go ahead, I want to hear what you found."

Jack explained, "I'm Catholic, too, but the son-of-a-bitch, excuse me, Sir, the bishop, he's lying. First, we asked about Father Leclerq and his family and why he was gone. You know, where he was, but the vicar general made light of it and talked about Father Rene being a private person. They said that all information came through confession. Bullshit. He insisted that the diocese had no information about Father Rene's family. They wouldn't give us anything. You know that they have records of their priests. What organization wouldn't?"

Maggie grimaced, "They also told us they had no information on the woman who burned up, and I don't believe it for a minute."

Jack continued, while Maggie consulted her notes, "Father Loren reported that the burn victim wasn't a street person and later indicated she was. The whole conversation was back and forth, piss and un-piss. This female person wouldn't be sleeping snug as a bug in the bed of a priest without his knowing, Sir. In his bed, not in the guestroom. Not in the living room. In his bed. With all the scandals that are going on with priests right now, finding a woman in a priest's bed is not in the best interest of the diocese. Neither is all the lying and cover-up that seems to be going on. Loren also insisted that none of the other priests knew her. Now, if the priests are as tuned in to the disadvantaged souls of the community as they'd like people to think, they would come up with a name. DNA's gonna prove something. We just don't know what, Sir."

"Hmm, that is interesting. What else?" Chief Tucker inquired further, "Have you gotten anything from ballistics, and when is the DNA report expected?"

"We submitted the DNA sample Friday afternoon, and the lab is performing some of the tests locally," Jack reported. "Since the Reno lab is pretty small, additional tests will have to be done in Las Vegas. Our lab said they will complete what they can today. The Vegas confirmation will take a few days more. They have a huge database and lots of inquiries, so we have to take our turn. We'll check before we go out again."

Maggie consulted her notes before continuing, "Before visiting the diocese, we had gone over to the Harte's house. They're the ones who are keeping those babies who were found. They informed us that the principal of the high school, Father Matt Hope, they call him 'Iron Man,' admitted that this type of blanket," she handed the chief the blanket, "was issued to all the wanna-be priests who go to the seminary at Holy Mount Seminary. The bishop played dumb or lied and told us that they weren't issued. We're gonna call Holy Mount Seminary and find out about these blankets. Then we'll head over to Thomas More High School to visit with Hope again to verify what he said. I don't think the Harte woman was telling tales. She has been very cooperative about this whole thing. She's caught in the middle. She has her own kids yet took on these two babies. She seems to be getting the run-around from Health and Welfare, and the church isn't doing diddlysquat to help her. We've been over there a few times. Nice lady. Nice family. In my opinion, these guys, holy men or not, can't be trusted."

"How long has the Harte family had these babies? There hasn't been anything in the paper about them. Has the media contacted you?" Chief Tucker queried.

Jack answered quickly, "Negative. That's another thing. We don't know how it has stayed out of the paper, but nothing has come out. I think the diocese sealed this up somehow, but we don't know how. They are tight."

Chief Tucker smiled, "The church has had 2,000 years to learn how to keep things secret. They are very good at it."

"Yeah, they're very good at it all right. We asked the bishop and his sidekick about Leclerq's disappearance. It was his house that burned down with the woman in it. He's a case in himself. Anyway, they won't give any information about him. Where he is or when he'll be back. Like Jack said, they are claiming confessional privilege. They are messing with us, Chief. I can feel it. You get a feeling when people aren't telling the truth. I'm not Catholic and don't have your roots, but they are messing with us big time," Maggie added.

Chief Tucker said, "Damn, I hate to see the diocese involved in a cover-up, but it sounds like something is going on. It's worth investigating. It isn't the first time the church has been involved in covering up the misdeeds of one of its chosen. In fact, it's not even the first one this year or this month. The Catholic Church has had its share of bad press this year. You'd think they'd learn to come clean. Why don't you check on the DNA and see what's cooking with that? This could be a big-time political nightmare for us if we're wrong and for the diocese if we're right. If the diocese is covering things up, the mayor needs to know as well, and you need to keep your ducks in a very tight and straight row. Don't even think about doing something that isn't by the book," Chief Tucker advised. "And keep that twenty grand in mind. That's off, really off."

Chapter 69

Father Josey
Monday

Josey was sick. Marcy would be back tomorrow. How was he going to explain that Our Lady had zero dollars in its checking account? He needed advice. He needed someone to talk to. The bishop had advised him to visit with Father McGraeth since he was the past chair of the diocesan finance council. He could also talk with the vicar general. He was amicable. Maybe he was the one to talk to.

He checked his stocks and email exactly when the stock market closed in New York. The value of the stock remained at $.63. Thank heavens, it hadn't fallen any more. He searched the chat room for DBLUP to see if he had gotten out of jail. No such luck. He checked his email, and there was a message from stocksonline.com, the group that hosted his stock trading:

Dear Mr. Zabalapeda. It has come to our attention that your account, number B45839, is currently in arrears. Funds in the amount of $333,800 must be deposited immediately in your brokerage account. In addition, there is a ½ percent convenience fee of $1,669. The current interest rate of eight percent per annum will be charged from the day you charged the margin until it is fully paid. That amount will be sent in a separate billing. Please deposit the designated amount of $335,469 into your brokerage account by midnight tonight. Sincerely, Guido Silvano

Josey started talking to himself, "Guido? I don't believe it. Guido. Talk about pressure. Are they going to come out and break my arms? Or will it be my legs? Doesn't he know that I am a priest? With a name like Guido, he must be Catholic. He's going to have to wait because I need to go see Ralph Loren. If he can fix speeding and parking tickets, he can surely fix this."

When he arrived at the diocese, he dashed upstairs to the throne to visit Ralph. He hadn't made an appointment. According to the other priests, Ralph was easy to see. No appointment. You might have to wait for a few minutes, but that was okay. Glenna could keep anyone entertained.

Glenna was not at her desk, and the two office doors were shut. He heard voices coming from the bishop's office. Ralph and the bishop were louder than usual. He anticipated that what he had to tell Ralph would cause him a great deal of added stress. It sure as hell was causing Josey stress, and he didn't want to increase his own issues by interrupting their conversation. He would wait.

Glenna came back and greeted him with a smile. "Hey, Father Josey, what kind of tears are you crying at Our Lady? Anything good going on? When does Marcy get back?"

Josey looked down at his hands before answering, "She returns tomorrow or the day after. I'll be glad to see her. I can't keep up when she is gone." He dreaded having her come back. She would look at the bank statement online right away and know that something was amiss.

Glenna encouraged, "Marcy is a great administrative assistant for you. God really gave you the finger in getting you two together. The fickle finger of fate, that is. You don't know how lucky you are. I'd like to have her work here. Of course, if she were here, the bishop and the vicar general would be eyeballing her and wouldn't get their work done. They'd have the glibido effect: talking and strutting. Anyway, I don't know when they'll be done with their conversation. Who did you want to see? Con or Ralph? Can it wait until tomorrow?"

"I want to see Ralph," Josey answered quickly. "It can't wait until tomorrow. It's sort of an emergency."

Glenna winked at Josey and purred, "You got it, Honey Lamb, I'll phone him to see if I can break him free. He's been wound tighter than two balls in a nutcracker today. I don't know what's going on. People have been calling and calling; Ralph has spent way too much time on the phone. The police—who were very rude to me, by the way—showed up without an appointment. I think this thing with the woman in Father Rene's house has everybody wound up tighter than an ass in alum. I hope Rene comes back soon." She punched in the number to the bishop's office.

"Vicar General, Darlin'," Glenna crooned, "can you come out? Father Josey's here and says it won't wait. It's an emergency. He looks as nervous as a lobster eyeing a pot of boiling water."

A few minutes later Father Loren appeared and barked, "I've got a few minutes. What's the big emergency?" They passed into his office, and Josey pulled the door shut. Ralph sat at his desk but did not ask Josey to sit down.

"Uh, there's a little problem. It has to do with money." Standing before Ralph was like standing before God in Josey's mind. Despite his diminutive stature, Ralph was the big kahuna, the ramrod of the diocesan dude ranch. Everybody knew that Ralph ran the show.

Ralph looked annoyed, "Is that all? Do you need an advance on your salary? If that's it, go see the business manager. He'll give you what you need. Tell him you talked to me, and I approved of it. Most priests go through some lean days during their first few months in a parish. It's no big deal but be careful how you spend your money. Use it for you, not for Our Lady of Perpetual Tears."

Josey was perspiring. He wiped his hands on his pants, and uttered, "You might say that. Uh, yeah, you might say that I need an advance on my salary."

"How much do you need?" Ralph inquired.

Josey stared Ralph in the eyes and blurted out, "$335,469."

"You mean $335? Piece of cake."

Josey looked at him dropping his eyes, "No, I said it right, $335,469."

"What? Three hundred and thirty-five thousand dollars? What are you talking about, Josey?" Ralph looked at him wide eyed and stood up.

Josey explained what he had rehearsed in the car, "I, uh, you see, I did some day trading, and the stock was going gangbusters. I was up over $1,000,000, nearly 1.5 mil., but then the CEO got arrested, and the stock fell, and it's worth hardly anything now. I got an email this afternoon from somebody named Guido telling me to pay up now. Of course, it could go up again. I've been praying and being fruitful and was multiplying. But now…"

"Guido? Are you kidding me? Guido? Fuck." Ralph was incredulous.

"Yeah, but I haven't told him that I'm a priest," Josey assured him. "Do you think he will drop it if I tell him I'm a priest? People always give priests special deals. Just like the mayor fixes speeding tickets. Maybe he will drop it."

"Oh, Josey. What have you done? Trust me, he won't drop it. Guido won't drop it. Tell me exactly. Tell me everything," Ralph pulled out a yellow pad and began taking notes.

Josey laid it out: the money he had inherited from his Basque sheepherder father, the parish money, how DBLUP had duped him with a pump and dump scheme, the margin call, and Marcy wanting to paint the rooms. When he had finished, Ralph had covered three pages on his yellow pad.

"So, it looks like we owe around $300,000 plus $7,800 to the parish plus another $1,600 for 'convenience?' This is not convenient, I assure you. You are a perfect idiot. You'll have to eat your own $26,000. That's your problem. The diocese will have to cover the rest. If we don't, Josey, you will go to jail. I can't have a shit-brained priest going to jail. We, meaning the bishop and the diocese, are going to cover this. Didn't you listen to your professors in your finance classes? Didn't you listen to the seminary classes on ethics? Truthfulness and integrity? God, Josey, you have breached nearly every code of ethics we have. Did you go out and diddle kids, too? Is there anything else that I need to know? You didn't leave anything out, did you?" Ralph was angry. He didn't need this today—or ever.

Josey looked at him and slowly stammered, "No, that's about it. Nothing much else." He paused, looking down at his feet. "Actually, there is one more, tiny, little thing."

"What's that? Interest on the margin call? I'll cover that, too. Is that everything?" Ralph had not lost his cool with Josey, but he was drawing closer.

"Yes, there's that. DBLUP predicted that the interest for buying on margin wasn't much, just eight percent per annum. That is probably $400 to $500 if we pay it back soon," Josey choked out. He was nearly in tears.

"Right, Josey, we…"

"But there is one other teeny, little issue. I did charge a little bit with the credit card offers that came in the mail," Josey choked out. "I don't think I'll have to pay them back, because they can write it off to charitable giving. I figured it out and checked my old textbooks. I haven't talked to them yet, but I will, first thing tomorrow. I thought you should know."

"Credit card offers. What credit card offers? You didn't mention anything about credit card offers." Ralph was standing again.

Josey replied, "The ones that come in the mail all the time offering free, 0% interest loans. We get them all the time. Even the mail carrier says they are a good deal."

"How much, Josey? How much did you charge?" Ralph demanded.

"I accepted four offers for Our Lady and me. Two in my name and two in Our Lady's name," Josey confessed. "I also got two for the diocese. I guess six offers in all."

"And how much was that?" Ralph drew out his words slowly. He dreaded what might come next.

"$50,000."

"$50,000? You charged $50,000 on credit cards and bought stocks with them?" Ralph was appalled.

Josey stammered, "Yeah, sorta, uh, no, not exactly, I mean, uh, I charged $50,000 on each of them. I think it is closer to $300,000. Probably exactly $350,000. But it's free money. Zero percent interest, don't you see? I'm sure they will write it off. Charitable giving. They'll make that much in tax relief. I checked it on the Internet."

"Oh, Josey. You'll never be a bishop. And now, thanks to you, neither will I." Ralph moaned as he sunk into his chair.

Chapter 70

Vicar General Ralph Loren
Monday

Ralph returned to the bishop's office. Con had helped himself to another piece of banana bread that Glenna had brought to work and was buttering it. "You are not going to believe this one. You'd better sit down."

"What did Josey want? You were gone a long time," Bishop Con asked Ralph.

"On top of all the other crap that has come in here today, Zabalapeda put us in a financial crunch. It seems our resident baby Basque priest decided to day trade."

"Day trade, what's that?" the bishop wanted to know. "Is that like the eBay thing I heard about?"

Father Loren gave him the basics, "No, this isn't eBay. It is much worse. At least it is worse today as far as we are concerned. Day trading is buying and selling stocks over the Internet instead of using a mainline brokerage."

"You can do that? If you buy or sell directly, can you avoid the broker's fees?" the bishop asked. His eyes lit up. That much he understood. He could save a bundle if he didn't have to pay brokerage fees.

Ralph couldn't believe it, "Yeah, you can do that, and Zabalapeda did it. He bought on margin and charged the whole thing on credit cards."

"On credit cards? How much is he in debt?" the bishop wanted to know.

"He's not in debt, Bishop, you are," Ralph answered. "You are in debt to the tune of nearly $700,000, give or take a few dollars. You gave him a parish, and you put him on the diocesan finance council. He did this in the name of the diocese. Welcome to hell, Bishop."

Chapter 71

Father Matthew Hope
Tuesday

Maggie and Jack drove to the high school mid-afternoon on Monday, but everyone was gone, and the doors were locked. They returned early on Tuesday morning. The office staff had not arrived yet, but Father Hope had come early to watch the football camp running through its paces at their summer training camp. He was sitting in the cool morning sunlight on the bleachers with a bottle of water and a protein bar when they arrived. His arm muscles bulged beneath his tight black shirt. He wore black shorts and Birkenstocks. Indeed, he looked like the Iron Man. His white collar was loose at his neck.

"Good morning. We're looking for Father Matthew Hope. Is that you?" Maggie asked.

"You found me. Who are you?" They introduced themselves and shook hands.

Maggie began, "You gonna have a team this year?" She loved football and was a fan of the local college team, the Dolly Vardens.

"TM always has a good football team," Father Hope bragged. "We have been in the state playoffs for the past 10 years. Coach Blanchard is a graduate and a top-notch coach. The public-school teams would pay him *not* to coach. He's that good. These kids out there will work for him when they won't work for anyone else. They'll even do their Latin without arguing, if he tells them their football position depends on whether they can translate Latin to English."

"We came to ask you a couple questions," Jack began. "Maybe you can help us. We are investigating two cases that are connected to the diocese: the case with the babies who are with the Harte family. She teaches here, right? And the fire and the death of the woman in Father Leclerq's house. Are you familiar with both those cases?"

"Sure. It's weird, isn't it? Last week I didn't know anything about any crimes in our area. Now I am in the loop about two. Life is strange." Father Hope opened his protein bar and began munching on it.

Jack started the interview, "Let's talk about the babies first. You've been to the Harte's house and seen the babies?"

"Yup, they're little, aren't they? No bigger than my hands." The priest held his hands out in front of him and flexed them. "You always forget how little babies are. I don't know how anybody could go off and abandon them like that." He gazed out at the field and stood up. He raised his voice, "Did you see that pass? That kid can throw. He is a sophomore. We're going to have winning seasons for at least three years."

Maggie encouraged, "Does he go to school here?"

"Yes, he does. He played varsity tight end last year as a freshman. The coach moved him to quarterback for this season. If he keeps that up, he'll be the starting quarterback," Father Hope observed.

She turned back from the football field and looked at Father Hope. "Yeah, leaving babies would be hard, but a lot of people do it. Do you have any idea who they belong to? Gwen Harte suggested that you knew something about rosaries and blankets. Those seem to be about our only clues."

Father Hope chuckled, "Gwen Harte and her kids wrote down what they knew about the babies. They put them on cards and named them clue cards. Did you see them?"

Maggie continued, "They listed several things, but let's start with the blankets. Mrs. Harte indicated that you had some knowledge about the blankets."

"Maybe. I have a blanket like the blue one you have." Father Hope related his story about the use of the woolen blankets at the seminary. "Holy Mount Seminary issues every priest-to-be a wool blanket, pillow, and sheets. They also give them some basic black shirts, sort of uniforms, to make everyone equal. Someone leaves the seminary, quits or graduates, he keeps the bedding, including the blanket. It isn't much to work on. I think some of the military services might give them out, too. My brother worked for the Forest Service, and he received green ones."

The two police officers looked at each other and said, "Thanks for that information. That helps a lot. Is there anything else that you can think of that might help us learn more about the babies?"

"Not really, I'm mostly the principal of the high school. I'm out of touch with the comings and goings of the diocese."

Maggie continued, "Now, let's talk about the woman who died in the rectory. Do you have any ideas about her? Was Father Leclerq seeing anyone? Does he have a girlfriend?"

Father Hope responded, "You must be kidding? I don't think Rene has a friend, let alone a girlfriend. A better question would be, 'Does he have a boyfriend?' I never thought of Rene as a sexual being, but rather as an asexual being. He didn't have time for sex. He was too busy running things he didn't know anything about. I feel confident that the girl or woman in the house wasn't his girlfriend. I don't know where Rene is, but he needs to come back. Summer is my vacation time, and I don't want to be reciting his Masses all summer."

Father Hope continued without being prodded, "Rene has made some accusations about the mother of those babies. He claims that April Harte, Gwen's daughter, is the mother. I don't think that is true, but he made some noise about it before he disappeared. When he returns, I'm sure he will make an issue of it again. He made some caustic remarks to me. I told both Gwen Harte and the bishop about the remarks. Gwen was furious, and I don't blame her. She is a great English teacher, and I don't want to lose her. When I told the bishop, he just moaned, 'Oh, my God,' and closed the door in my face. This was odd for our bishop. He's a happy guy who likes to talk and be the center of attention. Rene, on the other hand, doesn't want to talk about anything except what he wants to talk about. He can be a real hermit. It is his way or the highway. I don't think that way."

The officers finished their visit and watched the boys hike the football to each other in formation for a few extra minutes. There would be a scrimmage later in the day, if they wanted to watch, the priest said. The TM Boosters would provide free hot dogs and soda.

Chapter 72

Detective Maggie Monroe
Tuesday

Maggie called the forensics lab to see if there were any findings with the woman's DNA. The lab didn't have anything yet, but maybe they would later in the day.

Jack phoned the fire marshal and the crime scene team to find out what they knew. Both confirmed that after sending the body to the morgue, they sifted through the remains of the house. They did not find much. They had concluded that multiple candles positioned throughout the house had started the fire. A few distinguishable pieces of charred clothes in and around the closet were discovered, presumably Father Leclerq's. They found no evidence of any woman's clothing and determined that she must have been a street person with no belongings. The closets and cupboards were piled high with his belongings that were black from fire and smoke. Several bloody towels lying in the bathtub hadn't burned and the investigators sent them into the lab for tests.

Maggie next called the medical examiner to ask about the autopsy. The medical examiner performed the autopsy on Monday, but the burned body was fragile. They had to take extra precautions to gather enough information to continue the investigation. The cause of death was two gunshots to the head: one in the throat and one in the temple, both shots were with a .22 long.

The medical examiner reported that the victim died before the house was set on fire. The team could find no distinguishing identifications on her, such as tattoos, scars, or birthmarks, and they determined that she might have given birth, possibly recently, but couldn't know for sure. It looked like some stretch marks on part of the skin, but her charred torso made the findings inconclusive. She had eaten some Cheetos and had drunk a little wine, maybe two or three glasses, and had remnants of Tylenol or something that looked like Tylenol in what was left of her stomach. They took DNA samples and sent them to the local forensics' lab, hoping the staff would be able to run them. If not, they'll send them to Las Vegas to be processed there.

Chapter 73

Gwen
Tuesday

Clancy and Gwen spent Monday night talking about how to handle Father Rene's accusation about April being the mother to the twins. April's reputation was at stake, not only her immediate high school reputation, but more importantly, for her college years. A bad reputation could affect college acceptance, friends, social events, or scholarships. It certainly would affect her relationship with the church. It was already affecting their relationship with the church.

Clancy and Gwen did not tell April of Father Hope's concerns and his take on Father Leclerq's accusation. April's friends had heard the scuttlebutt and turned her into a pariah, but Gwen hoped her friends would be back to their normal selves when school began. With the current rumors, however, perhaps April ought to leave the school of *faith, hope, and charity*, and take her chances at a public school.

They still didn't know much about the babies, who they belonged to or what would happen next. They agreed to take the babies for "two-three weeks max," but the babies were worming their way into their hearts and becoming a part of their family. The thought of giving them up was something Gwen couldn't fathom. But Gwen also saw that little progress was being made all around. The Harte and Associates Detective Agency could be named the Inspector Clouseau Agency. They hadn't discovered much, but Maggie and Jack hadn't either. Violet must have been on vacation because she hadn't called for a week. Father Leclerq had disappeared, and the police had a murder on their hands.

Clancy made a decision, "We need to do something. We need to consider DNA tests for April and the babies. You and I both know that April isn't the mother. However, the diocese and school act as if she is the guilty party. I think that this level of DNA testing can be performed right here. I'll call the state police to see how it works, if they can do it locally, how much it costs, all that. I know the captain of the state police. He'll get me to the right person."

Gwen was less certain, "I dunno, Clanc. Do we want April in a DNA database? That's intrusive. I read that people in some places in Europe don't have an option of whether they submit to a DNA test. I don't want April's DNA to appear on the computer every time something happens. Isn't there another way?"

"There is. A doctor could determine if she had given birth, but our doctor's kids go to TM, so another rumor could emerge if the doctor ignores HIPAA. The priests could stop this train, but apparently, they have no intention of doing so. Leclerq knows that April is not the mother, and Hope does, too, but they are more interested in politics and covering their six, in Crotch terms." Clancy liked to use the term "Crotch" for Marine Corps. "Maybe I should go to see the bishop."

Gwen related, "I told Father Hope that I wanted to go with him to see the bishop. His response was, and I quote, 'The bishop won't see parishioners about trivial things. If he did, he would be seeing people all day long.' Father Hope deemed this was too trivial for the bishop. Isn't his job to see people?"

"I doubt if he'll think it's trivial if I sue the diocese's ass for defamation of April's character. And I might," Clancy loved being a lawyer. While the thought of going to court intimidated Gwen, Clancy thrived on lawsuits. His eyes always lit up when he talked about going to court. "Give me a set of facts and turn me loose. I'll have the judge begging the jury to release my client," he often bragged.

Clancy called Gwen later with the facts about DNA testing. The DNA lab was on the west side of town. If they took April and the babies to the lab, they could run the test while they waited. They could do an immediate test on the three of them comparing their DNA samples. They promised to destroy April's DNA sample but didn't know about the babies. Maybe it would help to find their parents. If they needed to send the samples to Seattle with a larger database, maybe they could find the babies' mother and father. While the cost of the test was not exorbitant, they learned that the police required another fee to destroy the test. This sounded like a bribe to Gwen, but it would be worth it. Maybe Health and Welfare would pick up the cost of additional testing if nothing here matched. Her returning mantra was, "God forgives all time spent in the trout stream and on the golf course." *If only I had gone fishing with Clancy instead of going to Mass last Saturday.*

Gwen decided to talk to April to see how she felt about it. She told her everything about Father Hope's conversation and their idea about DNA testing for April and the babies.

The tears flowed through the talk, but she answered, "Yes, Mom. Yes. I'll do it. I can't stand this. I don't have any friends. Yesterday, Audrey hung up on me. She called me a liar. Jenny hasn't called all summer. I don't want to go back to TM, because everybody thinks I'm a liar. Father Hope could stop this, but he won't. I never liked Father Lacking-in-Charisma and like him less now. He's a first-class jerk. If I lied at school, Father Hope would suspend me. Why can priests lie but other people can't? Are there special rules for priests?"

Gwen didn't know the answer to that question. Perhaps many other people had the same question considering all the pedophilia cases that the church had swept under the carpet. Gwen called Clancy to find out when they could have it done.

They loaded the babies into the car seats that Health and Welfare had given them and made their way to the police station. Multiple bags containing diapers, creams, bottles, blankets, changes of clothes, and reading material also made the trip into the forensics lab at the state police headquarters.

The civil servant who accompanied them to the DNA lab could have been Jack's twin, except he was a foot shorter. He, too, had shaved his head bald and wore a blue serge shirt and pants that appeared to be a police uniform issue but weren't. He had multiple gadgets attached to his belt and headphones with microphone attached. As he walked them to the forensics areas, they could hear him say "Roger, 10-4," and various alpha numerals that made no sense to civilians. He wore a silver metal nameplate reading, "PK Diamond, Civil Servant" as well as a ring on each of his ten fingers. The large rings flashed like brass knuckles, but they were rings, mostly made of black gold. His long, darkened fingernails revealed that either he seldom washed his hands, or he had spent the last month scraping grease out of his garage. He remained with the family during the test, standing at parade rest, hands behind his back, head alert, eyes front.

The lab technician took a mouth swab from April first, followed by Marie and Louis. In only a matter of moments, they had the results. As they already knew, April was not their mother. The technician gave them an initial printout and promised that they would send the formal document as soon as it was ready. Gwen gave them a check and reminded them to destroy April's DNA sample. April pocketed the results to present to Fathers Hope and Leclerq up close and personal.

Civil Servant PK Diamond snapped to attention and escorted the Hartes out of the building, talking to his radios with an ongoing secret commentary, "Check," "cross check," and "delta 200."

When they got into the car, they all doubled over with laughter. The name PK Diamond would be etched in their brains as a synonym for someone who was overzealous. At least they could laugh again.

Chapter 74

Father Josey
Tuesday

Josey did not sleep Monday night. He roused at 2 a.m. and gulped two cans of beer before going into the church and reciting a trifecta of Hail Mary's. Neither put him to sleep so he crawled out of bed for his 4 a.m. morning run. He hoped he would tire and be able to fall asleep for a couple hours before serving morning Mass and Marcy's return to work.

"How could this have happened to me? I prayed that my investments would be fruitful and multiply. Why didn't it work?" Josey tried to justify his actions to himself. "I was doing it for Our Lady. We need money badly. I had good advice and went through all the right steps. What I might have done wrong was using the credit cards, but that's gonna get fixed. I'm sure of it. Ralph said I was an idiot, but that's because it turned out bad, that's all. Who hasn't had a bad turn of events at some time or another? Bad luck can happen to anyone. At least I didn't create it. I am not an idiot. It isn't my fault."

When he returned from his run, he flipped on his computer and prayed. He kept thinking of a quote from Shakespeare or Steinbeck or Poe or one of those other guys who he had read in high school which said, *Call back yesterday, bid time return*. "What I wouldn't give to call back yesterday," he brooded. "If only I could turn time back."

His computer screen looked the same as yesterday. GrayBonePhone7 was floating at 63 cents. A couple of times it rallied all the way to 65 cents, followed by a steady downhill trend. He checked the chat room. Maybe DBLUP would be there. God, he needed to talk to DBLUP. The chat room was fuming with gossip about DBLUP and his scheme. Josey was not the only one who had lost some money. There were plenty of others, and they were all mad as hell. They were talking about suing DBLUP and the company for their losses.

His computer chimed a cheery "You've got mail" tone when he opened his email account. He had four messages. The first was a note from Guido Silvero:

Dear Mr. Zabalapeda: We have not received the promised deposit for $385,719. Federal Security and Bank regulations require that you pay your margin debt immediately. If it is not received by 10 a.m., we will call you to arrange to collect it. Guido Silvero

He had a second email from a corporate bank:

Dear Mr. Zabalapeda: Our records indicate that you have signed up for multiple credit cards within a four-day period. While we make multiple offers of credit cards, people are restricted to one offer. Please call to arrange to return all but one of the credit cards. No credit card use will be honored until you have called us. Ruth Lesley

And another:

Dear Mr. Our Lady of Perpetual Tears: Our records indicate that you have signed up for multiple credit cards within a four-day period. While we make multiple offers of credit cards, people are restricted to one offer. Please call to arrange to return all but one of the credit cards. No credit card use will be honored until you have called us. Ruth Lesley

And a third:

Dear Mr. Diocese: Our records indicate that you have signed up for multiple credit cards within a four-day period. While we make multiple offers of credit cards, people are restricted to one offer. Please call to arrange to return all but one of the credit cards. No credit card use will be honored until you have called us. Ruth Lesley

Chapter 75

Father Paul McGraeth
Tuesday

Paul slept late, nearly missing his own Mass. He rushed through the ritual and informed his administrative assistant that he was going on vacation. He told her to arrange for a retired priest to recite daily Mass for two weeks, maybe three. The Holy See moved slowly. He packed enough clothes to last him through October and could buy other warm clothes as needed. The rest could go to the Catholic Charities or the landfill for all he cared. He packed all his vestments and religious paraphernalia and would take those, too. He had packed everything he needed for six months into three bags. He was flying first class, but might have to pay extra for three bags, but that didn't matter. Getting out of town with three bags for a two-week trip would not evoke suspicion. He boxed up the remainder of his personal items and stored them in the closets. He looked around the house, there was nothing else he would need in Fairbanks. All his personal treasures were in the closet and the furniture was good enough for the next priest assigned to this pitiful parish. He would go to Alaska and never come back.

One last glance around the house, and he noticed the computers. He had forgotten the computers and needed to do something about them. There were plenty of snoopy people in the church, and some wouldn't understand. He drove to the computer store and bought a new computer case, large enough for his laptop and all the extras, discs, and thumb drives he had. He bought a couple thumb drives, too. He couldn't take the PC, it belonged to the church, but he would clean it off and no one would be suspicious. He had a massive number of pictures saved on it and didn't want to lose them, so he could transfer them to the laptop and his new thumb drives.

He would carry this case on the plane to help pass the time. He found his passport and placed it with his computer. He found the replica of the bishop's ring and put it in the suitcase. It wouldn't be long until he had the real thing, and he could toss this imposter.

He did feel badly about leaving. He had enjoyed his time at Holy Father's despite the deplorable people he worked with including the nuns, deacons, and all those revolting senior citizens who came to his Masses, not to mention the RFs. He enjoyed the mountains, the dry climate, and the moderate temperatures. The church was old but gorgeous, and he had decorated his rectory to his impeccable taste. He had been able to play computer games without anyone bothering him. That alone was worth something. The bishop did not know about his sexual exceptionality or any of his other issues from his time in Minnesota. It had never come up, and he saw no reason to tell anyone. In a few hours, he would be catching salmon with his brother, awaiting the call from Rome about his selection as bishop of Fairbanks. Life would be sweet.

Chapter 76

DNA Lab Team
Tuesday

After the Harte family left, the forensic science lab once again got busy with their DNA testing of the female murder victim. Maggie had called twice asking if the DNA test was finished. On Friday, they received the DNA sample from the burned woman found in the priest's house. They hadn't processed it and had started entering it into the database as the Harte family arrived.

The tech team was curious about the young woman and the babies who had DNA testing that morning. No one gave an explanation. The director ordered, "Run the tests," and they did so with no questions asked.

PK Diamond, Civil Servant, was an avid Catholic who attended St. Gertrude's Saturday night Masses with his parents. He heard about Mrs. Harte finding the babies, as well as Father Leclerq. His incessant around-the-clock monitoring of police scanners kept him in the loop for most things that happened. He took his role at the forensics lab very seriously. After the Harte family left, he returned to the lab area and offered the forensics team his services. It was a one-sided conversation reminiscent of Joe Friday on the old police show *Dragnet*.

"Harte, Gwen, found twin babies on Saturday, 7 June, at St. Gertrude's 1700 Mass. Husband, Clancy. Two babies, two races, live births, no known parents. Thursday 12 June at 0330 unidentified female dies. Priest, Leclerq, Rene disappears. No witnesses. Male and female babies tested for DNA comparing markers with Harte, April, daughter aged 17. Let's tie this all together, boys." The forensic team stared at him and mock-saluted answering, "Roger, Civil Servant Diamond, Roger," and continued to monitor the DNA computer program.

After PK left, the team made a few jokes about PK Diamond and his Dragnet-ese manner. One of the team called him an ignoramus, another called him stupid and crazy. They joked about priests and sexual abstention. They speculated and what-iffed for a while and decided to bump other requests until later and run the DNA samples tied to the two cases linked to the Catholic Church for the hell of it. "This is just too weird and too tempting, and let's give PK some answers," one of them said. They hoped to match the test with someone within their limited files.

Within the hour, the program made three hits from the DNA samples of the twin babies that had been entered. A male pedophile from Minnesota whose name was recently registered, a Paul McGraeth. He was accused of abusing altar boys 15 years ago but had moved out of the area before he was charged. As the nationwide demand to register pedophiles grew, Minnesota complied and sent all their records to appropriate states. Part of the records included information from the DNA database.

The second hit was from the DNA sample they had just run, of a burn victim. She was a local woman, a Rene Leclerq, who had DNA testing as a part of the new requirement for those working with children. Her role at St. Gertrude's Catholic School was Chairman of the Board. Nearly all the markers matched on both babies with both hits.

The third hit was for Connor Llewellyn, the Bishop of the Catholic Diocese. The DNA of Rene Leclerq linked to Connor Llewellyn and both babies showed markers linked to Llewellyn with 90 percent accuracy.

This was amazing. The forensics team ran it on a lark, partially in jest of Civil Servant PK Diamond, but also because it was intriguing, something they had never run into before. They called Chief Tucker with their results, but he was out for lunch. They left a message requesting that Maggie and Jack come to the lab to look at the results on their computer printout.

Chapter 77

Detective Maggie Monroe
Tuesday lunch

This case was wearing on Maggie. What started off as a fairly simple who-abandoned-the-babies case had turned into much more. A murder with lots of ramifications.

Through the week, they had met most of the priests in the diocese, but they were missing five: Shannon, Zabalapeda, Murphy, McGraeth, and O'Grady. She wanted to cover all her bases and maybe they would know something, so she called Glenna for phone numbers and after some resistance, Glenna reluctantly handed them over. Maggie called all five priests but was met with silence. Probably at lunch. She left voicemails but didn't expect a return call.

Jack had gone to lunch, and she found a second cup of coffee and pulled out the sandwich Brick had made for her before she left that morning. As she ate, she leafed through her notebook, wondering what they had missed. The whole thing with the bishop and the vicar general puzzled her, as they talked in circles and anytime the conversation honed into names and dates, they shut the conversation down.

She had finished her sandwich and her coffee when her office phone rang. "Restricted," it read, but she answered it anyway.

"Basin Police Department. This is Detective Monroe speaking. How may I help you?" Maggie said.

"Oh, good, Detective Monroe, I'm glad I caught you. Chief Tucker gave me your name and number. This is Julie Wright with the National Center for Missing and Exploited Children in San Antonio. We've received a tip about a man who is exploiting children in your city and Chief Tucker said you are an expert in that field. Is this a good time to talk?"

Maggie was an experienced law enforcement officer, but she didn't consider herself an expert in the field of child exploitation. The twins were the closest she had come to dealing with abused children, and they hadn't finished that case yet.

"Sure, this is a good time, but I wouldn't consider myself an expert," she said, "I have a single case of abandoned children that is pending, and although I've been involved in law enforcement for over 20 years, I haven't had many cases dealing with children. I was a sheriff in rural Nevada, so my experience was finding kids when they wandered away from their parents while fishing. I am not an expert by any means. Are you referring to those abandoned babies found in a church, the twins?"

She was puzzled that Chief Tucker had named her as an expert, but she was the only female on the force, so he probably figured she knew all about it.

"Well, no, I don't know anything about abandoned twins. This tip comes from a person in your town and deals with an adult, a male about sixty who spends his time watching kids on the Internet. Kiddy porn. According to the tipster, who didn't give her name, he's been doing it for quite a while. She gave us an address, but also did not give us a name. She was coy about it and said she didn't want to be involved. She decided to report it when she found out he might be moving," Ms. Wright explained. "It's an uncomfortable situation and always upsets me. I'm at the regional center of NCMEC. We don't have an agent or counselor in Nevada and need local law enforcement to check out this tip. Can you do it?"

"Sure, we can do it. What's his name?" immediately realizing that Ms. Wright said they didn't have a name. "I mean, what's the address? My partner will be back from lunch soon, and we'll go then."

"The tipster said his address was at 1650 East Meadow Drive. She said it was between a park and a church, but that's all she said. You can call me when you get done. We are an hour ahead of you, but we have a 24/7 answering service." Ms. Wright gave her phone number and said goodbye.

Chapter 78

Bishop Connor Llewellyn
Tuesday

Maggie and Jack had two stops to make, the DNA lab and 1650 East Meadow and decided to go to the DNA lab first. They were stunned to learn of the links between Rene Leclerq, Connor Llewellyn, and a priest they had not yet met, Father Paul McGraeth. Maggie thought it was surreal, but she began to understand the reluctance of the diocese to answer questions. Llewellyn knew a lot more than he let on and Loren probably did, too. Jack had heard of Father McGraeth but had never met him.

They next went to the house at 1650 East Meadow, ahead of the diocesan visit. Kiddy porn was a serious charge, and they didn't know what to expect, but no one was home. Jack looked through the window and said, "We should come back soon, there are a lot of boxes sitting in the living room and three suitcases by the door. Let's get a warrant." This would require another stop, this time at the courthouse, so they called Chief Tucker on their way and explained about the call from NCMEC and told him about the DNA tests results.

"You don't have a name? The judge will want a name. I'll make a call to the assessor and see if I can't get a name. I'll call the judge, too," Tucker said.

When they arrived at the courthouse, the clerk met them, but she was sorry, the judge was still at lunch, and would want to talk with them before issuing a warrant, so they diverted again this time toward the diocese. The clerk promised to call the minute he returned. He was lunching with an old friend, and it might be a while.

Maggie and Jack arrived at the diocese and were anxious to hear what the bishop would say after lying to them at their last meeting. It was time for him to face up to the evidence.

"Good morning. Is the bishop in?" Maggie greeted Glenna cheerily. "We need to see him."

"He sure is, Honey, but he's with someone. You can wait if you want or come back tomorrow. He has a 3 p.m. tee time and will leave about 2 p.m. Trust me, darlin', you don't want to mess with his tee time. He gets his knickers in a knot when you do." She smiled as she talked to the officers. Glenna was an interesting character. She could be as sweet as pie, or she could knock your shorts off with her crass sayings. Sometimes at the same time.

Jack raised his eyebrows and asked curtly, "Well, then, how about Ralph Loren, the general vicar? Is he in?"

"Vicar general. I regret that he, too, is tied up for the moment. He should be free in a few minutes though. Why don't you rest your buns?"

Maggie sat while Jack assumed his usual parade-rest waiting room position. They listened to Glenna answer the phones with occasional Glenna-isms, mostly when she was talking about one of her two bosses' schedules: "He can't call you back this afternoon, Honey, his dick is in a time-noose, and it's tightening every hour," or "He's been running a de-caffeinalon today, and it shriveled up his little ass. He'll call you tomorrow, first thing." Every metaphor was different. Her vocabulary was a work of art.

After a few minutes, the bishop entered the waiting room from his office. "Oh, Officer Maggie and Detective Jack, good afternoon. Yes, I have time to talk, but not too long. I have a meeting at 3 o'clock, but need to leave for it by 2," Glenna smiled and winked at the officers. "Let me get Vicar

General Ralph Loren in here, too. I've been tied up, and he's been handling some things."

Maggie looked him in the eye, "I'm the detective, Sir, and I'm running an investigation. Officer Shetland is an officer, a very experienced officer."

The bishop answered, "My mistake, Detective, I get mixed up sometimes."

They entered his office and noticed his golf club leaning against his desk, and an office-putting green gizmo in the corner. Tied up, my ass, teed up, would be a better description. The officers looked at each other rolling their eyes.

In less than a minute, Ralph entered the office, and Maggie took a seat across from the two church leaders while Jack stood near the door. This time, the priests did not offer the officers anything to drink or eat. Ralph smiled a frozen smile, "What can we do for you?"

Maggie reported, "We want to let you know that we've made some progress today. We got three DNA tests back and found some interesting things. The first was on the dead woman who was in the priest's house. Her name is Rene Leclerq, the same as the priest. In fact, they are one and the same. Interesting, don't you think? She seems to have been masquerading as a priest. Did you not know that Father Leclerq was a woman?"

Ralph Loren paused and asserted without blinking. "No, that's wrong. That's dead wrong." Ralph was determined to protect the reputation of the diocese at all costs. "Father Rene is on a retreat. We told you that. The DNA can't possibly be right. There is no way that Rene Leclerq can be a woman. He is a priest, a man of God. It can't happen."

"Say what you want, but the evidence says otherwise. You can see a copy of the forensic report if you like," Maggie pulled out a file and offered the bishop a copy of the first report. "Coincidentally, the Clancy Harte family, the people who are taking care of the twins, had DNA run on the babies, trying to determine who the mother was, and that DNA result confirms that Rene Leclerq is the mother of the two babies who were left at St. Gert's."

"What? Rene, a woman with babies? What babies are you talking about again?" the bishop inquired innocently.

Maggie was about up to her eyeballs with the bishop's cover-up game. She stood and moved to where she could look the bishop right in the eyes. "It's right there in black and white, Bishop. Don't play coy. You remember what babies. The different-raced babies the Harte family has. Perhaps we should go downtown to talk. Maybe being in the police station will help you remember things a little better."

The bishop's eyes widened, and he frowned, "Downtown? Are you kidding? Are you arresting me? I am the bishop of the diocese. I have done nothing wrong. Why would you arrest me? We have fully cooperated. We don't need to go downtown. We are giving you the information that you need."

Maggie stopped him, "Calm down, Bishop. Tell us the truth, and nobody will arrest you. Yet. As soon as you tell us the truth, we'll go on our way, and you can go golfing or whatever else it is you do. But you need to give us the information we need, not the information that you want to give us."

"I wasn't clear about what babies, that's all," the bishop explained haltingly. "There are babies everywhere in the Catholic Church. We are a family church with family values."

Maggie had heated up. "Right. What we are telling you is that Rene Leclerq is a woman and is the mother of a set of twins, an African American baby girl and an Anglo baby boy. Leclerq has been masquerading as priest."

Father Loren interrupted, "You are crazy. No one will buy that cock and bull story. The parishioners will never believe it. Catholics don't work that way. We don't deceive and don't lie. Rene Leclerq might have been a lot of things, but he was a priest and certainly not a woman masquerading as a priest."

Jack continued, "I'm a Catholic. I am a member at St. Gert's, and I'd believe it. How do you know Rene Leclerq was a man?"

The bishop answered, "For one thing, he wouldn't have made it through the seminary as a woman. It would have been impossible to hide that fact in the close quarters we lived in. It couldn't have happened."

"Did the dorm dads do dick checks every night? I'm asking you again: How are you certain that he was a man?" Jack didn't pull any punches with his questions.

"No, there were no 'dick checks' as you crassly put it," the bishop countered, "but there were psychiatric tests and physicals along the way. And again, there would be no conceivable way to keep that hidden from all the other seminarians. In addition, the classes were too tough, far too tough for a woman to take."

Detective Maggie affixed her eyes on the bishop and narrowed them. Her muscles tightened and she appeared ready to go in for the kill. Vicar General Ralph Loren reached over and carefully patted the bishop's arm while tactfully interrupting him. "Bishop, I don't think you want to go there." To Maggie he stated, "What the bishop means is that the classes were tough. Women think differently than men. Women would have understood the material easily enough, but they wouldn't have answered the same way as a man. The professors would have picked up on it. You are wrong with your idea that Rene Leclerq is a woman, that's all. He was a man, and he is on retreat and will be there for a while. He left after having made a confession. That's all we can say." He rose and moved toward the door ready to escort the officers from the room.

Maggie asked, "Interesting you should say, 'was a man and is on retreat.' If he or she is on retreat, give us the name of the retreat place, and we'll check it out. Rene Leclerq is smack dab in the middle of this whole situation, and we want to talk with him or her. Where is Rene Leclerq, Sir?"

"We told you. We can't divulge his whereabouts. He told us where he was going in confession. We will keep his confidence," Ralph Loren answered.

"Who did he confess to? You are using 'we,'" Maggie remarked pointedly.

The bishop and Ralph looked at each other, and neither answered. Ralph crossed his arms over his chest and retorted, "We can't say. Confessional privilege."

"Okay, have it your way," Maggie offered, "but our report will read that the dead woman, Rene Leclerq, was apparently masquerading as a priest and was the mother of the babies. She was murdered before the fire, with a .22 long from a rifle or pistol we haven't found yet. We came here out of courtesy. This might be a political nightmare for you, but I guarantee that it will be worse when your cover-up hits the papers."

Now, Ralph Loren was hot. He remained standing and rubbed his hands together. "No, we aren't covering up anything. You are wrong. Our parishioners will lose faith in the police. You should think twice about making these accusations. Do you have any idea who the father is?"

"Well, we are just getting to that, and it brings us to the second part of our visit. DNA tests confirm that the father is also a priest, a Paul McGraeth, and we have a few questions to ask him. We are going over to see him as soon as we leave here," Maggie told them.

Father Loren sat back down. Bishop Connor Llewellyn's mouth dropped open. They stared at each other for a full minute before the bishop spoke. "Oh, my God, that can't be true either. Paul's the priest at Holy Father's, one of our biggest parishes. He's a star. He's on the short list for bishop in several dioceses throughout the west. I had a call yesterday. He's being seriously considered as bishop of the diocese of Fairbanks."

"And, Gentlemen," Maggie related, "the last part of the DNA testing is the most interesting part. Bishop, your DNA popped up as a link to both Rene Leclerq and to the babies. Are you Rene Leclerq's father, Father?" She didn't want to smile, but her brain formed a big grin in her mind.

Chapter 79

Bishop Connor Llewellyn
Tuesday

When the officers left, Bishop Connor Llewellyn paced the office while Vicar General Ralph Loren sat quietly, his thoughts racing. "How many fucking scandals can one diocese have at once? The situation with Josey and now this. What else can happen? We have to make all of this go away. This must be shut down. Who do we know?"

Ralph requested, "You are good buddies with the mayor. Call him. Aren't you playing golf with him this afternoon? Bend his ear and have him get the police to back off. Maybe the police will quiet down if some demotions are on the line. None of this needs to come out. The mayor goes to St. Gert's, so I'll call O'Grady and tell him to remind the detectives not to malign the church. The mayor will have to deal with the woman. I don't care if she is a police officer, she and her partner can't talk to us this way. The police need to be shut up. They can ruin everything."

The bishop nodded. He understood. His mind wasn't on golf, but he picked up his putter and headed out the door to play 18 holes with his buddy, the mayor.

VG Loren caught him before he left, "Somebody must talk to McGraeth. What the hell did he do? Why would his DNA match that of the babies? He's got to be moved. Do you think we can get him out of here today? His brother lives in Anchorage, so I'll get him a plane ticket and send him on his way. We can pack his stuff before the police have time to see him. It's the only way to go."

Chapter 80

Father Paul McGraeth
Tuesday

Paul was nearly finished. That morning, he purchased several new cardboard boxes for packing, along with tape and bubble wrap. He didn't want other people going through his private things. He cleaned out all his drawers and closets and emptied his bookshelves. He packed everything neatly in the boxes and moved most into his closets, stacking one atop another. He ran out of storage cartons and was on his way to buy extra boxes when the phone rang.

"Paul, this is Ralph. I must talk to you for a minute. We've got a hell of a mess here, and it involves you. Can you talk?"

Oh, shit, Paul thought to himself. *Just what I need, that tight-assed bishop sycophant.*

"Sure, I was leaving for the store. I've been trying to clean things up around here. I'm packing to go on vacation. I'm going fishing with my brother in Alaska."

Ralph exploded, "Perfect. You should go fishing with your brother. You've got to get out of town. The police were just here about Rene. And those different-raced babies. And you. They informed us that you are the father. The babies' DNA matches both your DNA and Rene's. Do you have an explanation for that?"

Paul sat silent on the other end of the phone.

Ralph continued, "That's impossible, right? The DNA tests must be wrong. The police say that Rene was female. Oh, shit. I don't know anything anymore. Impossible. How the hell could that happen? How could a woman have gotten away with masquerading as a priest? And how could you have screwed her or him." He didn't tell him the third bit of news: that the bishop was Rene's father. "Paul, are you there? Did you hear me?"

Paul stammered, "Yeah, I heard you. Shit, I didn't think they would figure it out. The police are incompetent. I mean that Rene was a woman. He wasn't really a woman. He was a slimy, asexual being. And a fucking moron to think he/she could be a priest. Rene was a fucking deviant moron."

"That might be. In fact, you are probably right. Another matter is that the police could arrive at your house at any time, even in the next half hour, to try to decipher what you had to do with the babies and Rene's disappearance. They announced to us that they have evidence that Rene died before the fire started. With .22 long bullets. Paul, do you have a rifle that shoots .22 longs?"

Paul answered quickly, "No, I don't have a rifle like that." That part was true, he owned a .22 pistol, but not a rifle. And he had hidden the pistol as soon as Leclerq died.

Ralph breathed a sigh of relief. "I hoped you would say that. I don't believe that you killed Rene, but the police are going to try to make that connection. Do you have a good lawyer? Is there one in your parish?"

"There are probably a dozen lawyers in Holy Father's, but they are all ancient. They probably practiced law with Abraham Lincoln. I don't think they would be much help."

Chapter 81

Detective Maggie Monroe
Tuesday

Maggie and Jack stopped at the police station to report their visit to the diocese to Chief Tucker. It was after 3:00 p.m. and they still had three stops to make before the day ended, to get the warrant from the judge, to see the alleged kiddy porn guy at the Meadow Drive address, and to see McGraeth. They wondered if it would involve one arrest or two.

"Let's stop to see Tucker, he might want to send someone else to do the kiddy porn arrest. The police station is on the way to the courthouse," Jack suggested. "And I need water or coffee. As a Catholic, the apparent involvement with the diocese is upsetting."

They pulled into the police station and parked, and as they did, Chief Tucker stormed out of the building, "Let's go. We've gotta go now. We'll take two cars."

"Monroe, come with me. Shetland, follow. We're going to 1650 East Meadow Drive."

"Lights and siren?" Maggie asked. "That's the kiddy porn guy's address."

The chief looked at her, and said, "Monroe, you've got your hands full, because 1650 East Meadow Drive is also the address of Paul McGraeth, and it's my bet that he's on his way somewhere. Jack mentioned the boxes and suitcases in the living room. We want to talk to him before he boogies. Lights and sirens."

Chapter 82

Father Paul McGraeth
Tuesday

The doorbell rang, and Paul didn't hang up the phone but peeked out to see who was at his door. "It looks like they are here. One's a woman, and the other's a goddamned ape. And the third, I don't know who he is but he's a cop, that's for sure. God, do I have to talk to them? They won't find anything out. I won't say anything. Can't you bottle this up? You've done it before, Ralph. I am going to Alaska."

Paul answered the door after the fourth ring. "I was on the phone. I'm sorry to keep you waiting. How can I help you?" He invited the officers in and apologized for the condition of his home. "Things are a mess. I've been packing, heading off on a fishing trip."

Chief Tucker introduced the three of them and Maggie handed Paul McGraeth the warrant, saying, "We have a search warrant and need to look at your computer. Could you open it for us?"

Paul was not expecting this and looked at Maggie with a puzzled look on his face. "Computer? No, I've already packed it. I'm not going to unpack it for you, I'm on my way to the airport. My flight leaves in an hour. No, you can't see it."

Maggie pointed to the warrant, saying, "This warrant, signed by the judge, says I can. Open your computer, now."

Officer Shetland noted the multiple boxes in various states of being packed, "You are packing for a fishing trip? Are you taking all this stuff with you? Where are you going fishing, Sir?"

McGraeth was happy to divert the conversation from his computer to his forthcoming trip. "Alaska. I have a brother who lives there, and I am going to stay with him for a couple of weeks. The salmon are running, and we want to catch a few. We also might go halibut fishing near Kodiak. I haven't had a vacation in a while, and you get to a point when you need to do something different. Kodiak is a wonderful fishing spot. Have you ever been to Alaska to fish, Officer?"

Maggie didn't like him trying to divert her request, "Father McGraeth, don't change the subject. Either open the computer or I'll pull out the handcuffs and we will take both you and the computer downtown."

"I'm kind of in a hurry, because I have a plane to catch, but how can I help you?" Father McGraeth offered. "Is this about one of my parishioners? I can't imagine what you are looking for."

From his reaction and strained look on his face, Maggie's inner feeling said that he was deeply involved with both the death of Rene Leclerq and the kiddy porn, and she wondered if he might try to bolt. She stood ready. "We are looking for a couple things. First and foremost, kiddy porn. Today the National Center for Missing and Exploited Children contacted us saying they had a tip about a kiddy porn operation from this address, so we simply want to eliminate you from the accusation. Secondly, we are investigating the death of Rene Leclerq, and twins that were found at St. Gert's and how your DNA has appeared with the twins."

Jack said, "Both of these are about you, Father McGraeth. About you as a father, Father. But there is a third issue. Your DNA sprang up regarding a sexual misconduct complaint from Minnesota a few years ago. As a sex offender, you understand that you are required to register with law enforcement, don't you?"

Paul McGraeth gaped at them. He was expressionless, yet the officers observed a dark anger moving toward his face. "What are you talking about? Me? A sex offender? That's lunacy. No one ever made accusations against me. I don't know where you got your information, but I have a sterling reputation in the church. Sterling. The people all love me. Who? Who would say that?" His mind was bouncing off the walls. Who knew he liked to look at pictures? He didn't do anything but look and what's wrong with that? Who would have called the fucking hot line for exploited children? Other people had pastimes, why couldn't he? Using his computer online was only a hobby, nothing wrong with it.

Maggie continued while Jack stood erect guarding the door. "That's not exactly true. Not everyone loved you. We looked up the report from Minnesota. It reported that three pre-teenaged boys accused you of molesting them. The Minnesota authorities took DNA samples, but before they formally charged you, the diocese transferred you out here, but somehow those DNA samples disappeared. The lab recently discovered them, taped to the bottom of a desk, and forwarded the results to the DNA lab here. They found it when they were researching a molestation case of another instance involving a priest. They think someone, maybe one of your parishioners who worked in the lab, hid them on purpose. You've been here about 10 years with no complaints alleged against you. We didn't realize you were here."

"Why would you believe those kids? A couple of prissy altar boys lied, saying I did something to them. But I didn't. About that same time, the bishop moved me to the Pacific Northwest for my health, you see. I have an exceptionality that is... well, I have an exceptionality, but that's really none of your business. I didn't do anything. Kids lie about anything and everything. I was active in all the groups, including the youth groups. I was showing them how to tie their robe sashes correctly, and they said I touched them inappropriately with my hands. It didn't happen. It was a pissant charge and would have destroyed my reputation if it had gone to trial. I would have lost my parish and my retirement. Maybe I would have ended up in jail. I don't use altar boys out here. No way. They are trouble waiting to happen."

Maggie and Jack looked at each other and didn't say anything. They had heard the I-didn't-do-anything story many times before. Maggie smiled and said, "You can tell your story downtown." Maggie pulled out her handcuffs and headed toward him. "We need to talk with you downtown. You are under arrest." She put handcuffs on his wrists and read him the Miranda statement. "Jack, take care of the computer and find his cell phone. Box it up, along with any thumb drives and see if you can find something that looks like a list of passwords in case he doesn't cooperate."

Father Paul McGraeth's rile erupted. "You must be crazy. Rene Leclerq was a man, a priest. A man of God. This is un-fucking-believable. What you are saying is insane. You are saying that I, a priest, screwed another priest, who was really a woman, and babies were born of this 'relationship?' Impossible. I am not going anywhere with you two crazies. I have rights and I am going to see my brother. My plane leaves soon, and I have lots to do. Tickets are bought, and my bags are packed. I'll be back in a couple of weeks. Even you idiots ought to have this untangled by then. I'll talk to you when I get back."

Officer Shetland crossed over to the priest saying, "Your plane might leave tonight, Father, but you won't be on it. Let's go downtown, Sir."

Chapter 83

Bishop Connor Llewellyn
Tuesday

Bishop Connor Llewellyn returned from his golf outing before Ralph went home. "You're back early, aren't you, Bishop? I didn't expect you to return at all today."

The bishop looked beat, "I only played nine holes today. I couldn't concentrate and couldn't putt worth shit. I had three bogies and a double, and three-putted twice. I can't believe what the police think they've found." Defeated, he sank into his chair.

"I talked to the mayor about all this. He's going to see what he can do. He agrees with me that this must be a bunch of lies. The police don't like Catholics, never have liked Catholics, and this is another sign. Hopefully, he can pull some strings, and we won't be bothered by those police officers again. Maybe he can fire the chief or something. I think that woman officer had something to do with all this."

"McGraeth called. He's been arrested, just one more fly in the ointment. I need a drink," Ralph pulled out a bottle of Irish Whiskey and poured each a glass. "Bottoms up, what else can happen today?"

Chapter 84

Detective Maggie Monroe
Tuesday

The officers drove Paul McGraeth downtown to where the prosecutor was waiting. Jack remained with McGraeth in an interrogation room while Maggie visited the prosecuting attorney in a separate room. The computer sat on Maggie's desk, and she had called a tech.

"Did he do it? Did he kill her?" The prosecutor wanted to know.

Maggie began with what they knew, "Probably. We didn't ask him though. We brought him in for questioning for two or three issues. DNA showed that he was the father of the babies. The DNA lab found an old report from Minnesota that showed him as a sexual predator. It was evidently taped to the bottom of the desk at the DNA lab. We don't know who did this or how they found it, but it had never popped up before. He moved here from Minnesota more than a decade ago, somebody covered it up, and we have nothing on him all that time. Lots of good Catholics in law enforcement cringe at seeing a priest accused of anything. The Catholic Church hierarchy is powerful. The lay folks consider the pope to be a direct descendant of St. Peter, and the bishops are in line to him. The priests are not only men but holy men. There aren't very many cradle Catholics who will question the bishop or someone else in church hierarchy, and they think a governmental agency should turn its head at anything that reflects badly on a priest. The

Catholic Church is infamous for its ability to jostle things around to make them look good.

"Another thing, I got a call from the National Center for Abused and Exploited Children today, about kiddy porn. They only had the address, no name, but the address was his house. We picked up the computer and I have a tech opening it up right now.

"It looks like he is on his way out of town, so we brought him here until we can check everything. Things are all boxed up as if he was getting ready to move. He admitted he is going on a two-week vacation. But everything is in boxes: kitchen utensils, bath towels, knick-knacks, everything. I asked to use his bathroom and looked in the cupboard. It was empty, not a towel or bar of soap. Jack got a drink of water, and he had to drink it out of the tap. Everything was packed. I don't know anybody who packs all his towels and water glasses for a vacation. We think that he planned to get the hell out of Dodge and never return. The diocese didn't tell us about him leaving. They indicated that he was being considered for a position in Alaska, not that he was going there today."

The prosecutor observed, "Interesting. Did you ask about weapons? You need to question him regarding any weapons he has. See what he says. We can get a warrant to search the boxes, but we don't have much to go on. See if you can find some more."

Chapter 85

Detective Maggie Monroe
Tuesday

Jack and Maggie entered the interrogation room, and they began their conversation with Father McGraeth. Jack clicked on the recorder, introducing everyone, "Why didn't you register as a sex offender?"

"I am not a sex offender!" Father McGraeth screamed. "I don't know why you think I am. I have never been to jail, and my record is clean. Even if somebody mistakenly thought I was a sex offender, the police department never said anything about registering. I haven't had a speeding ticket since I moved here. You want speeding tickets, talk to O'Grady. He's the one with the lead foot. It's probably from all those antacid tablets he eats."

Maggie asked, "Do you have any weapons, Sir?"

"No, of course not. That's ridiculous. Why would I have a weapon? To chase off the little old ladies who want to fuck me at Holy Father's? Why are you asking me about weapons? I thought this was about being the father of those abandoned babies," McGraeth retorted.

"You don't have any guns, pistols, or rifles, anything like that?" Officer Shetland continued.

"I told you, no. I thought this was about being the father of those babies," Paul McGraeth answered.

Maggie said, "It is in part. What can you tell us about the babies, Sir?"

Father McGraeth answered rapidly, running his words together, almost as if he had rehearsed the answer. "Someone told me that a couple babies were abandoned at St. Gert's, and their mother was killed in a fire. The victim was nude and sleeping in Father Leclerq's bed. The fire was started with candles that were lit throughout the house. She had been drinking wine. A couple cats died. I don't know anything else. Only what I read. I wasn't there." He crossed his arms defiantly and leaned back in his chair with a look of disgust and impatience on his face. "Are you satisfied?"

Jack paused before answering, "You got everything right, too right. You knew she was nude. How did you know that? We kept that out of the papers. And the cats? That information was not released to the general public either. You knew the fire was started with candles, which was in the papers, but not that there were candles in every room. Were you in the house when she died? Did you kill Rene Leclerq, Sir?"

Father McGraeth stared at them. "No. You must be shitting me. Absolutely not. I was not there."

"We are going to search your house, Sir. For a weapon. For a .22 rifle or pistol. Do you have anything to hide?"

Father McGraeth's answer rose to a state of uncontrolled anger and his profanity increased. "Of course, I don't have anything to hide, but I finished packing, and I don't want your frigging ape officers rifling through my personal belongings. What I own is none of your fucking business. You can take your investigation and shove it up your ass. I am not answering any more of your fucking questions. And no, you cannot search my house. I am going to Alaska today, and you are detaining me. I want to finish what I was doing and get on with my life." He rose and started toward the door.

Jack blocked his way with his massive body, "We don't need your permission to search, Father. Based on your comments about her cats and being asleep in the nude, we can obtain a warrant and search for a weapon.

You are going to miss your flight. Maybe you want to call the airline or your brother, but I'd suggest you call an attorney first. Sit tight, Sir. It's going to be a long night."

Chapter 86

Father Josey
Tuesday

Josey confided in Marcy about some, but not all, of his doings. It wasn't any of her business. After all, he was the priest. He thought she should know that the checking account was empty before she tried to pay bills. She nodded saying she would use the building fund money that was held in a CD. "That is gone, too," he explained. "Don't worry. The diocese will put us back in business."

Guido Silvero called Josey Zabalapeda early Tuesday afternoon. Guido was very adamant.

"When are you repaying this money? Your deadline was 10 a.m., and we expected payment by then," Guido demanded.

"Guido, I mean, Mr. Silvero. God bless you for calling. I intended to call you this morning, but I got a little busy. You see this is not my fault. I got some bad advice from a financial guru. As it turns out, he's in jail right now. Things are a little tight, but I talked to the bishop's office. I can pay you by Friday. Maybe Thursday morning. Today's Tuesday. I'm sure they can cut you a check this week. How about Wednesday? They've got a lot going on. Are you Catholic? If you are, you understand that we are good for the money."

Guido was forceful, "You don't get it, do you, Partner? The money is due today. It is past due, as we speak."

"I'm good for it," Josey reassured him. "I'm a priest, and priests don't fudge on their debts. You can be certain of that."

Guido responded, "I don't care if you are a priest. I don't care if you have a lot going on. I don't care if things are tight, Padre. I do care that you owe us $335,469, and it is due now. Pay up or you'll end up living in jail. Comprende usted?"

Chapter 87

Father O'Grady
Wednesday

The police returned to Father McGraeth's house to look for the murder weapon. While on the way, Officer Jack received a phone call.

"Jack, Father O'Grady, here. How are you today?"

"I'm fine, Father, and how are you?" Jack answered thinking about this coincidence, wondering what his priest needed.

Father O'Grady began to speak. "Fine, thank you. The bishop requested that I call you. I understand that you are concerned about the mother and father of the babies that Mrs. Harte found at St. Gert's. I want to assure you that you shouldn't be worried. The Harte family has them and will make good parents. You should not look any further. God has put those babies in the right home. If you try to mess with the situation, you will cause the Hartes grief. You don't want to cause anybody any pain, do you, Jack? Besides, your mother wouldn't want you to cause trouble. She would say, 'Do the right thing,' and this is the right thing, isn't it, Jack?"

Jack started to respond, saying, *"But Father..."*

O'Grady interrupted, "Listen, Jack, the road to heaven is paved with good intentions, but God has already intervened, so your good intentions aren't necessary. Not needed. Do you understand? You shouldn't bother with this case anymore. As for Detective Monroe, you can deal with her, can't you? She's just a woman. She'll listen to you. Talk to her. Tell her how it is. God bless you, Jack."

"What?" Jack was shocked and confused at the tone and content of O'Grady's monolog. "I think it's a question of right and wrong, not..." Before he could finish his thought, Father O'Grady hung up.

Jack was furious at these comments and immediately shared them with Maggie, "Shit, you'll never believe what Father O'Grady wanted. They are trying to cover these cases up. These idiots are guilty as sin. Let's get over to McGraeth's." He didn't tell her all the details of the conversation, especially the one about her being "just a woman."

Before long, they were searching Paul McGraeth's house for a rifle or a pistol. They opened the sealed boxes first, box after box, and found nothing. "It's got to be here," Maggie speculated, "It's here somewhere. Did you check the suitcases that he is carrying with him on the plane?"

Jack answered her, "He can't be as stupid as to think he could take a pistol or rifle on the plane. Do you think? However, I didn't think O'Grady was so stupid to call me and tell me to cover this up. Everybody knows that you can't take weapons on a plane. Priests are educated, you'd think they would know about that."

"From what I've seen, they are also arrogant," Maggie said. "Perhaps he thought he could put it in his checked luggage?"

Jack looked in the largest satchel, which appeared to hold fishing gear. In his Henry's Fork Fishing Vest, mixed in with the hooks, lures, and fishing gloves, was a .22 pistol and three boxes of .22 longs.

"Holy crap," Jack shouted. "Holy crap. We found it. The father did it. I knew it! Holy crap." They returned to the station and arrested Paul McGraeth for the murder of Rene Leclerq with a second charge of not registering as a sexual offender.

***

It was after 6 p.m. when Jack and Maggie returned to the diocese. "Let's see what they have to say about obstruction of justice," Maggie said.

The bishop was alone in his office, and the janitor let them in. Glenna was gone, and they rapped on the open door. He was talking on the phone, nodding and smiling. When he hung the phone up, he bowed his head in prayer.

"Bishop, we would like to talk with you," Maggie said firmly.

The bishop jerked his head up and began to ramble. "I have been on the phone with the woman who found the babies, Gwendolyn Harte. She told me about the DNA testing. Her daughter was exonerated, which I already knew. She told me that she and her husband have decided to adopt the twins, God willing. Their home will offer lots of happiness. Solid parents. I understand there is a grandmother. Grandparents should be a part of the lives of their prodigy. Did you know that I am a grandfather? I never accepted the role of father because I didn't know I had a child, and I'm sorry about that. I fell in love once with a woman named Marie. The same name as the baby. My mother wanted me to be a priest. I never wanted it. After I met Marie, I thought about marrying her. I could have married her, but she left. I don't know what happened. I have been praying that the Harte family would adopt the babies, and God answered my prayers. I hope I can see them sometime. I never felt bonded to any children, but with these twins…," his voice trailed off. "You see, it's odd, I know, but I would like to be a part of their lives. They seem to tug at my heart. They truly are gifts from God." He realized that he was rambling, "It's been a long day. Please come in."

"Bishop Llewellyn, we've got some good news and some bad news. The good news is that we arrested a suspect for the murder of Rene Leclerq. The bad news is that we arrested Father Paul McGraeth. You should also know that we charged him with not registering as a sexual offender. Were you aware that he was accused of abusing children before he was assigned to your diocese?"

"I didn't know until today. I learned about it this afternoon. It isn't my fault. When I arrived three years ago no one told me. It isn't as if I didn't ask. I approached each of them in turn asking, 'Is there anything that I need to know about you?' Each answered 'No.' In hindsight, I probably should have queried them further. Priests are supposed to be holy men, men of God. Men of God aren't supposed to lie. I assumed they were telling the truth. Here I am with a pedophile and possibly a rapist on my pastoral staff. I honestly didn't know," the bishop shook his head slowly.

Maggie said, "Another thing, on McGraeth's computer we found site after site of kiddy porn. He indulged in some very nasty things, things you wouldn't believe. We will fully investigate, of course, but you should prepare yourself. It's much worse than I ever thought anyone could do. McGraeth is gonna end up in prison," she declared to the bishop.

Maggie took a deep breath, "The final part of the bad news is that you are under arrest for obstruction of justice. It pains me to arrest a bishop, but I have no choice." Jack pulled out his handcuffs, cuffed him and read him his rights. The bishop sat down and bowed his head.

Jack continued, "Is the general vicar here? We'd like to talk to him."

"You mean the vicar general?"

"Yeah, the vicar general. Is he here?"

The bishop looked at him with vacant, sad eyes. "No, he had to go on an errand to our Lady of Perpetual Tears. That young priest, Father Josey Zabalapeda, has been selected for the bishop track and is leaving for the Vatican." Figuring the budgetary crisis that Josey caused would disappear if he was out of the country, Ralph Loren called in some big favors in Italy.

"Father Loren and I recommended him this morning, and it came back, affirmed by email. The church moves slowly, but not in this case. I don't know how Vicar General Loren did it. He is helping him pack as we speak. Zabalapeda will catch the late-night flight to Rome. It departs at midnight.

"I might have made a mistake about Father McGraeth and that will reflect poorly on me, but Father Josey is a wonderful young man. He has made some mistakes but hopefully this new assignment will be exactly what he needs, plus Father Loren says he is a whiz with investments," the bishop smiled. "He's a fine young man. He'll be a cardinal someday."

Epilogue

The week's events had changed the lives of nearly everyone involved. The Harte family had strengthened their family commitments. Clancy spent more time at home finally realizing he didn't want to miss another minute of his kids' childhood. April didn't resent babysitting anymore. She especially enjoyed helping with Louis and Marie and taking them for car rides. Andy and Michael thought it was cool to be big brothers and were anxious for the babies to learn to ride bikes and play football. Gwen thought about becoming a stay-at-home mom but decided against it. Everyone agreed to pitch in and help with the babies and the added housekeeping. And they did.

Detective Maggie Monroe testified at both Bishop Llewellyn's trial and the murder and child pornography trials of Father McGraeth as the prosecution's main witness. Each time the courtrooms were filled to capacity with many of the faithful, and with tears and red eyes, they heard the accusations made by those who testified.

Brick continued his up and down days, but the up-days became fewer and farther in-between and the down-days more common. The daily care became more than Maggie could handle and when he fell in the shower and she could not get him up, the VA counselor suggested that he stay in the rehab center until his health improved. He went, but his health didn't improve.

Chief Tucker moved Maggie into the position of lead detective and added "social services," rationalizing it that it would make "caring for her husband easier." He promoted Officer Shetland to detective and gave him a service award, and Maggie finally got a new desk. Her efforts in the Diocese case did not go unnoticed in the adjacent jurisdiction, Reno, and the Chief of Police of Reno offered her a position as Chief Detective, homicide division. Maggie accepted.

School started again in the fall, and Gwen returned to her teaching career. Marie and Louis had grown through the summer and were becoming active and needing extra attention. They worked with Violet to formally adopt the twins, and they quickly became a real part of the family. They were hungry all the time, and everybody took their turn feeding them. Changing diapers was less popular, but they all learned to do it. Gwen's students were inquisitive about the babies and wanted pictures and updates. She brought the babies to school occasionally, and her students doted on them. April's social status improved as the DNA results were shared and other students learned of her summer's adventure. They were interested in hearing about Louis and Marie, and these new friends accepted her.

Gwen's mother decided to retire from her job as a real estate broker and volunteered to care for the babies during the day. She had missed April, Michael, and Andy as babies and was thankful to have a second chance.

Bishop Connor Llewellyn was fined $10,000 and sentenced to a year in jail for obstruction of justice, both of which were suspended by the Catholic judge. He realized that the many cover-ups throughout his career had finally caught up with him and retired from his position as bishop to play golf and enjoy his grandchildren. However, when he requested visiting rights to see his grandchildren, the court denied him, but he appealed the denial, which went nowhere. He never saw them.

Father McGraeth was found guilty of child pornography and would spend the next 25 years in prison without appeal. The charge of murdering Rene Leclerq was reduced to manslaughter, and the church removed his status of priest. After four years of incarceration in the maximum-security facility, the prison gave him the job of washing dishes in the prison kitchen. He never achieved his goal of becoming a bishop.

Ralph Loren managed to avoid being a part of the cover-up scheme and skirted legal charges for obstruction of justice. With McGraeth out of the way, he transferred himself to Fairbanks and quickly became bishop.

Junie May became totally befuddled over the events that had transpired and tried to make sense of them all. In her quest to unravel some version of the truth, she latched onto more gossip strands to continue being the Mother of All Gossip.

Josey went to Rome and was designated a monsignor by the pope, because of his superior service and the hearty recommendation by Bishop Llewellyn via Ralph Loren. He was named head of the Vatican's Department of Treasury and was given complete freedom to manage the Vatican accounts. He had learned about the adage of *putting all your eggs in one basket* from his day trading experience and moved 500 billion euros to banks throughout Europe. Unfortunately, half of the money fell into the Sicilian Mafia, and the news media went crazy. He confessed to this sin, and the pope gave him absolution. The church defrocked him, but he was given a large annual stipend to remain quiet and he moved to Bilbao, Spain, where he renewed his Basque heritage.

Coming soon: Maggie's next adventure is to address human trafficking, specifically the Missing and Murdered Indigenous Woman issue.

Read on for a sneak peek at the next book in the *Maggie Monroe* series: **Murder on the Rez**

Maggie shivered when she got in the car, as the temperature gauge read 15 degrees with a wind chill factor that her iPhone said brought the temperature to 8 degrees. She wasn't yet used to this kind of weather as it several degrees colder than it would be at home. At least it wasn't snowing, she thought.

She hit the road again, and at this time in the morning, few cars were on the road, and despite the wet roads, she increased her speed. Three hours later, she saw a sign for Big Timber and another Cenex station. It was larger and housed a McDonalds, and she stopped to fortify the Jeep, Riley, and herself. "Stay here, Riley, I'll see what they have. Maybe a Big Mac or something like it will hit the spot for both of us," she said.

She used the bathroom and was shocked to see three identical signs in lime green on the wall reading:

ARE YOU **MAY ROSE**?

Human Trafficking Is Illegal

If you are being held or moved against your will,

tell the clerk of this store that your name is **MAY ROSE**

and someone will help you.

Your information will be CONFIDENTIAL.

Maggie had seen many signs warning against human trafficking, but this one struck her. It was simple. She wondered how many people read it and whether it helped. The human trafficking issue had grown since she had begun law enforcement, although she had little experience in that area.

She paid for her gas, bought coffee, a bottle of water, two Egg McMuffins and two donuts to split with Riley, and started to step into the Jeep. She stopped cold as she saw that Riley had moved to the back seat and in his place sat a young woman, dressed in distressed jeans, a short-sleeved white T-shirt, and lightweight tennis shoes, maybe the Hey Dudes she had seen advertised. The girl didn't have a coat or even a sweatshirt and was shivering. She was slight and almost disappeared into the back of the seat.

"You're in the wrong car," Maggie asserted as she looked her over. Her eyes trailed downward, thankful that her pistol still sat in her dashboard holster, along with a hunting knife and scissors. She regretted that she had not locked the car.

Maggie looked out at the gas pumps wondering where the girl had come from. Twelve gas pumps were scattered in front of the C Store, but only seven vehicles were getting gas. A variety of people walked around the gas pump area, some entering or leaving the C Store, some stretching from being cooped up in car, and a couple getting ready to pull out. "Which car did you come in?" Maggie asked.

The girl squeaked, "Please, Ma'am, take me with you. I need to get out of here. That guy in that white seed cap over there, I don't want to go with him. Please, Ma'am, and can we hurry? He just came out of the C Store, but he will be looking for me as soon as he doesn't see me in that green pickup. Please, Ma'am." She pointed at a shiny F-150 pickup two lanes over. The top half was forest green, but the bottom was mud-covered. It looked new, but the mud disguised its age. Montana's muddy March, Maggie remembered the boys saying. The license plate was caked with mud, and she couldn't make out the numbers, but noted part of the State of Montana imprint. At least from this angle, she thought it was Montana.

Maggie cocked her head, wondering who this girl was. "What's your name, Girl? Who's that guy, your dad?" Maggie, as a former Nevada sheriff and detective thought she had seen and encountered everything, but this was new. Should she go? Or should she wait? None of her law enforcement experiences had covered this situation. Was the girl telling the truth or scamming her?

Acknowledgements

Murder in the Diocese has been a work of love for me, and I have invited many people to read the manuscript. With their input, I have made many corrections, additions, and deletions. The manuscript, as I write it today, is 92,000 words. I probably wrote another 92,000 words before it went to press.

It's a tough subject, and I needed lots of help. Some of the people who have helped me along the way:

Robert Mitchell
Linda Alden
Cole and Pam Cushman
Deb Decker
Janice Decker
Carol Evans
Donaleen Frye
Bernice Harris
David and Judy Hume
Elizabeth and Chris Hume
Neil and Linda McCarthy
Anna McHargue
Nan Scheiber
Sandra Soine
Anita Stephens
Eric Hendrickson
Especially Robert, Tom, and David
And countless others…

Thank you!

About the Author—Helene Mitchell/Gail Cushman

Born and bred a small-town Idaho girl in the beautiful intermountain west, my life has been a myriad of adventures. I am a Marine Corps officer, a former high school principal and superintendent, and I love to write. My readers may recognize that I write my blogs, my *Wrinkly Bits* series and newspaper columns as Gail Cushman, my birth name. I love writing these humorous stories and enjoy receiving the fond feedback. My heart is full when I read your comments. Thank you!

Before I penned my *Wrinkly Bits* series, I had written a serious mystery and crime series revolving around a female sheriff named Maggie Monroe in rural Nevada. Now I find that I need to switch hats, from the silly, flowery bonnet of Gail Cushman to a new hat, a detective's fedora, for my nom de plume or pen name, Helene Mitchell. One cannot wear two hats at the same time, so when I put on the humorous hat of Gail, I write funny nonsensical stories that occur in everyday life, and when I put on my detective Helene hat I write about murder and mayhem. Every day, I choose which hat I will wear as I say good morning to my computer.

I hope you enjoy this third book in my *Maggie Monroe* series. And watch out, I have several more in the pipeline. Enjoy life, my friends because as Scarlet O'Hara said, "After all, tomorrow is another day!"

Gail Cushman's books

- *Cruise Time*
- *Out of Time*
- *Wasting Time*
- *Flash Time*
- *Bits of Time*
- *Loving Again: A Guide to Online Dating for Widows and Widowers* (co-author Robert Mitchell)

Helene Mitchell's Books

- *Murder in the Parsonage*
- *Murder Almost*
- *Murder in the Brothel*
- *Murder in the Diocese*
- *Murder on the Rez* **Coming Soon!**

gailcushman.com

Made in United States
Orlando, FL
12 November 2024